Saline District Library

W9-BUB-675

Mystery Sha
Shannon, John, 1943-
A little too much : a Jack Liffey
mystery

A LITTLE TOO MUCH

The Jack Liffey Series by John Shannon

* available from Severn House

A LITTLE TOO MUCH

A Jack Liffey Mystery

John Shannon

SALINE DISTRICT LIBRARY
555 N. Maple Road
Saline, MI 48176

MAY -- 2011

This first world edition published 2010
in Great Britain and in 2011 in the USA by
SEVERN HOUSE PUBLISHERS LTD of
9–15 High Street, Sutton, Surrey, England, SM1 1DF.
Trade paperback edition first published
in Great Britain and the USA 2011 by
SEVERN HOUSE PUBLISHERS LTD.

Copyright © 2010 by John Shannon.

All rights reserved.
The moral right of the author has been asserted.

British Library Cataloguing in Publication Data

Shannon, John, 1943–
    A little too much. – (A Jack Liffey mystery)
    1. Liffey, Jack (Fictitious character)–Fiction.
    2. Private investigators–California–Los Angeles–
    Fiction. 3. African American actors–Mental health–
    Fiction. 4. Missing persons–Investigation–Fiction.
    5. Detective and mystery stories.
    I. Title II. Series
    813.5'4-dc22

ISBN-13: 978-0-7278-6991-3 (cased)
ISBN-13: 978-1-84751-323-6 (trade paper)

Except where actual historical events and characters are being
described for the storyline of this novel, all situations in this
publication are fictitious and any resemblance to living persons
is purely coincidental.

All Severn House titles are printed on acid-free paper.

Severn House Publishers support The Forest Stewardship Council [FSC],
the leading international forest certification organisation. All our titles that
are printed on Greenpeace-approved FSC-certified paper carry the FSC logo.

MIX
Paper from
responsible sources
FSC
www.fsc.org **FSC® C018575**

Typeset by Palimpsest Book Production Ltd.,
Falkirk, Stirlingshire, Scotland.
Printed and bound in Great Britain by the
MPG Books Group, Bodmin, Cornwall.

For Alex and Becky, new friends are sometimes the best.

Acknowledgments

I want to thank Dr Leanna Wolfe, for sharing some of her large store of knowledge of human sexuality and its varieties and of the defunct Sandstone Retreat in Topanga.

I also want to acknowledge, of course, Gay Talese and his book *Thy Neighbor's Wife* that featured the Sandstone Retreat prominently, and Alex Comfort's 1973 *More Joy of Sex* which did the same – until later editions of the book eliminated all mention of the retreat. I also want to acknowledge the video 'Sandstone' from 1975 by Bunny and Jonathan Dana.

In addition, I relied upon innumerable newspaper and magazine articles about Sandstone by Andrew Blankstein, Mark Dery, Jeff Booth and many others.

Topanga, a rustic mountain canyon between Santa Monica and Malibu, where I now live, started out as a refuge for artists, writers, musicians and exiles from the Hollywood Blacklist (including Woody Guthrie and Will Geer), full of owner-built cabins and houses made of found lumber – sort of a ruder rural version of Greenwich Village. But, like the Village, the lawyers and dentists moved in later and eventually changed the character of everything they touched, helping make an earnest seven year long sexual experiment like Sandstone no longer tenable. And despite Sandstone's claims at the time, I remain skeptical of the healing powers of polysexuality.

In the heartland of wealth and liberation, you always hear the same question: What are you doing after the orgy? What do you do when everything is available – sex, flowers, the stereotypes of life and death?
– Jean Baudrillard, *America*

PROLOGUE
The Damaged Ecology

Jhon Orteguaza tugged on the conical white knit cap as soon as he parked the Range Rover. He'd found the cap amongst his mother's meager belongings after she'd died of TB a month earlier in Hospital San Juan de Dios in Baranquilla, Colombia.

'What's that ugly old thing?' Amari Santander said, chuckling.

That was a big mistake. Orteguaza stared so hard and so long at the dark-haired beauty in the car that she started to get truly frightened. Red bloomed on one cheek as if he'd struck her. Perhaps he had.

'Do you believe sex and violence are linked?' he demanded.

'What?'

'Stay here now. When I come back, I will either *coge* you or kill you. You can choose.'

He stepped out into the dank alley. Orteguaza figured that the traditional cap of an Arhuaca holy man would get a rise out of the *santero* whose advertisement he'd also found in his mother's single cardboard carton of possessions – the sad gleaning of a lifetime.

Inside the shrine, which was really just a garage off the alley, the grizzled little man squatted in front of a bonfire on the cement floor. Orteguaza sat down cross-legged facing him across the fire. When the *santero* looked up, he shouted and swept the cap off Orteguaza's head like a bad idea.

A night of grave mistakes. Oh, little man.

'Them mountain *mamos* is stupid fuckers,' the priest said in an ugly Spanish that swallowed the middle of every word – so very Caribbean. *Mamos* just meant priests but it meant a lot more if you were Arhuaca. 'You an *Indio*, son?'

'You knew my mother, *pendejo*. She was Drunvala, a full-blood Arhuaca,' he said. He had scheduled a session because he half believed in the powers, just as he was half *Indio*, but he wondered if he was going to let this little faker live.

Drunvala Orteguaza's people had been one of the three famous tribes holding fast to the old soul in the inaccessible Santa Marta Mountains of coastal north Colombia. They had expelled the Capuchin missionaries plus the Spanish teachers and others sent by the state. In 1990, they had sent their one fluent Spanish-speaker down from the high mountains to demand that a BBC crew at work nearby follow him back up to document their mamos' warning to the entire world about the ecology that had become so fatally damaged that their regular ministrations might no longer be able to repair it. Remarkably, the BBC crew had agreed, and they climbed the mountain to make *The Elder Brothers' Warning*, a ninety-minute documentary.

'Them mountain beliefs is shit. Forget the sierras. Your mother's true Orisha was Oshun, the goddess of love and passion.'

Orteguaza was mildly embarrassed that his sense of his own *Indio* people existed in his mind only back in the mists, images built up from the crudest daily journalism in gutter papers that called them *primitivos* plus a little of the BBC film that he had seen, yet the tribe lived only seventy kilometers away. His mother had migrated down to Barranquilla on the lowland coast two years before he was conceived, where she'd worked as a domestic for rich supermarket owners and car dealers. She had gradually taken up many of the local servant beliefs of Caribbean Santeria, dancing herself to exhaustion at night in a stewed-together worship of African gods, their equivalents in syncretist Catholic saints and fading memories of her own Arhuaca yearnings toward mother-earth.

Jhon had been her only child, an accident of religious intoxication from dancing too near a tall, handsome Colombian wrestler. The boy grew up headstrong in Barranquilla and was repeatedly thrown out of the city schools. Eventually he'd grown himself up on the port-town streets, and like so many of the urban self-taught, this handsome and short-tempered half *Indio* had been left to believe everything and nothing.

He'd eventually fought his way to *jefe* of a cocaine distribution gang that was now richer than most Swiss banks and used low-flying airplanes, home made submarines, and go-fast cigarette boats, plus a hundred other smuggling ruses to transport the priceless powder into North

America. Inevitably, he came to owe allegiance to the powerful Medellin cartel.

Orteguaza ruled the *cuates* and thugs of his *klika* with a rough hand, and they followed their *Gran* Jhon and his occasional religious eruptions without question.

The *santero* surreptitiously tossed powder into the small bonfire on the garage floor, and it erupted into orange flame.

'You have done something wrong to someone,' the *santero* stated, in what suggested an oracular voice.

'*Chingada*,' Orteguaza said dismissively. 'Doing someone wrong is universal. Tell me something real.'

'Is a minefield outside, yes. Give me my coca now.'

That had been the price of the consultation. 'The talk isn't over yet, *padrito*. I need to know about my next biznis.' He used the English word, or something near it. 'Señor Stone has been straight with me up to now, maybe. But I have a strong inner feeling of betrayal. Give me some of that magnesium powder or whatever it is you use to dupe the fools.'

The *santero* tried to stare him down to reestablish his authority. Orteguaza grabbed the man's wrist hard and wrenched his hand down into the bonfire.

'*¡Caballero, po' 'avor!* Aiiiii!'

He let go and the *santero*'s other hand went into a small leather pouch and offered a palmful of silver powder.

Orteguaza took it and tossed it all into the flames, which blazed up like a brushfire sweeping through something very dry. He watched the shape of the flames with intense concentration and saw something unpleasant there.

'And what does that sign say to you, little man?' Orteguaza demanded.

'My Orishas do not always see the future as unmistakably as the stupid star-chart in *El Heraldo*,' he said with dignity. He was rubbing his singed fingers hard against his thigh.

'Then what good are you?' Jhon Orteguaza declared. He pressed his 9mm Glock against the forehead of the *santero* and pulled the trigger. The man shrieked like a bird as he fell over backwards.

'You see now whose gods are strongest, *pendejo*? What stupidness. Never insult a man's mother.'

He collected his precious mamo's hat and the tiny leather bag of magic powder and looked back at the flickering fire. Maybe this love-and-sex goddess Oshun could still tell him what to do about the troublesome woman in the car outside, and, most important, about Señor Stone in *El Norte*.

ONE

Salt of the Earth

It was probably the strangest job that had ever swept Jack Liffey into its orbit, and that was saying a lot. There must have been quite a few malign planets sliding into conjunction or whatever during that week. He didn't believe in that crap, of course, but several of the participants in this drama did. His worries had begun in earnest just after his wife (his live-in womanfriend, to be accurate, though he had begged her many times to marry him) had taken herself off for a while with a lover, his daughter had just about got herself killed by L.A. SWAT as she was so characteristically trying to rescue a crazy armed kid at UCLA, and a Colombian drug-runner's gang had dropped out of the blue and were running wild in town, shooting, bombing and maiming so outrageously that they pushed the sexual scandals of a TV preacher right off the news. May we all live in interesting times, a friend had saluted him – that old Chinese curse again.

They say life-changing drama generally begins Jesuitically, which is to say, it sneaks aboard your life in an extremely elaborate and dishonest manner. All this had started for him with an innocent visit to the ramshackle house his daughter had just rented with some classmates, not too far from her new college, UCLA.

'Man in the house!'

Jack Liffey burst into a grin. He hadn't heard that cry for forty years, not since the dorms at Long Beach State. He'd walked up the dirt drive past three cars, all girls' cars on various forms of evidence that a good detective would notice, including a bobble-prism hung from the mirror and a box of Kleenex on the front seat.

'Bunny, put something on! I think it's Maeve's dad!'

'It is,' he said mildly. 'An evil old man trying to cop a quick peek.'

The blonde in the wraparound green housecoat grinned back at him and then flashed him her breasts. They looked large and firm and quite remarkable.

'Oh, Jesus, don't!' He shielded his eyes. 'The spirit is willing, but the heart is weak.'

'Why don't you wait in the kitchen, Mr Liffey? In fact, why don't you call ahead?'

He grimaced. 'I'm sorry, I don't have a cell. I'm afraid I'm the last Luddite.' He padded gamely toward the messy kitchen. Once again he noticed that girls living together were less tidy than boys.

'I'm Axel,' she said. 'It's short for Alex.'

Not very short, he thought. 'Pleased to meet you. I'm Jack. Please wrap up tight.'

Like so many of the older Topanga cabins he had visited over the years in his job as a missing-child finder, this one had long passed its peak, with the yellow and green kitchen tile peeking from under piled-up dishes that were nicked and stained, and the linoleum on the floor no longer mimicking wood very successfully. He sat down obediently at a built-in table. Three flat boxes that said *Rocco's Pizza* were pushed against the wall, reeking of grease.

Sad, he thought, looking at the cracked sash window and other signs of neglect. So obviously a rental. No one had loved this bungalow intimately for many years.

Not wanting to do things the usual way, of course, Maeve had rejected living in the UCLA dorms and had found two girlfriends right off the bat to share with. They'd hunted down a place that was a thirty minute drive from campus, along Sunset and then down Pacific Coast Highway. Topanga Canyon had been a famous hippie and artist retreat, but much of it had slowly surrendered to the invading battalions of those with real money.

A very tall athletic-looking redhead wearing a dark complexion and very little else but a towel sat opposite him, staring fiercely. 'Maeve, you didn't say your dad was so dreamy!' she shouted. 'In an old and rugged sort of way.'

'Next time I'll call, I promise,' he said.

'My name is Bunny Walker. I'm drama. "Time rushes toward us with its hospital tray of infinitely varied narcotics, even while it is preparing us for its inevitably fatal operation."'

'You've got a while before you have to worry about the big sleep,' he offered. She might have been a junior, twenty at most, and pleasantly large and overweight. The flaming red hair looked real. 'Was that O'Neill?' he asked.

'Tennessee Williams,' she said. 'I played the older woman in *The Rose Tattoo* at the Raging Stage last year. I'm big, so I can get away with it. A woman of appetites, soiled, desperate for one last love.'

She batted her eyelashes and luckily Maeve arrived abruptly to rescue him. 'Hi, Dad.' She hustled Bunny out of the room. 'Beat it, beautiful. Get dressed. This one is all mine.'

Maeve came back and hugged her father more reticently than he was used to. He supposed that was just part of the long slow separation of the lander module from the main spacecraft. All parents knew the pain. 'Tea? I only have ginger and green. How's Gloria?'

'I'll try ginger. Thanks. Gloria's fine. I'm sorry to bust in on you, hon, but I seem to have a job up here.'

'In Topanga?' She began fussing in a cabinet.

'Well, isn't that where I am? I'm a bit disoriented by your roommates prancing around in the altogether.'

Her tone was slightly distant. 'You know, Dad, I think I can imagine back in your day, and what it was like for you. All that sexual repression. Maybe I just listened too much to you and Mom. But that's all just a joke for us now. At college, they have coed dorms. Nobody outside Kansas worries much about sex or nudity any more.'

His daughter had had an affair with a gangbanger in East L.A. and got pregnant, agonized for a while and then had an abortion, then she'd had a tumultuous affair with an ultra-smart high school girl who'd eventually pushed her away – so he guessed she had a perfect right to a blasé attitude, if not a complete renunciation of sex. But he knew she was more sensitive than she wanted to let on. He knew, in fact, with great pride, that she was a far better human being in many ways than he was.

Not everybody recognizes me. I guess I should accept that, but it makes me feel so vain. I mean, how deep in a cave do you have to live not to recognize a guy who's had three Oscar nominations, and has his face on billboards and buses all over town? And just to jog the memory a bit, I'm pretty clearly African-American.

'Coming up, son,' she cries.

I sit on one of the two sun-scoured white plastic chairs that I discovered on this bald knob, trying to make sense of the complicated hillside vista of overlapping canyons and spurs below.

The stocky woman follows her two q-tip dogs on leashes laboriously upward, her tennis shoes slipping on the soil. The dogs are more sure-footed. Better this bustling woman than one of my own Skinnies. For sure.

'Hooo-wee,' she exclaims with a gasp.

'Is this your place?' I ask.

'Heavens, no. Somebody left these chairs here long ago. This hill is known as "the chairs". Do you mind if I take the other one?'

I grew up in a polite era. Moms always said, What goes around comes around, Tyrone, it's lock and stock, nine times true. Be kind.

Moms. She'd actually repeated sayings from Richard Brautigan, too. She was just about the last hippie, bless her soul.

It's a funny feeling, not being recognized, and it lets me relax a little as I haven't done in years – but at the same time it annoys me. I've come up here to try to get my bearings from the one photo of Moms I can just about put a place to. After the early winter rains, the canyons and slopes facing us are mostly fuzzy green. We're on the Malibu side of Topanga Canyon, remarkably sparsely populated for being so near the city, maybe five miles west of my own house in Brentwood where Paulita, my long-suffering third wife, will be waiting for me, annoyed. I don't always tell her my doings. And I have a feeling this is the start of something special today – off on my quest. Why? Who knows?

'You live nearby?' I ask the woman. Damn. One Skinny rears up to peer at me out of a crack in a granite outcrop. Shoo-fly, sucker!

'You can't see my place.' She waves vaguely to the left.

The woman takes a really good look at me at last. Ah, shit. Here it comes.

'Do I know you?'

'Everybody says I look a lot like the actor Tyrone Bird, but I really don't.'

'I don't know him. Is he on TV?'

'I think he used to be.' I do my best to put on my light-skinned everyman face. Slack, uninterested, weary.

My head is starting to weigh a ton, which isn't a good sign at all. I'll be seeing a lot of Skinnies soon. I notice a hawk and mockingbird circling and shrieking, straight out over the canyon. The mockingbird is harassing the much bigger hawk, driving it like a biplane in some World War One pic. I suppose confidence and aggression always win out. It's the hardass way most of the pissant film directors work.

'Do you know which of those houses down there used to be the Sandstone Retreat?'

That makes her take a closer look at me.

'You got some interest in it?'

'Just curious, I heard of it.' In fact, I saw it once, but from this angle I can't tell.

'Sandstone was a wicked place,' the woman says finally. She tugs the dogs closer to her, as if I might infect them.

'Sure.'

'I mean, people got hurt. Oh, them sixties.'

Just point it out, *please*, I think. I don't want any rants.

'What made you ask about Sandstone?'

Be nothing but innocence now, I think. Can I ever relate to ordinary people in some direct way, some honest non-actory way? *Read* me now, woman. Trust me, trust me.

'No reason,' I say innocently.

She wiggles a disapproving finger toward a big ranch house on the near side of the canyon, far below us. There's nothing special I can see from this far away, but it has a lot of open land around it. It does look like the picture I have.

'It was a rental before the sex-kooks took it over.'

I can hardly hold my head erect. I should probably go back on the meds for now. I can't act for a film on the meds, but I think I'm going to be AWOL from the set until I learn something. This new urge has really taken me over.

'What a time,' the woman says. 'It was either jump in a jacuzzi with naked people or jump in a church.'

The official beginning of Jack Liffey's job had been marked by a fairly rude phone call from a gruff voice that had identified itself simply as Reston, as if he should know the name. 'Are you free right now, Liffey?'

It was a pretty tricky metaphysical question, but he decided not to take it that way.

'Sure.'

'They say you're damn good at what you do, which is what we need. I like guys who're good at what they do. So many of them aren't.'

OK, Jack Liffey thought, I'm supposed to sit still for this shit. That kind of arrogance usually meant good money.

'Reston, look. I need to know a bit. I don't do rough stuff, I don't hurt people, all I do is find missing kids.'

'That's the deal. Let's meet for lunch; I know a great place we can discuss this.' He gave an address, and the rest of his name and title: Meier Reston; Associate Producer for Monogram. Jack Liffey bet he knew the intimate place Reston was taking him to – the sort of 'secret' place everybody in town always knew.

The usual handover spot for the drugs was about as public as you could get in L.A., at the northern edge of the immense Costco parking lot and directly across busy Century Boulevard from Hollywood Park Racetrack. Despite its evocative name, Hollywood Park and its Cary Grant Clubhouse were actually in the largely black city of Inglewood, at least forty minutes south of Hollywood, though only three quick minutes from LAX, which was probably what the Colombians had in mind, since LAX still landed private jets as well as commercial ones.

Harper parked the Caddy Escalade two slots away from the spot the beaners had marked out themselves two years ago.

Marcus Stone sighed. 'You got some kind of Louisiana hoodoo says coming here for a look so early will help?' Stone was his senior by almost forty years and sometimes the old man would put on these airs that dissed you a little. He'd supposedly taught some shit at a crappy little junior college once, but as far as Harper was concerned he was just another old school banger who needed foot-soldiers, though he rather liked the old man.

Harper eyed the weird marking fifty feet away. The Colombians had painted on the asphalt a heart with shepherd's staffs on both sides. The windows of the Escalade were down

and the parking lot smelled like it had been scrubbed down
with piss.

'I'ma tell you got a bad feeling about this, too,' Harper
said.

'It's always wartime with big money in the picture. But I
want to keep my spirits up.'

'I can get the Rollin' Seventies here, Stoney, all strapped
out as you want. Even AKs and shit.'

The Rollin' Seventies Hoover Crips were Harper's old street
gang, the owners of the 'hood where they'd both grown up
south of Slauson, and only a few miles east.

'Too many street bangers get trigger-crazy,' Stoney said.
'Can you get four or five of the best?'

'Done. Where you want them to deploy?'

Stoney made a face as Harper used the military word, but
the old guy could stuff it, Harper thought. He'd done his two
tours in the damn Eye-raq, and he knew war and death and
all that kind of shit up front and for real.

'Not too close. These *vatos* would notice. They're not stupid,
Harp. Let your homies know that a lot of these *vatos* look
like brothers. Colombia's a funny place down there, with lots
of blacks. So we don't have any misunderstandings.'

'Yeah, I'll be picking these fuckers up at the plane, like
before. Their chief is a crazy peckerwood, looks Mex on a
good day, and the rest of them are Spanish niggers.'

'We'll work it out. You "deploy" your homies. Why is it
you think you-'n'-me both got bad feelings this time? They
been cool so far.'

'The big guy is spooky, Stoney. He's always talking angry
gods and shit. You can't never trust gods.'

Sure enough, Reston brought Jack Liffey through the crowded
front room of Joe Jost's tavern in Long Beach, crunching on
peanut shells, into the quieter pool room in back. They decided
on a far corner, a bit smelly, too near the free-range men's
urinal. Reston ordered two beers and two specials – Polish
sausage and sauerkraut wrapped in rye bread. Jack Liffey
acted impressed. It cost him nothing to pretend he hadn't
been here twenty times before. As usual, he didn't touch the
beer.

Reston seemed to be struck reticent, staring at his sandwich that was slowly unwrapping itself like a time-lapse flower opening up.

'So, what is an associate producer anyway?' Jack Liffey asked.

The man tore himself away from some inner concern that was needling him. 'The old joke is it's the only guy who'll associate with the producer.' He didn't even pretend to laugh. 'There'll actually be four of us up on the credits, but I'm the guy who does the big worrying. I bring in the paper bags of dirty money from unmentionable sources and I bury the bodies.'

'You got a dead body?'

'No no no. Manner of speaking, Jackie. I got a young superstar who's absconded that I need found. Everybody's sitting around on rotting money while he's gone.'

'I prefer Jack.'

'Sure, sure. You heard of Tyrone Bird?'

He had, of course – an ingratiating African-American actor who'd started fast in stand-up comedy, then some popular sitcom on TV, hip-hop music, and he'd finally made it sideways into really big budget movies. 'I think so, but help me out. I don't get exposed to a lot of pop culture.'

Reston looked at him like he was a Martian. 'OK, *Jack*, what you need to know is that the real irony of this whole perishing decade is that the only two actors capable of opening a movie, as the Trades say, and then selling it in Iowa and Tajikistan are both spooks – Will Smith and Tyrone Bird. No more Nicholson and Pitt, forget it. And we're two generations past Jimmy Stewart and Hank Fonda. Bird may be fucked up deep inside, the way the tabloids are always hinting, but up there on screen he smiles and makes your fucking aunt and uncle in Nebraska feel like good non-racist Americans. They see Ty, and they can pretend they voted for Obama.'

Jack Liffey thought for just a millisecond about his dad voting for Obama. Inconceivable. Declan was probably still writing in Strom Thurmond's name. 'Can I ask what movie you're making?'

'Our director Joe Lucius has a bug up his ass. You probably never heard of it, but there's this damn book by a guy named Chester Himes called *If He Hollers Let Him Go*. Of course we can never call it that. Studio wants it to be *Getting Over*.'

Jack Liffey let out a slow breath. It was like being told they were making Ralph Ellison's *Invisible Man*. No sane Hollywood studio would try it. He couldn't help saying it. 'Yeah, I know the book. What were you people thinking? It's the angriest book about the black American experience that's ever been written.'

Reston nodded ruefully. 'It was Ty's idea first, and Joe insisted. You know Joe may have made *Vampires from Mars* once but he's top of the A-list now. And his dad worked assistant on *Salt of the Earth,* and didn't give a shit about the blacklist – they got money from some drugstore chain. Monogram's got Joe Lucius under contract for two more action movies, and he insisted this little sidetrack is Academy Award material. A little prestige along the way never hurts.'

'Have you actually read the book, or only the plot summary?'

Reston's eyes narrowed. 'You want this job or not, Jackie? What we desire is Tyrone Bird back on the set and one hundred per cent cooperative. We're losing – well, lots of gelt every day. We don't want anybody in the press sniffing after Ty's blood. That's the whole truth, so help me God.'

A little of this bonanza of studio money would sure help out with his finances, Jack Liffey thought. 'You know I mainly find missing children. He's not a kid any more, but I'll do my best. You have to tell me what you know about him taking off on you, all of it.'

TWO
The Cord is Cut

They'd put him with the director Joe Lucius so he could get the whole story about Tyrone Bird, whatever that meant. It was one of those ridiculously opulent location trailers reserved for the big boys, and Lucius clearly didn't want him there. He was concentrating on a woman who was exercising on a ski-machine in black underwear and nothing else. Some notoriously expensive single-malt Scotch called Glen Garioch was on offer all around, but Jack Liffey demurred for his own reasons.

'They say you're good friends with Bird,' Jack Liffey said.

The leprechaun-like man scowled. 'Nobody's good friends in Hollywood, boss. My family knew his mom.' The man caught a glimpse of his own face in one of the mirrors scattered all over the trailer. 'Unaccommodated man,' he commented with a scowl.

'Why are you so eager to make *If He Hollers*?' Jack Liffey asked, trying to turn the focus around. 'It sounds like your dad.'

That got his attention. A lot of emotions passed over his face then. 'I don't know why I'd tell personal shit to some over-the-hill shamus.'

'Nobody says shamus, man. It makes you an old joke.'

'Must be a bit drunk. They sent you here because I'm the only one on the set with the guts to tell you Ty is a fucking schizophrenic. He has amazing eyes, and I can usually tell when the bastard is using his schizo eyes. The camera goes crazy for them. What was your name?'

'Jack.'

'Jack, OK. And you're Jack who doesn't drink. Good on you. Ty is high functioning when he stays on his meds, and that's good enough for me. Happy now?'

'Not especially. But it helps excuse the rudeness. I actually like your work, and your dad's.'

The director thought about that for a moment, taking a deliberate breath. Then his eye went back to the woman, skiing and skiing, her buttocks reciprocating in semi-transparent black panties. 'It's really not rudeness, on some level.' He held up his shotglass. 'On such a day . . .' He downed it all at once.

'I take it that's one of your meds.'

He smiled. 'Dad was a red, I'm a drunk. Maybe it's the same thing in the film world, functionally. Send them all back to Russia. Or rehab.

'Don't give yourself too much credit,' Jack Liffey said, trying and failing to suppress his annoyance. 'Your father never worked again after *Salt of the Earth*.'

'Not quite true, Jack. He did TV under another name, mostly that tiresome *Robin Hood*.[1]'

'Please tell me what you can about Ty,' Jack Liffey said.

'His mom cleaned our kitchen. Later, Ty and I were friends when he was a stand-up comic stealing Haldol so he could get over. You know, it's almost random when the damn disease hits you. He was maybe twenty-two. Before that, he was antsy, like most comics, but the one thing that seemed to calm him down was photographs. He kept a pocketful of photos of his mom that he'd spread out on a table and stare at like a poker addict looking at his hole cards. She was a real hippie – a caw-casion, you know? Beautiful chick. One photo was even nude and she had huge tits, taken at some commune. Ty would study the pics and become quite peaceful like somebody'd just hit him with a big Thorazine dart.

'He has a face to die for, you know that. Men, women – you just can't take your eyes off him. The cheekbones, the skin like milk chocolate. When he's on screen, it's like a cobra next to a baby. He just kills anybody he works with, like Steve McQueen fussing with his hat or tugging at his ear.'

The woman stopped skiing and dried herself with a towel.

'Do you know why Ty left the set?'

---

[1] This TV series, shown on CBS in the late 1950s but shot in England and produced by a company partially funded by the American Communist Party, became famous, *sub rosa*, for employing blacklisted writers like Ring Lardner, Jr., Waldo Salt and Adrian Scott (under pseudonyms, of course). Steal from the rich, give to the poor, after all.

'I'm just a movie director, so I deal with the outward aspect of things, Mr Detective. I don't know very much about Ty's inner resources. I'd guess they're pretty thin.' The director waggled his eyebrows in some Groucho-like gesture so odd that it gave Jack Liffey a chill. Intelligent but cold-hearted, he thought. Narcissistic.

'I'm not his keeper, boss. But I'll tell you one more thing, and then I want you out of my space because I got other plans. I had Tyrone back to my house the day before we started shooting this film. We had a drink, which he doesn't usually do, and then he froze me where I sat with those black eyes. I thought a truck had hit me.

'He said to me, "I'm not really under control, sir. In order to act in this movie, I have to go off my meds. I'm getting scared about it. Help me get over."'

He waited a beat or two. 'I never helped him, boss. OK? What was I supposed to do? Tell me.'

Then the woman came and wrapped her arms around Joe Lucius, cooing, and Jack Liffey left.

Jhon Orteguaza walked to the doorway of the makeshift Santeria shrine, jumped overhead for the broken rope and yanked the roll-up garage door down so it slammed shut. He was almost unmoved by the killing he'd just seen . . . or was it committed? The only clarity was in absolutes, and not always then. Life was like that.

The bitch hadn't fled and was waiting stiffly for him in the Range Rover, though she looked frightened, and one side of her face was still red as a beet. How could anyone be that stupid to hang around?

'What's your decision?' he asked as he tore open the door. He really wanted to be alone to figure things out. What had just happened and what did it prefigure about Señor Stone?

'You're serious?' she asked.

'Don't push.'

'You know you can fuck me any way you want, *querido*. I'm your girlfriend, and I take every drug you want. I'm your slave.'

'Then what good are you?' Orteguaza reached inside his jacket for the Glock. Oddly, the metal was warm.

* * *

'I mean, look at that,' Maeve said with awe, nodding to the remarkable view. 'I've never been to Italy, of course, but Axel says it looks just like Tuscany.'

The girls had a flat sandstone patio off the back of their house, with a nearly unobstructed view across the canyon to rugged hills, dotted with houses and stands of trees. One diagonal fire road ran as discreetly as it could up through the hillside. The patio came equipped with three plastic chairs and a cheap plastic table, where two teacups were giving up their last wisps of steam.

'This part of Topanga is called Fernwood,' Maeve said. She repeated some local lore she'd just heard about the TV show *Fernwood Tonight*, but Jack Liffey wasn't really listening. He knew he should leave the girls alone.

'I hope the view of Tuscany doesn't interfere with your schoolwork,' Jack Liffey said.

'Noon bus to campus!' Bunny yelled from the house.

'Not me!' Maeve called back, retreating to the kitchen for a refill.

Forty years ago, the view from his Long Beach State apartment had been of a cracked alley with toxic-looking pools of water. He wondered if she took him too seriously, with that straightforward gaze of hers, seeing only some imaginary pillar of grown-up strength. No one was that strong. Recently he'd come to feel that his life was winding down without ever quite panning out in the ways he'd once hoped. Except this incredible, precious daughter.

Maeve had her own problems now, he thought, and that was as it should be. Worldy-wise in her peculiarly innocent way. He loved her energy and bedrock integrity and her high spirits, and wished he could be twenty again to experience her as a pal.

'You'll do OK here,' Jack Liffey called to her in the kitchen. 'I just stopped back to see if you'd run into anyone yet with a big store of knowledge of the canyon. I need some seventies lore.'

'Dad, you know you came here to check up on me.' He smiled a bit sheepishly. 'Not true. If I don't trust you by now, it's way too late.'

She stepped back outside and fluffed her dad's hair, before sitting and sipping with two hands. 'Sorry. I'm a bit wound up still – college is so new and scary. How's Loco doing? I forgot to ask.'

Loco was their dog, who had recently had serious surgery and some horrific chemotherapy for bone cancer. 'Loco is the thing itself. He's always got that. He never stands back and wonders, what if I'd been born a zebra or maybe to a richer family? He's a little slower these days, but he's OK.'

'Wonderful.'

'How's school?' He'd just noticed a little powdery residue on the table that looked suspiciously like the lost tail of a line of cocaine.

'Overwhelming. UCLA is a very big place, you were right.'

'I thought you might have more fun at a small college, but your hypothetical circle of friends is a lot bigger here. How do you like Axel and Bunny?'

'Give me a little time. We met off a notice board. But they seem OK.'

When she wasn't looking, he ran a forefinger over the residue of powder, then waited until she looked away again and wiped it quickly against his gum. Yep – the abrupt chill and then the speedup. It had been a long time for him, but he'd once known it well, the bad years after Nam, and then after the loss of his safe tech job and the breakup with Maeve's mom.

Get yourself out of here, he thought. She'll make her own mistakes, in her own way, and you'll still be there for her.

'Dad, when you're right you're right. I did meet a local blowhard if you want to talk to someone. He was walking his dog. He insisted on telling me everybody who'd ever lived in this house over the years. He's in the little orange house uphill, the one that looks a bit like a Taco Bell. There's a horse in back.'

'Thanks, hon.'

The taste of hammering defeat rose suddenly in Jack Liffey. He wondered if he'd find a guy much like himself at the Taco Bell house; a know-it-all, aging without grace.

Jack Liffey got home to Chicano East L.A. before dinnertime and decided to cook something. Lately, Gloria had been bringing half her lunch home or just pulling out a frozen burrito at random, if not just drinking her dinner in Coronas or Tecates – and who could blame her on the LAPD's twelve-hour shifts.

He found a number of likely-seeming ingredients in the pantry, the ear-shaped pasta, sun-dried tomatoes, artichoke hearts, and some dry salami he could fry up to bring out the flavor. Gloria loved strong tastes. A little onion and garlic and a couple of jalapeños and they'd be fine with the Mexican-Italian concoction and a salad. He missed Maeve dropping in for dinner now and then, carefully picking the meats out of whatever he cooked, but it would still happen, he was sure.

Loco's yellow eyes watched him from the door, probably wary these days that all he loved could be yanked away from him without much notice.

'Hey, dude, you need a new doggie girlfriend.' Loco had never been spayed, but the chemo had pretty much put an end to the random appearance of his pink appendage. 'Anything you want from me, just speak up.' He dropped a round of salami that Loco sniffed at suspiciously.

Once in a while, entirely justified by events, he'd growl a little, but that was it for speaking up.

Jack Liffey was surprised to hear Gloria's RAV-4 coming up the drive early. He was amazed how much the prospect heartened him. Nothing wrong with loving someone, but he knew you had to be careful about counting too much on their presence.

Jack Liffey had a deep superstition that relying on anything too much drove it away. Gloria had been assailed by so much of her private grief recently that she'd almost stopped touching him for comfort.

He heard her come into the front room, fuss with her holster and pistol, set it aside, and then take a little more unaccountable time dealing with something. She had been raised by foster parents who hated her Indian heritage, but even that never quite seemed sufficient for her deep inner rage.

He overdid his banging around in the kitchen on purpose to attract her. He knew she had to come his way to get her first beer.

'Hi there . . . Jackie.'

She could barely force his name out for some reason, and it hurt him down deep. 'Bad day?'

'Always.'

'You're early,' he said as brightly as he could.

'They gave me some time off because there's a . . . thing they want me to go to tomorrow.' At the old avocado-colored fridge she got out a long-neck Corona, then bashed the cap off on the edge of the wood counter top. Her *macha* gesture.

'Thing?'

'Police conference, up in Fresno. The role of thirteen-region DNA in rape investigations. Jesus, who wants to go to Fresno?'

'But you get to go through Bakersfield. You could say hello there.' That was a touchy mine he'd just planted on purpose.

Their eyes met for a moment, though she couldn't sustain it. A year and a half ago, he'd summoned her up to Bakersfield to help him rescue Maeve from a real mess, and he was pretty sure in the course of it all she'd connected in some way with Sonny Theroux, an investigator he'd been staying with, a smart guy from New Orleans he'd once liked a lot.

'God, no,' she said. 'That was a bad time and place for all of us – especially Maeve.'

What a lousy liar she was, he thought – at least on this level. Was this going to be it for him? She was twelve years younger than he was, and so was Sonny, a clever and appealing guy, who was still as desperately lonely as any man could be and almost certainly in love with Gloria.

Jack Liffey knew he had a tendency to leap to farfetched conclusions, especially sinister ones, and he did his best to calm himself down inside. 'How long will you be gone?'

'Tomorrow for travel, and then the weekend.'

'I'll miss you a lot. Feel like some whatever pasta tonight?'

'Let me unwind and have a couple. But sure. Thanks a bunch, Jackie. You're always a real prince, and I love your cooking.' She gave him a half kiss on his cheek, then harder on his lips, and he knew something was going downhill. 'You'll be all right here?' she asked.

'I won't starve. I saw Maeve today.' Even when your imagination starts to give up on something, you still go on counting on it, he thought.

'Tell me in a minute. I have to regroup.' She headed out to the front room with her beer.

He'd betrayed women enough times in his life to know all

the faint signs of bad faith. But he wasn't done yet. Sonny, we were friends once. But I'll fight to the death for this woman.

The phone rang as they were eating dinner and he ignored it, as usual. A police emergency for Gloria would come in on her cell. After five rings, the monitor squawked so loud they both winced.

'Liffey! Pick this fucker up now if you want to keep your assignment. We're losing a million dollars a day and we expect you on the job twenty-four seven!'

'People with a lot of money really are assholes,' Jack Liffey said equably, without budging an inch.

'Threatening people is nuts,' she said, frowning. 'You back yourself into a corner. Every cop knows that. Either you got to really fuck them over or you got to admit you can't. Go on, Jack, get it.' Part of her seemed to rejoice that he was being drawn away from dinner, and away from her.

But he shook his head. He'd call Reston later. This is Jack, you prick. Eat me!

Gloria was frowning. 'Jack, Jack. You can't let your ego get in the way of the job. They taught us lots of brilliant stuff like that at the Academy.'

'Oh, can't I?'

'Is something eating you?' she said, cop instinct.

He had an indelible image of a moment where something had passed between her and Sonny Theroux while he was watching. He held out one finger on each hand and then drew an imaginary square around himself. 'That's where I sit, Glor. That's all I've got. If I give it up, I'll never get it back.'

'Oh, don't be so full of bullshit, Jack. I back down every day when it's for the best. Even with assholes.'

He didn't know how much to say, so let it pass. 'Maybe I'm just a little upset because I can see Maeve is gone for good now.'

'Not very far.'

'No, but the cord is cut. It's the way it's got to be, I know it.' You always lose what you love, he thought.

I slip on my red eyeshades and check into the Tiki-Tai Motel on Ventura Boulevard down in the San Fernando Valley. I use my Alan Smithee credit card – it's the name directors use when they're so ashamed of a project they want their name off it. If I'd gone over to the Malibu side of the canyon, where the movie culture was a lot stronger, that name would have been recognized for sure.[2]

I have a secret affection for anonymous motels in anonymous towns so the Tiki-Tai makes me happy as a clam. Fame really does suck – you'll never know. I never appreciated that when I was younger. To remain impeccably polite to some old hag or a group of giggling teens – and you have to explain the same crap over and over. Yes, I loved kissing Beyoncé in *Permanent Tourist*. No, I didn't do my own motorcyle stunts in *Ride to Live*.

In ten years, there was probably one intelligent and challenging question: how did I first learn I was black? Jesus! That's the whole fucking deal, you know? With a kindly white Moms and no dad in the picture, it takes a while to figure it out. What age? I just don't know. Go ask your President, kiddies.

I slip out of my room in the motel past the ridiculous Easter Island head and make my way across the umpteen-lane Ventura Boulevard to a Fatburger restaurant in a mini-mall. They're legend in L.A. – the Valley's one big contribution to high school cuisine, and I've never even sampled one.

My head is getting heavy again, and I don't know how long I can hold off the Skinnies. My meds are at home in Brentwood, but so is Paulita, and wouldn't this sudden compulsive dive into my past be nice to try to explain to her?

I collect my plastic number tepee and wait patiently for my Fatburger. A young girl out on the street with spiky green hair glares in the window at me, possible recognition, and her boyfriend with his Popeye arms and big tattoos throws me a possessive glare. Maybe even racist. One of the heartbreaks

---

[2] Scores of disowned films have come out under Mr Smithee's aegis since the name was invented to resolve a dispute over the movie *Death of a Gunfighter* in 1969. This name was long used by directors including those of *Cool Hand Luke, Ronin,* and a hatchet-like TV recut of the brilliant Oscar-nominated *The Insider*, that was actually directed by Michael Mann. But the name is becoming too well-known now after writer-producer Joe Eszterhas ruined it by making the horrible mess *An Alan Smithee Film: Burn Hollywood Burn* – and doubly ironically making the real director Arthur Hiller take his name off it.

of being African-American in America is always having to deal with that, and never knowing when it's coming.

Jesus, man, I wouldn't do that freaky girl to save my life.

I wonder if I'll ever get any closer to understanding Sandstone, or Moms – or finding a useful hint about my father. All I really know is she got impregnated at that sex club, when she was fucking who knows how many men, night after night after night. (For a moment, I feel sick.) And, of course, I know Mr Lucky was black.

Moms – Donna Wisecki, Donna Freedom, Donna Robin's-egg, Donna Bird, Melanie Bird. She went through Students for a Democratic Society, then some tiny Maoist group in Santa Monica, Esalen, Rolfing, Gestalt Therapy and Primal Scream – just about everything but a really bad religious cult. She told me she'd actually heard the Manson Family play some ragged rock music at the Topanga Corral. Thank God she didn't get caught up with them. I wasn't really around, of course, but the only thing left of all that time now seems to be a lot of ruined lives, a lot of regret and a few prison sentences. And me.

For just an instant a Skinny peeks in the window of the fast-food place and I look away. These spooks come from that time in Sydney, Australia – shooting *Southern Lights* – when I chose to sneak off to the museum and I saw the spindly stick carvings of what the Aboriginals call *mimis*, mischie-vous unbelievably scrawny spirits who slip in and out of the cracks in rocks to bedevil men, or help them – as they choose. I'd been seeing my own *mimis*, the beings that I called Skinnies, for two or three years by then, and every wooden image stopped me in my tracks in that museum and rang my bell.

The waitress brings my oversized drippy burger and greets me insincerely, with a backward glance of 'maybe I know this guy.' I almost tear my jaw muscles taking a bite, then choke a little.

We don't want you to hurt yourself, a chirpy voice says right into my ear.

Are you guys included in the budget of this crappy pic? I ask.

The Skinnies emit their rapid giggles, just out of sight somewhere. Their intrusion leaves a smell on the air like patchouli oil, as usual. They all tell me their goofy names, but I never learn them, on purpose.

My drugs. I need them. But they're so far away in Brentwood, man.

Trust us, a Skinny says. Look at us. We always know what's best for you.

For some reason, a number of painstakingly restored nineteen fifties cars begins passing slowly on the boulevard outside, blessedly diverting my attention. Amazing – they turn off into my own motel, one after another. Is this real? Of course it is. What is more real than a 1957 Plymouth with maybe the tallest tailfins that ever rumbled down an assembly line?

Skinnies, you have nothing to say about car culture, do you? Nor anything else about the ordinary world. That's your weakness. You live in a world of illusion. You little shits never pay attention to the birds and the flowers.

'Dis de way Americans live?' Winston Pennycooke asked, looking contemptuously around the small, furnished apartment that Harper had rented for him. His eye fixed on a small old-style picture tube TV.

'There's a bad recession going on now, my man,' Harper said.

'I-an-I not care about any recess.'

It was uncanny. With the floppy three-color knit cap, the gold silk shirt and the checkered bell-bottoms, he was a near perfect clone of his dead brother Trevor whom Harper had worked with a few years earlier. Even the height – six-seven or so. 'Tomorrow, maybe, you get the big Beverly Hills mansion. For now, you prove to us you're bad Tony Montana. Your brother was my right-hand fixer for a year and he was cool, he was down.'

'Straight way I get to your country, ma'an, you stick me in the slavehouse. I dunno. I give you half my wage back if you put my tongue in some real Jamaica brown rum tonight.'

'Winston, man, how much younger are you than Trevor?'

'Call me Ratchet, ma'an, with respect, like we all say "Terror". Din't know no Trevor person. I seven year younger. I-an-I nineteen las' mont'. Terror my idol. I got to find the one that kill him.'

'Don't worry about that now, Ratchet. I'll have work for you soon.'

'Cha, look, my mind run to de romantic. An' I don' mean

no kissin' t'ing. I mean like de ol' knights of de Round Table. I got to venge Terror.'

'All in good time. I'll find out exactly what went down. All I know now is a man named Jack Liffey was with him at the end. We need a real man with no fear. You help my business, and I help yours.'

Harper knew his man, or boy. He took a bottle of Mount Gay Eclipse rum out of a paper bag and handed it to Winston Pennycooke, who did his best to keep his eyes from going wide as saucers.

'Super you bring dat, boss. Oh, dat de bes'.'

It was a long drive from East L.A. to Topanga, but Jack Liffey had shortened it some, or maybe not, by waiting until after the last tardy bustle of the rush hour and then going up the Hollywood Freeway and across the Valley. He'd called back and cursed out Reston for threatening him. 'Do that to me again, motherfucker . . .' He'd always had a strange-rooted need to challenge whatever had the power to hurt him, but that didn't mean he wouldn't get on with the job. Almost out of spite.

Just before he hit Topanga Canyon Boulevard at the Valley end he passed a big tiki motel and just to nail it all down, its parking lot was filled with lovingly restored 1950s cars. A complete time warp, he thought.

Without trouble he found what Maeve had described as the Taco Bell house – just an ordinary bungalow with an added arch of orange stucco and a tile roof. The lights were on, and a battered Chevy stake truck, with tall plywood sides, was parked in front. The truck door said *Rolf's Rubbish Hauling* in crude lettering. OK, Rolf, you're it.

A big man answered the door. He looked straightforward and physical. Jack Liffey offered him his best version of a business card, which even had his real name and phone, but no big detective eyeball.

'My daughter lives down the hill, she's going to UCLA, and she told me you seem to know a lot about the old times in Topanga.' The dog Maeve had mentioned materialized behind the big man's legs, a bulldog growling gently.

'Hush, Gord. You want to talk to me because . . . ?'

On an impulse, Jack Liffey squatted to greet the dog on its

own level. It glared back at him. 'I just blew my entire 401K on my dog's bone cancer. May you both escape that fate.'

'If Gordie gets that sick, my 401K will buy him a Big Mac as a sendoff. You were about to tell me your business, Mr Jack Liffey.'

'Have you heard of the black actor Tyrone Bird?'

'Of course.'

'Let me ask one more question and then I'll answer anything. What do you know about the Sandstone Retreat?'

'Oh, Christ.'

THREE
A Failed Experiment

I sit in the saggy Danish chair in the motel room and I take the rubber band off my delaminating paperback copy of *If He Hollers* and open to a dog-eared page. I've read the book six or seven times.

> 'What makes me so mad,' Johnson said, 'is the white folks got it on you at the start, so why do they have to give you any crap on top of it? That's what makes me so mad.'

I can't tear myself away from those words. I can hear Skinnies mutter and confide, but all off camera, so to speak. There are whole types and species of them, to suit any kind of sadness or embarrassment or fear I have to endure.

They tell me their flowery names like T.S. Eliot's cats, but I refuse to remember them. Should I meet my hallucinations half way? Nobody in *Parade* magazine tells you the answers to questions like that. Boy, I need my meds. Lacking them, my only real option tonight is to drink myself to sleep.

Rolf looked about sixty now, but Jack Liffey could imagine a fit and handsome thirty-year-old, obviously desirable traits at a round-robin sex club.

The man handed Jack Liffey a bottle of sparkling water and they settled into canvas sling chairs suspended from the living room ceiling.

A big-head black pony looked in through the open French window from the paddock and whinnied, as if unhappy about being left out in the dark. The bungalow was a single big room, probably a converted barn.

'Jack, meet Enrique. He's a Peruvian Paso. One of the few naturally gaited horses in the world,' he said. 'He's small but he's got a sense of mischief.'

'Hi, Henry,' Jack Liffey said dubiously.

The pony flapped his lips and withdrew.

'Sandstone,' Jack Liffey reminded the man.

'It wasn't like one of those nudist ranches. Or The Swingers Club down in the Valley. Most of those places banned open sex. At Sandstone, sex was the name of the game. Upstairs, earnest lectures about its healing powers. Downstairs was what was called the ball-room.' His laugh honked a little unpleasantly. 'A big open place with a lot of mattresses. You'd go down there weekends and see bare butts hoiking up and down everywhere. There was a raised platform where somebody'd be laying and half a dozen folks would be rubbing them with oil. Lots of grunts and squeals.

'John Williamson and his wife were messiahs about how sex would liberate the world. Some folks came to get liberated. Some just came to get laid, and that was OK with John, too. Lots of celebrities. Sammy Davis, Orson Bean, Daniel Ellsberg and Anthony Russo, before they stole the Pentagon Papers. Hell, I remember Bobby Darrin and Peter Lawford, I think Dean Martin. The memory grows a little dim.'

He urged his suspended chair into a light swing.

'The big crowd would blow in on Friday night and fill up the dirt lot next door with cars. It was this weird thing John called "open weekends". There were lectures and events for the visitors. Maybe twenty of us actually lived there full time. We did gardening and construction and I guess absorbed it all. The celebrities just popped in for curiosity or for sex and sometimes stayed the weekend. It wasn't a cult. Nobody *had* to do anything.'

He told Jack Liffey that he'd taught French Lit at UCLA until he'd got caught up heavily in the anti-war movement. A girl from a march had taken him to Sandstone.

'Timothy Leary,' he said abruptly. 'I remember him one weekend. Self-important as shit. Maybe I'm too cynical. Male celebrities were allowed to pay a weekend fee and come in without a partner, but ordinary guys had to have a woman in tow.

'I'm still ambivalent. Maybe there really is something liberating about trying to get yourself past jealousy and possessiveness. But I think the place hurt a lot of people – maybe even damaged them permanently. It shook me up.'

Enrique poked his head in again and Rolf Fuchs levered himself up to give the pony a couple of carrots from a big plastic bag against the wall.

'Truth is I didn't recover from Sandstone for a long time. I married the girl who took me, on a whim, but she left with someone else. Williamson himself got bored and left, and another guy took over, some ex-Marine who wasn't as hang-loose.'

Dark had fallen completely, and the only light in the room was a kerosene lamp on the kitchen sink.

'I thought I might go back to college in history. I read up on free-love places. There's been a whole lot of them. Especially in the sixties after that book *The Harrad Experiment*. But you can go back a century to Oneida and Nashoba. Did you know Hieronymus Bosch ran a free-love collective in fifteenth-century Holland?' He honked his odd laugh. 'The Inquisition came down on them like a ton of iron bibles.'

Jack Liffey had let him run because the man had a strange manic undertow that interested him, but he hadn't got what he wanted.

'It's seven, my adult beverage time,' Fuchs said. 'Can I offer you a glass of cabernet?'

'No thanks.'

'A.A.?'

'I'm just proving something to myself. What do you do now, since you quit teaching?'

On a kitchen counter, the man fought open a bottle of wine and poured some into an ordinary tumbler. He dipped a carrot in the red wine and held it far out the window. Somewhere out in the dark the carrot apparently vanished. 'Clear weeds. And there's a third-rate private school up here called Village and Country where I teach French to spoiled not-very-bright kids. V and C gets me cheap. No credential.'

'No dreams for something else?'

The man dialed up the kerosene lamp and it threw a remarkable amount of light across the room. His eyes were fixed and expressionless. 'Dreams? Sure. To be able to play *In a Silent Way* like Miles Davis.' He choked off a laugh. 'No, Jack, to be honest, I think Sandstone killed my dream capacity. Drained me right down dry like unplugging a sump.'

He raised his glass in a pointless toast.

'Sex is too powerful to play with like we did.'

The horse whinnied outside, as if agreeing.

'You can't let yourself act out your deepest fantasies, man,' he went on. 'Trust me. It burns away something you best keep inside.'

'Are you OK?' Jack Liffey asked, suddenly a little worried about the man.

'Oh, yeah. I'm fine. Absolutely. No question. I can get along without fantasies. I could even sing it for you.'

'Please don't.'

'You asked me about Tyrone Bird. How does he figure in this?'

'Has he come to see you?'

'No.'

'He will. Bird was conceived at Sandstone – at least he thinks so. His mom was white as rice, so it's a pretty good bet his dad was black. How many blacks hung out there?'

Rolf Fuchs thought about that for a while. 'Not many. Have you got a photo of this guy?'

Meier Reston had given Jack Liffey a publicity composite, an unwieldy eight by ten with Bird in a half dozen costumes and poses. He'd done his best to fold it along the photo borders, and he brought it to Fuchs at the kitchen counter.

The man uncreased it flat. 'I've seen him. Can't remember the movies. Handsome bugger, isn't he? Like Paul Newman, dipped. Who was his mom?'

'I don't have a picture. Melanie Bird. She was never famous.'

'I don't remember a Melanie. When you get a picture of her, you show me. I can give you two names now; black guys who obviously hung out to hit on the white girls, but where they are now is anybody's guess.

'Donnie Spencer – he was an actor, student of acting, I don't know anything else about him. And the other's only a first name. Stoney. Maybe a nickname. Sorry. Wait. Stoney was some kind of intellectual, a show-off about it, a little older. This kid may be all wrong.'

Enrique put his big head inside again, and Jack Liffey got up and scratched between his ears for a moment.

'Bird will find you,' Jack Liffey predicted. 'Would you give him my card and tell him I'm on his side?'

'Are you?'

'I find missing kids, but I never take them home if they don't want to go.'

Rolf left the business card on his countertop and breathed softly into the horse's nose. 'Everybody's luck runs out sometime, doesn't it, Jack?'

It was time to leave. Rolf Fuchs' emotional life seemed like some kind of failed experiment, as if he'd been warned but gone ahead and sipped the forbidden brew.

Gloria parked about a block up the Oildale street from the house and exhaled very slowly. She should still be on the way to Fresno for the police DNA conference. It was late, dark already.

Jack was the best – she couldn't hope for better, really. Was she throwing him away? Yet, how did you walk away from a vibe that tingled this deep? An ex-cop with a grin, an honest one no less, who'd been fired for his honesty in the Deep South, clever and funny and hard, a guy who knew most of the same things she did. No civilian, not even Jack, would ever have that.

All they'd really done was hold hands briefly. But what a surge of electricity she'd felt – hunkered down in the midst of a police shoot-out. She recalled the shivering urges she'd had for Sonny Theroux ever since, and his pleas, notes, e-mails, even covert phone calls. Just one test, he insisted – they owed themselves one night to find out.

She let up on the brake and allowed her RAV-4 to idle slowly down the block to the ugly little ante-bellum slave manor somebody before Sonny Theroux had built there, almost as a parody of *Gone With the Wind*'s Tara, on the totally inauspicious no-sidewalk block of working class tarpaper bungalows in Oildale, across the trickle of the Kern River from Bakersfield. As her car drifted in front of the house and she finally braked to a stop, a bright lamp came on above the silly columned rotunda, flooding the front grass with light, probably a motion sensor.

She'd never been a coward, and she took the keys and walked straight up to the house.

'Gloria,' he said, pretending only mild surprise when he opened up. He was wearing his absurd satin smoking jacket, too effete to appeal to her deeper urges, but still.

'Sonny. It's been six months and thirteen days since we touched.'

She didn't really have to say anything more.

He nodded. 'I kept the bed warm.'

The UCLA administration had given Maeve a parking spot in lot eleven off Sunset Boulevard, which was a twenty minute walk from her anthropology classes at Haines Hall. In fact, they hadn't given her anything. The lot assignment was a hunting permit for a small quadrangle of asphalt large enough to park her Echo, and it had cost her almost two hundred dollars for the quarter. The decal was useless after about eight forty-five a.m., by which time every slot would be taken.

She was beginning to dislike her primary professor, Dr Clydesson-Browne, already. He rattled on and on about his own work on kinship systems among the Yao in central Africa. That had been fifty years ago.

What had interested her about anthropology – or so she'd thought – was how the modern world had evolved out of these older societies, what this prehistoric world said about being human, and what in that transition had brought about, or preserved, all the rivalries, distrust and wars. She didn't give a damn about how a second cousin felt about a mother's brother in Yaoland in 1966 – or 1066. What did their customs say about the position of women now? What did they say about who was in charge of the body politic and why? She wondered if she should have been in sociology or political science instead.

In the cavernous arena of the freshman auditorium, a boy she'd noticed before with an attractive dark forelock bobbing over his eyes leaned toward her and whispered, 'Is this as tedious to you as it is to me?'

'I hoped it would mean something,' Maeve whispered back.

The professor wore a radio mike and his voice boomed forth on the sound system, dry and practiced, the intonations falling in odd places, as if he'd learned English somewhere in Sweden.

The professor turned away from them to scribble on the giant whiteboard:

> In some instances, the sister's son has special rights over the property of his mother's brother. A vestige of a matrilineal society?

Before Clydesson-Browne could boost the movable portion of the whiteboard upward into better sight for notetaking, the boy beside her gave a sigh of discontent and slipped down the row and out of the hall. Without quite knowing what she was doing, Maeve grabbed up her notebooks and followed.

He was lighting a cigarette on a bench a few feet away. 'I'm Chad,' he said.

'Chad? You should have been knocked off a ballot card ages ago in Florida.'

He smiled dutifully. 'The many cousins of my mother's brother, I guess.'

'My name's Maeve. No backstory to speak of.' That was a lie.

He offered the pack of American Spirits, and she hesitated, then took one. Why not? Just one, she thought. Though it did violate her healthy principles. College was for new experiences, even if she'd pretty much had all the new experiences she would need for a full lifetime before getting here: pushing her near-dead father through a riot on a wheelbarrow to save his life; being held prisoner by a band of dim-witted motorcyclists, etc., etc. She hadn't yet been abducted by a flying saucer.

As he lit the cigarette for her, Chad said, 'I'll tell you my real name if you promise not to laugh.'

'How can anybody promise that – it might be Whoop-de-doo – but if I do laugh, I promise to do it with respect.' She just barely beat back a gust of coughing as the cigarette smoke burned down her gullet. It was actually her first tobacco cigarette. Only the experience of marijuana had prepared her for the raw rasp of smoke down her throat.

'My folks named me Templeton,' he said ruefully.

She smiled, then suppressed it hard. 'The fussy troublemaking rat in *Charlotte's Web*.'

'Can you believe they'd never read the book?'

'Then maybe you were named after their butler.'

'Nobody has a butler,' he said indignantly. 'We did have a cook, but her name was Marisol. I don't know where my name came from. But when I was thirteen, I told them I was going to stop answering to Templeton. I just dead refused. I told them my new name was Chad.'

'Why?' she asked.

'It seemed normal. I don't know.' He puffed heavily on the cigarette. 'That lecture, man – you know, last year I worked the Jungle Cruise at Disneyland.'

'"And now, the most dangerous part of the journey,"' they both recited in unison, '"the return to civilization."'

'Yuk,' he added dully. 'The only good part was when I got to shoot blanks at the big fake hippo. Now and again tour guys would vary the spiel and get fired for it. My pal Otis said, '"Oh, look, Uncle Walt's ass is rising out of the river!"'

Chuckling, she puffed cautiously, trying not to inhale.

'Off the port bow, ladies and germs, up on the cliff, the little mechanical monkey in back can be seen to be masturbating.'

'Are you an anthro major?' she asked.

'Organic chem,' he said. 'This is my general sci course.'

'I've heard organic's the hardest subject in college,' Maeve offered.

He raised one eyebrow. 'Lots of memory-work. What drew you to anthro?'

She shook her head. 'The average undergraduate doesn't have a clue what she's doing,' Maeve said. 'That's me.'

'The average human being is utterly blind to beauty. You're really, truly beautiful, Maeve. Want to hook up?'

'That's way too sudden, Chad. Be cool. When you see me again, ask me out to dinner.'

Slowly, waking and letting my eyes zig-zag across the mess on the floor, I remember drinking myself into alcohol-drenched sleep from a goofy little six-pack of fifty mil Chivas bottles, airplane bottles, bought from behind locked glass from a disapproving old woman at a drugstore. Now a whole platoon of little dead soldiers is lying on the beige carpet. I half expect one of the Skinnies to come into view, peer inside a tiny bottle and make a big O of his/her lips before winking at me in that snarky way they have. But remarkably, they're allowing me some morning peace.

Luckily I don't get physical hangovers. When I drink too

much, I just wake with baffling anxieties – like somebody who's being followed by a tragedy that's too hard to face. Amazing that I once thought money could take care of all my worries. I knew quite a few people, rich as sin, who were worried to death about what their money meant, as if it might just evaporate on them, or turn on them and exact vengeance for some great crime, but that wasn't my problem. I wasn't born with money, so enough had always been enough.

If only some over-the-counter drug could help with the rest. I'd walk across to the Rite Aid and buy some acetaminophen or Dimetapp. But the meds I really need are in Brentwood, in a carved soapstone box in the bedroom. Paulita standing guard like a banshee.

Then, all of a sudden, there's a banging at the motel door. I grab at my wristwatch on the bedside table, a plain Rolex Oyster, and find out it's just after eight.

'Hold on!' I yell. Polite to the last, even if it's my assassin. Yeah, that's Moms's doing.

I tug on my pants and answer the door, holding the pants up with a fist.

'Mr Smithee, sir. I'm so very sorry. The computer tells me your Visa has a problem.'

'You're not from Hollywood, are you?'

The man is an East Asian of some sort, with jet-black hair and a squared-off shirt with a lot of white-on-white embroidery. 'My family is from Gujarat, sir.'

'What a glorious place that is,' I say, offering my most winning smile. I have no clue where Gujarat is. 'I confess, the name Smithee is a kind of in-joke in Hollywood for remaining anonymous. I'm in the movies. I'll give you another credit card in my real name. When you're done with it, just slide it back under the door. OK?'

'Yes, sir. But if it is still not good with my service, we are in very grave trouble.'

'*You're* not in trouble, Mr Gujarat. I promise. But please leave the name "Smithee" on the card I signed.'

I hand him an American Express in my real name, wondering what has gone wrong with the other one, and I shut the door before this man can look too closely at the mess inside.

Maybe the *If He Hollers* production company is hunting me down, I think, and that bastard of an agent Ardak Sahagian

FOUR

A Place to Hold All the Failings

I drive out of the tiki motel as soon as I'm fully awake, so whatever rats are on the scent can't track me. *Gone, No Forwarding*, I think. It's the title of my second movie, made from a Joe Gores novel about a skip-tracer, and I can't remember a damn thing about it except the baby-faced director just out of film school who kept strutting around the set braying foolhardy orders until the production company pulled him off and brought in a reliable older action director, known to have better set-manners.

This morning I use all my credit cards to draw a couple thousand in cash from a whole string of banks all over the Valley. They can trace the banks and cards as much as they want, but best of luck tracking me now, assholes – I'm running on cash.

Then I drive up Topanga to Fernwood and up a winding lane to an overlook above Tuna Canyon. I came this route once before, maybe ten years earlier, and found that the Sandstone Ranch was nothing but a dowdy empty house awaiting a buyer. Presumably some sad soul owns it in absentia, unless the accumulated karma of its reputation has driven everyone away. Something says, this is a bad place, Ty.

I lean out of my car to press the button on the squawk-box at the gate and wait. A big slab of sandstone set into the rock gates announces:

Sandstone Ranch

'I think you made a mistake, pard,' comes back the electronic gargle.

I realize I have nothing to act on now, no connections at all, except this dream of finding my past through this sad benighted house. I can't be turned away. It's become a terrible mythic longing.

I know the house is two miles down a one-lane access road that isn't paved for the first half mile, a bizarre kind of deterrent to journalists and simpletons like me.

'I'm thinking of buying the place,' I try over the intercom. 'I'd pay a lot more than you owe on it.'

'That's a *nada*, pal. I'm just the caretaker. But you can spread a little green around, and the bank will never know.'

'A hundred bucks to look the place over,' I offer. 'That help any?'

'Make it two hundred, and you get the grand tour, pard.'

I know perfectly the sound of a sucker-raise from a yo-yo sitting on a pair of threes. There's practically nothing but poker on movie sets, and the stunt men I learned from can smell bluff like sharks on chum. 'Let's say a hundred, and if I'm happy with the tour, I'll make your day really memorable.'

'OK, big tipper.'

The gate buzzes, a slider rather than a swinger. The whirring goes on for a bit before the old gears use up their backlash, and the gate begins to pull open.

As I drive in I realize the place probably hasn't seen a crowd, or even a single heart-pounding newcomer since the late-nineteen seventies. Something aches inside me. The view as I crunch slowly down the gravel road is awesome, the greening winter hills falling away dramatically to the blue-green Pacific, choppy with tiny whitecaps far below. Darker kelp beds make big jigsaw shapes like something secret hidden in the depths. Even from up here you can see flights of pelicans cruising low.

The car bumps on to asphalt, cracked and weedy, and eventually I see the overlarge ordinary-looking building in the distance. Yet it's *the* building. I can't resist a frisson from Moms's tales and so many of my own imaginings – I see a dark first floor of unlit glass and upstairs the main floor with a house-wide balcony bisected by a fat white chimney.

I pass the flat field where so many cars must once have parked on weekends. There's no evidence of it now, and I stop near the house, beside a beat-up old Mazda 323 on the forecourt.

The house door is opened by a stubbly guy in khaki Sansabelt

pants and a wifebeater T-shirt, smiling as if the expression
hurts him. An aging Stanley Kowalski. He must be seventy-
five, and something about him suggests he's been ill.

'I'm Karl Rubin. I used to meet so many people right here,
in the nude, if you can believe it.'

'Why not?' But I want to say: Too much information, dude.

'And right on that spot –' He points to the wood floor about
three feet inside the door – 'Sammy Davis, Jr., started
undressing and dropped what must have been a ten-carat
diamond cufflink. He didn't give a shit.

'But his date, the porn actress, Marilyn Chambers, did and
she fell to her knees – no joke intended! – and grabbed it up
like a chipmunk. Then Mr Davis dropped a diamond-covered
cigarette lighter, and the woman grabbed that, too. Jesus! Next
time, I was going to go down on *my* knees, but the man
laughed and soft-shoed on into the living room. It was already
full of people, undressed and otherwise, yakking about the
philosophy of sex or some such. They were so intellectual
about it all.'

'Did you know Melanie Bird?' I interrupt his reverie.

'Mel, sure! She was Donna, too. She was here from about
halftime. A really nice woman she was.'

Once again I've run into someone who obviously doesn't
recognize me. I wonder if movie culture is disappearing among
older grown-ups, the way music and books have. In another
year or two, the only celebrities at the mall will be people
from reality TV – and Warhol will be right about the famous
fifteen minutes. The thought oppresses me, as if I'm pissing
my life down a drain. All this make-believe.

I snap myself out of this stupid funk before the Skinnies
can show up. 'So nobody wants to buy this place?'

'It's got twenty-five acres attached. That's like having a big
Albert Ross around your neck.' I begin to wonder if he's
pulling my leg. Albert Ross? 'The Coastal Commission doesn't
let you subdivide. Asking price is five-point-six mil. It's a lot
of bread for a pretty ordinary house and twenty-five acres you
can't use. The only thing it'd be really good for is a nursing
home or a rehab.'

The man leads me into a big darkish room.

'Tell me about Melanie,' I say.

'I think she came with a husband. Maybe. But a lot of guys freaked out at the scene and took off pretty quick. That was a long time ago, man. Here's the main meeting room. When we had lectures, everybody would just sit on the floor or on a bunch of old chairs. Most of the speakers talked about this big change that was coming to human consciousness, yada-yada.'

The room we stand in is a big echoey nondescript space; an old console TV faces one easy chair, a parody of a bachelor pad that's the size of a dance hall.

'I came as a handyman but I became one of the steadies. I got laid as much as I could on the big party weekends.' He laughs a fake laugh, but it chokes off. 'Anybody buys this place is going to want to put up some walls, I think, maybe rebuild completely. Unless he likes free-range bowling.'

'Did Melanie hook up with somebody?'

'It didn't work that way. At least, it wasn't supposed to.'

'Come on, people have special friends.'

'Get over that thinking, man. It'll keep you from seeing what this place was. Melanie had friends, sure, she hung with a woman named Joyce McDonald. Her guys, I don't know. She was pretty busy that way. I even had her a few times, but she was nothing special. It was kinda like – "You moved, did I hurt you?"'

The man didn't notice that I was doing my best not to cross the intervening space and strangle him.

'I hate to say it, but sex gets old. At least when there's so much of it going. I could use a little of the overflow now.' He laughs his suppressed laugh again, like someone profoundly alone.

I wonder if it isn't better just to come out and tell him she was my mother. He's getting hard to take – and I also worry if part of my annoyance isn't the fact that he hasn't recognized me as a movie star. Deep down, maybe it is.

'Follow me. I'll show you what used to be the ball-room.'

I know the joke, but follow him glumly down the wide stairs to another big empty room with brown carpet and no furniture at all.

'This was all mattresses and bare butts. Come look here.'

A large bathroom toward the back has flowery gold and brown wallpaper, and the caretaker beckons with a come-see finger. Up close the scrollwork resolves into copulating couples and threesomes and various other Kama Sutra notions. Shit. It makes the place seem so sophomoric.

'Cute,' I say. 'Listen, man. I'll give you two hundred if you just tell me any African-American men Melanie Bird hung with.'

Karl Rubin squints at me, getting it at last. 'You're about that age, ain't you, son? Well, it weren't Sammy Davis, that's for sure, if you got a golddigging mind. There was a few coloreds here, for sure, but there was one she seemed keen on. Marcus Stone was his name. He was a college professor, out in the Valley.'

I count out one hundred and sixty in twenties, crumple it all spitefully into a ball and drop it into a grimy toilet in the Kama Sutra bathroom.

'There's no call to do that, son.'

I remember a walkoff line from one of my early films that I never really understood. 'That's just the squid ink inside me.'

'Somebody's out looking for you, Stoney,' the man said at his door.

'You know this because . . . ?'

'My friends.' Harper pushed his way in.

'We don't have friends, friend. Beyond business, we have cunning and we have fear. Tell.'

'Speak for your ownself.' Harper gave him a long cool stare. Harper had made a point of not putting a shirt on over his huge buff chest, which he'd just shaved and oiled. 'It ain't business and it ain't payback. I think it's personal. I don't like it when your old-school life come and want to jitterbug.'

Marcus Stone pressed three fingers to his temple in the small pool house that was now his home, a gesture he had used for years to try to rid himself magically of trouble. Too many years. 'Nothing gets in the way of business, you know that.'

Harper did his best to prove Stoney's dictum about having no friends. 'Listen, old man, me and the Rollin' Seventies could swallow you with a glass of water if we have to. I'm your connect to everything you need now – your soldiers, your dealers, your heavy cash. I even brought in a new soldier from the Big J. I pick up the Colombians flying in today. Everything got to be smooth as silk. Convince me this guy looking for you now is no problem.'

'This the first I heard of it, child. Somebody from back in the day? How the fuck I know, dickhead?'

'You smell like a trunk full of dead cats, Stoney. You ever take a shower, man?'

'Don't be dissing me. Hear? Or we got to get down hard, you and me.'

'This the way it is,' Harper announced. 'If this mother-fucker gets in the way, I'm'a tell my new trouble man Pennycooke to take him down hard. It's just pest control. You with the program?'

Marcus Stone shrugged, thinking for some reason of his uncomplicated life way back in the day, teaching community college, staring intently at all the lovely short-skirt knees on girls in his classroom, when he was still righteous and clean and respected. He knew how he had spun so far off track, but wondered what fate had set it up. 'Go on then, if that's your mind. Bust a cap on this old-time mothah. I don't give a shit.'

Gloria woke first, in the sunbright bedroom upstairs. The light came through the gauze curtains, blazing across the room to a big painting of the French Quarter in New Orleans, all fili-greed iron railings and a half dozen people hanging over to wave and toss strings of glass beads. Mardi Gras, of course, she thought. She was surprised that it meant anything at all to him, but then she knew that some pretty corrupted Paiute Indian customs – even the Ghost Dance – still mattered a lot to her.

She studied Sonny, sleeping, so anguished and restless. He rolled and barked a few unintelligible words. It was hard not to reach out and gather him in, with all his torment. He'd been about as good a lover as he could be under the circum-stances, and she knew the circumstances included his timing things and secretly slipping into the bathroom for a Viagra. Everybody had issues, she thought.

Just then his wristwatch on the bedside table started alarming, a soft burring at first, then a little louder, a double-buzz louder still. He began to wake on about the fourth increase in tone. A twitch here, a knuckle rubbing the sheet, a leg shuddering. Sonny Theroux, you're a whole encyclopedia of nervous tics, she thought. She leaned over him to the table, and pressed a stud that seemed to silence the watch.

'Whoa. Early don't last so long.'

'Do you have to go to work?'

He shook his head, but he might have been clearing it. 'I just don't want to miss any precious time I get with you.'

She ruffled his hair, a bit hard. 'You're a tormented man, you know that?'

'Gentle, darling. A little too much fond-lick with your strength and I'm broke in two.'

'Don't get off into dialect with me, Sonny. You may have started off in some swamp, but I know you've et in hotels.'

He laughed softly. 'Very good one, ma'am. I enjoy the word-play but I enjoy you more. I really love those great big breasts hanging over me. Señora Hinojosa has the morning off, so we can cook breakfast for ourselves. Or whatever we have a mind for.'

'Well, first, for accuracy, this breast here is mostly silicone after I had the evil cancer taken out. Second, I've got to get myself to Fresno to register for at least some of this conference. Why don't you just fuck me once more right this minute, if you've got more of your joy pills.'

'Do I?' He got up and headed for the bathroom, but glanced back. 'I didn't know you'd noticed, but you're a helluva cop. You know the big social drawback of Viagra?'

She shook her head. 'The wait?'

'All those trophy wives. They got to actually screw the wrinkled old fart now.'

She smiled. Some day, she'd ask him what the problem was with him – if he knew. Maybe blood pressure meds. He certainly had a full plate of anxieties. But no questions now. Now she wanted to enjoy his erect penis, even if it took a bunch of elves cranking on the mechanism to get it up, and she wanted to distract herself from the whole dangerous game she was playing.

Jack Liffey let himself wake at his own tempo, which often meant he'd feel a bit groggy with oversleep for a while. He didn't even look at the time. He'd gotten used to waking beside Gloria and really missed her. He knew damn well she was probably experimenting up north, but what he didn't know was whether she saw some possible future, wholesome or otherwise, that did not contain him. And that idea scared him to death.

He could hear faint *banda* music on the block already, its polka-like beat normally an annoyance. But now it made him feel at home.

After he showered and fetched the *L.A. Times*, he saw that the answering machine was flashing. Screw 'em. It could only be the film company, riding his ass for instant results. Why were film people always such assholes, he wondered. It was almost a rule of life. He should have it tatted up on a sampler and framed: film people are assholes. It would sell like crazy in L.A.

He poured out a little cereal and ate it while scanning the headlines. The paper had been so thoroughly debased by a pinhead Chicago real estate tycoon that it was no longer worth reading much, except to note now and again a hint of something local buried deep inside that affected a case he was working on. For years he'd been on the knife-edge of canceling and taking only the *New York Times*.

Morning memories popped up. He remembered, during the divorce proceedings so many years ago, his wife's mother saying dutifully (it had been necessary then) that he was a lousy father, and it had really hurt him. It was part of the game the system had demanded back then, before the invention of 'the uncontested divorce'. But it had made him reconsider himself – the way any outside judgment did. Am I inconsistent? Am I loving one minute and then forgetting my family the next? He almost phoned Maeve that instant to reassure himself that he hadn't been that bad a father.

Jesus. All this morning misery suggested so many other screw-ups that he had squashed down deep into the hardened white space that he kept far inside himself just to hold all the failings. What had happened to make him lose his sense of humor about himself? Cool it, Jack.

Finally he let himself think of Gloria and wondered if she really had gone to see Sonny. How had he even guessed at that? A single glance between them that he'd observed six months ago? Her own eagerness to make the trip? And –

was he imagining? – a kind of understated retreat from him beforehand. No, he wouldn't reject her preemptively. Gloria was it for him, damn it. He wanted her, and he'd fight for her.

The toaster burst upward noisily and startled him, and he'd forgotten he'd even loaded it with a split English muffin. OK, he could substitute instant gratification – melted salty butter and strawberry jam – for the deteriorating tangle of his psyche.

I'm fine, he thought. She'll be back.

FIVE
De Whole Troof

Winston 'Ratchet' Pennycooke awoke with a splitting headache, not quite knowing where he was. He saw that a half bottle of Mount Gay Eclipse sat on the bedside table, and his brain worked things out quickly. He was finally in America, in L.A., in a crummy apartment for losers. He was following the footpads of his brother, Trevor, who had initiated him into Rasta when he was a nine-year-old back in Trenchtown and then taught him to break loose from the old ties of the West Indies – even the pull to all the cousins who'd emigrated to England. 'That place just a black-n-white movie now, Win,' he'd said and then sucked at his teeth. 'Cha, Uncle Sam got more future in his likkle finger than John Bull total body, and Sam, he right over dere. Dey even cook our food in America. Dey got good jerk meat in every big city, real plantains, ackee and saltfish, dirty rice. But no cow-foot stew. Forget dat.'

Winston Pennycooke, Ratchet Pennycooke, sat up on the edge of the bed and wondered about his woman, Yasmin, in Golden Spring. He wanted her with him. It wasn't much of a life yet, but from everything his brother and this new boss had said, it would be pretty good if he proved himself. But enough about himself. He had a duty, too. Trevor, brah, I here for you, ma'an. Trevor had been killed here three years earlier.

Walkin' down the road
With your ratchet in your waist,
Johnny you're too bad.
You're just robbin' and a-stabbin' and you're lootin' and
    a-shootin'
Now you're too bad.[3]

[3] The Slickers (Winston Bailey; Roy Beckford; Derrick Crooks; Delroy Wilson), 1972

The phone rang, startling Winston Pennycooke wide-awake.
'I-an-I present,' he said into the phone.
'Ratchet?'
'The very one. Dat Harper?'
'Now who else in this country know your location, my man?'
'His Imperial Majesty, Conquering Lion of Judah, King
of Kings of Ethiopia and Elect of God, Haile Selassie. He
know all.'
'Oh, Sweet Jesus. Forget that shit. I got a job for you.'

It was a drag that you couldn't go out to the gate any more to
meet people right off the plane, Harper thought. All this post
9/11 crap. The world had changed forever, as they say – but
most of it for about a week. Then he remembered that you
never had been able to go out to the gates in the Bradley, the
international terminal, where they herded arrivals through
customs and immigration first. He wondered if he should make
a big cardboard sign, Ortagwaza – however the fuck the greasers
spelled it – and stand there along the exit ramp like all the
chauffeurs and tour-guides.

Fuck it. He was the only black waiting there who wasn't
dressed like a bellhop, and he and the big O had seen each
other before. O was a light brown *blanco*, skin like an Indian,
and his pals would be Spanish niggers. Not too hard to spot
each other, Harper thought. Still, he was restless. He'd arrived
just after the Avianca flight's official landing time, and he'd
been waiting more than an hour. Another troop of foreigners
pushed their overloaded luggage trolleys out the glass doors
and came up the ramp, brown men in silky non-tuck shirts
with round women in tow. Could be Middle East, could be
Latin America.

Women, listen up – eat a whole lot less, Harper thought.
Men don't like chubbies, whatever they tell you. He was a
health nut and worked out twice a day to keep his abs solid.
As more little groups came out, he craned his neck not to
miss a single face.

A half hour later an angry little party of blacks in expensive clothes slammed out the door with only carry-ons. Their
eyes caught his right away.

'Or-tuh-guaz-a,' he said softly as they came abreast on the
ramp, leading their boss.

''Arper,' the tall one said, glaring with his black eyes. 'Or-tay-*hwa*-sa.'

No one said another word until he'd got half the steely-faced bunch into the black Escalade, and the other half into a mini-van taxi. He counted nine, no, ten with the boss. Jesus. Who needed ten ride-alongs for a dope delivery? Something was up. It was good he hadn't brought Stoney. He'd have flipped out.

The tall guy had a tendency to grind off sparks of suppressed rage at just about anything, and the other guys looked like a jumpy Secret Service detail ready to fill the air around their President with lead.

'Navigate us to the Beverly Wilshire,' the O Dude ordered.

'No trouble,' Harper said. He passed the word to the cabbie, some kind of Middle Easterner, who followed them north on Sepulveda. At least they couldn't possibly have any weapons, just getting off a plane.

'There's a bank called the Culver-Fed up ahead on your left,' Orteguaza said. 'Stop there.'

'It's changed,' Harper warned. 'Things is pretty unreliable in banks these days. It's a Wells-Fargo, now.'

Orteguaza glared at him as if the takeover was his fault.

'The big crash,' Harper shrugged. 'I lost some money, too.'

'I don' lose money. They lose my money, they die.'

A theory Harper rather liked, but he doubted if it could be enforced against Wells-Fargo. He was made to wait across the street, the mini-van behind him on a red zone, and the whole crew stopped traffic and trooped across six lanes of Sepulveda Boulevard, carrying empty handbags and nylon duffles. After a minute he slipped across and chanced a peek in the glass doors and saw all of them heading in through the grillwork to the safety-deposit vault. Shit, he thought. They probably could have stored anything in there – guns, small rockets, nukes.

When they came out, there was no question they were all strapped. Probably picked up some cash, too. Maybe the whole load of coke, or maybe that was later. He had Stoney's million dollars in rumpled twenties stashed away safe to pay them, but not in easy reach.

''Otel.'

'Let's get one thing straight,' Harper said, before he'd restart the Caddy. 'All a' you, I respect you guys all to hell, but I ain' no hired dingus chauffeur. I'm an O.G. of the Rollin' Seventies, the roughest social club in L.A. I'm due my props – my respect. I can see you guys are all fixed up with your armament now, and that's just fine, but we got a chemistry expert who's going to test any coke you give me ten ways from Sunday before I hand you a million real American dollars. Are we cool about that?'

Orteguaza tried to stare him down, and Harper took it as a challenge to his manhood and just wasn't going to look away.

Time passed very slowly.

'I feel the wrath in the air,' Harper said finally. 'You do understand English?' He saw the look in the tall man's eyes, the maniac expression of someone just about to go to war. 'Please calm down, *señor. No sea un tirón.* I'm not a beginner. I respect you. Everything is perfectly cool this end. I have the money, if you got the snow. This isn't Colombia or Mexico where there's a bunch of heads lying in the streets every morning. This is the U. S. of A., where we do our shit clean and on the up-and-up.'

'*No sea un* asshole, 'Arper. Drive.'

You could never get yourself so far away from this kind of macho that it smoothed out; Harper knew that. He'd have been happier just stopping in the middle of the boulevard and jumping out of the Escalade and killing all four of them right there, and letting the taxi-van behind go into panic. Money or no money. Driving around with a bunch of Spics showing off their I-gonna-keel-you eyes wasn't Harper's idea of a cheerful afternoon.

'I hear you got problems,' Orteguaza said out of the blue, almost no intonation in his voice. 'Maybe somebody wants to stick a nine in your boss's ear and take our *drogas* and your money.'

'That's your world,' Harper said. 'Not ours. Our end is all tied down. That shit don't happen. We got guys ready to fuck up guys that even think like that before they get out of bed in the morning. It's all cool. You and your boys have a good night sleep and go see Disneyland, and we exchange in two days.'

'No meet today?'

'The deal was day after tomorrow. It stays the same. No changes, none.'

Orteguaza smiled for the first time, but there was absolutely no humor in his rictus. 'You ever have a greased pistol up you ass, *cabrón*?'

Harper hadn't started the car yet. A gorgeous blonde was jogging right past them, her breasts too big for her sports bra, but not one eye in the back seat left Orteguaza and Harper.

It had taken Ratchet Pennycooke an hour of driving around in his rented Impala and asking questions – with dozens of other cars reacting in panic and honking rage at his oblivious, abrupt veers on to the left side of the street – but finally he found a four-pack of Reed's Extra Ginger Beer at a place called Trader Joe's Market. He'd learned a lot from his older brother, including the crucial importance of proper burning hot Jamaican ginger beer to interrogation.

The morning sun was blazing down, almost as uncannily tropical as home, an intense holy light, and it seemed to invigorate a very small horse that was prancing happily around a side yard of the orange cabin. Pennycooke parked on a section of shoulder that barely gave other cars room to pass, and carried the ginger beer under his arm to the corral fence.

'Horsie, how you like dis here yard? You look like you full of rambunctious.'

The horse stared hard and came to rest a respectful distance from the Jamaican, pawing a little at the dust. 'Sorry, ma'an, I-an-I got no apple or such. We see you later.'

He rapped on the front door, and before long it came open a few inches on a chain.

'Ma'an, you got such a fine likkle horsie.'

'Who are you?'

'Let's say I-an-I got a question for you.'

'I teach class in half an hour. Can you come back when I have some free time?'

'But you see, I got no time. Life go by as we stand.'

'You can't be much over twenty. You've got a lot of life left. Son, I really do have to teach, but I'll be happy to talk to you after four o'clock. Whether it's tutoring or accent reduction, no problem.'

'Cha!' Ratchet leaned back to kick at the door and his blow ripped the light chain right off the doorframe. Stepping inside, at about six-seven he looked big enough and strong enough to do a lot more damage than that.

'Don' hurt me, please. Take what you want. The TV is in the bedroom.'

'I-an-I ain' no t'ief. Sit and talk to me naow.' He indicated one of the sling chairs and set the four-pack of ginger beer on the counter. Pennycooke plucked one bottle out of the pack and began shaking it.

Rolf Fuchs sat down gingerly in the chair. 'I mean you no harm at all, son.'

'I know dat, sir. But you the man knows everyt'ing, dey say. I got to be certain we gettin' de whole troof, so help me *Ras Tafari*.'

Ratchet leaned forward and pressed his big hand against Fuchs' adam's apple to hold him against the canvas of the sling chair, but not too hard. 'Dis jus' my way to fin' what g'wan wit' you.'

'I wish I knew what you wanted, I really do,' Fuchs said.

'Get ready fe tek some questions.'

'Go right ahead.'

Ratchet smiled and shook the bottle of ginger beer even harder. He smashed the cap off against the counter. With one sweep of his arm he applied the spewing neck of the bottle to Fuchs' nose, and slid his other hand up to smother the man's mouth. The super-gingery carbonated brew did its job. The old man's legs thrashed as if he was dying, and his fists beat hard at the Jamaican until Ratchet backed off a foot to let him retch and cough and nearly vomit. A wagging finger warned the man about trying to get up.

'Yeeee! Yoooo! No more!'

'Mebbe you had you plenty, heh? Or mebbe you jus' be wicked. Firs' ting, who be asking 'bout my frens?'

Ominously, the Jamaican shook the bottle again with his thumb over the neck. He glanced at the label casually, as if making sure it was genuine.

'You like dis ting? Very good bev'rage, ma'an.'

'Stop! Christ! My sinuses are on fire! I'll tell you anything you want. Are any of your friends black men who used to go to Sandstone Retreat?'

'How I know dat? Be full serious, ma'an.'

'I thought Rastafarians were gentle souls,' the man said.

'I not on dat track. I-an-I a steppin' razor. A likkle reminder hyere.'

He rammed the bottle against Fuchs' nose once more, but let him off after a few seconds of spray.

'Eeeeee!' Fuchs brushed at his face and coughed and sputtered. 'No more! Please, I beg you!'

'De troof naow. You no penetrait it? Who de baldheads come 'round to see you?'

'Just one man. He was Jack Liffey, but he told me the movie star named Tyrone Bird was going to show up to see me. You know him?'

'You cyan be dance again,' Pennycooke threatened.

'No, please! Bird is really famous. Ask anyone. Jack Liffey's card is right there by your sodas. Introduce him to ginger beer. You tell your boss I'm your friend. I won't help anyone else, no one. Not even a movie star.'

Ratchet Pennycooke claimed the business card off the cracked blue tile. Liffey – oh, yes, he knew that name. The man who'd been there when his brother was killed. He glanced up at the old man who had streams of tears running down his face.

'Man who lie to me, I say, dem be wicked, and I-an-I boun' fe harm de wicked man.'

'Oh, no, sir. No, no. It's the one hundred per cent truth I told you.' The old man cringed back into the sling chair, and Pennycooke believed him.

Unaccountably Pennycooke set the bottle down and offered a friendly handshake. 'I-an-I sorry to give you trouble, sir. You no seeit?'

Fuchs seemed afraid to take the hand, as if it was a trick. The hatch in the wall was open and the horse looked in now and whinnied once. When the Jamaican glanced at the horse and smiled, Fuchs finally held his hand briefly.

'I give him a carrot?' Pennycooke asked. 'And you tell me 'bout dis hyere movie man.'

They'd met at the north campus grease-pit beside Rolfe Hall. It was one of those multi-cultural food courts that specialized in myriad ethnic stalls that mainly featured various forms of

ground meat and carbohydrates – with a few all-veg stands for the health-conscious. Chad had an Armenian pizza, known as *lahmajoun* – and Maeve had a salad, dressing on the side.

'What do you expect to do with organic chem?' she asked.

'I'm told with the degree and three bucks you can get a Starbucks latte anywhere in the U.S.'

'Nonsense, you can invent expensive drugs that sell for exorbitant amounts of money. Move to New Jersey where all the drug companies are.'

A madly bobbing flock of pigeons ruffled past their feet to close in on a discarded paper tub of french fries nearby, shouldering hard at one another and tearing at the rancid fries in a very uncomradely way, and she wondered what their cholesterol count was.

'I'm thinking of switching to lit, but I see a dead end there,' Maeve said. 'I don't know if I care though. I really love books.'

'They say that back in Greek times people our age used to hunt down sages like Socrates and just sit at their feet to learn from them,' Chad said. 'I wish universities were still like that.'

'Maybe they really are,' Maeve said. 'If we just ignore all the credits and grades, we could walk in on any lecture we wanted. Philosophy, chemistry, Greek, French 101. Learn whatever we want.' The sweep of her arm took in a whole lot of university, scores of big buildings on the four hundred or so acres of super-choice real estate, hard up against Bel-Air and Brentwood with some of the most expensive homes in the U.S.

'My parental units would kill me,' he said, 'if I didn't come out of here with a punched ticket for a good job.'

She toyed with her salad, not very hungry. 'I guess it's part of what we all face. You'd never guess my dad's job.'

'OK, but I get a kiss, with some tongue, if I guess right. He's a skip-tracer.'

'Criminy! That's just too spooky. How did you know that?'

He smiled. 'Axel. I saw her for a while, but we're over.'

'Really? OK – Dad hunts for missing children. I really admire him for finding something decent to do after getting laid off from aerospace. It's all kind of white knight stuff. What about your folks?'

'My mom is Polish extraction,' he said. 'She's blonde and slim and really smart, but that never matters when you say 'Polish.' Her family name was Nowicki, and they Americanized it to Novak. The jokes about Polish stupidity do get pretty tiresome. You know, Poland is an old and very cultured country. Even if a lot of farmer-peasants came to Wisconsin about 1900. The jokes are so brainless. But Dad was another story.'

'You think the Irish had it any better?' she said.

'You've had your Kennedy. I guess we're still waiting.'

Maeve was beginning to like the guy.

Suddenly there was an unmistakable gunshot, then several more, possibly nearing. People in the eating court looked at one another, and then about half of them bolted off their benches, abandoning their meals to head somewhere else.

'Why take a chance?' he said. She knew she was usually too slow to react to danger so she put herself in his hands, and Chad grabbed her arm and dragged her toward a sheltered alcove that was lined with vending machines.

Several more gunshots echoed in the eating plaza, closer now.

SIX
Death by Minimum Wage

'Most of the time when a T is required to make up the new DNA strand, the enzyme will find a good T and there's no problem.' The man in the ostentatious lab coat and goatee drew something on the whiteboard with a snap. 'After adding a T, the enzyme can go ahead and pick up more nucleotides. However, about five per cent of the time, the enzyme will get a dideoxy-T, and that strand can never again be elongated.'

Gloria's eyelids felt made of lead. She caught her head as it was about to nod against the cop in parade uniform sitting to her right. He was actually taking notes in the big lecture hall. His shoulder patch said City of Redding, which she was pretty sure was somewhere north of Sacramento and wasn't all that big a town. She'd bet they didn't even have a DNA lab.

Earlier, she'd gathered up a shopping bag worth of stapled handouts off the tables at the entrance to prove she'd been here, and to give out to the eager kids in the Scientific Investigation Division who all wished they were, instead of her.

'Call of nature,' she whispered, as she stood up, hoiked her overstuffed bag and pressed past all the bony knees in the Fresno State University's Peters Auditorium.

She had no doubt her new captain had sent her up here as a punishment. For keeping a messy desk, she was sure. He'd sent her several ludicrous memos about it. She had five murder books open, more than any other detective in the Harbor Division, but all Caesar cared about was a tidy office! The story was the man had messed up royally in Pacoima, missed a community meeting and then missed a court date that had let half a dozen bad boys walk. So they'd kicked him sideways to Harbor. She could hardly bear to think it, but the new central house downtown was probably protecting him because he was a Sanchez. Fuck that. There weren't any Old Boys in the headquarters to look out for Native American women.

In the lobby, she collected a few more handouts and her bag was so full she had to tuck the new ones under her arm. A uniformed cop stood nearby with his forehead pressed against the big glass lobby windows, ostensibly looking out at a grassy precinct of the college where a few students sat in little groups. He looked like he was about to weep.

OK, she thought, it's only us losers here, and we all know it. 'Are you OK, man?' she asked, against her better judgment.

His face came around, furious. 'I don't care any more,' he said. 'I just don't give a shit.'

You didn't always do what you ought to do in life, she thought. Even Jack Liffey relaxed his galactic-size sense of duty sometimes, she was sure.

She rested a hand briefly on the cop's shoulder, as if that made up for everything he was suffering, and walked straight out of the auditorium toward the parking lot. Sometimes she felt she was always fleeing her better angel, but she had her own problems.

In an hour and a half her little Toyota RAV-4 was parking in front of Sonny's house in Bakersfield, and bless whichever angel, his car was already in the drive.

'I can see pretty good through the hog wire,' he said at the security door. 'You're here early, and you got weevils in your wheat.'

'It's not your clever words I need right now, Sonny.'

He grinned. 'Ride a bug homeward.'

Chad stepped quickly in front of her and held her trapped between two vending machines as they saw the gunman sprint confusedly into the alcove.

The stubbly-unshaven young man held square black pistols in both hands, like some revenge movie poster. For some reason he also wore an artificial-looking long bright red wig, and he froze electrifyingly in front of Chad, his fidgety powder blue eyes lost somewhere far away. The last of the other students were noisily fleeing the machine room, and Maeve gently pushed Chad aside, not wanting that kind of protection.

'Let me get you a sandwich,' Maeve offered.

'No thank you. I've already eaten,' the gunman said in a quavery voice. He seemed to look straight into Maeve's eyes.

'Don't be upset, friend,' she said. 'Talk to me. What's your name?' Chad struggled to get in front of her again. Both pistols wavered vaguely in their direction.

There were squeals and shouts and the sounds of running feet out in the table area.

'I know I can help you out of this,' Maeve said, with great gentleness. 'If you put those things down on the ground, I'll buy you a Coke and we can sit and talk. I'm sure I can keep the police from shooting you. You know by now that they're coming. What's your name?'

Chad was startled enough by Maeve's intervention to keep his mouth shut and stop trying to force his way between them.

'I have to create my own luck,' the young man said bitterly. A pistol waved around, but it seemed he was only wiping sweat off his forehead.

'I have perfect luck,' Maeve said. 'You can have some of mine.' Her life had been implausibly punctuated by events much like this one, many due to her father's job, but she had learned a lot from Gloria, too. How to calm. How to de-escalate. How to get in touch. 'My name is Maeve. What's your name?' she tried again.

He seemed mystified, dazed, and she wondered if that was a step forward. 'Who *are* you?' he barked at her.

She said, 'Please put the guns down, friend. No one will touch them. I've helped a lot of people who really need to talk.'

'I'm sick unto death,' he said. 'I need death.'

There was a long break when the noises outside were hard to interpet.

'I'm from Lamar, Colorado, and my girlfriend is an Arab, and nobody cares.'

'What's your name?' Maeve asked yet again.

'Salaam Beyda.'

'Hello, Salaam, peace to you.' He didn't look the least Arab. 'Please put the guns down. Have you converted to the peace of Islam?'

'I want to! No one lets me!'

'You mean your parents?'

'They made me eat bacon!'

She thought she saw a tear in the corner of his eye. But just then a flash-bang explosion made them all jump a little, and a SWAT team in body armor and face shields like giant black insects came around the corner, high and low, left and right, pushing into the alcove quickly behind their short assault rifles. Salaam turned toward them with the pistols still in his hands.

'Stop! Everybody stop!' Maeve yelled. 'He's OK!'

At least five of the submachine guns fired at once, plus something with a deeper sound, much more powerful from farther away, probably a sniper rifle. Salaam did a little dance as he was struck many times from at least two directions. Parts of what must have been the boy's head splattered over Maeve in a wet sensation that she would never forget. That was it. It was done.

She brushed madly at herself to remove whatever it was that clung. There was just no question what had happened, no point wondering, no point at all objecting. She sat down disconsolately in front of a snack machine. Gloria would see it as a failure. Chad sat down next to her and put his arm around her. She realized tears were streaming down her cheeks.

'You did your best,' Chad said. 'You were really really incredible, Maeve.'

'Who are you?' a SWAT cop screamed in her face.

'Fuck you – you stupid macho killer.'

That was pungent enough to get them both thrown face down on the concrete immediately with heavy knees in their backs, and their hands cuffed behind them with plastic wirewraps.

'Man, I wish we didn't have no deal with no Colombians,' Harper said. 'All that I-gonna-keel-you bullshit.'

Stoney shrugged.

'Those pogues are just zombies of death,' Harper said.

'You were in Iraq,' Stoney said.

'You think?'

'Yeah,' Stoney said. 'In Nam, pogue meant people-other-than-grunts. Same-same? You know I studied linguistics – long ago, pogue was Irish prison slang for a queer.'

Harper shook his head. 'So don't drop the fuckin' soap in the shower. Always the bookman, ain't you? That old school stuff – it's all dead to me, Stone. We both got our fat lips and our curly chest-hair. Brah.'

The last word a bit sarcastic. They sat in the book-crammed pool house where Marcus Stone now lived out his austere and much retrenched life with seeming contentment. It had once been his own pool house to rent to others when he'd owned the big Woodland Hills home beside it. He'd been married then to Lilith Levy, the head of the History Department at Cal State Northridge, though he'd started calling her Lithium Lady, when he wearied of the interminable depressions and anxious tantrums. It had been a lifetime ago now.

'OK, what if we just shoot them down and take their snow?' Stoney suggested, not very seriously.

'They're up-armed like a SEAL platoon now, my man. Who thought you could store weapons in ordinary safe-deposit boxes in a bank? You go in a podunk bank empty, and you come out strapped like Chuck Norris.'

'What a sad thought. People flying here and subverting our fine capitalist banking system,' Stoney said. He poured out a little more rum and Coke for himself.

'Sometimes I ain't sure if you're gettin' up in my grill, Stoney.'

'If you did know, you'd probably have to kill me. Don't you worry, my boon coon. Tomorrow, we meet these South Americans. We be nice as mice to them, treat them like white men, and I test their product with my Captain Midnight chemistry set our college Jap taught me, and if the powder's not Boraxo, we give them the cash, and you run them back to the airport, and it's all over for another few months.'

'That's when things get the most squirrelly. All of us holding all that cash and snow at Costco.'

They ticked glasses. 'We'll let 'em keep the money. This time, anyway,' Stoney said.

Harper glanced around with a scowl. 'Is this crib where you gonna live forever, man? It sucks big time.'

'I'm a modest man of modest tastes.'

'I best think you ain't laughin' at me because you ain't laughin'.'

'On the real, Harp – back in the day, you do something you can't never ever take back, even if you want, against the Man. It's best to stay out of the light for a long long time.'

He reached over and squeezed Harper's shoulder. He hadn't touched the man in a long time. 'Forget this crib. You and me. I am where I am, and I'm OK with it. You know what a badass African party is?'

'No.'

'It's when somebody comes into your own home and disses you bad, and you're forced to stomp all over their ass. I don't like these guys not doing you straight with your props – you my brother, Harp – especially I don't like this O guy. Make sure tomorrow you got us a bunch of your old Rollin' Seventies pals nearby if we need the backup.'

'Dis yere be Mr Jack Liffey?'

Phone to his ear, he boosted himself straight up in Gloria's leather TV chair, where he'd been brooding – relearning the ways jealousy put you through a lot of mental adjustments and took you down funny little back roads you thought you'd forgot all about. She'd called only a half hour ago to say she'd be away another day. The caller-ID feature gave him six six one, which was Bakersfield, as if he needed the extra dig in his ribs. Fresno was five five nine.

This new voice was astonishing, so much like his dead friend Terror Pennycooke's that he wondered if the Jamaicans hadn't found a way to make the dead walk and talk. There was no percentage in letting on to anything, though.

'This is Jack's friend,' Jack Liffey said. 'I can reach Mr Liffey if it's important.'

'Cha, how many white men lie to me – I lose count.'

Even on the phone, Jack Liffey could hear the man suck his teeth. 'Friend, they lie to me, too, all the time. Tell me what it is you want.'

'Dis Liffey man, yes, he be dere when my big brother kill. He owe me.'

'Jesus Christ, man, Terror Pennycooke was my good friend and ally.' He shouldn't have said it, but he did. 'Afterwards, I got his girlfriend into a school. Who the fuck are you?'

Cunning came into the phone voice. 'Mr Jack it is, uh-huh? I require to talk to you, face on face.'

'Sure. And when we meet, if I even see a bottle of Jamaican ginger beer, I'll shoot you where you stand. Do you understand me?'

The man laughed a bit longer than necessary.

'Are you the little brother? What's your name?' Jack Liffey asked.

'Ratchet. Pennycooke. A name to be fear.'

'Where you staying? You don't have to give me an address. Just a city.'

'Some Ca-no-ga shit.'

'Canoga Park? They stuck you in the fuckin' Valley? OK, fine. Get a car or take a bus or run, and you find Lake Balboa in Van Nuys, maybe five miles east of you. I'll be there in an hour. Don't worry. I'll know you.'

'Cha, man, I-an-I done be nuttin' but civil wit' you. Don' be no evil-man.'

'Ratchet, if you're half the man your brother was, I'm your best friend. But I don't recommend staying in this city if you're working for the same people he did. There's no future in being a hit man for drug-dealers. One day, there's always gonna be more weight on the other side, and more cops.'

'You be dere, Mr AD-vice. Just don't do me no dirt.'

Business like this could ruin the nicest day, Jack Liffey thought. But he hadn't been having the nicest day, anyway. Somewhere way down in the madhouse they were playing the Jamaican card, right on top of his jealousy card.

'Don't be a rude boy, Ratchet. Your brother Trevor was a good man.'

It doesn't look any too posh, but using only cash and my one phony ID, I check into the Sputnik SurfRider Motel out here at the scraggly end of Malibu at Topanga Beach. From the road there's a tall pole with one of those spiky fifties emblems from the glory days of the leap into space that nobody's bothered to update as it rusts away. Inside the room, the kindest thing is to think retro. No clown prints, but the bed actually has a padded white leatherette headboard, held to the wall with brass buttons every eight inches. I don't care, of course. All I need is privacy, and sometimes, like any movie star, I have to pay a lot extra for that. Here I'm Joey Wilson.

I don't use my cell in case they've got the CIA or FBI on me. I use the house phone to call an old friend, Art Castro, who works at a detective agency downtown.

'Art, this is me, the guy you once chased off that stalker

for – don't say my name. He was starting to drop threatening notes. We clear?'

'How could I forget you, my man? You was a stand-up guy, and you slipped a kind word in my boss's ear. May have saved my job. You in trouble?'

'Not a bit of it. I'm just AWOL for a few days from a movie, and you know how hysterical those guys get.'

'Millions down the shit-can every second, yeah. What can I do for you? Anything, man.'

'I've got a name from way back in the when. And I want to find him fast.' In fact I have two names, but I'm pretty sure of the right one now, and I'm going to drop the other one. I can remember Moms talking about a Stoney. 'Marcus Stone. Stoney. Back in the day, he hung out for a while at one of those swinger clubs – the Sandstone Retreat in Topanga. I got reason to think he taught at a college out in the Valley and he was something special. OK?'

'I'm on it. . . . You want to stay "location unknown" and call me? Here's my prepaid cell. Untraceable.'

I copy his number down.

'I'll connect you two by sunset or no money changes hands.'

'Money is no problem, Art. Just do what you do, and you'll end up very happy.'

I hang up, staring at a bad painting of a surfer in an impossible curl, and wonder what it's going to be like if I actually meet this guy – my father. Will he even want to see me? He won't be a bum, knowing Moms – but what's become of him after all this time? He may have a huge family and be so uptight he doesn't want to know me.

She told me he was a Black Panther for a while, so I carry around this mental image of him in a big Afro and black leather jacket, like those sixties photos of Huey Newton or Bobby Seale. I remember trying to grow my own Afro for a while when I was eighteen and strutted around a bit in the mess – it just looked scraggly and stupid. Anyway, that won't be what Stoney looks like now, age maybe sixty, maybe sixty-five. He'll be gray as a dead TV.

Pacing the motel room, I nearly walk headlong into a vertical yellow surfboard that's been made into a floor lamp. Jesus. OK, I'm in Malibu. What a contrast from my Panther imaginings to this, I think. Those white kids of the nineteen sixties – I suppose it was their way of rebelling to risk death in the surf. But maybe everything I know is lies. Maybe Pops wasn't teaching at a college at all, maybe he was a janitor cleaning up the bathrooms at a McDonald's. Risking death by minimum wage.

It is what it is, I think. His drop of sperm did its work.

As Gloria was about half again his size and weight, and appeared a bit tired, Sonny Theroux did a lot of climbing over and around and over again to get at and make available all their erogenous zones. All this randy circling around on his part blew out a lot of the squat candles he'd started up in the dark-curtained bedroom. He hadn't worked so hard at loving in years. There was something about the way she mixed abrupt unselfconscious demands and a yielding to every suggestion he made that really tickled his fancy.

'I do believe you're the sexiest woman I ever sparked and larked.'

'Oooh, a little higher! Right there, sweetie! Hard now! Do it!'

After a while, they were both thoroughly worn out. Oversported, he thought.

'Gimme that slack gearshift to hold on to,' she said. 'I'll know when the motor's running again.'

'Woman, I'm'a take a pretty bad heartache after you.'

'I hope that doesn't mean what I think it does.'

'It means I'm crazy in love with you, Gloria Ramirez, you're so far past my best dreams that I been having fantasies about you for months. It's the big thing, the real thing. I want you to leave Jack and be all mine – right here, or L.A., or Paris, or Bangkok, or we can go live on your Rez. I don't mind.'

'Cool your jets. You're lettin' your head go runnin' around after your dick, Sonny. Let's enjoy the time we got.'

'I ain' never been a Tom-catter.' He tried to look her in the eyes, but she wouldn't meet his. 'I can't say it any plainer. I want to marry you forever and ever. He ain't married you.'

'Not because he ain't asked, Sonny, over and over, just like you. I told him no because I'm too fucked up and too angry inside for any man. You don't see that now, but you would.'

'I'm prepared—'

'Hush now,' she commanded. 'We still got an evening and a night and maybe a morning. Don't spoil it.'

She rolled over and began slow-licking the gearshift back into operation.

'Oh, jumpin' Jesus.'

It didn't take a genius to find Ratchet Pennycooke sitting on a bench overlooking placid Lake Balboa and hurling torn hamburger buns out of a bag to the pigeons surrounding him.[4] With his floppy tricolor knit hat, gold silk shirt and striped pants, Pennycooke was either a Jamaican archetype, or someone on a clown tryout. For all the flamboyance, though, the whole getup did look great.

Jack Liffey watched him for a while, amazed by the dead-on resemblance to his big brother Trevor, who was now dead. In fact, Trevor had fallen desperately in love with a young Paiute girl caught up in the 'adult entertainment' industry who Jack Liffey had been hired to find, and Trevor had become the victim of a three- or four-way feud for her loyalty. They had almost escaped a raging wildfire in Malibu when one of the angry rivals had shot Trevor from long-distance with a rifle, before dying himself in the fire.[5]

Jack Liffey had come to like Trevor quite a lot, and he hoped the younger brother had some of the same spunk and innate decency. He'd been told over and over by Trevor that Winston was by far the smarter brother, who got three A-levels in school. Now here he was, the big colorful man tearing up sandwich buns for the pigeons. Not a bad sign, really.

'Winston or Ratchet. I'm Jack.'

They shook hands, an amazingly normal handshake, no strange tugs or twists or fist-pops, and he didn't get up. He looked tired and a bit lost.

'Thank you for coming, sir. In this country anything can

---

[4] This is a lake that probably ninety-nine per cent of Los Angeles residents south of the mountains have never heard of. It's an artificial reservoir created after a real-estate bust in the early nineteen nineties, trying to boost local property values, set into a small part of an emergency flood catchment basin behind Sepulveda Dam. In bad rains the whole basin goes deep under water, but a big chunk of the Van Nuys area of L.A. has now been renamed 'Lake Balboa' and thus the developers have created a new reality, created 'facts on the ground', as the Israelis say. Fitting, since tens of thousands of emigrant Israelis live in the area.

[5] See *Dangerous Games*, 2005.

go wrong.' He seemed to have concluded that Jack Liffey
wasn't his brother's killer, which was a plus.

'And often does.' Jack Liffey sat down beside him. 'I really
liked your brother a lot. He was a fine man, a determined
vegetarian and I believe a true Rastafarian.'

Winston nodded. 'He posted I-an-I a raggedy letter that said
you were a good man, too, and this Red Indian woman he call
Luisa was his big-love.' With all the brag about Winston's
smarts, Jack Liffey guessed some of this rude-boy patois was
probably put on. He was almost certainly bidialectal with
Standard English.

'Yes. She's doing OK, now.'

Jack Liffey told him what he could about the way Trevor
had died, and that there was no need for the man to brood
about vengeance, as the killer himself was dead. He said that
Luisa was in an Indian school out in Riverside County, catching
up on lost opportunities, and he would set up a meeting with
her if Ratchet wanted, but not right away. Now he wanted to
get Ratchet away from the drug-dealers and gangbangers who
had presumably hired him and brought him here.

But that was going to be tougher than he thought. They'd
paid Pennycooke's way, and the large young man felt he had
an ethical obligation, which he took seriously. They talked
for a long time about what the gangs were like in L.A.
Apparently it was much more anarchic back on Jamaica.

'I understand your loyalty, son, but these men feel no obligation to you. They don't give a damn if you live or die.
You're just Kleenex to them. Please think of me as Trevor's
only real friend in L.A.'

Jack Liffey gave him his business card. 'Sooner or later, if
not right now, you should prepare yourself to walk away from
them. You're always welcome with me. Be warned that my
woman is a cop, but she's an honest cop. She'll like you fine.'
That is, if she still likes me, he thought.

'I-an-I suppose to be finding dis man dat's looking for some
friend of my bossman. Messin' up da scene for him at a bad
time. Dis commitment ain' got no flexible, sir. I got to finish
the job. Today I-an-I question Rolf Fuchs and dat's where I
got your card de firs' time.'

'Oh, no. You didn't use ginger beer, did you?'

Ratchet looked a bit chagrined. 'It don't leave no lasting hurt.'

'Except in the heart,' Jack Liffey said, and he pressed his finger very hard on Ratchet Pennycooke's chest, right where the heart was reputed to be. 'De people,' Jack Liffey said, with what he hoped was a Jamaican emphasis, 'somma dem fight and somma dem talk rough, but I hear Winston Pennycooke got him three A-levels from Knox College. Dis man yere smart as a computer, and he knows what's righteous.'

Ratchet grinned and chuckled. 'You Jackie-too-bad youself.' All at once, the Jamaican's black eyes lost a kind of glint, and he grasped very hard on Jack Liffey's finger that had been prodding at the center of his chest and moved it away from himself with tremendous strength as he stood up. 'Thank you, with my blessings, for looking after my brother and now for watching over me. I know who I am on earth, and it's no bad thing to let these wicked punters think I'm only the brainless country mouse. Right now, I got to do what they pay me to do. We know all about slave-time on J. I'll be seeing you one day soon as a free man.'

The last minute before his departure he had sounded like another man entirely who'd been brought up listening every day to the BBC.

Jack Liffey was caught up in an irrational worryfest about Maeve. For years he'd never watched the local TV news, but the *L.A. Times* had collapsed so thoroughly that there was no longer any hope of learning much about the city's day-to-day life in print, so when he got home he flicked on KCBS, the least awful of the local stations. They confirmed the brief burst of chat he'd heard over his half-broken car radio that there'd been another random shooting incident at a college, but he didn't catch where or much else.

How long do we have to go on paying, he thought, for our dysfunctional families and dysfunctional schools and our whole dysfunctional social order? He wondered where this shooting had happened – these things had moved on from post offices and now went off unpredictably in rich and poor areas alike, rich or poor schools, glitzy or shabby malls, fast-food restaurants, wherever people congregated.

Then his jaw dropped as, on screen, he saw Maeve, utterly unmistakably, and a handsome boy handcuffed side by side on their knees in front of a vending machine full of potato chip and pretzel bags. She didn't seem hurt at all, thank God. But how was she involved in this?

The sound began to come up as he punched madly at the remote's volume control.

'. . . reports of as many as three gunmen. Some students say the police went on a rampage looking for accomplices, but so far it appears to have been a lone gunman. He ranged across the north campus of UCLA, not far from exclusive Bel-Air, carrying two semi-automatic handguns. At least twelve shots were fired, most of them apparently up in the air. No one except the gunman appears to have been hurt. Police cornered the gunman and shot and killed him when he refused to drop his weapons. No notes have been reported, and nothing is known about his motives.'

On screen there was a human-size lump under a blue tarp, with the concrete area surrounded by yellow police tape. He flipped around all the channels, but there were no more shots of Maeve. What weird karma kept doing this to her?

Gloria had been trying to cook fajitas on his kitchen grill, but Sonny was kissing her neck, making her concentration on the cooking extremely difficult.

The phone rang three times, then coughed its way through Sonny's outgoing message, until they could both hear Jack Liffey's voice on the monitor thirty feet away. Gloria pushed him away gently and walked to the phone to listen.

'. . . I'm sorry to bother you, Sonny, but if you know how to reach Gloria, Maeve needs her help. She's somehow caught up in a shooting incident at UCLA. I saw a shot of her hand-cuffed on TV. I'm doing my best to find out what's going on, but a smart cop with connections can always do better. Please. Don't let anything else get in the way of this. Me or you.'

He sounded heartsick, and it wasn't just about his daughter, she knew that. Jesus, the fact that he knew where to call. He did have a sixth sense. OK, she thought, fuck him. He'd figured it all out, and now he'd have to live with it, and so would she. Some indescribable change for the worse had come upon her, subtle but momentous, as if the air in Bakersfield had just become twice as dense. Her senses were actually disarranged a little – by her raging hormones, and by her desire for the world to be back the way it had been ten minutes ago. But it wouldn't be. She had to ride this new thing all the way down.

'Sonny, pull yourself together.'

'It's hard.'

'Forget hard. There's only *do*. Wait ten minutes, then call Jack back and tell him you reached me, and I'm coming home fast. That's all. No more.'

'But I want you tonight, Glor.'

'I know that. If you screw this up, you've lost me for good. Get it right and maybe I'll be back. Think about that.'

SEVEN

Melanie's Son

'Why we wait a day on this?' Harper asked.

Stoney shrugged. 'Their original deal. I presumed they needed the time to meet their courier and collect the product. We can use it to plan.'

Stoney decided to make it clear he was war-captain. Harper may have done his famous two tours in the big Eye-raq, but Harper had never shown Stoney the most rudimentary tactical sense. All buck and bluster. Sometimes, he thought of it as the ghetto curse: better to look cool, than go the extra distance to be cool.

'Your four best homies – no loose cannons. The tight ones we can trust. Tell them to park at ten fifteen exactly, way back with Mr and Mrs Shopping Cart. They can move the car if they have to to keep a straight run toward us, but everybody just kick it and hunk down in the car except one good pair of eyes on point. If we need help, it'll be my signal, mine alone. I'll slap my neck.' He demonstrated, as if offing a mosquito. It was the perfect signal; natural looking, but almost nobody did it in L.A. 'Then they open a can of whoop-ass like maybe they the DEA or somebody the Spics don't want to mess with. Maybe get them blue cop warm-up jackets, with the badge printed on, the ones they use for the drug busts so they don't shoot each other.'

Harper acted out the slap himself, and Stoney nodded. 'It's all good. We'll pay them real money for a day's work, whether they got to roll up on the Panchos or just scrunch down and whack off all morning.'

Marcus Stone stood up and levered open the grill-cloth that covered his center woofer. He took out his kit with a rolled joint resting on top. He lit it with a Bic and drew twice. Was he starting to want it too bad? Like the booze-hounds?

'My go on the blunt, man.'

Stoney passed it to Harper who was sitting cross-legged on the floor.

'Know why this meet tomorrow gives me the willies?' Stoney said at last. 'I just heard trouble a second time – from that fat cop Ernie Keeler who thinks I'm gonna be his snitch some fine day. He go, "Just so you know, man, your crew from the Big South is said to be in money trouble. The Medellin chief's on their ass for some fuckup, and they need extra yayo bad. Maybe they think they can knock over a simple nigger like you." Course, Ernie's trying to play me, but I don't see any percentage for him in freaking me out.'

Harper smoked for a while, ruminating.

'My worry's different, Stone,' Harper said. He drew a last deep burn and handed the blunt back, almost down to a pinch. 'Sister's got this Chinese friend now, does us an eye-ching whenever we want, and, man, she always been right on. Don't be hate on me, man, I see you. It's for true. This Chink cunt throws the bones for me, and the bones say the dragon is flying. That's wack. Last time the dragon was flying, Li'l Tight-eye got himself capped.'

Stoney tried not to glare at him like the half-wit the man was turning himself into. Once he'd had hopes for Harper – he'd shown some real promise. Intelligence. He'd tried to get him into a community college, but the man was glued to the streets.

All of this made Marcus Stone feel doomed, trapped by the decisions he'd made long ago. It was as if his life was narrowing down around him now, closing him inside his own bad choices. Surrounded now by asshole street thugs who could barely tell time with a digital watch.

Growing up, he'd assiduously avoided the street as his mother had insisted – and here he was with all their para-noias and homemade mythologies and their dumb-ass ideas of the way the world worked. White Satans and black politi-cians taking bags of Jew money. Man oh man!

The dope brought back thoughts of his best girl Melanie, way back when. Damn, he'd blown that one for real – thrown away the best thing in his life. And just because she talked so half-smart; she couldn't make the fancy talk of revolution at his house parties.

'Where you head at?' Harper asked.

'It's all good,' Stoney said. 'We on top, don't you worry.'
The weed was maybe beginning to mood him up a little.

My cellphone offers its dull *tunk* for an incoming call, probably another plea from my agent or a raging threat from the
director or one of the producers. Fuck 'em all. My head is
heavy as a boulder, but I'm determined now to follow through.
I should let one of the Skinnies answer the phone, I think, let
him giggle down the line for a while like Jack Nicholson with
his head through the axed door. Hee-ee-re's Skinny!

Damn if they couldn't put their tiny heads through some
pretty narrow slits, too. Cool it, Ty. You know they're only
imaginary. Halloo – cinations. Luckily, right now they're still
off at the edge of my vision, investigating the Sputnik Motel.

Then I remember Art Castro. Said he's gonna get back to
me by sunset. I look, and there's a voicemail on the phone.
'It's Arturo, dude. I got what you think you want. Mr Marcus
Stone is the guy, all right, but watch yourself. He used to be
a big kahuna in the revolution business and now he's into the
drug business.' Art Castro gave him an address in Woodland
Hills – a Valley locale, but not hard to get to at all over
Topanga Canyon. 'That three-quarters number in the address
got to be an upstairs or a pool house. Honestly, pard, he has
all the props in the world for being a hard guy, so take care.
Oh, yeah, he drives a black Escalade, no pimp shit on it like
cow-horns or such. It's not sundown so I did my duty. I'll
take cash money, a check, anything negotiable works fine for
me. Break a leg, dude.'

A chill travels up and down my spine at thinking I have
my possible father's actual address. Could this be it? Melanie's
lover so long ago, and my real pops? It doesn't really bother
me what the guy's into now. I know perfectly well that half
the best minds in the black community are into bad business.
It's what you do when you're smart and all the doors are
closed.

Dads. Pops. Father. I try the words, but they don't sound
right.

Mr Stone, sir. I'm Melanie's son. Look at my face. Is it
yours?

I find myself sitting on the edge of the bed and crying, and
the Skinnies are going crazy all around the motel room, doing

summersaults and jumping jacks like anorexic clowns on
speed.

Gloria's little SUV was a case study in tense dead silence as
she and Jack Liffey drove over the Fourth Street bridge to
the brand new post-modern police headquarters, right across
from city hall. There was some kind of irony in that juxta-
position, he wasn't sure what. That glass box was where they
were holding Maeve. Sooner or later he'd raise the issue of
Sonny, he thought, but not before they'd got Maeve out of
the hands of Big Law. Maeve had a way of rubbing officials
wrong.

Gloria left the car in an official lot down a tunnel and hung
some kind of plastic label over the rear-view mirror.

'Stay here,' she commanded. 'Don't even think until I get
her out of here.'

'Understood.'

'Then we talk,' she barked.

'Got it.'

Shit. He watched her stride away purposefully. What was
there to say between them? Good-bye? You've got a week to
pack up, Jack? It was about as despondent as he'd ever felt,
and he found his life frozen into a kind of glacial melancholy.
There seemed precious little of his ego left.

He watched young cops coming in to work, hanging their
tags on the mirror-posts on their windshields, leaving pocket
items in their cars, taking away other things, stringing them
around their necks for good luck, probably Saint Christophers
or Iraq dogtags.

Jack, he told himself. You still want a life with Gloria. It
hurts like hell, but it's honest.

I don't know what I'm thinking, to tell the truth. I don't know
if I'll work up my nerve to go up there and knock on the
door, but here I am on Topochico Drive, my Porsche Targa
parked about two houses down from the address Art Castro
gave me. I'm watching the lights and shadows in what appears
to be the window of the tiny stucco pool house in front. Grass
and hedges and geraniums, a slightly nicer version of what
all the post-war whites had bought fifty years earlier.

I can see somebody's inside, moving around, and it makes

me feel cowardly just to sit here. But you can't take such a giant step all at once. Maybe he won't want to see me. Did he ever know I existed? Moms was a proud woman.

I flip the passenger sun-visor down and there's the photo of me a few years ago, smiling, with Paulita and her son Mikey from her marriage to Dan. I do my best to be Mikey's 'dad.' We're standing with a gray donkey painted hideously with white stripes to mimic a zebra. The latest item of Tijuana kitsch, a sad photo-op on literally every streetcorner along the Avenida Revolucion.

I was actually happy that day. In remission from all the Halloos. But being happy creates its own problems – it leads you to take on responsibilities you can't handle. A Skinny pokes his impossibly thin face into sight in front of my windshield, frowning. Time to go back to the motel, or time to force myself to meet him, or time to drive down to the movie set. Whatever – I'm not in very good shape.

Gloria walked out into the underground parking with Maeve in tow, looking a bit dazed.

'Why don't you stay with us tonight, hon,' Jack Liffey suggested as Maeve got in the back.

'Yeah, we kind of worked that out,' Maeve said in a half-dead, half-frightened voice. 'Gloria was pretty strong in there. She can sure talk the talk.' Gloria didn't add anything. 'Love you, Dad.'

'Me too.'

'Sorry, this time I was really shook up,' Maeve said and she leaned back and closed her eyes. She seemed to be trying to rub something off her face. 'I was talking some guy down from his muddle, I'm not sure. His eyes were just starting to focus. Then they killed him right in front of me.'

'Sweetie,' Gloria said – and she couldn't keep a harsh tone out of her voice. 'What you're calling a muddle was a crazy man shooting up a campus with hundreds of kids in range. Put yourself in the place of people trained to protect the public from threats like that.'

'I try to, honest, Gloria. But he was looking like such a confused little kid. I don't really blame the police. People do what they have to. But I don't think I'm some sort of outlaw for trying to save the guy's life.'

'Maybe we're a family of outlaws,' Jack Liffey said out of the blue. Jealousy was making him ridiculously contrary, he could feel it inside. All he could really touch was petulance. He had to get a grip.

'Shut up, Jack,' Gloria snapped. 'A man died today, and no one is happy about it. SWAT doesn't have celebrations when they have to kill somebody.'

Everybody was on edge, for various reasons. 'You're right. Every posture has its consequences. Including my bad moods.'

They all sat silently as Gloria drove toward home. Maeve opened her eyes and watched the two of them as if she sensed that something other than her own experience was going on here.

'Hush, everybody. I had a moment of hope there,' Gloria said. 'I'm trying to bring it back.'

'Thanks for interrupting your course to come get me out,' Maeve said, and when nobody took up the thread, she let it lie, knowing something was really wrong.

The sun wasn't up yet, but the Porsche Targa up the street whooped a few times as it started and then warmed up, or at least gave some hotshot the sense he was warming it up. Winston Pennycooke figured there was no longer any question that this was the guy who was dogging Harper's bossman. The guy had waited there in his hot car most of the night watching the house. Winston started up his own rental Impala. He'd never keep up with a Targa on a race-track, but the big throaty V-6 would be just fine for city traffic unless he got caught at a light, and he wasn't going to let that happen.

He almost criss-crossed the street to the wrong side as head-lights came uphill at him, but he got himself together in time. Remember to stay right side, ma'an. Luckily the Porsche had distinctive low pointy taillights that he could follow through the L.A. traffic.

Cha, my friend. This a great big dread American street cruiser and I can rumble with you bumpy little German turtle any time you want.

I'm pretty well disgusted with myself by the time I get back to the motel, the sun just offering its first eastern glow. Why go AWOL from the movie if I'm going to get right up on Pops's crib and then turn chickenshit? Today? Tomorrow, sometime – I got to face Pops, if it is Pops. I'll probably know just by looking at him.

I should probably call my shrink, Dr Rosen, to help kick me over this last bridge, maybe let him know I'm finally tracking the old man down, but there's a freedom in being away from the world of good sense and good advice. Rosen can't come with me on this quest anyway, firing his healing arrows at my head as we go – wap, wap, wap. No more running away, Ty – and maybe the Skinnies will hold off, too. Yeah, I see you peeking. All's I got to do is walk straight up to the man and say – what? Sir, I'm Melanie's son. Melanie Ocean Bird.

But I have too much imagination. Look kid, the man replies, every swingin' dick's got Melanies in his life. Did she play the skin clarinet? Was she that one-night stand in Oakland?

In my head the scene plays out in a dark doorway so I can barely see him.

I'm your son! Don't be so mean!

Do you really think I give a shit, kid? I got a hundred bastards just like you all over the country.

Several Skinnies saunter into the room, prancing around, too many to dismiss now. Fatherhood is nothing, they link arms and sing out in their falsetto chorus. But we'll always be with you. We're your pals.

Who are you to me? I say audaciously. You're all just halloos. Figments.

Ty, don't you know the truth?

That was the Skinny with the ghostly blue eyes. It smiles and dips its head as another takes its place, the one with the floppy hair. We always help you get home safe, Smart Ty. Your moms sends us. Have a drink right now to get your butt calmed down. Just a little one, and maybe another little one right after.

Look at me! I shout in my head. My father is real!

Maeve went off to cuddle Loco and drag the dog into the guest room that they kept available for her – still her room really. Which left them alone in the kitchen, and neither was sure they wanted to be alone together just then.

'Let me thaw some burritos for all of us,' Gloria said.

He nodded, not trusting himself to reply. The word thaw opened up too many possibilities of sarcasm.

She handed him a 7-up and opened a bottle of dark Indio for herself. For its name alone, she'd taken to drinking the hard-to-find beer from Monterrey in eastern Mexico. The wrapped burritos went into a plastic bag in a pot of water in the sink, and she sat opposite him at the green Formica table covered with its little flying kidney shapes. She worked assiduously on her first Indio.

'So?' he said.

'It's hard,' she said. 'I really care for you, Jackie. You been so very good to me.'

'Do you want me out of your house?'

'No no no no. Please. But I got to ask something even harder.'

He did his best not to panic. He tried to focus on what he knew of her dreadful childhood, her pain and her own needs, and her exact words now. You've made your mistakes, Jack. Atone now, he thought. It wasn't that easy. What about me and my needs, he thought.

'I'm asking you to be stronger than God,' Gloria said. 'Let me run with this thing a little longer and find out what it's about.'

'We'd better be clear,' Jack Liffey said. 'You mean Sonny Theroux?'

She nodded, and his heart plummeted all the way to the floor and then bounced sickeningly. A one-night fling with some handsome cop in Vice was one thing, but a smart guy that he respected and liked – or used to like – really frightened him. She was saying she wanted to go on fucking Sonny Theroux. 'Can you tell me about it?'

'Jackie, you're not Superman. You're not meant to sit there and listen to me talk about a guy. That's for some girlfriend. I'm really a mess. I have to get drunk a little to get over my shame when I see him.'

And when you see me, too, he wondered.

'I can say this much. He wants it to last, but I don't think it will. I don't think it can. I don't know what it is. Just an angry old woman's last infatuation? One last admirer before I fade to black. I'm a fat fifty-year-old, Jack. It's not even proper.'

She was silent for a minute, and he didn't know what to

say. I'm sixty-three and I'm really scared of being alone now, he thought.

'And that house of his is so comical – that pint-size *Gone With the Wind* thing. It's like being wooed in Disneyland.' She drained the beer, and he saw it wasn't the first drink she'd had tonight. He wondered where she'd got the others – if she'd started hiding bottles.

He smiled a little, before he realized he didn't feel very much like smiling. It had pleased him momentarily that she'd had the same reaction to that ludicrous house that he'd had. Alcohol would have helped him deal with this event, too, he knew that. Maybe he should make an exception. 'You're going to go back up and see him again?'

She nodded gravely. 'I got to, Jack. You know, the sex part maybe doesn't mean so much no more. It's not that.'

Yeah, Jack Liffey thought with dread. Sonny was trying to reach things inside her not many men had reached before, and he could only hope that the man failed. He'd sure tried hard enough himself. He did his best to be sympathetic – to force himself to remain in some suspended emotional state. Think of her.

Some acid was eating away at her self-respect way down inside, and he'd done his best to scoop it out. It didn't seem to help any more to say it was just being a Native American who'd been fostered by a couple of fucked-up old Latinos who'd taught her contempt for her own people. The pace of her life, a cop's life, the service to others, day after day, had made it almost impossible for her to examine her own feelings calmly and carefully. And she wouldn't go to therapy because she said it was the kiss of death to your career if word got out in the department.

Her, he thought. She's on a knife-edge, and you can be strong for her. If you want her, you've got to be. Demands won't work. Anger will make it all worse. He did his best to keep his ill will under control.

'I hope Sonny helps you learn something important,' he said, and he knew that saying those words, even in his most rigid, controlled voice, was giving his permission.

She fetched a fresh bottle of Indio and looked at him skeptically over it. 'Will you feel the same way when I drive away from here to see him?'

'I don't know, Glor. Don't ask me to be made of stone. I'll do the best I've got. I'm scared to death for myself, but I care about what you need, too.'

There was a bustling sound, and Maeve followed Loco into the kitchen just in time. 'I'm sorry, we're both dying of hunger, folks.'

'Mr Bigs Harper,' Ratchet said on the phone. 'I-an-I move forwud fe find dis guy bother you and de boss. Las' night he wait in his likkle Porsche at de man's house, sitting dere all night. But big surprise for you. Listen up. Dis Porsche guy, him a famous star in de movies, for true. You no wan' him tek some licks, I tink. Or you get all de coppers in Babylon mash doun on you.'

'Wait a minute, wait a minute, Mr Rude Boy. Tell me all this shit in English. I know you're a smart boy. You found our nosy guy?'

Ratchet was enjoying messing with Harper's head with the deepest Jamaican dialect he could muster. 'OK, dis de guy you wan'. Mr Big Movie Star man – name Tyrone Bird. You no see *Law'n' Disorder*? *Avenue on Fire*? I see all a' his movie back on J. I watch dis Tyrone Bird las' night. At Mr Stoney house in Woodland. Just sittin' an' a thinkin'. Him broodin' on somet'ing. I follow de ma'an back to his motel. You want I fe speak wid him and tell him back off – OK, I do it strong. But I know you no want no dread beat an' blood, not on Mr Famous. Dat bring da downpressor.'

'Jesus fucking Christ. Are you sure, man? Ty Bird? You're not fucked up on one of those two pound sticks of weed or something?'

'Nah true. No ganja for I-an-I. Dis big movie starman – I know him like me own mama. Tyrone Bird is tops in J, everywhere. He numbah one. You still wan' me fe tell him back off?'

'Jesus, no. Don't even go near him, but watch him. I'll talk to Stone.'

'OK, I'm ga'an. Me link you up layta.'

'Wait—'

The phone clicked off.

Pussyhole, Ratchet thought. He laughed out loud. We ragamuffin win dis likkle game all de time.

The only man he'd met in the States who wasn't an idiot was that old white guy – what was the name? – Jack Liffey. He didn't seem to need a pretend hard guy standing up inside him, like so many on the streets. And the man had helped his brother and his brother's girl. Honor, ma'an. I-an-I do what honor is all about.

EIGHT
The Deal

It wasn't hard to find the symbol – the heart with shepherd's crooks for handles – that the Colombians had painted on the parking spot at Costco. It was starting to wear away now but marked the place they had used several times as a handover point.

Stoney knew that Jhon Jairo Orteguaza and his boys would have rented a car or two of their own by now, and he and Harper had no real idea what to watch for coming through the entrance – except maybe that Porsche Targa that Ratchet had warned them about, the wild card. They'd been damned careful getting there. To follow them, this movie star, whatever his game, would have had to run a couple of red lights and then make himself pretty obvious by doubling around a suburban block, twice. Even high-priced stunt drivers couldn't get away with that.

Stoney guessed Orteguaza would be favoring a big Lincoln or maybe a ridiculous Humvee stretch limo, if anybody rented out those things any more. No Honda Civics. Nobody would ever accuse the Colombians of modesty. They were nuts about show-off commodities of all kinds.

Without making a point of it, Stoney lightly touched the Israeli Desert Eagle .50-caliber under his left shoulder, just for comfort. It was really too big a pistol to walk around with, but it would put a bullet right through any rental car door they were likely to meet, and then continue on through at least two Colombians and maybe even out the other side, so it did make him feel better. He knew Harper had his own comfort pistol, whatever it was, and probably an Uzi or a Steyr spray gun under the seat. Lord knows what his Rollin' Seventies pals had if they were indeed back there. He had forbidden Harper to turn around and look for confirmation, but they'd texted him of their presence on his BlackBerry. Probably they carried old rusted AKs and shorty MAC-10s.

Ghetto straps – cheap and wildly inaccurate, but intimidating enough with their rapid fire so they could blow away a few infants in the houses nearby.

'Man, you either trust your boys or you don't,' Stoney said. 'They said they're here.' They were both wearing fairly discreet bulletproof vests of Honeywell Gold Flex. It wouldn't stop a round from an assault rifle at close range, but it'd cope with most handguns. You just couldn't go around in Marine body armor without looking ridiculous. Stoney felt he'd done his due diligence on this deal all the way around. He'd arranged for everything on their side except artillery and air power.

'Did our Rastafarian friend give the slightest hint what this movie star in his Porsche is all about?'

'I thought it best to keep them apart, Stone. That Pennycooke family has a rep for squirting ginger beer up your nose to make you answer questions. You don't want no shit like that right now.'

Stoney turned to study his younger partner, all bright eyes and little glints of fear – that strange persistent blink he had – and he decided not to ask about the ginger beer. The man had been called Blinky on the street until he threatened to bust a cap on the next person who called him that. 'Harp, when you're right you're right.'

'This whole place is mad bait, Stoney. I don't like it here.'

Marcus Stone made a face. 'It's been cool so far. The Panchos have been straight. We've been careful and straight. It's so public nobody sane would start trippin' here. Of course, who says these assholes are sane. You want to do the talk when they come?'

'You not dumpin' me headfirst in some shit, Stoney?'

'Man, don't be paranoid. You my number one. My word is on it. I just want you to get some experience dealing with the big world.'

They touched fists below the level of the dash. 'Sometimes I worry about all that intelligence working overtime in there,' Harper said. He tapped a finger on Stoney's forehead.

It was annoying, and Stoney didn't forget the feel of the taps of that finger.

'You do the talk, Stone. You Mr College.'

*   *   *

A half hour ago, they were doing their best to lose me – or lose anyone. If I hadn't done most of the driving in the movie *Hard Down* they'd have lost me ten times over. Connie McKay – one of the world's great stunt drivers – with two Oscars and dozens of broken bones, was my tutor on that one, and I demanded him from then on.

He showed me all that splendid bold driving that old Hollywood specialized in before the computers took over – think ahead, Connie insisted, think every turn way ahead and every brake, anticipate every move. People are gonna tell you you're a terrific driver. You ain't. Nobody, not me, is too good to make a mistake. Guys did a little street racing in a rice-burner at eighteen and think they're hot shit. Driving hard on streets is a skill almost no swingin' dick values enough to work at it. Except stunters and some track drivers, mostly Formula One. Them Indy guys and NASCAR, they don't do shit but turn left and turn left again.

Connie let me in on a bit of the lore when he had to, but not too much. Figuring where a car was probably going and shifting a block over to hide yourself. Easy enough, he says, if you got a really hot machine so you can do a U-ey and catch up when you're wrong. Connie taught me the moon-shine-runner's handbrake turn, a hair-raising one eighty at full speed, yanking on the handbrake to rip the wheels loose. Making sure to keep far enough from the curbs so you don't tick them even a little in the turn and roll. Even with all that training and all the Targa's edge in acceleration and handling, I would have lost them this morning when they did a rope-a-dope twice around a block that would have shown me clear if I'd followed, but I just stopped to watch and here I am down in the parked-up mass of cars at the Costco in Inglewood. With Mexican families pushing big flat carts of goodies past me. Strange that these two black guys think they're so invis-ible sitting out at the periphery all by themselves in that Escalade. They look like giraffes sitting in a cathedral. And, strangely enough, in my silver Porsche Targa, backed into a slot between a big Tahoe and a Corolla, I'm the one who's invisible.

What I'm starting to notice is that two rows in front of me, on the aisle, there's an old Buick that's all wrong. All the windows are down for air, and every few minutes a bit of a

head rises enough over the seats to glance at the Escalade,
then another head. I don't like the look of this comedy at all.
An ambush? Some kind of takedown of a dope deal? What
an irony it would be to find my dad at last, just as he gets
killed in a drug deal going bad.

Naturally, one of the Skinnies has trotted up near the Buick,
and he winks to me, then starts doing cartwheels in the aisle.

I lean over to look at myself in the rear-view mirror and
there they are – my secret eyes. Nobody but the Skinnies, and
maybe Paulita, ever sees them. I used them very briefly a few
times in movies when I was desperate to get past some crappy
action-movie line, but no one seemed to catch on, no one
except a handful of other crazies who wrote fan letters to tell
me what they'd seen.

> Mr Bird, what Providence were you violating when you
> said in *Morgan the Magician*, 'I belong to those who
> are the great controllers of the universe.' I saw your
> terrible eyes when you said that.

These letters I burn. Who cares about a schizophrenic fan
or two who can see through the mask?

Oh, Paulita, maybe tonight I'll slip in, and you'll let me
get my meds.

That was some damn fancy driving, Ratchet thought – big up
onna you, Winston. He was still a little winded from trying
to keep up, a few blocks back, and cranking away at the
big sloppy Impala steering, throwing a bad scare into a half
dozen ordinary drivers along the way before he had to back
down. No hurry, really, since Harper had told him where the
meet was to go down. But, cha, it was good to watch Tyrone
Bird drive that low German car like it was glued to the road.
Truly like watching Jamspeed up at Discovery Bay. He
wondered if being in movies taught the man that. You de best.
I like you more and more, ma'an.

I-an-I gonna watch your back, you like it or not. But what
is it make you come here, with bad bwoys all over dis unhappy
place, and drug business come dis way fast? You remember
dat ting you say to Julia Roberts in de great film *Cracking Up*?
'Sometime you got to look at youself and judge youself from

a second place. You got to look at you dreams and see if they tell you back off what it is you doing.' I hear you good. I need dat second place, Mr Tyrone. Mr J. Liffey, maybe him got him one. Maybe he be pretty good fren', I say. The guy who know the score, like the guy with the checker flag at Jamspeed.

Jack Liffey had heard her murmuring on the phone very early in the morning out in the hallway.

Earlier in the night, as they'd gone to bed, he'd rested his hand on her bare shoulder, but nothing more. And when he'd taken it away without trying to do more, she'd said, 'Thank you, Jackie. I'll remember that.'

When she'd been on the phone, he'd listened closely for any talking-to-Sonny loving intonations, but it had sounded more like she was dealing with Harbor Division, entreating extra time off.

He certainly felt himself on the outside of things now. Looking in through cupped hands pressed to the armored and darkened glass. He wasn't planning on getting up yet, though it was far too late, and he hadn't slept much. What impressed Jack Liffey was the absoluteness of it all, his whole future. It was right there in front of him, and he had no control over a goddamn thing.

He watched her pack up her little duffle again, before it was even light outside. His heart did its dipsy-doodle down to his toes and back up part way, maybe as far as the knees. She was obviously heading for Bakersfield. So soon?

'So soon?' he said aloud.

'Come morning. Don't you think I should get it over with? Find out?'

'Well. When we all thought Loco was dying, the vet asked me if I wanted her to lie about it. I said, absolutely. Lie like crazy.'

Gloria looked over at him, where he was sitting up and holding the sheet to his chest like a virgin. 'Loco is still dying,' she said in her hardest, self-unforgiving voice. 'Just slower now.'

'Hell, we all are, Glor. Even Walt Kelly died, and Pogo should have lived forever.' As a child, the Pogo cartoon strip had been his shield against his father's rigidly racist writings and screwball neo-Nazi friends.

She turned thoughtful for a moment. 'My foster parents hated Pogo. They said it was too cynical and too smart. Not the animal, the strip. Smart always threatened them, I think.'

'I learn more about you all the time,' Jack Liffey said. 'I think it's my goal in life.'

'Well, I don't hate smart, Jackie. I hate not knowing for sure who I am and what I need. And what's going wrong.'

'I told you, any time you want to abandon L.A. and go live in a dusty trailer on the Paiute Reservation in Lone Pine, I'm with you all the way.'

She went back to packing. 'When reservations are that small, they call them rancherias. I don't think the options are that simple. Any feeling of loss takes me back to my childhood – but my childhood isn't really in Lone Pine any more.'

'What loss is it?' he asked, trying to ignore chills of fear.

'Don't ask me the hard ones right now, please. Wait for me to get through this.'

'You know I will.'

'I don't know a damn thing.'

I get out of my car and find a loose shopping cart in the huge parking lot, and without obviously looking at anything I push it past the Skinny who's making faces and plucking at me and then right past the primered and dented Buick Riviera with the front fender a different blue. Uh-huh, there're five young black guys in this old hooptie, all slumped down, and I see hints of weapons. A curved ammo magazine, a blued gun barrel.

I turn on acting mode for them – Oh, I've forgotten where my car is! And then – Oh, there it is! – back behind me, after all! If I can't convince half-assed gangbangers with the faintest gesture, I'm really not much good, am I? Of course there's nothing in the shopping cart, so if they're half-way sentient, they ought to realize I'm fucking with them. But then maybe I'm a store employee, out collecting carts. On several shoots back east, I've been amazed how many people actually return carts to their marked bays, almost all of them. Nobody in California ever does.

That damn Buick is bad news, I realize, as I climb back into the Porsche. Guns and goofs. I want to protect my dad – even if he isn't really my dad. Let me believe, gods.

*   *   *

There was a place on Sepulveda on the way to the airport that rented all sorts of high-end cars so you could impress your girlfriend or your contact, or whomever you were picking up, Stoney thought. That must be where the Colombians had rented what was probably the biggest, most expensive production car ever made – the Maybach 62 – that came rolling very slowly into the Costco gate. Harper's little cousin, B-Dog, had been coveting that damn thing ever since it had been introduced, replacing the Mercedes 600 in his fantasies. It looked like a Rolls that had fallen through some other dimension and melted a bit at both ends. Harper knew it cost over five hundred grand and was just Euro-shit, as far as he was concerned. He'd rather have a big-fin Caddy from the sixties with lots of chrome.

The Maybach chugged across the parking lot and finally settled precisely over the fading Indio emblem on the asphalt. Four eyes in the Escalade one space away watched maybe sixteen eyes in the Maybach suspiciously as the smoked windows hummed down.

'Welcome to the land of opportunity,' Stoney said out his window.

'*Tranquilo*,' an unidentified voice said. '*Somos todos amigos, amigos.*' We are all friends.

'I want to speak only to Señor Jhon Orteguaza,' Stoney said.

The tall lighter-skinned man in the back seat made some subtle signal as he sat upright and then nodded. 'We have met several times before, Mr Stone.' He was the lightest of them, but even he would have been taken by many bangers for a Mexican, though maybe a rich Mexican.

'First, sir, may I indulge my curiosity? What is it you gentlemen painted on this parking spot?' Stoney said evenly.

The Colombian showed no effect at all. 'It is personal, *amigo*, but out of my great benevolence I will tell you. It represents Oshun, the Orisha of love and sex. She is kind, but she has a terrible temper. If you use her too hard, she will take vengeance. She became very special to my mother, who acquired an interest in the powerful Caribbean deities.'

'Believe me, Mr Orteguaza. I respect you totally and I respect your mother and her deities; you have all props here. We have never cheated you, and you have never cheated us, and that goes a long way in this world. But I need to know why people telephone me from Medellin and Cartagena late at night and say, *Cuidado, señor*. This Jhon Jairo needs a large infusion of cash money quickly and trust him only if you wish to die.'

'These are my enemies, Señor Stone. What can one expect *enemigos* to say? They wish to make you suspicious, of course – to make very hot water for me and to destroy our deal. When I get home, I will crush some of these enemies.'

'I would, too. But your enemies call my private telephone number, and that worries me a lot. We're both simple honest men, sir. I do not doubt that. This is just business we are talking about. We're not into waving our dicks to see who is the big dog here, but I'm fully and completely prepared, if that's what you have in mind. Please don't doubt it. This is nothing but an honest business deal, with many many people watching over it.'

Harper was so relieved that Stoney hadn't asked him to do the talking. Jesus Christ! You could cut the tension with a dull knife. This was way way over his head. He'd never seen Stoney push a deal so hard and look so worried. He reached across the seat very low and touched Stoney's knee to warn him that he was scared.

'I don't know all your idiom, Mr Stone. I think I can guess about waving dicks. Anything can be purchased, these days, even private telephone numbers. Perhaps from your corrupt DEA. But tell me, you don't work sometimes for your police? Just to confuse them, perhaps. Maybe a man named Keeler?'

A small electric go-cart with SECURITY written on the side chose that moment to tootle around the periphery of the lot. The old black security guard inside was doing his best not to look at things too hard, and they all fell silent for a bit of mad-dogging as the cart buzzed past.

'People have been hurt for suggestions like that,' Stoney announced. How would Orteguaza know such a thing? He was getting a bigger and bigger premonition of trouble ahead. The air seemed to grow thick around him.

To show his cool, Orteguaza lit a slim brown cigarette. Everything, from both sides, was being done with a slow formality. 'Times are hard everywhere, señor. Your drone aircraft watch everything we do in our country, even my ranch on the coast, your government poisons our coca fields with phenoxyl esters, and even the price of gasoline for transport goes up.'

Stoney began to wonder at what point trading these veiled worries and veiled threats had started to seem like a good idea to the Colombian. At that point, you couldn't roll the dice again.

'I go to the gas station, too,' Stoney said. 'Tell me straight, señor. Are you bumping the price on me?'

'No, sir. The price is twenty-five thousand a kilo, for all forty kilos, exactly as we arranged.' Orteguaza blew strong-looking smoke across the facing seats and into the front seat of the Maybach, and his boys up there turned their heads away discreetly. 'When I make a telephone call –' he displayed his cellphone as if Stone might not have seen one before, '– a kilo of powder will be transported right here, as if by magic, and your boy can test it.'

Harper stiffened, but didn't react further. He was 'the boy' now. He'd paid his USC chem student a lot of money to teach him how to test cocaine, and he had everything he needed in the back seat to do the titration himself. Why carry a cherry kid along? But that wasn't what was worrying him.

'We are all honorable men,' Stoney said, 'but we don't want to leave open any possibility of mistakes. Once my boy tests the kilo that you have chosen for him and pronounces it one hundred per cent correct, then, perhaps, some confederate might cheat both of us and deliver thirty-nine kilos of baking powder.'

'You suggest we are cheaters?'

'I want only the custom we have established. As is our custom, you bring the load in your pickup truck or your old car or whatever your delivery guy is going to use, and I get to choose the bag to test.'

'I don't think that is going to be possible today.'

For the first time, Stoney was really alarmed. The million dollars in rumpled cash was taped up in Ralphs' bags in the trunk, as he'd never done it before and shouldn't have done it this time, and that left him terribly vulnerable to a skunk-and-run.

Why had he changed precautions? He'd just felt that with Harper's pals out there in their car, and the unknown Ratchet in his car, and the Panchos in at least two cars, one or more hidden out there somewhere – with all the unpredictable Costco shoppers to-ing and fro-ing and the little whirring security cart rounding the perimeter – he'd assumed the Colombianos would make the delivery as usual and let him select a random baggie to test.

The goddess of love was painted on the ground, OK? No goddess I know sends trouble, Stoney thought. She deals with trouble.

'Suppose, when I'm happy with my one kilo, I bring you one bag of cash money to count, say twenty-five thousand dollars. The rest will be delivered to you later.' This was all going bad far too fast.

Maeve got up late, which was understandable after her ordeal at the college and the police station. Luckily Chad had never given the cops any lip, and they'd let him go right away.

'Can I make you a late breakfast?' Jack Liffey asked.

She was still a bit bleary looking. 'What is a late breakfast? I picture little tombstones over fried eggs.'

'You're not Leo Gorcey.' They'd once had pun contests, and she'd always loved the Bowery Boys in the old old reruns, howling and rolling on the floor at the man's malapropisms and self-importance.

'Thank God. And I'm not Groucho, either. You know I'm the only person my age who knows who those guys are?'

'That's a true loss to the country. That goofball humor was the high-water mark of American Culture.'

'You used to say that was Bugs Bunny.'

'Him, too. Oh, yes.' He knew her one fast-food weakness. 'Two frosted raspberry Pop-Tarts coming up.'

'Oh, thanks, Dad. I'm not so into that any more, but I can do it.'

While she was in the bathroom, he toasted three of them, thinking he'd make a show of eating a late breakfast with her. She came into the kitchen in an old chenille robe of Gloria's, sleeves rolled into big wads at her elbows, and he almost wept. He poured some coffee and served the tarts on Gloria's colorful *talavera* plates.

'Glor at work today?'

'Probably,' he said. He hated lying to her, but he would if it was best – though he wasn't very good at it.

'I don't like that answer.'

'I don't much like daughters attaching themselves to random gunmen and getting on the wrong side of SWAT teams.'

'We pretty much talked out that subject last night, I think. If you remember. Is this Gloria's big thing that's going on?'

'Big thing?'

'She warned me weeks ago that she might be away for a while, looking into something that she said "might change a lot for us," and she said I had a right to know that much. Jesus, you guys get dramatic at the drop of a hat. It's got to mean another guy.'

'Let's just see what happens, hon. I'm doing my best to normalize here.'

She put her hand on her father's wrist as he was about to pick up the Pop-Tart. 'Don't eat that.'

'The poisons in it?'

'I want it, and I know you don't.'

Everything just gets harder and harder, he thought.

Harper was getting even more nervous as the face-off wore on – clutching a handful of Stoney's shirt from the side. Stoney pointed calmly, drawing everyone's mute attention to the little electric security cart out at the perimeter fence, like a distant moon of the planet Costco, coming around again. Whatever went down, Stoney thought, this was absolutely the last time he'd do business over a fucking Caribbean magic symbol.

'I know what's wrong here,' Orteguaza said calmly.

'All of it's wrong,' Stoney said. 'There's no powder here, and no money. Because there's no trust.'

'That's the word. Trust is not here. My English is so weak.'

'No, it's not. We all want to go home in one piece to our women, right?' Stoney suggested.

Orteguaza met his eyes firmly, and it was like looking into the mouth of hell. Later he would swear to himself that the eyes glowed red from deep within.

'Women are just cunts,' Orteguaza said. 'Señor Stone, consider your skin being flayed off your bones for many days while my doctors keep you conscious and alive. This is not the way to do business among honorable men.'

Stoney heard the Escalade door open behind him. He glanced around involuntarily and saw Harper get out and slap his neck. He wanted to shout to stop him, but it was too late now. Harper was carrying a Steyr assault rifle in one hand and he hunched down behind the hood of the Escalade. When Stoney glanced back at the Colombians, metallic glints were appearing in the interior twilight of the Maybach, too, weapons dragged out of jackets and grabbed from the floor.

Orteguaza raised his eyebrows. 'Let's not ruin such a nice car.'

'Then go in peace,' Stoney said. 'I permit it.'

'You say you permit it.' The voice came like a rumble from deep in the bowels of the earth, but before it was out, there was a squeal of burning tires some distance away – he guessed it was the Rollin' Seventies' car coming on fast, with bangers hanging out the windows holding their armament. Sure enough he heard automatic fire start up – with about as much chance of hitting his Escalade as the Maybach.

Stoney saw Orteguaza shake his head slowly at him, like a Roman emperor disdaining a petition for mercy. 'Flayed. Think of that word.' And the word from hell did stay with him.

The big car's engine roared to life, and by now there was no percentage in letting the Panchos drive away in a vengeful state so Stoney rested his Desert Eagle on the window ledge and put repeated shots into the place where Orteguaza should have been. The huge car had lunged forward faster than you could imagine something that big launching – six hundred turbocharged horsepower – just as Harper's Steyr opened up over the hood of the Caddy, thut-thut-thutting.

There was the sound of a car crash far behind them, but Stoney was busy lining up his sights on the smoking right rear tire of the overpowered Maybach limo and he fired again and again. He didn't want anyone who used the word 'flay' in relation to him to walk around freely on the same planet.

The Maybach swerved and slowed and a Colombian leaned out the rear window aiming the cone-shaped nose of a rocket-propelled grenade straight at him.

Jesus Christ! Stoney dived across his Caddy and scrambled out to tackle Harper and take him down flat on the parking lot. But the rocket either wasn't for them or wasn't very accurate.

Looking behind, he could see that the old Buick had been driven into a line of parked cars by what appeared to be a side collision with a fancy Porsche Targa, just as the rocket flamed past them all, leaving a trail of smoke, and a parked Ford Taurus lifted one wheel off the ground and erupted in flames.

He got up quickly and put two more shots into what should have been the driver of the Maybach, but the thing was accelerating so fast that God himself couldn't have hit it.

Harper stayed down low, and that was just as well.

Stoney watched the Maybach exit the parking lot in a squealing drift around two slower cars using the exit lane, and then blow a light on Century Boulevard to turn right, strangely away from the airport. Damn good driver, Stoney thought. He hoped they weren't planning on staying around in town. He could have tried one more shot as they came past on the boulevard but it was too far, and the pistol was too powerful, and he knew he might have hit somebody at the racetrack.

He put the big pistol back into his shoulder strap as he heard the Porsche engine scream nearby in too low a gear. As it passed him he locked eyes briefly with the driver, a handsome light-skinned black man who looked strangely familiar. No time to think now.

'Baghdad two point oh,' Harper said, sitting up.

'I wish you hadn't signaled, Harp, but maybe you were right. Who knows? Things weren't going down kosher. Let's book before the heat shows up.'

'What about my homies?'

'They seem to be mobilizing.'

Their old Buick was wrenching out of its mess, backing away from the smash-up with wheels spinning smoke.

Stone headed diagonally across empty parking slots toward the exit. 'Tell me again about this actor your Jamaican muscle has been watching.'

Ratchet had had the Impala running the whole time, but he'd had no sense of who was who in the fight – except the Escalade, maybe. That he'd seen at the pool house. It wasn't clear who was uppressor and who was downpressor, and he wasn't sure his poor movie star knew, either. Though Ty Bird had sure made up his mind fast and drove a great run to smack that Buick unexpectedly off course, and making a rumpled mess of his own front end on that nice Targa. Only a man with too much money would do that to a fine car.

He wondered what Trevor would have done in his place. His brother had always been impulsive, and as much as he'd loved him, he'd worried that Trevor would get himself hurt or killed one day. And that was apparently the way the gods had intended it.

He had to talk to Harper now, but maybe, really, he better talk to Mr Jack Liffey.

NINE
Immortal Is Way Too Long

Jack Liffey was just going out the door to help set Maeve's life as gently as possible back on its track by driving her to her parked car at UCLA lot eleven when the phone rang. Somehow, it carried the imperious resonance of Gloria calling, burring impatiently. He had no idea why he thought that, but he was utterly certain of it, so it shocked him when he picked up the phone to hear a string of glorious West Indian vowels.

'Big up onna you, ma'an. Blessed.'

'Top of the day to you, too, Winston.'

'Dis Mr J Liff?'

'It is I. Do you prefer Ratchet or Winston? I never asked.'

'Dozen a one, half a six of de udder. I need to talk wid you.'

He could hear the urgency, and some kind of quaver in his voice. 'I'm at your service, son. I have a chore at UCLA right now. Are you anywhere near there?'

'I forward dere easy.'

'At the southeast corner of campus there's a botanical garden. Meet me there in forty-five minutes. You know southeast?'

Jack Liffey heard a scornful laugh. 'Kingston southeast of Montego Bay, ma'an.'

'OK, fine. You go to Le Conte and face the campus and it's all the way to the tip of your right fingers.'

'I nah say I know sou'east? Everyting cook an' curry.'

'Smell the flowers by the stream. I'll be there.'

Maeve was looking back into the open front door at him, curious.

'Just work,' Jack Liffey told her. 'Not life asserting itself.'

She came back in and hooked her arm through his and squeezed. 'Oh, Dad, it'll all work out. I know it will. You're such a sweetie. She has to know that in her heart.'

'This whole thing wasn't my first choice for my life,' he

said. The jealousy shamed him in front of her like a minor crime. 'But thank you, you always manage to make it a sunny day.'

'What do we do now, Stoney? Those greaseballs are really lunchin' out.'

'Have you heard from your friends in the Buick?'

'You know I haven't. You an' me been together all morning.'

They were sitting out back at Woody's smokehouse on Slauson. It was comfortable and always a busy place and you could bring in beer from just down the street, and no Colombians would ever sneak up on them there.

'You might have got a text,' Stoney sighed. 'We were balls deep with the Panchos, and they were going to take us down, no question. Why? I think we can kiss any future deals with that crew good-bye.'

Harper looked at him like he was crazy. 'Man, I hope you got an idea more than that. These trippers still here. I want to live to see my kids go to high school. You my ace boon, but I didn't sign on for no peeling off my skin if that word flaying is what you say. Mr Big señor had eyes like a vampire.'

'Ever since the Mexican drug guys started chopping off heads, people been trippin' on threats. Put piranhas up your ass, sew it up. What the fuck's wrong with the world? This was just business.'

'Maybe when there's too much money, business always go crusty,' Harper suggested. He used a plastic knife fastidiously to loose one baby back rib from the rack they'd ordered.

Stoney nursed a beer in a brown bag and picked at a small cardboard skid of sweet potato fries. 'Interesting thought. You know, we've still got the buy money. We could go put it in the First Bank of Janky Old Peckerwoods and make two per cent on it. Or we could find another supplier of flake fast. I didn't get that green from some payday loan over by the donut shop. Ooops. Here's your money back, sirs, but we ain't got no interest for you today. So sue us.'

Harper rested his forehead on his palms. 'Ah, shit-sakes.'

'Ten per cent a week, brah. I didn't teach math-a-matics, but I've got enough fingers to count how dead we're gonna be when DJ Potter wants his vigorish. You can come visit me on life support at County. Unless . . .'

Stoney sat up straight. Harper saw he'd had an idea, as clearly as if he'd held a lightbulb over his head like Wile E. Coyote.

'OK, you zonin' now,' Harper said. 'What it is?'

'Get that Rasta man of yours over here. He says a movie star's been doggin' us. Don't know why, don't know who – but movie stars mean big money, and they got lots of pals that got the hard-on for the good drugs. Maybe we fix up a whole new business scene.'

'Man, it's a relief not to see the failure in your face no more. I din't like it.'

Jack Liffey let her off by her car at lot eleven just off Sunset Boulevard, under a bright clear sun like a promise that the world might just go on functioning favorably. The TV news that morning had said they weren't shutting down the campus and everything was back to normal.

'So, you going to class?'

'Not today, Dad. I'm still discombobulated. I'm going home to Topanga to regroup.'

He couldn't help himself. 'Please don't regroup by sniffing powder off a mirror, that's all I ask.'

'Dad, Dad. OK, you are a detective. I didn't know Axel for five minutes when I signed on for my share of the cabin. Please don't generalize to me.'

'Sorry. And thanks for easing my heart.'

'She has a lot of excuses and reasons. Next time maybe you can help her. You're good at that.'

He wanted to jump out of his pickup and clasp Maeve in his arms for a moment, or maybe an hour or two, to comfort and cosset and protect her from all the world's dangers. And soothe himself. 'You'll never be this age again, hon. Enjoy it all.'

'Dad . . . ?'

'Yeah?'

'You'll never be this age again, either. Think about you and Gloria.'

'Do you think I ever stop?'

Sonny walked Gloria down to the shores of the Kern River, not two blocks from his house. Not so romantic a spot, but the best he could do in Oildale, unless he wanted to take her over to North Chester Avenue and the famous redneck fist-fighting bar called Trout's.

It wasn't exactly picturesque down by the depleted river. Scrubby clay and sand, patches of water willows like buggy whips stuck in the sand, and the pung of stagnant water.

'Lovely,' she said. Directly across what there was of a little gurgling stream, the rich of Bakersfield lived on top of the high cliff, with a picturesque view not only over the slum where the oil workers lived but also over a hundred square-mile complex of wellhead pumps and storage tanks, all lashed together by raised silver oil pipes, the Kern River Oilfield, one of the biggest in the world. 'Just takes getting used to, I guess,' Sonny said. 'Devil take the hindmost.'

'Leave us not speak of devils. You know why.' It had been a crazed devil-worship hysteria in this town that had swept up Maeve and brought them all together to save her. They sat on a rotting ponderosa log that had been carried down the Kern Canyon from Lake Isabella in some unimaginable flood long ago. 'All man's creations are admirable,' he said. 'A Bako oilfield and Bourbon Street and the Champs-Elysées.'

'I don't know the shomz eeleezay, but I love the Eastern Sierra. Mostly because there's so little of human creation. It's the greatest mountain view I know, open high desert below, all creosote and greasewood, and snowy peaks up above you at fourteen thousand feet.'

'There is that point of view as well. But does any of that help you know why you're so unhappy now? You're a smart woman. I know you've got both oars in the water, but you still row in big circles.'

She looked away from him. 'What a sight you are in your white linen suit, Sonny. You should be named after a Southern State. Alabama Theroux.'

'You're changing the subject off of you-all, as you always do. You're afraid to look ourselfs in the face.'

That got her back up. 'I'm a near full-blood Indian, Sonny. Southern Paiute. My mom died drunk in a gutter in Lone Pine, fucked to death in winter by no-account cowboys for drinks and spare change. At seven, I was fostered to a Mex family that said Injuns was all dirty and I should pretend I wasn't an Indian. At fifteen I was in an Eagle Scout group in L.A.

run by the cops, and I fell in love with a cop, and I had to abort his kid because he was married and it would have ruined his career. It was a bad surgical job and it ruined me for having any more kids. I made my own way in the world since, and if you think Jack is the top prize in the ring-toss, think again. But for some amazing reason, Jack seems to care a lot for this fucked-up cigar store woman, almost unconditionally, and it astonishes me so much I still cling to it.'

'I do believe you and I want to get beyond that; to another place that's better for you,' Sonny said.

'I don't know about that,' she said. 'You don't always sound so dependable yourself.'

'I think I can take you where you really need to go.'

'Can you tell me ahead of time where it's at, Sonny? I really need that. Not just over some fucking rainbow.'

'Give me half a chance, Glor. I know I'm a guy who's good to cross a stormy river with.'

'This river?' A few yards away the remains of the Kern were about two feet wide and frothy with chemicals.

He winced. 'Don't be mean. I promise you a beautiful day today, a beautiful sunset and a wonderful night of love. And lots more talk – as much as we have on board. I love your busted-up soul more than you can know.'

A huge bird rose from somewhere unknown and flapped lazily past them, bigger than any bird should ever be.

'Blue heron,' he said. 'We salute you.'

'Watch how it labors along. Jesus. It's looking so old to me.'

'We've all got immortal longings,' he said.

'Nah. Immortal is way too long for me.'

Jack Liffey parked in the UCLA hospital structure and paid his nine dollars, resenting every penny of it. There was a whole neighborhood of rich people's houses nearby, but it was zoned for residents only. Those bastards could park in front of his house in Boyle Heights for free any time they wanted.

But it was an old umbrage. He simmered down and walked along Tiverton to Le Conte, where he froze all at once.

At least thirty young women who were nude except for paint and panties jogged out of the botanical garden, right past him, seemingly driven by snappy whipcracks from a handful of slightly older women in black balaclavas. The driven women wore garish paint to disguise their breasts as eyes, targets, tiger stripes, brick walls.

'Eros and Thanatos!' a woman shouted.

'You *will* learn to sing,' one of the whip-crackers cried out.

It wasn't altogether unpleasant, he admitted to himself, but still rather unsettling. When the group with their naked unpainted backs had run around the corner at Hilgard, up into sorority row, he realized that across the road three older matrons carrying shopping bags had stopped to look at him querulously, as if the bizarre display might have been his doing.

'What on earth was that?' one of them called.

'"In wildness is the preservation of the world,"' he called back. 'It's Thoreau.' It was often misquoted as 'wilderness', but Jack Liffey liked it better the original way.

One of the matrons laughed. 'I wish my boobs looked half that good.' She chucked a forearm under her breasts as if to firm them up.

He walked into the Mildred Mathias Botanical Garden at the corner. OK, Winston. I've had my infusion of oddity for the day. Let's do this thing.

I liked your brother. I helped his girlfriend, and I'll help you, too, and I'll help Maeve's roommate, and I'll help – God, I do believe there's a limit to what I can mend. Now and then, there were dark days when Jack Liffey felt that maybe he'd been issued the wrong tools for life – a hairbrush along with a hammer, say. And here he was now, still brushing away at the hammer like mad, hoping it might do something. Life is such a blind rush to death, I hope there might be some kind of recompense for all the pain, but I know better. What he really meant was: Gloria and Sonny are fucking away in Bakersfield while I'm alone here.

He followed the path down to the bottom of the botanical garden where the artificial stream burbled away. Isn't there something in all this disorder of life for me? he thought.

He'd had his midlife crisis, some time back. You don't get a second one, sport. Sorry. The best you can do now is buy a spiffy little car, but you can't even afford that. Enough. The steady drip of self-pity made him sick to his stomach.

A garden crew was raking and weeding up the slope, moving at the pace of those for whom work was largely physical and poorly paid. Somebody had left a worn push-broom on a bench built into the lovely WPA stonework by the stream. He moved the broom to the side of the bench and sat primly to watch the flitting of a few dragonflies. Their haphazard zig-zags calmed him immensely, following a course all their own.

'Blessed,' the deep voice announced, and then Jack Liffey saw Winston striding up the path. 'Whoa, I-an-I see a true Bobo Shanti!'

'Hello, Winston. What the hell is that?'

The tall Jamaican smiled and stopped before Jack Liffey like a large materialized djinn, arms on his hips. 'Dat one of de many mansions of Rastafari. The Bobo Rastas wear turbans and carry brooms to signify dey cleanness. Dey followers of King Emmanuel, who ima dead now.'

Jack Liffey glanced at the broom he'd moved to the side and, superstitiously, he pushed its head farther away from the bench until it passed the tipping point and clapped down loudly on the path.

'What say you sit down beside me and relax a bit?' he said to the Jamaican. 'I need a relaxed friend. Don't try so hard to be Mr Outsider. I'll bet we can finish this whole conversation in Standard English.'

'Wicked bet.' Winston sat beside him and grinned.

'All those smart A-levels. Trevor said you were too speaky-spokey for your own good.'

'Trevor said that?' He laughed softly. 'It's true. Back on J, I go the opposite way entirely, and I sound like the gov'nor-gen'ral. I enjoy deviling people a little.'

'It's not such a terrible plan, but give me a break now, Winston. I've had a bad morning.'

'Yes, sir, indeed. But you seem strong and *tallowah* to me. And I need your help.'

He let the strange word go. 'That's why we're both in this lovely garden in the middle of the city, I believe.'

Winston's cellphone went off with a jaunty little reggae backbeat. He glanced at his pocket, but let it stay put and finally run down.

'Is that the problem?' Jack Liffey said, meaning the call, or whoever was on the other end of the call.

'All is problem, man, when you don't know the customs.'
He told Jack Liffey about coming to America in Trevor's foot-
steps, hopefully to solve a family money crisis, and once he
got here, his assignment to find out who was tracking down
a certain Mr Big, probably a drug-dealer, and how he'd found
out the tracker was the movie star Tyrone Bird. He said he
liked Bird a lot, he'd always liked his movies – and Winston
insisted that there was everywise a decent but troubled man
inside every role he played.

One of the Latino workers wandered down the grassy hillside and reclaimed his broom.

'*Buenos*,' Jack Liffey tried to greet him.

The man just nodded, and they all stayed silent until he'd
moseyed on up the slope again, dragging his broom behind.
Contrails from a jetliner leaving LAX scraped the powder
blue sky, and a few crows jumped from tree to tree complaining
angrily.

Something more was worrying Winston. 'This morning,
Mr Bird went someplace where he should have stayed far
away. You'll be seeing it in the paper. A big bad deal was
going down in a parking lot. Guns were all over the place.
And Mr Bird drove his silver Targa right into the middle of
it – I don't know why. Ty Bird shut the deal down. It was
all drugs and money, I'm sure – I'm no pickney just off the
farm. People started shooting every direction. One guy even
fired one of those Middle East rockets. Now, I think these
guys I work for are going to want Ty Bird dead, Mr Liff. Or
want him somewhere so they can twist his arm hard. I won't
do it.'

'Why not, Winston?'

'In my heart I didn't come to the States to follow my
brother's footpads as a criminal, but to avenge him. Or maybe
I can serve his memory. I had to pretend I was a rude bwoy,
just like Trevor, but that's not me, sir.'

'You want to tell me the name of Mr Big?' Jack Liffey
asked.

'Oh, sir. Then you step hard onna burning bag of shit, too.
Like a prank we use to play.'

'OK,' Jack Liffey said. 'Here's the curveball. Or what do
you call a deceptive bowl in cricket?'

'Googly or an arm ball.'

'Great, here's the googly – I believe Ty Bird is on a search for his father. Is your Mr Big dope-dealer about the right age for that? Say, fifty-five to sixty?'

Winston's eyes went large with thought. 'I only see him from far. I deal with his lieutenant, call Harper.' He pronounced the military title British fashion – leftenant. His cellphone rang again, and again he let it play on and on, then thunk into message. 'Damn, sir. Everything go so bad. I don't want to be part of something I don't understand – or overstand, as the Rastas say.'

'I'm with you, and I'm on your side, Winston. I know this city better than you ever will. Tell me the name of Mr Big, and let me deal with it all, and I'll give you a place to hide, and then I'll get you home.' Can I actually mend something this complicated? Jack Liffey wondered.

Winston made a face. 'Man, they lit that parking lot up, those guys with all the guns. I've heard that racket in Trenchtown, too, but never so bad as that. It was war. I don't care about this job any more. I know my brah's dead and gone. Cha, everyt'ing in the States start to feel wicked.'

'Then let it go.' He rested a hand on Winston's muscle-hard shoulder. 'Hand the weight to me. This is my country.'

Winston Pennycooke's face wrinkled up as if in pain. 'I don't know why so, Mr Liff. I feel maybe I can help Mr Tyrone Bird. If I go hide, they'll just send somebody else after him, like me, but real mean and unstoppable. Maybe I can help Mr Bird for Trevor. No, sir. I not budge on dat.'

'You're making a mistake.'

'I got to do it.'

Jack Liffey could tell when a man had settled into place, into some groove in which he considered his inflexible honor ran. 'I'll help you.'

'No, ma'an, I been lucky forever. I know I got to do this thing my only.'

'I can see you're determined,' Jack Liffey said. 'Move fast if you want to save Ty. Find him and talk to him. And call me if things go bad.'

'If you was a girl, I'd hug you,' Winston said.

'In this country, it's OK.' But it wasn't OK with him, apparently.

*   *   *

The sun was up and warming. It seemed precarious to step on to campus again, as if a killer could hop out of any crevice. But she changed her mind about going home and went back to the anthropology lecture, to give the professor one more chance. Classes were going on as if nothing had happened the day before. She had until Friday to drop the class.

Amazingly, Chad was in the huge lecture hall, too, near the back and the seat beside him was empty. On the whole, she'd rather have sat somewhere else, but felt it would be rude after all they'd been through.

She had her notebook out, but she recognized the same thing that she'd learned a dozen times before when she'd given other things a second or a third chance: a book that really bored her to death but somebody insisted was the best; a foreign movie that seemed so pretentious and talky, but some pal had said was better than Fellini. In her experience, the second chance was always just as bad as the first. Maybe one day it wouldn't be like that, who could tell?

'Let laughter flee,' he said softly to her.

'Pardon?'

'Nothing. I'm probably out of here in a minute or two. Is your life always so eventful?' He looked a bit chagrined.

'Pretty much, yeah.'

'I guess we all figure we're somebody different until the Grim Reaper shows up. I really had the bads about that guy.'

Heads came around and glared at them, and several people shushed them. He nodded apologies and collected his books and notebooks.

Maeve hesitated but followed him out and tried to let the big door wub-wuff as softly as possible behind her.

'Let's go to the union and you buy me a beer,' Chad said. 'I've never seen anybody stand up to a gun like that. Shit, I mean, what was the idea? He could have blasted all of us, who knows? Maybe you're just a lot braver than I am.'

'He was a sad case,' Maeve said. 'They shouldn't have shot him so quick. People like him go nuts when they can't look straight at things. Or won't. You've got to help them look, that's all.'

Marcus Stone and Harper were still waiting restlessly behind Woody's, nursing another few tubs of fries and two more beers. They hadn't meant to kill off the morning quite so thoroughly, but they were both worried about returning to any known haunts. The Colombians would undoubtedly fly out of L.A. pretty soon, but they feared nothing would prevent a little ultra-violence on their way out. That big guy was a vampire. The idea of being flayed alive was enough to freeze your blood.

They both had feelers out everywhere – a carload of maniacs in a big Maybach was about as hard to miss as a steam locomotive on the freeway. Though the Panchos might have switched to a couple of plainer cars. They weren't idiots.

'I hope that guy in the Cubs hat doesn't try to chase us out of here,' Harper said. He meant the guy at the serving hatch.

'He probably thinks we're married and is leaving us alone.'

Neither of them found that very funny.

'Call that useless Rasta of yours one more time,' Stoney said. 'I want to know if there's something bent about this movie star. That was him for sure coming on hard in his little Porsche, and maybe he works for the Colombians. If so, I'll bust a cap on his ass myself. Maybe do it anyway for getting in our face.'

Harper sighed and thumbed in the speed-dial, which hadn't been answering.

'Ratchet! Man, where you fuckin' at? Don' you go bein' off the grid like that.'

Stoney could just hear a tiny voice from the cell, like a man trapped in a bottle: 'My bad, Mr H. Dis detective man bucked inna me an' I hadda stay quiet on de cell.'

Marcus Stone grabbed the phone from Harper. 'Listen here, Mr Rasta. I'm the boss. The buck stops here. I require your presence now, and I want to know about this movie star you talk about.'

'Wa' mek you so vex wid me, ma'an? I-an-I do good work fa you on dat rough scene today. So where I come see you?'

Yes, where, Stoney thought. Shit. He couldn't announce it over a cell. Even the CIA could be listening. 'You come to a place I keep.' He didn't want to say it was his crib, for too many reasons. He hinted at the pool house and found out the Jamaican already knew about it. Jesus, did everybody in L.A. know where he lived?

'I forward, naow.'

Winston hung up before Stoney could ask him more about the movie star.

'OK, then. Let's go deal with your Rastaman before somebody else does.'

'We can go home, Stone?' He'd heard Stoney hinting at his own place in Woodland Hills.

'I don't like the idea, but he knew the place. We park a block over and go through the yards.'

'These Mexes are stone crazy.'

All Latinos were Mexes to Harper, even Colombians. Stoney sighed. 'Fo sho, brah. Keep your strap handy.'

What a day, I'm thinking – considering the nasty wrinkles in my Porsche's front end – not to mention the rocket-propelled grenade that had passed about three feet from my head, unless that was a hallucination, too. A screeching high speed object I never want to see or hear again. I'm back in my motel by noon with a bag of In-n-Out animal burgers – the only consolation I can think of this early in the day. Too soon for a margarita or I'll start dancing nude with the Skinnies. Luckily they all seem to be sleeping it off.

I use my Swiss Army knife and dig out the grout, then lever out a tile in the bathroom wall high above the tub. I dig out a hollow between studs and hide the cash I've managed to withdraw. I regrout the tile with toothpaste and who knows how good that's going to be, when the *moza* starts washing down the bathroom. I hope she's inefficient.

I'd better make friends with her, I think. Though my Spanish is pretty crappy. Why did I take French in high school? I mean, like I live one hundred miles from France or something and I'm going to be driving there every few months. To be honest, back in Dorsey High School I got scared about competing with all the Mexican kids in their own language. Dumb reasoning. Who cares about grades now?

I gobble down one of the burgers, cooled off to room termperature so it's past the point where it tastes all that great. Still, that beef flavor, hit with extra salt I asked for, gives me a shot of nostalgia. Moms bought burgers and fries almost every day, even when all her buddies went veg. It was amazing she didn't turn into a blimp, but that was probably from being on her feet so much as a waitress, and later, of course, the cancer.

Beside the bag is the old Himes novel, open like a tent, and I pick it up on impulse and flip to one of my permanent dog-ears:

> I began wondering when white people started getting white or rather, when they started losing it. And how it was you could take two white guys from the same place – one would carry his whiteness like a loaded stick, ready to bop everybody else in the head with it; and the other would just simply be white as if he didn't have anything to do with it and let it go at that.

Man, you can probably say that about a lot of blacks, too, I realize. Some whites seemed to get a lot less tense about it all after Obama. Like they'd finished a test where they'd got at least a respectable C and the whole nightmare of studying was over for good now. Weird. Voting for Obama made so many whites forgive themselves. A lot of blacks I know just got more worried. Maybe it's about all that hate spilling out of the wingnuts now and lots of them have guns.

There's a heavy rapping at my door.

'Who's there?'

'Open, ma'an. I done be your brudda an' your keepa for days.' It's clearly a West Indian voice, and it sounds incredibly sincere. It's such a lovely accent; I've always wanted to be coached at it. 'I gotta favor you or I gotta flee dis stoosh city naow, ma'an.'

I draw in a breath and then open the door on a handsome Jamaican kid who's well over six-and-a-half feet tall and maybe twenty years old.

'Ooooh. I seen all you moovies, ma'an,' the young Jamaican says. 'You de bes ob all. You all heart inside dere.'

OK, I'll take a chance. My big weakness. Right, Skinnies?

'Come in, tell me why you're my brother. Other than being a big fan and all.'

This guy steps into my room without a hint of embarrassment. He carries a brown bag and draws out a half-filled bottle of dark rum, a brand I've never seen. Mount Gay Eclipse.

Weird. 'Dis a treat, ma'an. We get us some Coke and Chee-
tos from de machines, an' I-an-I serve you like dat Mr Saxton
fellow in *Jookman*. You 'member him?'

The butler who'd suited me up in the movie and carried
all the weapons that made it seem like I had real superpowers.
Tom McCarthy, with a nice phony English butler accent. The
first movie wasn't too bad for a spoof of the genre, but the
scripts became increasingly ludicrous, as usual – worse than
the worst of the junk superhero movies – and I nixed *Jookman
III.*

Two of the Skinnies are starting to get curious about this
giant Jamaican, peering around the bathroom door.

'Cha, I gotta say, ma'an, I wit' you forever and ever and I
will defend you to de death. But you in some big trouble wid
de drug chaps here. I go get the Co-cola and we talk.'

Orteguaza had all his guys booked into big adjoining suites
on the top floor of the Airport Radisson, and they were clus-
tered in his huge twelfth floor suite now, smoking cigars
importantly as they watched their boss negotiate with his cop
contact in L.A., Randy Sem, Colombia-born, who was now
a sergeant in the Inglewood Police Department.

All business was conducted in a rough and ready Norte
Spanish that disgusted Orteguaza, but Sem's parents had immi-
grated when he was only six. You worked with what you had.

'OK, how long will it take you to find this Marcus Stone?'

'Don't worry about it. That's all as good as done. This ain't
no third world country, man. Money makes us all smart.'

'And the other thing?'

Sgt. Randy Sem made a shrug. 'Somebody who can lay off
a million bucks to wholesale for a new guy with pure snow,
all in one day? *Madre*. And pay cash on the spot? And trust
you because he trust me? Let's talk again about my cut.' In
English, Sem added, 'Ten big wans don' seem hardly adequate.
Ol' fren'.'

'You got me at a bad time,' Orteguaza continued in English.
'You act good for me now and I remember it. You be diddly
shit, and I remember that, too.'

'Don't try and scare me for no phony friendship. You already
gone an' fucked up big time in my country. Shootin' up a
Costco! Shootin' a RPG! No, my gentleman, we ain' frens no

more, not like the old time. You give me twenny-five big wans, and we back to frens for life.'

Orteguaza glared at him without making a sign. Streetlights were coming on in the dusk outside in long rows of haloed green embers behind this gypsy-market haggling Latino cop.

TEN
The Day of Creation

Gloria read the blurry printed image over his shoulder with a frown.

> The tall guy (Dr Lenny?) goes, the more probes you use the greater the odds you get a poynter that just goes to one suspect. But two many probes cost a boatload of money . . .

It was a fax of a six-page report Sonny had got out of a friend in the Bako PD. The typing – actual typewriter typing – was full of strikeouts and words scrawled between the lines.

'DimTim Maloney can just barely see through a bob-wire fence,' Sonny said, 'but you can crib enough from his junk prose to write a legible memo that says you were there.'

'Thanks, Sonny.' She just couldn't bring herself to run back up to Fresno. The drive itself, up truck-infested Highway 99, the ugly old city with its three absurd brown high-rises from the 1940s, the whole crappy conference. 'They only sent me to the thing as punishment.'

'And there's me here, too, along the way.'

'Sorry. I just don't know what I'm saying,' Gloria said. She turned to look at him beside her in the front seat, a pretty unlikely lover she would have thought, so much shorter than her, almost comic in his tropical suit, but there it was. He gave her a pang in her heart. They sat in his van behind the police station, watching a shift change, cops drifting out to their Corvettes and big American SUVs.

'Can we do something innocent for a while?' Gloria asked. 'No unruly sex. No drinking. Maybe some mac-and-cheese. I need to stabilize. It'll help me more than you can know.'

'There's a little zoo up the river five or six miles. A bit sad compared to the big city zoos, but they're rescued animals

and it's a nice drive, anyway. And I'll show you one thing
there that you'll like.'

'Haul me up there, Mr Man.'

'You're sounding awful down.'

'Let's not talk about anything real, OK?'

'Then I'll be a close chewer and a tight spitter.'

'Oh, stop that, honey. I'm really sick to my stomach.'

Maeve and Chad carried their book bags up into the sculpture garden that was scattered across north campus.

'I'm gonna drop the class,' Maeve said with finality. She didn't
look at Chad much. He was so damned square-jawed handsome.
She was determined to lay off the romance for a while.

'That'd just about finish you off as an anthro major,
wouldn't it?'

'Probably. They assigned me a counselor; somebody named
Betty Cherry, if you can believe it. I'll go talk to her.'

'Quite a name.'

'Oh, let it go.' They were passing a sculpture of long slowly
wind-bobbing lances that she liked. 'What's your favorite
sculpture here?' she asked, trying to find neutral in his gearshift
and calm him down.

'I never thought much about it. Maybe that one way over
there. There's something tough about it.'

'My dad liked that one, too,' Maeve said. 'I remember it's
called "A bird goddess". He used to bring me here for picnics.
To be honest, I like that Deborah Butterfield horse best. I love
horses and I love her horses.'

'The one made of sticks?'

'It only looks like sticks. It's all bronze.'

'Cool. So what's the rest of your college life gonna be like
if you drop anthro?'

'Are you staying in?' she asked.

'It's boring as hell, but I can get a gentleman's C. For
organic chem I don't need any better.' He scratched the top
of his head, almost like Stan Laurel.

'You know, Maeve, that was a fine mess you got us into. You
talk kindness to a stone crazy kid, then you piss on the cops.'

'You've gotta try to help, especially the clueless.'

They sat down on a grassy hillock beneath a wonderfully
curved abstract torso.

'I risk my life just being near you. I think that deserves a real date. Want some hummus and pita?' He took a paper bag out of his book satchel, and pried open a Tupperware.

'A real date? I've seen you pretty close with a redhead.'

He made a face. 'She isn't really into me. And I'm not very crazy about her music or her taste in books. Man, oh, man. She wanted me to read some vampire book, for Chrissake. What's all this attraction girls have with vampires? Isn't life nasty enough without imaginary bloodsuckers?'

Maeve smiled. 'Why do boys spend hours playing video games about shooting everything in sight?' She gave a mock shudder.

'I never did, but I hear you.'

'I don't read vampire books. But I think I can guess what it touches in young girls. Vampires combine something like sex with a shudder of fear. They come through your bedroom window late at night. Girls may not want to be overpowered for real, but we all have fantasies.' She dipped up some garlicky hummus with a triangle of pita. He had good taste in snacks.

Chad touched her wrist gently, as if accidentally, when she went for more pita.

'Vampires,' she said, trying to ignore the touch. 'They're our generation's beatniks. They subvert all the normality our parents worship – science and religion, or at least decency, and getting home by eleven. No, wait.' She chuckled at her own sudden thought. 'They're all Heathcliffs, undead Heathcliffs. Promising girls a wild ride.'

'Clever deconstruction,' he offered.

'They're tormented alpha males. Are you an alpha male?'

'Doubtful, sorry. Not if it means I played football. Or went out in the woods and shot deer. You don't really want me slipping in your window at night to bite your neck, do you?'

'You do and I'll bonk you with a baseball bat.'

'Don't worry,' he promised. 'If we get together, it's not going to be like that. They made us take this really serious pledge in high school, signed and all: the word no from a girl means no.'

I can tell we're both getting a little woozy with this wonderful rum of his, decanted none too gently into fizzing Coke cans in my motel room. 'Man, friend, that's really good rum.' I'm so relaxed one of the Skinnies is doing jumping jacks with his back to us.

'Cha, now, why youself be interferin' at Costco this morning, ma'an? Dat a very bad place, you no seeit? I almos' have to save you ass.'

A chill takes me hard, and instantly a whole bunch of Skinnies start peeking around doors and chests. Before this moment, Winston has given me no hint that he was there at that mess, though he said he's been babysitting me. Did the production company send him, or is he just another star-stalker, after all? 'Get out of here, guy, before I call the cops.' I hand him back his rum as several Skinnies clap with appreciation.

'Fool. I de only pro-tect you got. Dere a waar out dere. Like Af-gan. I-an-I no fook around naow. You got to know you do de very wrong t'ing dis morning. De drug heads wan' me to smoke you ass right now or bring you in for de big questions, ma'an. No worries, I ain' go there. But why you stick you head up?'

It's hard for me to a get a read on this guy. I wonder if he can be my friend after all. Most of the Skinnies in the room get frightened and retreat to the bathroom. 'Tell me more, Mr Winston.' He wants me to call him Ratchet, but I refuse, I don't know why.

'You tell me why you be like likkle dog an' run after dis big drug man.'

'You mean Marcus Stone?'

His eyes opened a bit as if I'd spoke a name that would call down the gods of vengeance. 'Hol' it down. Sight!'

What the hell do I have to lose? I think. 'Look, Winston. I think Marcus Stone is my father, and I want to meet him.'

'Sufferation! Wa mek dis idea?'

I can see Winston is pretty drunk, too. We're both a bit hazy. This is no way to be negotiating my future.

'Dis all fuck-up.'

'If you're going to kill me, Winston, kill me now.' I open my arms to make myself as vulnerable as possible.

Weirdly, the man goes down on his knees in front of me with open palms. 'No, no, no, ma'an, I beg. I-an-I good man. Check it out as deep as you wan'. You can call Jack Liffey and ask him.'

'I don't know this Jack guy and I don't care. I need to meet Marcus Stone. Can you take me to him?'

He sighs. 'Cha, I got to talk to him firs'. An' his Minister of Defense, he call Harper. Got to prepare de way for Jesus to enter Jerusalem on his ass.'

'Don't be sacrilegious, Winston. Be my friend. I can use a friend.'

Li'l Joker's stomach began to cramp up after they'd let him out of the rust-red Buick with all the gunshot holes and the big fresh dent on the driver's side. He'd like to get his hands on the driver of that Porsche who'd hit them this morning before they could get to Stoney. Everything had gone so wrong that it was giving him bad indigestion, the way his body had always objected to things like math tests and asking girls to dance.

Most of the day they'd hung out at Marletta's watching old movies, *Scarface* and *Terminator 2*, waiting to word-up, but then Stoney called and said everybody go home. They dropped Li'l Joker two blocks from his home on 73rd, as he insisted. He left his Uzi and his old Browning .38 in a sports bag under the seat so they could take them back to the clubhouse. He was twenty-three, but his mom still browbeat him mercilessly about 'bad companions' whenever she saw them. To her, he was still little Deon Le-Vaughan Wilkins, smart boy in school, ahead of his class in reading, and he had been all that to himself, too, until his rebirth as Li'l Joker after they'd jumped him into the Rollin' Seventies.

He'd walked a block and was just about to pass a strange looking dark chocolate guy in a really expensive coat when a .357 Magnum was poked hard into his stomach. Then the chocolate brother opened his mouth, and Li'l Joker could immediately hear the Spanish in his voice.

'Get in *el coche* or die now, nigga.'

Another black Latino with a scowl held open the back door of a battered Ford Taurus – not the huge Maybach that he'd seen this second guy hanging out of that very morning with a gun.

A shove had him in the seat and another one had him moving to the middle. His stomach cramped hard again and he tried to blame it on the all-and-all pizza from Dac's. He'd tried to pick them off, but vegetables always tore up his stomach.

'No hard feelings, gentlemen. Why you Jews so interested in me?' He smiled for calling all these weird brothers Jews, but none of them smiled back.

The car smelled bad, as if they bathed only once a month. The pistol was held hard against his ribcage and he tried to ignore it.

The white guy in front turned in the seat to look at him. 'Forget the Jew shit, *pendejo*. I can't see how you rate no real gang. You just Bobo the clown.'

L'il Joker estimated one second to grab the pistol away from the guy, and then another two or three seconds to kill them all.

'*¡Golpéelo!* Hit him!'

The guy on his left whacked Li'l Joker's cheek hard with a big square .45 auto. '*No te doy color.* I hit you more if you move a milli,' this voice said. It was so weird, hearing black guys talking normal Mex.

'I think you got the wrong guy,' L'il Joker said. 'Chris Rock is over in Hollywood.'

'Shut the mouth.'

'I'm feeling a little sick to my stomach now. Why don't you guys come back some time and talk to me when I'm feeling better.' He really did feel like throwing up in the car.

'Get your grips,' the white guy said. 'We got to show your chiefman to do us right. Is he getting greedy?'

'I hear it was you dudes changed the deal. Nobody can't work with that shit.'

'Life is all change, *pendejo*. Some smart guy deals the cards over again and we all make adjust. You tell Señor Stoney, for me, that respect is not no painted-on mustache.'

Li'l Joker didn't know what he meant. 'I'm not in that track, man. I'm really sick now.'

'Ignacio, drive to that church we seen.'

The car set off eastward, and the fact that they'd mentioned going to a church helped Li'l Joker a little with his worries.

Just as dark was coming, Ratchet found Stoney home alone, sipping a single-malt Scotch and writing in a book with black pebbled covers. Ty had desperately wanted to come along, but Ratchet had insisted he had to stay away until the ground was plowed.

'Where the fuck you been, Haile Selassie?' Stoney seemed to have no intention of getting out of the doorway.

'Ease up, ma'an. No be rude wid dat name. I no Rasta man, but I got respek. I come in naow.'

Stoney stepped away and let him in. 'Next time, you go to Harper first.'

'I-an-I got news jus' for you: dis ma'an dat been close to yo' business – him say him want to meet you bad. Him say prepare because him your real an' true son. Him say, you got to remember way back – and he make me say dis – Donna Wisecki, Donna Freedom, Donna Seagull, Melanie Bird.'

Stoney sat back down in front of his big black book without giving any indication he'd been affected by any of the names. 'So, I got to care about some peckerwood bitch from the seventies?'

Ratchet almost smiled at him. 'Ma'an, who dat say to you "peckerwood bitch?" Who dat say to you "seventies"?'

'Didn't Harper tell you to eliminate this person out of our lives? We got trouble enough.'

'Cha, I tell you, sir, wit' respect, dis man some really *big* movie star, you no seeit? Dis a Arnold Schwarzy or Will Smith. You no wanna' be in dat place, hurt dis guy. His name Tyrone Bird. He jus' make *Good Cop, Frat Cop* wid Bruce Willis an' Sarah Jessie Parker. Man, dis movie so big all over de known an' unknown world. Anyway, I say Tyrone a good man and a vex man, and he need to meet his pops.'

'You been hanging out with him?'

'Yes, I see him, Mr Stoney. I vouch. I protect you every minute for sure. You no wan' see you son? Dis be roots. You be knowing de truth in you heart when you see him. I feel it.'

'Why didn't you bring him here right now? Don't you trust me not to shoot him?'

It took Ratchet a moment to figure out an answer to that question that worked. No, trust wasn't very big in the picture. 'Him say him desperate fi a fadder. An' you already sucking yo' teeth like mad. I got to run ahead like John de Baptiss. Make sure all is prepare.'

Stoney started to laugh, but it was one of those laughs Winston had heard from late night drunks that sometimes just stopped dead with a punch or a knife. Finally, Stoney ran down and jotted a note in his book.

'OK, you're John the Baptist. Which makes the kid Jesus

Christ, and makes me . . . what? Who can algebra that? Let's
get it over with. How soon can you get Jesus here?'

'He scare. I scare, ma'an. Morning good for you?'

'Mrs Wilkins, can you jus' have Deon Le-Vaughan call Harper
when he come in?' He thought for a moment. 'I got some
money for him, for fix up my car.'

'You ain't part of that bad rollin'-rollin' gang, boy?'

'No way, ma'am. Deon and I go back to Manual Arts High.
Please, I need to pay him before I spend the money.'

Harper hung up quickly. He hadn't been able to reach any
of the crew he'd brought to patrol the drug exchange. It was
as if they'd scattered to the seventy winds.

Harper put his cell away. For the first time in a long time
he felt at a real loss. He wished he had the kind of confidence
in his decisions that Stoney had. It was so good to watch, but
he didn't feel he was learning much about how to do it.

Something had gone bad, and he just wanted a big do-over
for the day. He found a roach in the lint in his pocket. Short
as it was, he lit it off a paper match, holding it with a scorched
alligator clip, but one good hit wasn't even going to dent the
badness of that day.

'So how's Jack and Maeve?'

'They're dead, Sonny. It was that commuter train wreck
out in the Valley.'

'Very funny.'

'I wasn't sure you were listening. Or cared.'

Sonny took her seriously about staying focused on innocent activities. They'd used up a lot of the day picnicking in
a lonely place along the river edge with what they could buy
at a mini-mart, including a bottle of bad red wine, dusty and
Greek with a turpentine flavor, and smooching just a little
now and then. Then they'd wandered most of the sad little
zoo for wounded and abandoned creatures until it started to
close up in the dusk, with somebody in authority shouting out
for the stragglers to make their way to the exits. But he was
tugging at an inch of her shirt, keeping her from leaving.

'Woman, I never don't listen to you, not even when you're
sulling.'

'Am I sulling now?' she asked.

'You're gone inside, I can see it.'

'Of course I'm worried. I been with Jack more than six years, and I love both of you. I've enjoyed about as much of this freedom as I can stand. Something tells me that you always tend to fool yourself when you have an affair – you think you're getting away from all the old problems, and you pretend the new person doesn't got his own problems. But you do, don't you, Sonny?'

'Gloria, meeting you was like being hit in the face with a bag of nickels. I can't help what I feel. Don't make fun of me, please. I think you feel the power of this thing, too.'

'Come on, show me this amazing beast you been promising, and let's get out of here. I don't want to get locked in.'

He took her hand and led her to a tall wire enclosure about the size of a two-car garage. Oddly, nothing was visible in the murk within except a fat dead forked tree right in the middle.

'A big dead tree. Hey, amazing.'

'Don't be some dumb cop. This is a class act, even if the cage isn't. The enclosure is too small, I know that, but let's let the obvious go to hell for right now.'

'You're the boss.' She glanced up where he pointed, into the wire roof two stories up, and thought she made out something dark in the shadows, stirring.

Sonny whistled, and all at once a huge presence fell like a big car out of the wire roof, flubbed audibly once in the air, and swung in a tight arc so it landed hard on the limb of the dead tree. For a few moments the giant wings stayed open after the landing, nearly the length of a police cruiser.

'Jesus H. Christ,' she said. 'You see its picture but you never know!'

Then the head swiveled around, feathered white on top as the whitest rice, with a golden beak hooked over like something caught hard in her psyche. And of course it was only one possible creature – an American bald eagle. You were probably never prepared for seeing one up close, even in a crappy too-small cage, she thought. There was some quality to that mighty presence of the predator that ran down deep in her. She wished she knew its name in Paiute. And then from out of her distant past, inexplicably: *toha tsopege ggwe'na'a.*

'*Toha tsopege ggwe'na'a*,' she said aloud, addressing that presence. 'Welcome among us. I wish I could let you soar.'

The bird said nothing, did nothing, but one of its stern white eyes rested on her, head in perfect profile.

Sonny's hand was on the back of her neck, squeezing, and she left it there, animating the intensity of it all deep in her sex.

'That bird can kill with a look,' she said. 'Look at that eye. Angry, Angry, and Angry.' And in that moment, she knew she would not leave Bakersfield without releasing this incredible creature from its revolting prison.

'So magnificent,' Sonny said. 'Like the day of creation.'

Maeve and Chad were both parked a couple of curves above her rental house as the very last of the sunlight went off the eastern crests of the canyon. Both cars were parked off the pavement, though she'd swapped over to his more spacious Ford F-150 with its bench seat to talk and share some cold beer they'd bought from the liquor store at the bottom of the hill. He had a fake ID. Neither of them wanted to confront the girls in the house just then.

'Man, this looks just like Italy,' he said, looking out across her at the steep hills, almost mountains, all pricked out now by the scattered lights of habitation coming on one-by-one in the dusk.

'I've never been to Europe,' she said, thinking of the one time her dad had promised to take her, but had ended up stuck in hospital with a collapsed lung. Another of his jobs gone wrong. 'Have you?'

'Sure. You're special, Maeve. I know you won't die before you see Venice.'

'That's one city I can imagine pretty clearly.'

Chad had a big chug of beer. 'I went with my best friend one summer. There's nothing else like it.'

'You said your dad was blacklisted.'

'Yeah, but he wasn't one of the famous ones. When they came with their subpoena, he'd only had one script produced, a cowboy movie called *The War on Powder Creek*. The usual – the big evil ranchers against the little homesteaders. He was with the homesteaders, of course. Dad was a supremely defiant man. I love him to death for it. This all happened before I was born and before the more famous stuff in Washington in front of the cameras. The Un-American Committee came out here, I think it was in forty-seven, maybe forty-eight, for a first crack at scaring lefties, and they met at the Biltmore downtown. Most of the witnesses that first hearing were what they called "friendly". But Dad sure wasn't. He just stood there all by himself and said, "Screw every one of you, I don't talk to fascists." Even his Communist pals told him not to do it. Don't be an idiot, Sam. Take the Fifth.

'Eventually it got him a year and a half in the slammer for contempt of Congress. Weirdly, he ended up doing his time in the same Danbury Prison as the head of the committee, J. Parnell Thomas, who got caught stealing public money. By the time Dad got out of prison, working in Hollywood was out of the question any more. We moved away and he went back to selling shoes at Henry's Shoe-Horn in Reno, where I grew up. Later some of the better-known writers got their fancy Hollywood jobs back, but he never did.'

'I'm so sorry.'

'Don't worry. The family found ways to live with it, or make jokes about it. We were Tolstoy's happy family and I loved Dad to death. He had me pretty late with his third wife, but I did get to know him, even as an old man. He did a couple of children's books later. But Reno wasn't such a bad place to grow up. Probably healthier for me than Hollywood High.'

'Who knows what's a bad place to grow up – as long as it's not in the middle of a war?' Maeve said. 'I feel privileged that I was near the beach. And I love my dad to death, too.'

'I feel super right this minute, too. I guess I mean being with you. I'm really crazy about you, Maeve.'

'I like you a lot, too, Chad, but let's slow down. It's good that we don't really need to cure each other. Of whatever.'

'Can I kiss you?'

Maeve stared at her hands for a while. 'I don't think it's a good idea, Chad. I'm coming off some pretty heavy stuff. I've had a serious gangbanging boyfriend and a girlfriend. And I've had an abortion.'

'Can you make it clearer what you mean about girlfriend?' Chad asked.

'It's not rocket science, Chad. I don't have a girlfriend right this minute, but the feelings are all there.'

'I guess it's a bigger deal for a guy to like guys.'

'You all say that. But I'm not so sure. Gore Vidal always insisted there was just love for a person, and there didn't have to be a gender strait-jacket.'

'It's a bit scary,' he said. 'You'll let me know if you decide to settle down on the female side.'

She laughed. 'You'll be among the first to know.'

They'd punched Li'l Joker a few times, randomly, in the face and chest to make him more compliant as they drove, and then they dragged him groggy out of the car toward the white clapboard church called St Stephen's African Methodist Emanuel Church of God in Christ near Central Avenue. Somebody was obviously working on its exterior, repainting or repairing, because there was scaffolding half way up the blank east wall, which was probably the chancel wall.

'I'm still not up to speed, guys,' L'il Joker said woozily. 'Maybe you got it all wrong. Did you think of that?' He kept his eyes on the streetlight nearby and tried not to do anything they'd think was either a kowtow or a challenge. Somebody was trying to remove his wallet and having a hard time at it.

One of the Panchos kept pointing somewhere and saying petulantly, '*Donas. Quiero donas.*' I want donuts.

'If you get to see your boss, tell him what I telling you now,' the head guy insisted.

L'il Joker did his best not to look at the man. He knew they were trying to scare him, and the best thing was not to admit that it was working and making his stomach sick as a dog's.

'You tell him, adjust the deal to the times, *pendejo*. Anybody doesn't do that is stupid all the way down to the bones. But, really, I don't think you get to see him no more.'

They turned on a compressor sitting on the ground that throbbed away with power. Then they hauled L'il Joker up the scaffolding, and, forty-five feet in the air, they crucified him to the clapboard wall with the air-powered nail gun that had been waiting there. He vomited out into space and screamed before he passed out.

ELEVEN
Stupidity For Dummies

Now and again car headlights washed over them as they talked. It all made her a bit nervous and uncomfortable, being with handsome Chad. She'd been so into girls recently, and she still fancied Bunny quite a bit. Was it possible to be more confused about life? Maeve thought. I'm going for the record.

'Tell me some more about your dad.'

'Beer?' he offered.

'No thanks.'

He snapped a fresh can for himself. 'He got kind of private as he got older. I mostly remember him pretty old, Maeve. He was sixty when I was born. He worked on a novel for a while but nobody ever saw it.'

Cars became infrequent, and she relaxed into what seemed the creepy absoluteness of the dark outside. Vampire dark. She noticed the tiny lit homes on the slope opposite and the faint glare of the city reaching up into the southeastern sky. But no moon, no streetlights, no houses at all nearby.

'When I got older, maybe fifteen,' Chad said, 'I tried to talk to him one night. By then he only had a year or so left to live. Diabetes was killing him, but that was not to be mentioned; never. It was a strange situation that night. He got up really late while I was watching some old movie on TV. I heard every sound from the bathroom. All at once I had this weird certainty that he was looking in the medicine chest for something to commit suicide. I have no idea why that idea hit me, but it yanked me right out of my teenage funk – I mean, how would I feel later if it was true and I didn't try to stop it?'

'I don't get it.' Maeve's dad had absolutely never been suicidal.

'I don't either. God, Maeve. I want you so bad.'

'Please tell me about your dad.'

'OK. We weren't relating so great then, maybe our ages, maybe it was my problem teens. I must have come at him out of left field. He looked in the TV room and I said how much I'd always admired him and his courage, which was damn true. And how his . . . I don't know, his furious perfectionism sometimes made me feel inadequate, which was also true. I thought it'd be one of those meaningful moments, you know? Life-changing or something. But he didn't get it. He just didn't. Generations, I guess. He said I was a perfectly fine kid and I should go back to my TV and stop fussing. I felt like I'd taken a really difficult step toward him, and he wouldn't make even a half step toward me. But, hell, he was seventy-five then, and we all knew he was dying.'

'That's so sad.'

The intimacy that he'd offered and the velvety darkness all around made her feel at the vital center of something new. Yes, I'm selfish, Maeve thought. I don't need Chad. And I'm OK. She could have fun with Chad, if she wanted – but she could discard him, too, if she felt she needed to. She didn't even need her dad any more, not really – and that was a new thought, almost terrifying, but empowering, too. She was alone now. She could do life her way, on her own.

'Dat dere Mr Jack Liffey?' the voice on the phone said.

'Oh, knock it off, Winston. How many Anglos do you know in L.A.? And how many Jamaicans do you think I know?'

'You know de mos' importan' one, ma'an: me.'

He laughed softly. 'OK, what's up?'

'You warn me of dis. Tyrone Bird – he in big trouble. A bunch a' de drugsters want him in bigger trouble. He still insist to see de Big Man for dat father t'ing. But some a' dese guys, I sayit, they reasoning ain't so innocen'.'

'Can you bring him to me first?'

Jack Liffey stared at his yellow shorthair half-coyote, who was still recovering from the chemo and trying to get in a good chew on Jack Liffey's last good sweater hanging off the back of a kitchen chair. He was too softhearted to interfere with any pleasure the poor beast had left to him.

'I don' know,' Winston said.

'*Try*, man. You can't do this babysit alone, not in this town. I'll come to you.'

There was a pause, and Jack Liffey could sense there was another issue at work.

'Mr Sir, I know you help my brotha, but I need to know for sure you OK. I feelit, you got somet'ing bother you, somet'ing da matter. I no wan' you run out de door while us hold a big bag a' shit.'

He had pretty sensitive radar, this Jamaican, Jack Liffey thought. Somehow he must have sensed what had been preying on him: Gloria. We all live with fears, even me, and we all still die tomorrow, he thought. Everybody goes on living in some relation to his nightmares.

'Winston, yeah, I have some personal problems, but I won't run out on you. I was there for Trevor to the end. The guys you got to watch out for are the ones who tell you they're Mr Brass-balls, and they got no problems at all. Bring Ty to me if you can. This can be your safe house.' He gave his address.

'Oh, ma'an, I just spy a shooting star. Dat a good sign.'

Jack Liffey could see to the west out the open back door of the service porch, and he didn't see how anybody could make out a heavenly body in that radioactive yellow dome of city-light.

'You'll both be safe here,' Jack Liffey said. 'That I can promise.'

'Everyt'ing dainty,' Winston said before hanging up.

They'd had a pretty good time in bed, both doing their best to stay in the present through the lovemaking and not worry about her having to leave in the morning. Gloria had been careful as hell about the word 'love', but he'd tossed it around a lot, and they'd both tried a few sexual wrinkles that they rarely had before. 'No taboos,' Sonny had insisted. 'This is the real *laissez-le-bon-temps-rouler* thing.' The famous New Orleans Cajun motto: let the good times roll.

After one last surge of energy, Sonny became so exhausted that he uttered an incomprehensible Cajun exclamation and passed out on his back, soon snoring like a bandsaw. It hadn't exactly been her plan to take him to exhaustion, but it fit in fine.

As near as she could tell it was about three a.m. Gloria got up gingerly and dressed in cautious silence. And then she realized that for all practical purposes, she was sneaking out like a one-night stand and might never see him again. She shoved her belongings into the holdall bag and found a notepad on the dresser.

> My Dearist Sonny,
> This will always remain one of the gratest weekends of my hole life. I am not leaving your house early to escape you. Please beleive that. I have a job to do before I leave this crummy town.
>
>   I know you respect Jack and will not plagge us with letters and calls. But I will find some way to stay in touch. Do not be angry at me but I must stay with Jack for so many reasons that I cant even explain to myself. Just keep hoping for another time next year. I do not promise but I do not dare deny I have these desires too. You are very presious to me. And, funny as it is, Jack likes you too.
>
>   Your too passiunate friend

Discreetly, she decided on leaving no signature, not even an initial. Who else could it be, the maid?

Maeve and Chad stood on the edge of the cliff beside his car. She was letting him hold her hand, as they looked out over the night hills, with house lights going off now, a village gradually turning in. She figured he was probably given to grand declarations of his feelings, like most men, and she hoped he would just hold off for now.

'What a lovely night,' he said.

'*Muchacho*,' she said. She smiled to herself. Odd word to choose. 'Let's be cool and let things settle inside us now.'

He turned to look at her.

'Don't ask me anything now. You know I love women, too, and I don't know how you'll deal with that.'

'I tell you, this guy a Johnny Whiteguy, for true, but he can help all of us,' Winston says to me, standing right there like a colorful genie out of some lamp I rubbed.

I want to go talk to my pops, hopefully my pops – for the first time in my life, like a normal human being, and I want this Jamaican shadow gone out of my life for now, and I don't want all these Skinnies doing trampoline jumps around us. It's sad to see them teasing him. He's an honorable guy, and I know they're part of me, so they must be acting out some of my inner resentments toward him. Hear me, Skinnies – I despise your mocking.

'I can't do it, Winston, sorry. Some white guy who says he's a detective, my protector? Got an office with a big eyeball on the door, I bet. Breaks up marriages by peeking through windows. Think how primitive his soul must be. He's barely above a polecat. He's pond scum.'

'Nah, ma'an. I done met him up close. He no wicked like dat. He can help us, and dese other guys you like so much dey down deep in de world of debbils and drugs. I knaoit.' He made a pained face, his emotions all oversize, like the young man himself. 'I suppose to be work for dem, but day all craven baldheads.'

Three Skinnies cartwheeled between us just then, and I had to smile. I love this Jamaican's speech patterns and his amazing earnestness, but right now I want him gone. I suppose that's what the cartwheels are about.

'Give me a night to think on it, Winston.'

'I dunno, man. Everybody try to kill everybody in dis big action movie. Dey all see your fancy Porsche dis morning. Don' count on dem be stupid.'

'I hope I don't. But you know I'm a bit crazy, don't you, Winston? I mean, true men-in-white-coats-drag-you-away crazy. *Cuckoo's Nest* crazy. Jack-Nicholson-with-a-knit-cap crazy.'

'What you say?'

'Oh, yes, mon. I am afflicted with a schizoaffective disorder, with hallucinations – the diagnosis code is two-nine-seven. I'm officially Daffy Duck – woo-woo-woo – and my medications are all back at my house. You've got a nutcase on your hands, Winston. What you want to do is go away tonight and come back tomorrow morning, after I've had a good night's sleep. I'm worst when I'm tired. In the morning I'll be fine for a while,' I lie to him. I look in the mirror and there they are – my God, I'm using my secret heartfelt eyes on him, solemn enough to convince even me a little.

Winston seems to undergo a transformation of his own. 'I ain' no buffoon to dismiss like Tweety Bird, Mr Tyrone. I got three good A-levels. I don' know if you know what that means, but at home it means I can go to a university in England if I wish. You needing help, just ask me.'

'You're going to have to let me do things my way, A-Level. What's your full real name?'

'Winston Churchill Pennycooke. I only use Ratchet for the street. Pennycooke is a proud Kingston name. My brother Trevor died here in your city helping a young girl run away from the whoremakers. This man Jack Liffey helped them. That how I know he's not worthless.'

I notice that the Jamaican dialect is gone, though the lovely rich intonations are still there. For a moment all the cavorting Skinnies hold their poses, as if hit with some new and alarming news that just might send them skittering into hiding.

'Tomorrow morning I want you to tell me all about that. Right now I have to sleep, Winston.'

'You lie to me now?' Winston asks.

'No, my friend. I swear on my sacred honor, I have to sleep now or I'll keel right over. It's the curse of this disease I carry.' I can feel my secret eyes hard at work to reassure, convince.

'Cha, I t'ink of all da t'ings I shouldn't hab done in dis life,' Winston says, a lot of the street flooding back into his voice. 'Too much trus' was in all a' dem. But Ima trust you, my fren'. I-an-I step out nao. I hope you ain't try fi put me in some big joke book call *Stupidity for Dummies*.'

The stucco wall was intimidatingly tall. She'd had to go over something similar in full batbelt, with ammo and pistol, baton and flashlight at the Academy in Elysian Park, to prove she was as physically proficient as any male recruit, but she was carrying quite a few more pounds now, and quite a few more years, too. OK, use the noggin now, Glor.

She got back into her car and backed the little SUV around. Gingerly she drove it over a row of stones and then over a cactus until the rear bumper thumped the stucco wall lightly. She hadn't seen a night watchman anywhere, and how many people ever broke into zoos, anyway?

Gloria retrieved her bolt cutter and the Pelican LED flashlight from under the passenger seat. It was the official issue plastic flashlight of the LAPD now, designed to be too light to deliver a real Rodney King beating, unlike the Maglite that had hammered him down in 1991. She dialed her cellphone down to vibrate, for good measure.

Gloria climbed up the front bumper on to the hood and then boosted herself over the windshield on to the flat roof of the Toyota RAV-4. That put the top of the wall at waist level so going over would be fairly easy. But then she looked over and saw the drop and knew there'd be no easy way back out. She'd find a way, she thought, if she had to kick down a door. *Toha tsopege ggwe'na'a*, I'm on my way.

She tossed the cutter inside first, but carried the flashlight. It was a painful jolt to her ankles coming down hard on the clay path, but she didn't think she'd done any damage. She was a little disoriented about the layout of the place but started toward where she thought the big bird's cage was located. There was no moon, and as she walked, she poked the tail-switch of her flashlight for the merest instant now and then to orient herself. Something made her think of Sonny Theroux, and then of course, of Jack Liffey. Her head was in an uproar. They were both such good men. Jack had given her worries and heartaches over the years, but almost always getting into trouble in service of somebody needy, and often enough his daughter.

Love's a hardship, always, she thought. Her old partner had said love had a whiff of mortality built in. I guess it's all the complications we know about in the man we're with that makes us grasp for a simpler, unfussy love, but that's just an illusion. Every person on earth comes fully equipped with troubles.

She passed the big new cement hill they'd built for their single lame brown bear, and she knew exactly where she was. Around the path to the left now, she thought.

How was she going to forgive herself for the adulterous episode? She'd never before had trouble forgiving herself – she was so intense and self-focused that she'd always been the center of her own universe, the one who mattered. But this was a new kind of trouble, with poor Jack right there, so aware of her infidelity, and Sonny so demanding and needy – and so loving himself. Men were no easy task, for sure. She wanted to keep her spirits up for the liberation of the bald eagle, but she couldn't get any distance on her own crisis. She had to find something to make it all bearable in the end.

She flicked the flashlight and there it was, the wire atrium, maybe twice the size of the creature's full wingspan. A big dark shadow stirred atop the dead tree in the middle.

'*Toha tsopege ggwe'na'a*, my apologies for taking so long. I'm here now. May your spirit please bless this action.'

She tapped the flashlight button again, and the bird stirred in the flash of light, but did not visibly come awake, its glorious white head lolling forward to rest on the middle of its chest. There was a kind of airlock double-door portico made of chainlink at the back of the cage to let a keeper enter. She debated attacking these doors, but wondered if the great bird would be willing to waddle out the low doorways. This was not going to be as simple as she'd thought.

Her bolt cutter could shear the chainlink easily so she decided to open a big inviting window up high right in front. She reached up and began snipping. The only sounds she heard were the downhill winds from the mountains to the east rushing over the trees in the zoo, a faint chittering that might have been a restless squirrel, and the nasty snip of her bolt cutters as she worked hard at the wire. Her palms began to smart with the pressure of the cuts, and reaching upward with the heavy tool made her arms ache.

Then she heard a metallic clang somewhere not so nearby and halted for a moment. Sounds could often be deceptive. Maybe a bulky animal shouldering into its cage wire, an antelope or the bear. She told herself not to be so anxious just because she was jeopardizing her whole career to free a bird. She knew there was no love lost between the Bakersfield cops and LAPD, and particularly her. They would cut her no slack at all up here – since she'd solved one of their own cases, quickly and easily, making them look inept.[6]

She went back to work, panting a little with the effort and promising herself to return to her daily exercises, at least one round of the machines in the exercise room at the station and a good mile jog after work. She was always after Jack to do something similar.

There was enough starlight now that her eyes had adjusted, and her grappling with the cage had awakened the creature

---

[6] See *The Devils of Bakersfield.*

inside so she saw the hooked beak and the fierce appearance of the bird's white head, turned profile so its big eye could watch her. My heavens, *Toha tsopege ggwe'na'a,* aren't you something! Sacred to my people, but no more sacred really than all life – even a cane rat caught along the banks of the Owens River is sacred. Her aunt would always apologize at length before cooking and eating any wild animal.

Eagle, I apologize for my species. You shouldn't be held in a crappy little toaster-oven like this, even if your wing is lame. It's dead wrong.

She had about two-thirds of a big flap cut free from the wire and wondered how she could induce the bird to grasp its freedom. Maybe it would be afraid of the open air after so long? But she hadn't been afraid to exercise her freedom from Jack, had she? Enough, woman.

With her palms on fire from the rubber handles of the bolt cutters, she sliced the last few links of the cage fencing, then she used the bolt cutter to grasp the big overhead flap that she'd made and yank it wide open. It was certainly big enough to release her bird. She shone her flashlight on the opening, then on the eagle, on the opening again, and made chirping and tsking sounds of encouragement. 'Mr *Toha tsopege ggwe'-na'a,* come on out now!' she urged. 'Bald Eagle, dammit, fly!'

She wished she had some meat or live bait as an inducement, but she hadn't thought she'd need an inducement. She wondered if she was such a great cop after all if she hadn't thought this rescue through.

There was another clang in the distance, and the shriek of a bird circling overhead. She hoped it was another eagle, offering companionship. Please! Go out for a little sex, big boy. Or big girl. She realized she had no idea. She heard the air-rush of big wings overhead and tried to catch whatever it was with a flash of her light but couldn't. The light was like a beacon up into mist, a bit creepy.

The eagle stirred, and she showed her flashlight on the opening again, the bird doing a little side-to-side dance on the dead limb.

'Oh, come on, do it now. Fly! It's your fucking nature! This is your chance. Things that you leave undone are the ones you regret.' Was she sure of that?

The huge bird ripped open its wingspan, as if posing for a

postage stamp, spreading the black wings an unimaginable width, but still it hesitated. Then it launched itself in a leap to the edge of the window she had cut open and perched there unsteadily on the wobbly edge of the wire, glaring out.

'Yes. GO!'

At that instant, all the overhead lights in the zoo came on, and she knew immediately that she was totally screwed. She took the clip-on holster off the back of her skirt and laid the .40-caliber Glock gently on the path behind her. She set the bolt cutter beside it, then the Pelican light. She wanted to live. Tetchy cops vs people holding firearms rarely worked out well. All the complications rose like angry ghosts before her – the reaction of her own captain to this depradation in a faraway city, Jack's reaction, of course, but most of all, memories of the last time she'd been up here and badly insulted a couple of the dimmer Bako cops. Let's just hope those dipshits weren't shifted to nightside, she thought.

'Go, eagle!' She shook the wire cage below it, and the shudder only startled the bird, and made it hop back inside on to its perch, her heart dropping inside her.

'No, No! Out! *¡Pendejo!* Don't forsake me!'

The eagle screeched once at her in complaint – of what? – and then a squad of cops came around the corner of the bear house with guns drawn.

What did they expect? An international animal thief?

'Freeze!' somebody shouted.

'I'm frozen, gentlemen. I'm an L.A. cop, out of my jurisdiction, and my pistol is on the ground there behind me. My badge is in the dark blue Toyota. I'm sure you saw it outside.'

'*Ruca*, are we being invaded by the tactically and morally superior forces of the famous Los Angeles Police Department?' It was that very voice, she thought with a terrible chill. What *was* the name?

'Please don't get your back up, man. I'm the one who's in the wrong here. You've got me.' What were the odds, for God's sake? She was sure it was the Basque one, the mean-spirited racist sheepfucker. She couldn't come up with his name.

'On the ground, bitch! Down now! Hands spread.'

'You don't have to do this, sir. My pistol is on the path behind me. I don't carry a throwdown piece.'

'GET DOWN NOW!'

She sighed and lowered herself full length onto the gritty walkway with her arms spread out inoffensively. For the first time, she felt the faint chill on the air, a breeze wicking under her skirt. She wished she'd worn trousers, but this was meant to be an official trip to a semi-formal lecture. What impressed her was the absoluteness of her predicament and, of course, her own stupidity to bring it about. Once the LAPD fired her, what job could she take? Security guard at a bank? Even Jack Liffey might have trouble understanding what this was all about. She had a bit of trouble herself. She wanted to look up and curse the bird, but didn't.

'I'll frisk her! Look for other burglars.'

'We should wait for Carol, Tom.'

'Bullshit. Not with officer lives in danger.'

Tom, oh yes. Tom Etcheverry, she remembered. The barrel-chested asshole who'd always stood with his hands on his hips, leering at her. And she knew he had every reason to hate her guts. She'd probably cost him a promotion and some salary by showing him up and solving the crime he was making a real mess of investigating, tromping all over the evidence.

A heavy man knelt beside her and ran his hand slowly up the inside of her thigh, forcing up her skirt, bunching it higher and higher until he pressed two fingers hard against her pussy, then worked them under her panties and began rubbing. Unfortunately she was still a bit wet from Sonny.

'That a weapon you got there, *ruca*?'

She knew better than to sass him, but there were others around. 'Gentlemen, this officer is feeling me up. He's about to penetrate me with his fingers. That's a felony in this state. Is there anybody in charge here?'

Nobody said a thing, but when she turned her head back to the cage, she saw the big bird dance on the tree and one of the other cops using her bolt cutter to push the window of fencing closed. All for nothing.

The cop worked his two fat fingers into her wet vagina and his thumb pressed hard on her rectum.

'I can lift you like a bowling ball,' he joked.

'You try and you're a walking dead man.'

'Anybody hear that? She just threatened me.'

Who knows what else they could take away from her that night, she thought. And the great bird was still a prisoner.

TWELVE
Our Rise-Up-Angry

I park the Porsche Targa as quietly as I can several doors up the road from the pool house that I've already seen. A hint of moon has just appeared and it's throwing its usual licentious silvery light. I see no stalking guards with big automatic weapons, or even snoozy men on chairs with bulges under their coats. Now an owl hoots or a coyote bays. It's so far I can't tell which. This isn't like an action movie at all. Just a pool house in a suburb. No second unit director to tell me what to do.

Tyrone Bird here – I take my heart in my hand and walk alongside a row of redwood roundels set into the grass, quiet as I can. Only one Skinny tiptoes along with me, emoting caution like a mime on speed. Something is keeping me from looking straight at what I'm doing, and I know how long I've been waiting for this. All my life, really. If I make no noise at all, I can turn around and flee at any moment and deny to some big ear in the sky that I was ever here.

There's a low wall I go over cautiously and a bell-push beside the door, and I pause and argue with myself over ringing or knocking. The decision is made, finally, to make noise and disturb the universe. But is ringing too assertive for this time of night? Knocking softly is what fools do, the weak. What's my motivation? Calm down, kid. You're overthinking it.

In the end I push the button, hearing a single bleep-bloop in the house. I wait, as the distant owl/coyote announces itself once more, and then I push the button again boldly. There's one of those fish-eyes in the middle of the door and I see it darken almost imperceptibly. I display empty hands. Oh, man, am I so very innocent.

Finally a number of chains and bolts are withdrawn noisily, like a New York door.

The door draws open a few inches, and a handsome older

black man stands there in a bathrobe, an astonishingly large auto pistol in his hand, pointed vaguely in my direction. I offer both empty palms again as I study his face intensely. Could it be?

'Sir, I'm no threat to you. None at all.'

'You're the sucker in that Porsche. If you have plans to go home alive, you better explain yourself.'

'I believe there's a large chance that I'm your son, Mr Stone.'

'Bullshit.' I can see he wasn't told back in the day. Moms and her pride.

'The Sandstone Retreat, sir. She used a lot of names: Donna Wisecki; Donna Freedom. Later she dropped Donna, too. Melanie Bird was the Moms I knew. I bet she never told you she was pregnant.'

The man's eyes look me over in a new way, head-to-toe. 'I heard this fairy tale from my own man. It was the hip days. Everybody was fucking everybody, fool.'

And you never used a condom. She was always careful. Except with you. 'She said you were a philosopher, a college teacher, her liberator from white skin privilege.'

With a sneer, I think he recognizes something he may have told a lot of white girls. 'Cool out, nigger. Take this thing real slow. Why do I feel I've seen you? I felt it this morning when I saw you drive past in that two-year-old Targa. My man says you're a big movie star. Is that right?'

He sees cars better than genes, I think. I name several of my bigger movies. 'I'm not here to extort money from you, sir. I probably have more in my 401K than this whole neighborhood. I just want to meet my pops – if he wants to meet me.'

'Shit, fool, I said slow down.' Marcus Stone rubs his forehead hard with the side of the huge pistol. 'Come in out of the dark. Very slow.'

'If you want a DNA test, it's done,' I offer.

As I enter, I can see one of the Skinnies already inside, beside a tiny fridge, making a big-mouth O at me. I look at the man, and a bit of ancient resentment stirs. Moms fucked you like pure madness, discarded her protection, and you didn't really think about her at all, did you? I bet she loved you.

But one could forgive almost anything of a father. Isn't that the way it's supposed to work? How would I know?

They erected a couple of xenon crime scene lights and a lot of POLICE LINE DO NOT CROSS yellow tape, but the area had been pretty badly despoiled by the first two beat cops to arrive. What they hadn't stomped all over, they'd vomited on several times. The first detective to arrive thought he was tough enough for anything but did more of the same with a fresh spaghetti dinner.

In fact, not one of the cops at the church knew what the word 'flay' meant. The captain of detectives, arriving about five a.m., sorted that out for them and sent everyone outside the tape until the SID forensics truck could get there. The only remaining question for most of them was whether the poor guy who'd been crucified to the clapboard siding of the church on Central Avenue had been dead before someone had made a clumsy effort to skin him, and every one of them hoped fervently that he had been very dead first.

A note fixed to the wall with the same nail gun used on the victim was addressed to 'Rocky,' and suggested Rocky learn his lesson *muy rápido*. The name 'Rocky' was not of much use to anyone, since even L.A's City Attorney was nick-named Rocky, and there were far too many others. They'd also nailed a driver's license to the wall, but it was two-thirds covered by the note and no one was touching it yet.

Gloria sat as confidently as she could in the interrogation room – she wasn't even sure whether it was the Kern County sheriff's headquarters or the Bakersfield city P.D. She wondered if this bilious yellow-green room was where they'd held Maeve and a lot of other kids and terrified them to death about being devil worshippers.[7]

There was a single rap on the door, and the fat fuckhead – Etcheverry – strode in to screech his aluminum chair out from the table and sit hard opposite her.

'Fraudulent destruction of property, four-fifty-eight, B-and-E, four-fifty-nine, resisting arrest, one-forty-eight, assault on an

[7] See *The Devils of Bakersfield*.

officer of the law, two-twenty-one. You want to deal with all that shit?'

'Sodomy with penetration, two-twenty-zero, assault under color of authority, one-forty-nine. I know the California Penal Code, *pendejo*. Yours are worse.'

'Just erase all that, *ruca*. Nobody in this town is going to believe you for a minute. No judge, no jury. And I can drag in your new boyfriend in Oildale for conspiracy to enough crimes to get him twenty years, even if you get off.'

She let out a slow breath. That did scare her. How did they know about Sonny? 'You sound like you want to give me options. I haven't even had my phone call yet. Where's your partner, Lieutenant Efren Saldivar? He always had sense.'

The abrupt grin was frightening. 'You remember Effie? He's out on disability, *ruca*, playing poker with all the other tired cops. Must be nice – except for the screams of all that wife-beating. I like Effie, I still do, but he has a tendency to wait around for his bosses to tell him how terrific he is. Not me. I want what I can get now.'

'How about my phone call?'

'You get to listen to me first. I'm doing you a favor. I don't want you to lose all your L.A. luck, sergeant. If you call a lawyer right now, everything is etched in stone, you know that. You're booked, printed and slammed. I file my report and that's the end of you. You lose your big L.A. job, for sure. You probably go to the can for a while, too. That was one stupid stunt at the zoo; what got into you? As I say, I can even take that little Cajun prick down on something.'

She noted a tiny indicator light up in the corner of the room and it wasn't on. Oh, God. Her heart sank. This was the wages of her sin, she thought. 'You're not running tape on the interview.'

'Oh, my. How negligent of me.'

'What is it makes this all go away?'

'Real simple, *ruca*. You're no virgin rose. You come to a nice comfortable motel with me and have a few beers and do what I ask for twenty-four hours. Willingly and with enthusiasm.' She wondered if she could do this and then kill him later – or even during. It sounded like a plan.

'And I'll take a few nasty photos and mail them off to a pal just in case you want to get back at me later.'

'You sure know about power, don't you?' She figured it would flatter him, and it did. He grinned and leaned back in the chair. She thought she could probably launch herself across the table and kill him right now with a single knuckle to his larynx, the way she'd been shown – entirely in theory – by one of the ex-SEALs teaching at the Academy. But nothing would go away if she did that. How could she have been so damn stupid? For a bird! She could barely stand to look at this oily fuckhead. 'The guy in control of the game calls the shots, doesn't he?' she said.

'Of course, bitch. I want a down payment. Get on your knees under the table.'

'So Moms wasn't lying to me?'

'We called them junior colleges back then, but it was the real deal. I was department head and taught "Historiography of Philosophy", "Directed Study in Existentialism" and "Kant, Hegel, Marx". I doubt if they teach any of that any more. It's probably all "Ethics in the Business World" and "New-Age Religions".'

'What happened to you?' We're sitting in the tiny living room, drinking beers from long-necks, and two of the Skinnies seem to be drinking beers, too, playing with our discarded bottles and squatting with us like hippies.

'You mean, did I get fired?' Stoney says.

'I guess.'

'It's hard to fire a teacher, but, yeah, I suppose I did. It was another era, Ty, and I got caught up in what you could call revolutionary thinking. I met one of the L.A. Panthers, Bunchy Carter, and he was a friend of Huey Newton, but then Bunchy got himself killed by the black nationalists or maybe the FBI. I don't know, I don't care any more. We were all asking for it, really. Think of it. Carrying rifles into the statehouse, challenging cops to their face. But Bunchy's murder made me so angry back then I think I was almost clinically insane with it.

'I made my way to Mozambique for a while. I wanted to train with the ANC militants for South African raids. *Umkhonto we Sizwe.*' He laughs. 'They didn't want some dipshit radical from the States who couldn't speak a word of any African language. If I'd been in the army, I could at least have bartered some military expertise. There don't be a lot of guerillas just crazy to learn existentialism.'

Both the Skinnies giggle. They seem to like the guy's utter honesty, and so do I.

'OK, you walked away from a tenured teaching position.'

'I came right back with my tail between my legs. It was six months later but everything had changed. The left had blown itself up. The world was closing in. It's crazy, but I went on pretending to a lot of folks outside that I was still a teacher. I thought maybe I could get back in at Pierce, but I couldn't. The new head of the department hated my ass, for good reason. You have to realize that in the midst of all that, this Sandstone place and all that bleating about sexual liberation was really not very important to me. It was like a burger joint I visited from time to time. There's only so much of people looking at you like Mandingo you can take. I don't mean Melanie. She was too cool for that, but. . . .' He shrugs. 'I lost track of her. Kid, I had a dozen girlfriends at Pierce College, of every color. I don't like telling you this now, but honestly your mother didn't mean that much to me, and I never heard from her afterward. That canyon place was a freakshow. I'm sorry.'

I notice he's given in to calling her my mother. 'Tell me more about the time at Sandstone, please, sir. It's all I've got.'

'No – you've got me now. I can't really be your father, we won't make that mistake. I know it's too late for that. But maybe we can be . . . good buddies or something.'

For the first time, I start to wonder if he might be after my money. He obviously isn't living too high on the hog here. It's not a worthy thought, but actually I'm more than willing to help him out a lot. Even if that's the bribe that's necessary to get him closer to me.

'That was a drug deal this morning, wasn't it?' I say.

Stoney frowns. 'Ty, don't judge me. I got two degrees in philosophy from L.A. State. With that and three dollars, you can buy a fancy coffee at Starbucks. A black man who wrote mostly about Marx back then? Ha. Who wants him? I did the high school teaching thing, a substitute on day rate, and then I got an emergency credential and taught social studies to a lot of kids that didn't give a shit. It wasn't a way for a man of ideas and action to live.'

'And selling drugs is?'

Both Skinnies scuttle backward in fear, as if I've just whacked the old man with a stick.

'You never did anything you ain't proud of? All your movies ranked with the best literature?'

'I apologize. No, sir. My first movie – this is still a big secret to the fan mags – was a bit part in gay porn, and then a dumb TV movie about a detective who dresses like a pimp. But I'm working on a Chester Himes now.'

'No shit? Which one?'

'*If He Hollers, Let Him Go.*'

'God, that's a great great book,' Stoney says. He smiles at me, proud-like, and it means enough to send me into seventh heaven. I find myself tearing up a little.

'My own son, bringing Robert Jones to life.'

He's said 'son.' I heard it. 'Yeah – it's something good in the world, isn't it?'

'Come here.'

Stoney moves first, and we hug awkwardly in the middle of the small room. 'That's way too cool, boy.'

'Then I really got to say something hard, Dad, see if you still so proud.' It hurts so bad to own up. Maybe I'd rather die. 'Something happened inside my head when I was about twenty. My mind – it just wasn't working right any more. I have to take these powerful medications to control it.' I sigh. Here comes the word. 'They say I'm schizophrenic. That doesn't mean I split into different people, like so many folks seem to think. It means the dopamine chemicals in my brain are out of whack, and sometimes I see things and hear things that aren't there. Aw, let's face it – it means I'm crazy.'

The Skinnies are all fled out of sight for the moment, but making soft hooting sounds to remind me they're still there.

I can tell Marcus Stone doesn't know quite what to say.

'Another hour and I'd have to of booked you.' Etcheverry held on hard to the handcuffs he'd affixed behind her back, then stressed her shoulders with a nasty upward pull as he nudged her up the steps of what looked like an abandoned dope house in some rotten area near downtown Bakersfield, everything gone bright and hard-edged in the new sun just coming up over the Sierras. The front door was screened by a torn-open steel grid, and inside there was nothing personal at all, just beat-up Salvation Army furniture and rubbish on the floor. The smell of meth chemicals from somewhere in back.

'We don't want no records,' Etcheverry said. 'This is the real nowhere.'

She still had the sour taste of him in her mouth and kept trying to imagine ways to kill him discreetly. But she knew he could as easily kill her and dump her down some abandoned Central Valley waterwell or rural sinkhole. Nobody here would ever even look for her – except maybe Sonny. She was taking quite a risk to try and get out of this mess clear.

In what had once been the living room of the abandoned house, he pushed her down on to an iron-frame double bed with a stained mattress, and he relocked one cuff on to the frame.

'Get some sleep. I'm not a bad guy, Miss Gloria. I'll bring us some doughnuts and beer later, and we can have us a party.'

She knew better than to say a word. Her temper was her worst enemy now.

Winston phoned Jack Liffey and insisted he turn on Channel Nine, where the TV crews were covering what seemed to be an extraordinarily gruesome execution in South L.A. It was hard to work it all out with all the queasy euphemisms the morning TV host was using. Apparently somebody had been nailed high on the side of the church in the night, a mock crucifixion; that much was clear. And then – who could tell? The poor guy had been repeatedly stabbed? Skinned? A crucifixion alone was enough to send the city's media into the stratosphere, but there was clearly something even more. Something about torturing the poor man.

Shit, I'll probably never know what this is about until Gloria gets back, he thought. She could always get the real dope. And that made Jack Liffey realize Gloria was running late. Given her relationship with Sonny, he wasn't too surprised, but there were such things as car accidents, too. So he felt he'd better call Sonny, as humiliating as it would be.

'Didja seeit?' Winston's voice barked surprisingly in his ear. Jack Liffey had forgot he was still on the line. 'I know who that guy is,' Winston said.

'Good for you. Call me back in fifteen minutes.'

'Wait . . .' Jack Liffey hung up and punched in the 661 number that was scribbled on a laundry receipt in the alcove.

'Sonny, this is Jack.'

'Good morning, Jack. It's good to hear your voice.'

'Let's get to the point. You can have the luggage sent on later. She isn't back yet. Should I know something that's going on? I mean beyond what I'm already not supposed to know?'

There was a deadly pause. 'As far as I know, Gloria left town last night. She said she had a job to do before leaving.'

'Said – how?'

'A note left behind.'

'Would you read it to me?'

'No, Jack. You have to trust me that the only part you need to know is what I just said. Here's the very words: "I have a job to do before I leave this crummy town."'

'I may come up there and make you eat that note right after I read it all. Will you go out and look for her right now?'

'Of course. I'm not without resources in Bako.'

'Good for you, Cajun. Here's my note to you: I thought you were my friend. Fuck you plenty. You keep Gloria out of any heavy-duty shit up there, or I'll hold you responsible.'

'Understood. I'm no coward, Jack.'

'I don't give a damn about that. I want Gloria home. Or safe. If she's lying right next to you and safe, you tell me now.'

'Her duffle and car are gone, I swear it, Jack.'

Jack Liffey hung up, and he was all alone in the dim hallway with his heart pounding hard.

We've been talking enthusiastically about our lives for what seems hours, and fresh sunlight is leaking through the curtains. God, what a wonderful gift – a gray-haired, thoughtful, intelligent, kindly – dare I even think the word? – father. Sure, I know he deals, but choices are limited when you're black.

A father. It's like being given a whole new set of tools for life. Last night has been like one of those orgies of talk with a new summer girlfriend who you think, finally, is going to work out. It doesn't really matter if she doesn't in the end. It's still such a delight – there's nothing in life better than a summer romance. Can you have a romance with your pops?

'What steered you to movies?' Stoney asks me. He isn't
even fortifying himself with cognac any more.

'Pure accident.' This is the official version, leaving out that
one day as an extra dick on the gay porn shoot. Maybe he's
forgotten that I mentioned it. 'A friend took me up to Universal
one day to be atmosphere. That's what they call the people
who just sit around in the background. I was a spectator for
a boxing match, and some second assistant director ran his
finger down the row and stopped at me. He yanked me out
of the seats to dress me up as a defeated boxer who passed
the star in the hall. I had a single line: "I'm too wiped out to
count, man." That's my first movie line, Dad. I guess it's
historic.' The word 'Dad' feels funny in my mouth, but I work
at it. 'This was *Second Comeback*, that Mike Douglas boxing
movie that nobody liked very much. Man, was he a shit to
me when I tried to say hello.'

'I loved his dad,' Stoney said.

'Everybody loves Spartacus,' I say. 'Nobody loves Gordon
Gecko. What a stupid name. Did you see *Second Comeback*?'

'Sorry.'

Now and again the Skinnies peek out at us from fissures
between things, but they're hanging way back, and I thank
them internally, deeply. 'Dad. *Dad*. Pops. Father. The words
feel funny. You tell me which one you'd like. Why don't we
take all the money both of us've saved up and run away and
start a ranch in Montana or an ice cream parlor in New Jersey?
Buy an internet company, I don't care. Something new and
clean. A fancy steakhouse.'

I want to save him from the drugs. Stoney makes a contorted
face, but smoothes it out in thought. I can tell it's probably
hit him too quick. 'Sounds interesting, Ty. But we might have
to wait a little.' That's when the first Skinny comes back into
the room with that big snarky look they get. 'Everything I
have,' Stoney said, 'is tied up in the mess in the Costco parking
lot. I can't walk away now, too many people are in on it. It's
the tar-baby of all deals.'

The phone rings and we both look at the old-fashioned
landline instrument. I can't remember the last time a phone
at six a.m. was good news.

Stoney picks it up with great reluctance, and he listens
for a long time. 'You sure it's Li'l Joker?' A few other

Skinnies gather and pretend to listen secretly to the phone
– oohing and aahing to me silently. 'Oh, shit.' Before my
eyes, my father changes into someone else. The softness is
gone and he's all business now, rising on the balls of his
feet, ready to move fast. 'Get your crew. You know where
to come.'

I try not to feel that my new dream is burned away, like a
rose in a pizza oven, but it's the way life has generally dealt
with my dreams. My father hangs up gently, far away in
thought.

'Can I help?' I ask oh-so-reluctantly.

'No, Ty. I don't want you involved in this at all. I'm up
against some real beasts. I think one is a psycho-killer.'

'Would money help?'

'Not right now. But thank you. Don't follow me when
I go.'

My father puts the big pistol that he set down long ago into
a harness under his arm, and then reaches through a curtain
under the sink and takes out a long gym bag that in my imagination can only contain a small submachine gun.

'Wait here five minutes, then go somewhere safe. Copy
down the number off that phone.' He thumbs toward the landline. 'I monitor it. We'll get back in touch, Ty. I promise.'

He hugs me quick, which is uncomfortable with all the
metal. Then he's out the too-bright door, and I'm alone again
with the Skinnies, who are all shaking their heads with ghastly
comic sneers.

'Fuck you all,' I say aloud. 'My father will work out.'

Sonny drove back across the wide sand riverbed to downtown
Bako to the tidy craftsman home of the lawyer he'd worked
with for years, Jenny Ezkiaga, a hefty and commanding Basque
daughter of the town who was allowed pretty much to be
herself because she grew up there in an old family. Her partner
Teelee Greene was playing some game with plastic ducks in
the side yard with her eight-year-old daughter Catalin. Jenny,
Teelee and Catalin had driven joyously up to San Francisco
in that brief interlude from February 12 to March 11, 2004,
when same-sex couples had been allowed to marry legally
because of the mayor Gavin Newsom. Legally married or not,
there was a curious don't-ask-don't-tell standard at work even

in tight-ass Bakersfield, as long they were all locals and they didn't French kiss in public.

'Teelee,' Sonny called. 'Jenny inside?'

'She sleeps late.'

'Not today,' Sonny said and double-hopped hurriedly up the porch. He rapped on her bedroom door. 'Sorry, dearheart! It's an emergency.'

It didn't take long. 'May you die painfully and soon.'

'I'm sure I will. Are you decent?'

'Too much theology at this hour, Sonny. Come in.'

There was a sheet that did about all it could do for her abundant body, but left the imagination gasping. Sonny explained about the missing Gloria Ramirez, whom Jenny knew well from Gloria's help in ending the devil-worship hysteria.

'And you learned she didn't make it home directly from Jack?'

'Yes.'

'That must have been a barrel of fun.'

'Let's leave fun out of it. He'd probably like to kill me with a stapler, to make it last, but that's another story.'

Jenny grinned. 'Oh, I'll need to know about the fun, too, but go away now and talk to Teelee while I dress and make some coffee. Want?'

'With chicory?'

'Sorry, I don't do that bayou shit. Strong French is the best I can do. This sounds like a mess.'

'You know Gloria. Nobody is one hundred per cent innocent.'

'How do we know that was Li'l Joker on the TV?' Stoney asked his dirty cop on the phone. He was doing his best to act confident and in command, but he was worried. Apparently the Colombians weren't about to jet home, the deal written off, as he'd expected. What could they want, except some kind of all-out war for no reason? It's not logic, it's not business. It's not even wounded pride. He'd done nothing to them. The guy was nuts.

Oddly, a part of him welcomed it all. Now he would be the Umkhonto we Sizwe commander that he'd once aspired to be in South Africa. The Spear of the Nation. It was such a great name.

'The Colombos nailed his drive license to the wall, Stone,'

Sergeant Ernie Keeler of the Torrance Police Department said.
'TV news say the name Deon Le-Vaughan Wilkins. That him?
You think you the guy in the handwritten note? Rocky, Stoney
– these guys ain't Einstein.'

Stoney settled back, thinking, and held the phone against
his chest, looking at the Rollin' Seventies. 'Those who didn't
see the TV, they found Li'l Joker dead at that church they're
fixing up near his mom's crib. They hurt him bad before they
kill him.' He repeated a little of the description for them and
they all made awful faces. None of them normally gave a shit
about the daily news.

Keeler went on: 'These Colombians got somebody knows
this town pretty good – knows me and you – knows the whole
Rollin' Seventies. They got some dirty spic cop who can look
in the files on me and you. Means they probably know the
whole set. And know where the crib is at.'

His eyes went warily to the painted-out windows of the old
used furniture storefront that was the Rollin' Seventies clubhouse. So Li'l Joker was dead. Every neighborhood soldier in
the room already had his very best strap in hand – an Uzi, a
smuggled M-16, an expensive Austrian Steyr, a Russian AEK,
an M4, a couple of Ingram M11s, even an old M3 greasegun
from World War II. Stoney figured these twenty-three gangbangers could put an awful lot of noisy metal into the
surrounding air fast, though not very accurately.

'Take care, Stone,' his own dirty cop said. 'If the Colombianos
are outside now, you all blown up, boo-yah, in 'bout one half
second. These guys ain't amateurs. They got what they need.
What went bad?'

'It's all shifty, E. I guess these Colombia-heads be like any
tweaker. They just always want more than you got. We played
them fair.'

'I hear you.'

'Stay in touch.' Stoney hung up.

'Be strong, gents. I'm on top of it. We got our cop, too.
And we got the element of surprise. Maybe. Go hang out
somewhere you never been, go to a library. Then meet me at
Woody's at noon. And keep your best straps with you. Let's
all go out the alley door right now.'

They started to stir.

'And keep Li'l Joker in mind. We can't let no Spanic

motherfuckers dance into our city and punk us out.' He meant it, and they could all hear he meant it. 'Get anything else you got, even old throwdown pieces, get your pals. Get bazookas. Get dynamite. This is war. Let's make what these fuckers did to Li'l Joker be our rise-up-angry.'

THIRTEEN

While the Sierra Madre is Still a Virgin

'We don' wan' no more of these Li'l Joker *pendejos* to beat on,' Orteguaza said fiercely, one drink too far lit, though few had ever openly acknowledged seeing him that way. 'You give us Marcus Stone. The man himself.'

Randy Sem fingered the plastic nameplate on his Inglewood Police Department uniform. Something in the room smelled like skunk. What a fucking genius he'd picked for his first foreign payday, Sem thought. With all the bright boys running contraband out of Colombia and Mexico and Belize, he got the one with a brain like a rattlesnake caught in a wood chipper. 'Lately, Stoney has been keeping hisself off the grid,' Sem said.

'What the fuck's "off the grid"? You a real cop or some kind a pussy just puts papers in the files by alphabet?' The whole Colombian gang had massed in Orteguaza's big suite on the twelfth floor of the Radisson, shouldering like kids for the best northward view of the huge overseas 747s descending gracefully into LAX right across their windows.

'I told you before; you guys should be looking for a new distributor for your nose candy. I can help with that. Have you called the guy I said? No. I tell you again, revenge is amateur hour. It don't pay no widows.'

Orteguaza stared hard at him. '*Norteamericanos* don' never see how important this thing is – this respeck. We don' never back off, *hombre*.'

Randy Sem shook his head. The last thing he wanted to get into here was a dick-waving war. 'Then every chicken-shit who ever stepped on my shiny shoes in junior high I got to hunt him down and kill him dead, and I'm waiting on Death Row right now.' He saw the man's puzzled look. 'Never mind that, here it is: this very day, I think I can get you a new sales rep for your best base or I can find you the whereat of Mr Marcus Stone – so you can shrink his head to the size of a *béisbol* or boil him in a big pot or whatever you headhunters do with your enemies. I can't do both at once. You decide.'

'No, you get me both, Sergeant Sem. You wanted twenty-five big wans. You get a partner with the good stuff, you don' ask for no twin beds.'

This asshole would require a real mental adjustment, Sem thought. He'd have to dump him in the end, but he wanted a big goddamn taste first. You flow with it or you flow against it, but a guy like this, you just never find a way to get out of his wake. It was too much like Iraq. His captain had said the only way to live with Fallujah was to re-up right away and never expect it to be Nashville.

The big black Colombian guy in the corner had been talking soft all the time – Special Forces soft – into one of those bulky satellite phones that cost a fortune and didn't go through the cell towers. He made a noise to get Orteguaza's attention. They spoke in a slangy Colombian Spanish, as if he was too dumb or too *norteamericano* to follow. '*Jefe*, the devil-man tell us, No, don't make no move on the Stone clowns if we don't got to. Unless we can grab their shiny gold. Finish our biznis while the Sierra Madre is still a virgin.' He snickered.

Gloria had no idea what time it was when light began filling the room, but it felt far too early to wake up. She turned face down and tried to pull non-existent covers over her head.

'Party time!' Etcheverry called brightly from the door.

She opened one eye and saw the fat cop holding up a six-pack of Coors, as if that would interest her at all at that hour, and in her condition. Coffee, maybe. Her right arm hurt like a bastard and she realized her right wrist was cuffed to the bedframe. This was just way too much. Gone way over the high side of her toleration.

The bed gave as he sat heavily beside her and started to unbutton the cotton police blouse, her best. 'Let's see what you got under here.'

She flailed at him with her free arm, too awkward to do any harm, and he caught her wrist in mid blow and twisted it back hard. The asshole was damn strong. 'Honey, I said you got to have enthusiasm for the party, or you just might end up down an old mine shaft. We got lots of them in the hills here.'

'If you stop now, Tom, I'll forget all about this. I promise,' Gloria said. Until the moment I jam my pistol into your mouth, you stupid fuck, she thought. I swear you're going down. But she knew about establishing rapport, being respectful, de-escalating. She'd talked several raging suspects down. It had just never been this personal before.

'Mister John Doe, come in here now. See if you think a piece of this is worth fifty bucks.'

Another out-of-uniform cop sauntered in, almost as big as Etcheverry. This had to be the headquarters of the Dumb Club, she thought. You could always tell a third-rate cop, she thought. The swagger and that aura of entitlement to power.

'Man, you don't want to be part of this, believe me,' she said to him.

'You're that L.A. cunt who caught the devil-man and dissed our whole department. Yeah, I remember you. They said you joked about us. You said they'd got to send us out on patrol in threes: "'cause one of us can read and one can write and the third guy watches the dangerous intellectuals." Actually, it was pretty funny.' He sniggered.

The smile evaporated and his forehead furrowed. She knew that look, a man going to war.

'John Doe' turned to Etcheverry. 'Can I beat on the bitch a while before we fuck her?'

'Another fifty buys what you want.'

Jack Liffey knocked on the chartreuse green motel door of the Sputnik SurfRider in Malibu. He didn't realize motels came this downmarket along the beach, but it was still probably expensive, every rat and roach itemized.

It was Winston who opened, looking bleary. He'd called and given Jack Liffey the address. Tyrone Bird was sleeping fully clothed on the Roy Rogers bedspread, down for the count. Jack Liffey had seen the bunged-up Targa out front.

'He phoned me a while ago – he needs help – and that's when I called you,' Winston said.

'I get it.' Jack Liffey had got even a bit more than that already. He had to push Winston gently to get past into the dreary room. 'You have a car here, too?'

'Yeah. That Impal'.'

'Good. Drive west, that's to the right on PCH, until you see a good coffee place. There'll be one, trust me. Starbucks is OK, or Coffee Bean or some local. Get us three strong coffees and whatever sugary pastries they sell for chewing on in the morning. You have money?'

Winston nodded.

'I take it you don't know much about Ty's meeting with his dad last night?'

'Nah, sir. He collapse. But he say his old man in big trouble – shooting-type trouble.'

'Don't worry, I'll take it from here, but I can use your help.' Actually, he didn't have a clue, but Winston looked so hangdog that Jack Liffey's heart cried out to reassure him. 'Between you and me, we can handle this.'

Winston smiled weakly. 'Thanks, Mr Liff. I know you worried, too, but I need to hear all fruits are ripe.'

'Go on now. I need coffee.'

As soon as Winston was gone, Jack Liffey sat down with the room phone and called Jenny Ezkiaga in Bakersfield. A year earlier, she'd functioned brilliantly as his lawyer, getting Maeve and a lot of other kids out of trouble. No noise so far seemed to make Tyrone even stir on the bed.

'Jenny, this is Jack. I bet you remember me.'

'Of course. Sonny's here, worried about Gloria, too.'

'OK, Sonny and I both know you're the go-to gal in that town. I assume you're both about to go out looking for her. Would you call my home number every couple hours and leave a message? You know I don't have a cell.'

'Join up with the twenty-first century, Jack, you big weenie.'

'Just keep me in the picture or I'll be right up there, riding your ass.'

'Don't even think about it. They hate you worse than Obama in this town, Jack. You got their favorite Evangelical minister killed, even if he was going nuts and sponsoring book burnings and was about to shoot you. They got wanted posters all over town with your picture, saying, "Kill this man – win a prize."'

'I don't think so, but the sentiment is probably right. It's a hardshell town.'

Tyrone gave out a buzzsaw snore. Then the young man

rolled over and slammed the mattress once with a fist. Still deep in a troubled sleep. What a disturbed kid, Jack Liffey thought.

'And Gloria wasn't as nice to the Bako cops as I was,' Jack Liffey said.

'We don't have nice up here, Jack. We've got Jesus, instead, but our Jesus isn't into turning the other cheek.'

'If Gloria gets hurt, nobody up there gets to turn the other cheek, I really mean it.'

'Yeah, you tough guys always mean it. I'll call.'

The snore got even louder, the fist hammered a few more times, and Tyrone Bird rolled on to his back again. Jack Liffey decided he'd better wake the man before he detonated in his sleep. He always hated waking someone who was sleeping soundly – nothing was more precious than sleep, but this ragged state of Tyrone's didn't seem all that precious. He shook Tyrone's shoulder.

'Sorry, man, the feature players are all on the set. Time to go over your lines.'

One eye snapped open – an eye so turbulent that for about five seconds it seemed to be able to drag the world down into infinite darkness. Then the eye closed for another count of five, and reopened as an ordinary eye. 'You're Jack Liffey, I bet. I need sleep. Why did you wake me?'

He was quick, Jack Liffey thought. 'You can keep that as a grudge if you like. I sent Winston for coffee. We need to talk before he gets back.'

'Can I wash my face?'

'Sure. And I'd get rid of everything to do with that dream, if I were you. It scared me as much as it must have scared you.'

'Nobody told you I'm schizophrenic?'

'I always reserve judgment, son. Others say you're a good man.'

'Wow, I wonder who.' He went into the bathroom and locked the door. The water ran.

Jack Liffey wondered how much of the half-empty cognac bottle on the bed he'd had recently. Probably enough.

There were no rats visible, but the room was a foul yellow-green, and a big thrift-shop painting of an impossibly tall wave with an intrepid surfer was screwed to the wall beside

the bed. The glass bead lamp beside the bed was off, which was a mercy. Plenty of morning light came in through the double layer of gauzy curtains.

Tyrone drifted back in with his face dripping. He actually had wet his face, Jack Liffey thought. That was refreshing in a city where 'wash my face' usually served as a euphemism for re-upping on cocaine.

'Winston says you can work miracles,' Tyrone said.

'Only on Sunday. Tell me fast about your dad. Our Jamaican pal works for your dad's friends, and I don't completely trust him yet, though I think he's probably OK.'

'I'm sure he's OK.'

'You let me decide that. Let me decide most things for a while and I'll get you over, I promise. What did you learn about Mr Stone?' He was guessing, but pretty sure he was right. Jack Liffey could see Tyrone focusing on things in the room that he couldn't. The young man tried not to let on, but it was hard for him to ignore whatever it was that he was seeing.

Tyrone gave him the short version of Marcus Stone's life: teaching philosophy, the Panthers, Africa, 'Now he's one of those guys who makes his life hell by blaming the system but really blaming himself. He's got all the smarts to make money as a bottom-feeder. He knows he can outthink the gangbangers, and he can use them. He was never away from that old school anger long enough to find anything else that worked.'

'Good quick read. I can see why you're a big deal in Hollywood, son. But something is bothering you in this room. Are you seeing things?'

He didn't answer right away.

'Do you need some medication?'

'You bet I do. There's one of my fragile buddies sticking his tongue in your left ear right this minute.'

'Where do we get the meds? Have you got the scrip?'

'There's a whole plastic bottle full of them at home up Mandeville Canyon.'

Jack Liffey nodded. 'OK. Winston should be pretty good at fetching those after he gets back with our coffee. Will you miss your fragile buddies if the meds work? I'd rather not have a tongue in my ear.'

Ty grinned. 'Don't ask me that. Just be my co-star for now and keep me functioning.'

'Tyrone, trust me. You're my total focus.' Jack Liffey realized that ironically enough he was back on the job for
Monogram Pictures and Meier Reston, babysitting Tyrone.
But after seeing that bottomless hell in the poor man's eyes,
he'd be happy to help him for his own sake.

'You have to help my dad, too,' Tyrone insisted, as if privy
to his thoughts.

'That goes with the deal. Tell me more.'

'That prick Etcheverry arrested her last night, but somehow
he's keeping her off the books. Apparently she broke into the
zoo on a mission to release the damn bald eagle.'

Jenny was covering the mouthpiece in the kitchen as she
informed Sonny who was sitting across her Formica table.
Sonny buried his face in his hands.

'Shit, shit. I took her there yesterday. That raggedy-ass bird
can't even fly. They clipped his wings.'

'You do remember she humiliated Etcheverry to the whole
police department?'

Sonny nodded disconsolately.

Jenny uncovered the phone: 'Thanks, Tomasita. If you learn
anything more, let me know.'

She listened for a while more and then hung up. 'Some
other cops were there at the arrest last night and said the thing
was a bit dicey,' she told Sonny. 'I'm not sure what Tomasita
means by "dicey". She only works on the switchboard and in
records. But Gloria's not in the system this morning. There
was no booking. God only knows.'

'What would that old cooter do?'

'You don't want to think about that, Sonny. Let's go see
his partner, Efren. He's been keeping that moron out of trouble
for years. He's out now on disability with a broken foot.'

'I wish we'd just stayed in bed,' Sonny said.

'Let's not get into that. I always figured God gave a billy
goat like you a hard head and a clear conscience. That doesn't
seem to be working out for you.'

'Somebody slippin' on his game here, I think.'

'We balls deep, brah.'

They'd gathered at the plastic tables behind Woody's, sharing
beers and a few paper plates of ribs just to look like they

belonged. Each had a sports bag or some other container full of weapons at his feet, a few just supermarket paper bags. Stoney could see that a lot of the guys were not in a trusting mood. In their heads, they'd been reading papers and working the TV news about Li'l Joker to death and they were scared and angry.

'The best defense is a good fuck-you up in the grill,' Crispy said. He was the oldest of the active Rollin' Seventies, maybe twenty-five.

'We got the word out,' Stoney said. 'We only got to find where these Colombians are hiding out. This our country. We got our own cops looking.'

'Man, I hope our cops are better than their cops. The Spics can pay more.'

'I don't understand why they wanna catch a fade with us?' Crispy said. 'We chopped drug for them for three years, and we never took them off, not a damn penny. What is it? They way too butt-hurt in this.'

'They just crazy *putas*, man,' Stoney said. 'What you expect from way way south? They so far down there it make Mexicans look like eskimoos. They upside down on the earth. They suck they own dicks 'cause they hang up. You gotta know foreign assholes ain't the same at all.'

A couple of them chuckled.

'Stone, you been a good money-man so far,' a young banger said. 'I know you was a Rollin' Seventy back in the day, but don't you be hate on us 'cause we ain't been to the big college.'

'You always my homies, son. I don' forget that. If Ima be warlord here, I wanna know what we got that shoots. Nah – don't be showin' me. Tell me anything more interesting than the piece you took out of your momma's purse this morning.'

One by one, they mentioned the assault rifles and machine pistols that he already knew about.

'OK, I got me a M203 grenade launcher for my M-16, and I got six cluster rounds,' Crispy said. 'Those rounds cost three bills each at Spanky's.'

'Tom-Tom, you got you a big grin.'

'I got me a CS tear gas Cobray. They ain't be expectin' no gas bombs.'

'Too bad it's not nerve gas, but let's all be ready for a little windy blowback. That stuff will make you puke on yourself. Keep your hankies wet.'

Harper patted his long duffle. 'I got me a D-64 frag grenade launcher, made to protect submarines against fucking frogmen.'

'Good, good.'

'It ain' over till the G-Dog bark.' G-Dog was the tallest and most deeply, quietly angry of the Rollin' Seventies, and Stoney had never figured out whether he was thoughtful or just lost somewhere deep in all that rage.

'OK, G, what you got?'

'Dart gun they use on the fuckin' tigers in the jungle, with M-99 darts. It's mad bait. The mother you hit go right to la-la and some duck-sucker can stand over him and shoot him dead.'

Jesus Christ, why not shoot him dead in the first place? Stoney thought, but what the hell. Better an enemy out cold. He'd hoped for a little more armament, maybe some more explosives, but it would have to do against South American *cholos*, who might not be able to get much more in L.A. than rusty revolvers from some Mex gang or whatever they could buy quick. Though they had retrieved that RPG from some big deposit box at the bank, the one they'd fired off at Costco. Couldn't have been much more than that in a safety deposit box, he thought. No tanks, no nukes.

Stoney's cell rang, and snapping it open, he saw the number was his police snitch.

Sonny parked the mini-van in the nearly forgotten enclave of old money out in east Bakersfield south of the country club. New money had gone out to the western periphery across Highway 99, but the houses here were large and Spanish or even pseudo-Tudor, on curving roads without sidewalks, built in the 1920s or some other prehistoric time before the sprawl and white flight from as far as L.A. had swollen the old south valley townlet of maybe thirty thousand on old Highway 99 up to half a million.

'You want to take the lead in talking to him?' Sonny asked.

She nodded. 'This is as touchy as it gets.'

'Look at these houses. How did a cop buy here?'

'That's a little luxury of knowledge we don't want to get into right now,' Jenny Ezkiaga said. 'They are nice, though.'

'I don't get over here a lot.'

'Why would you? These folks don't hire people who run at our speed. They own the stores, they don't rob them.'

They both got out of the car, shutting the car doors softly, as if to minimize their presence in the super-quiet neighborhood.

'These are the ones who rob you with a fountain pen, as Woody Guthrie said,' Sonny added.

'The legend says he was quoting Lincoln,' she offered, as they started up the long rising lawn.

'Can we trust Saldivar?' he asked.

She puffed through very tight lips. 'Can we trust the sun to rise tomorrow? I'm in the lead here, partner. Stand down.'

But before she could steady herself for the task, Efren Saldivar stepped out on to the screened verandah with a frown and a black aluminum baseball bat, limping a little on a big plaster cast over his right foot. They knew his on-duty accident probably didn't bear a lot of scrutiny. They say he'd been moving a desk in the police station and dropped it on his own foot. An alternate version had his partner Tom Etcheverry doing something incredibly stupid during the same move, like stopping abruptly to tell a joke and causing the accident. Almost everybody liked the second version best.

Saldivar was still young looking, maybe late thirties, and darkly handsome, with the usual tidy cop mustache. He wore expensive casual clothes, a nice polo and a pair of gray sweats that would pull easily over the cast.

'Freeze, motherfuckers!' Saldivar said, probably out of habit, or just a joke, as he rapped the bat on his porch. But they both froze, a good ten yards short of the steps.

'I'm sorry to hear you were injured, Efren,' Jenny said. 'It looks painful.'

'Thanks so much, Jenny. I know you've come here about my foot's welfare. You, too, Sonny.'

'I wish you only well, L.T.'

Saldivar just glanced at him, and then returned his gaze to Jenny, knowing where the real muscle lay.

'No, you can't come up on the porch. Every time you show up, woman, one of us got to worry about an abrupt end to their career. Yes. The foot hurts like a bastard. Thank you. For the first time in my life I feel really impaired.'

'It's not you we're here for, Lieutenant; it's about your partner. You know perfectly well he's not playing with all fifty-two cards. You've been walking after him in the park with a pocketful of doggie bags for years.'

Saldivar looked like he was about to say something nasty,
but a motorcycle came noisily past and seemed to change his
mind. His eyes took on the aimless resentment of an old snapping turtle, and he shrugged and rapped his baseball bat on
the wood again.

'Do you want to know what's happening with Tom or not?'
she asked. 'His ass is in your hands.'

'Oh, probably not. Just try me half way.'

Something had got her back up, and Sonny liked the result.
'Remember that L.A. cop, Gloria Ramirez? Of course you do.
The one who came to help Jack Liffey and his daughter and
humiliated the whole department by mounting a real police
investigation all by herself. Look, I know I'm over the line.
You can get angry now and not learn anything, or you can
let that drop. The woman was sent up to a conference in
Fresno last week.'

'That damn DNA thing.'

'Uh-huh. She was in town here on the way. Never mind
the details – your partner ran up against her and arrested her
when she was pretty far off balance, but he never took her in
to Truxton to be booked. I think a worst case is happening
right now or just about to.'

Saldivar's eyes went to Sonny. 'What's your part in this,
pendejo? You dally a little with the bitch?'

'Sir, she's a friend of mine, and she's missing. You'd do
your best, too. I been a cop. Long ago, in Louisiana.'

'Your manhood isn't much to me, guy, but I guess to you
it feels like the real thing.'

Jenny whacked Sonny's arm with the back of her hand, and
he shut up. 'Sir, you've got to know by now your partner's
a bit of a sociopath. With a bad grudge against women, especially this woman.'

Saldivar glared at Sonny for a moment, then turned back
to Jenny. 'Have you got any real reason to be spewing all this
manure?'

'She's been gone overnight, Efren. No official arrest. No
paperwork. Price admitted Etcheverry drove away from the
scene with her in the car. Things happen in the dark of night.
One of your buddies who was there says privately that
Etcheverry was sticking his hand up her skirt pretty hard after
he arrested her.'

'OK, shut up now.' The cop glanced down at the baseball bat that still dangled limply. 'It's failure that you never get over,' he said, as if to himself. 'Tom's been a failure from when we was both in the second grade at Bessie Owens school.'

He looked off into the sky and sighed, the sigh of a man foreseeing something truly unpleasant. 'I got to deal with this, not you. You get that? Just go home, peeps.'

'We can't do that.'

'Get in my way today, and I'll shoot you on sight.' Saldivar hopped to the screen door and shoved it open hard, and the pneumatic closer rebounded once before banging shut behind him.

Maeve led him up to 'the chairs', both of them huffing and puffing a bit along the last forty-five degree stretch of crumbling asphalt roadway and then a slippy-slidey climb up dirt and sand.

'Have you ever heard of Sandstone Retreat?' she asked.

'Huh-uh,' Chad said. Chad had insisted on coming back in the morning to see how she was, so she took him for a walk to keep this all away from the girls. From Axel, actually.

They settled with sighs on to the white resin chairs on the knob. They grasped paper coffee cups with plastic caps that had gone a bit misshapen and disappointingly cool during the long ascent.

'You don't think a street can get any steeper and then, wham, it does,' she said.

'Steep enough,' he said. They sipped the coffee as they caught their breath. He frowned and poured his out on to the weeds.

'I just heard about this place,' Maeve said. They'd driven to the only parking spot at the base of the hill.

'Which house is this retreat you mentioned?'

'I think it's that long gray building down there. Back in the day, it was some kind of sex cult, even had celebrities coming from all over.'

'I bet sex cults are all pretty much the same. Like religious ones. It's amazing when you read those old guys and they go on and on about their penises. Henry Miller. Mailer. Roth. It's like they had to kick the world hard, like some stingy Coke machine, to get their share of sex.'

Maeve smiled, once again having to look away from the tug of Chad's dazzling beauty. She wondered if his dad's third wife had been some beauty queen starlet. 'I bet you always got your share in high school.'

That statement seemed to annoy him a little, but she couldn't help that. She bet it was true. The detachment made him seem unreachable for the moment.

'I had girlfriends. I really didn't think of high school as a big reality show with some squeaky announcer keeping score. Did you get your share?' he asked.

'I'm sorry if I said the wrong thing, Chad.' She was feeling generous toward him and let the hostility go. 'Do you think there's such a thing as having too much sex?'

He frowned at the puddle of coffee that he'd discarded. 'Maybe if you're buying popularity with it, it's probably the wrong currency and it'll bite you on the ass.'

'I think we can both agree on that. That'll kill something in you pretty fast. But . . . I don't know. I'm thinking of a place like that that makes sex a big fetish. What happens to you if you turn sex into a recreation? The old in-and-out, as guys used to say. Two, maybe three partners at once. Or doing it ten times a day. Do you think it hurts something in you?'

He looked at her in a way she couldn't interpret, and then shrugged and looked out over the hillside. 'I'll bet some people do fine and others get freaked out. Like going to war and killing. Some do fine, some don't. Californians have made whole junk cultures out of skateboards, and surfing, and custom cars, and pickups that jack themselves up and down fast. We can probably do the same with sex.'

'Is a junk culture anything poor people choose to do?' she said slyly.

'Is sociology just the anthropology of white people?' he countered.

'Touché. Thank god you're no dope, Chad. For all the crazy things I've got caught up in in my short life – and I've told you some of them – I've never done what must have been Sandstone sex. Sex without even the pretense of affection.'

'Is this an elaborate way of blowing me off?' he asked.

'Why are you asking me that?'

'Radar,' he said. 'I feel the start of a freeze-out.'

Maeve watched a pair of mockingbirds dive and soar,

harassing the hell out of a red-tailed hawk. Defending their
nest, probably. What was more understandable than that?
'Life's not all about you, Chad. We both just started college,
and I'm a little overwhelmed by it all.'

'I thought we were doing pretty good, actually,' he
complained.

Chad was like a dark room to her, and part of her wanted
to know what was in it – but not terribly urgently.

'I think we're good friends,' she said.

'I thought so, too, until you started to worry me.'

'Let's not hurry life. I don't even know what high school
you went to,' she said.

'Reno High, right in Ward One downtown. With all those
poor people and junk cultures.' He smiled halfheartedly.

'What else was special about it?'

'Nobody there had heard of the blacklist. So I could have
a regular high school life. Regular is pretty much OK with
me,' he said gently. 'I think I'm regular. That's why I'm not
at Princeton.'

The abrupt softening in him affected her. 'You do attract
me, Chad. If that's what you want to hear.'

FOURTEEN
Life Is Sugar, For True

For a savvy cop, Saldivar was pretty oblivious to having a tail. Maybe it was the urgency of his concern for his partner. And it helped that Sonny was following in a fairly anonymous white mini-van. Bakersfield wasn't the most complex city-plan around, so it wasn't that hard to follow Saldivar's 1969 fastback Mach 1 Mustang, with its louvers over the rear window and its black bent-wingtip-spoiler over the tail. They trailed him out of the country club streets and then across the grid – toward the oddly bypassed chunk of Old Downtown that had pretty much been abandoned to druggies and punkers. Saldivar seemed to know right where he was going.

'How are we going to keep Jack out of this if it's bad?' Jenny said. 'I don't want him driving supersonic over the Grapevine with murder in his heart.'

'Let's worry about Gloria right now,' Sonny said.

'I have a feeling she can take care of herself. Look, Saldivar's pulling over.'

They slowed as the Mustang turned hard and stopped in the driveway of what looked like a meth house, a stucco box with a dead lawn in a really bad neighborhood, steel doors and oversize burglar bars everywhere. Jenny didn't know what Etcheverry drove, but there was a beat-up Camaro out front, and a big Ford pickup, too, probably the most anonymous vehicle in all Bakersfield.

The steel drug door had been torn open long ago and the regular door must have been open, too, as they watched Saldivar work his way up to the porch on his crutch and go straight in. They parked a half block up the road and shut the engine off as a tattooed kid on a skateboard clattered past and gave them the finger, then both fingers.

'Can I shoot him?' Jenny said.

'Suit yourself. It'll save somebody trouble later. Nice neighborhood.'

'Not much worse than yours.'

'Point taken.' Sonny's Oildale, an oilworker and poor-white ghetto only inches above the mud flats of the Kern River, was an unincorporated district so scabrous that even Bakersfield refused to annex it. This area was Bakersfield proper, but the city had pretty much disowned it.

In a moment, Saldivar hopped back out the door of the ratty bungalow, kicking at nothing in particular, except maybe life, with his heavy foot-cast, which almost threw him off balance. He stared in supplication at the heavens for a moment or two and then sat hard on the stoop. He put his face in his hands.

'If I didn't think such things were excluded from our world, I'd say he's crying,' Sonny said.

'The imagination reels.'

At the Airport Radisson, Orteguaza was announcing to his men that if Sem didn't call back in ten minutes, they'd go and show him how a partner ought to behave.

But Randy Sem called back in five minutes. 'You want a reliable distributor for your coca, here's the number to call; ask for Gideon. He's ready to go.' He read off a number. 'On the other hand, you only want violence, God help you, go to Hillside Memorial Park and set yourselves up. It's a Jewish cemetery right off the 405, not far. I can send Stoney and his boys to meet you there. Which is it going to be, Mr Man-o-war, business or pleasure?'

As usual, he felt at the center of things and in control, even though he suspected this man's nonsensical way of addressing him was not meant to be respectful. His mentor, Abelardo Rubio, had long ago taught him never to worry about what worms thought of you. And also never to move on in life without wiping the ground clean under your feet. 'Are we supposed to dig his grave in this Jew place?'

'He ain't been bar mitzvahed, *Colombiano*. Just think of Hillside as a big grassy place with no cops in it where you can shoot someone. If that's your choice, you pighead madman, don't ever call me again. I want a reliable business partner.'

'You send Señor Stone, *amigo*.'

The line went dead.

'Get ready to move,' Orteguaza snapped to the room. 'We got to pick up the heavy stuff from *Dieciocho*.'

Jack Liffey let Winston in. He was juggling a big cardboard tray of paper coffee cups, little cream canisters, and a selection of the asphalt-hard confections that these franchises called scones.

'Trash 'n ready. You all tek de fruits.'

'Calm down, Winston,' Jack Liffey admonished. 'Let's speak ordinary English. Eat a little sustenance yourself, because we have work for you.'

'I et some dry bananas from the market – a terrible swap for the good little red sweet Jamaican bananas – and two mangos that tasted like they been soaking all week in petrol.'

Tyrone Bird drank down a whole cup of the black coffee. 'Oooh, man. Yes. Dear, doctor. More of that.'

Jack Liffey handed him his own cup, and Ty gulped down about half of that, too.

'As you can see, our man here needs something strong. And he knows where the real thing is.'

Tyrone Bird wrote out a note to his wife, and told Winston where to find his house in Mandeville Canyon, not so far away. Winston showed no reluctance at all.

'Thanks from the bottom of my heart, Winston,' Tyrone said. 'I don't forget favors.'

'I-an-I no Jah man like my brah – none o' dat Rasta perturbs me, but I b'lieve we all climb de good mountain together. Both o' you good men.' His deep black eyes met theirs with something like devotion. He seemed caught up in his shaky self-image and his dialect again.

'Three Musketeers,' Tyrone said with a smile.

Jack Liffey wondered if he'd fallen through some crust of reality into a high school play. But why not? They grappled a clumsy three-way handshake.

'OK, de wicked got to be injure. De Musketeer – dey vanquish dere foe.'

'Go, friend,' Jack Liffey said. 'Don't kill anyone right away. Call me first if there's trouble.'

Winston hurried out the door with a big infectious grin, tucking the note to Mrs Tyrone Bird in his shirt pocket.

'Utterly amazing,' Tyrone said. 'What a wondrous people Jamaicans must be. If you could pick up that island and set it down in Kansas, the whole middle of the country would vibrate with their energy.'

Jack Liffey nodded. 'His brother Trevor was one of the most un-selfconscious heroes I've ever met. Always weirdly off the wall, but always with a heart of gold and the will to make things right.'

'We all need something,' Tyrone said. 'What are we gonna do about my dad? I think he's in big trouble.'

'Don't let a sense of hurry take you over. Your dad's been in trouble for thirty years. Some of the guys I knew back then came down off the Panthers into social work or a college or a small business. Your dad chose drugs. We can try to help him, but it's the most self-destructive choice there is.'

'Please.'

'Of course, Ty. I'll call the only cop in L.A. who's willing to talk to me right now, and see if she can find out what's going on about him.'

He picked up the motel room phone and called Gloria's best friend Paula Green, feeling immensely guilty about not driving straight to Bakersfield to try to help Gloria. He'd thought about it and figured his presence might just make things worse – the cops there hated him so much. Gloria and Paula had been through the Police Academy together – black and brown sisters, back in the nineteen eighties when female cops-of-color had been a whole lot rarer.

'Paula, this is Jack.'

'Hi, Jack, not now. Give me five. I'll give you a callback at that number.'

'Of course.'

You never knew what a cop was up to when you called their cell in the middle of the day – handcuffing a suspect, beating him over the head with their baton, or lying like mad to a clueless field superior about it all.

Jack Liffey looked back at Ty, and he was once again watching something going on in the room that the rest of the world couldn't see.

'Anybody licking my ear?' Jack Liffey asked.

'How do you feel about kisses? Two of my Skinnies are at your cheeks.'

'Seems pretty crappy that I don't get the benefit. We'll get a callback about your dad in a few minutes, I'm sure.'

'Thank you, Jack. I feel I'm on the edge of pissing away everything that I ever wanted to matter in my life. But those crappy action movies – who cares?'

'You regret risking the Chester Himes?'

'Yeah, I hope I can pick it up again.'

'Not much longer, I reckon.' The last time Reston had called him from Monogram, he'd been pretty angry. He was threatening to kill the whole movie if Ty Bird wasn't back in ten minutes, yesterday, whatever.

Jack Liffey realized he hadn't checked in with Reston in quite a while. Life was overfull. Nor had he called Sonny and Jenny in Bakersfield about Gloria in a while, nor had he touched base with his own daughter, whatever trouble she was getting herself into.

Not for the first time, he wished he were three or four different people so he could watch over everything that needed watching over.

'I started keeping a diary last week,' Maeve said, as they drove back down the hill.

'Doesn't that feel a bit egotistical?'

'If you don't write down what you're thinking and force yourself to move on, I have a feeling that your thoughts just recur. This way you're pushed into reflecting on something new every day.'

Chad smiled.

'It's pretty ambitious, I guess,' she admitted. 'But adults don't think we know anything. It's better to try to be fresh, don't you think?'

'I don't know, loneliness is so inescapable,' Chad said. 'I ride a bicycle a lot, really long rides, and I love it. Nothing takes you into solitude more than a bike but that's not the same as loneliness. You can be present in the world, in the city and nature.'

'Maybe you could show me.'

'You've got to be fit. I don't dawdle.'

'I could try to catch up. It sounds great.'

'What are you going to do about our dreaded anthro class?' he asked.

She shook her head. 'I don't know yet. Have you got a second bicycle?'

'Not here. You'd have to get one if you want to come along, a real road bike, not some crappy beach cruiser.'

Sonny and Jenny strolled cautiously up to Lieutenant Efren Saldivar sitting on the stoop of the dilapidated bungalow with his face still in his hands, oblivious.

Jenny Ezkiaga raised her eyebrows and nodded to Sonny a rudimentary go-ahead. Apparently she was no longer so sure of her relationship with the man.

'Efren, Lieutenant, it's Sonny Theroux. Don't spook. We're here to be helpful.'

The officer lifted a reddened face from his palms, revealing a fierce glare.

'What the fuck you two doing here?'

'We followed you,' Sonny admitted. 'You look like a man who needs help.'

'Oh, yeah? You both want to go back to your car and commit a double suicide? That would be my taste in help.'

'I'm sorry we followed, sir. We're really worried about Gloria. Just being in this part of Old Town can taint the nicest day for anyone.'

Saldivar gave a short bark of a laugh, with no real humor in it. 'Go on inside, midget, and then come back out here and bleat some more about how you plan to help.' He turned his death-eye on Jenny. 'You, too, dyke.'

She chose not to reply. There was a freedom in knowing that she would never cure him of his attitudes – despite the fact that she actually liked him. She and he both knew that he would be forced to hew to his small-town cop world-view forever, and if he deviated by so much as an inch from the prescribed sensibility and attitudes and jokes, his brothers would punish him mercilessly down to the very end of his days on Bakersfield's thin blue line. Perhaps it was all inevitable, she thought – stiff men of authority protecting the ancient yardstick of the normal.

'May we go in, sir?'

There seemed almost a malicious gleam in his eye. 'Be my guest. I hope you haven't ate recent.'

'Cut, aw fuck, cut.'

On Terminal Island, Joe Lucius had just craned up on another long angle using Tyrone Bird's double walking out

of the shipyard in a mass exodus, head down, full of anger
and disgust. Hard to convey at a hundred yards. It was just
about the last establishing shot that Meier Reston could find
for him or invent for him.

As the big Chapman crane with its heavy Panavision camera
descended silently on its pneumatics, Lucius leapt down
impatiently the last few feet. 'Meier, you look like you got
news.'

'I hear our guy has found Bird.'

'Yeah, you think so? Where is he?'

'That's still a problem.'

'Get the Bird here or crucify your detective on the side of
a church, like that guy in the papers. And yourself, too.'

'Done, Joe.'

'I want to shoot scene twenty-one A with the real live Tyrone
Bird tomorrow morning or I'll walk, and you can shitcan the
film. Tell me what Friedkin thinks of that.'

'He'll be here, Joe.'

Lucius stopped and turned back furiously. 'If that black
gentleman isn't standing right there at nine a.m., you take a
room deep in the funhouse and don't come out.'

Winston Pennycooke knocked softly at the rustic door of the
long white California ranch house crowded uncomfortably
close to the road on winding Mandeville Canyon. By L.A.
show-off standards, it wasn't much, but in Kingston it would
have been top of the line.

A chocolate-skinned maid in a frilly apron came to the door.
'How may I assist you?'

'Sistah, you a sight to make fine muzik.'

The woman squinted at him. 'I can tell you arrive on these
shores recent, sir. Let there be no mistake. I am from Bell
Gardens, South L.A. I am American. You remember that, sir.
What you want here?'

Winston smiled because he'd distinctly heard hints of the
musical vowels of Kingston under the American black accent
that she was working so hard to adopt. 'Cha, I mean you no
problem, sistah, but I got a letter from the man of the house
to the woman of the house. I'm sure she want to see it.' He
handed her the note. 'I got no wickedness caught up inside.'

'Goody for you. You stay out there now.' She took the

note and closed and latched the door on him.

Crows squawked at him and a squirrel running along a phone wire chittered. Oh, I'm on the outside here, all right, he thought. Even in the eyes of the wee animals.

The door opened again. An imperious-looking white woman in a tightly cinched bathrobe. She had long blonde hair, different from her brown eyebrows, he noted, and she was getting overweight. He figured this had to be Ty's wife.

'If you think you can waltz in here and steal my husband's drugs, you've got another think coming. Who are you?'

'That not Ty's real signing on that paper?' Winston pointed.

'Never you mind. Where's my Tyrone, if you even know him? If you and your pals aren't holding him for ransom, or for dead.'

'You write a letter to him and I take it back with the pills. That's all he say to do. I do my duty to this man I love.'

'Serena, call the police!' she shouted over her shoulder, but somehow it didn't sound quite serious. 'You know what an NIB is, boy? You're up shit creek. That's the worst crime there is to our patrol. Nigger in Brentwood.'

He didn't really expect this from the wife of a decent man like Tyrone, but he knew the white world was full of these bumbaclots. This bodderation had started out low-class for sure. He didn't expect much help from Miss Bell Gardens, either. Probably the opposite.

'Last chance for you to contact Ty, Mrs Bird. You ain' give me no medicine, I ain' take no note,' he said. He turned and started to walk away.

'Ah, you a smartie one, ain't you?'

He got half way back to his car.

'No, stop! Come back, man. Forgive me, *please* – with Ty gone off on me, I'm all hard of heart. I got my own crown of thorns to deal with, please understand. Tyrone isn't the easiest, and he's been gone for days.'

'Yeah, wanderers is real hard to live with,' he said. 'But he trying to help his dad he found just now.'

Her eyes rolled, and he wondered if he should have said anything at all. 'He won't let go of that old dead dream,' she said sadly. 'He's found himself another wino with a square jaw that wants to get into his money. Hell, let him babysit this one a while, too. They all need it more than we ever. What's your name?'

'Winston.'

'Winston, you get Tyrone back to me in one healthy piece when this dad dream of his goes to hell in a handbasket, and it's worth a thousand dollars.'

'Mighty kind, ma'am, but I get him home to you in any case. He got another man helping, too, a really good man, I promise you. Big up onna him. Could I have the medicine, please? If you want him home still cool and instyle, I think he really need the stuff.'

'He needs it, all right, Winston. Come in.' She let him wait in a large foyer, alongside Miss Bell Gardens, arms on her hips, keeping a fierce watch so he didn't pilfer any of the African masks or the Aztec pottery.

'Dey a bran new breed back on J now,' Winston tried out. 'Dey get dey A-levels and plan for college. When you leave home?'

She smiled, just barely. 'All I remember is rude talk and fighting.'

'Ah, nobody on J no more say – the only way be blood, the only way be violence. Different time now, different talk.'

'I hope. It's not so great for us here, neither.'

'Oh, sistah, you sound so sad and lost.' Mrs Bird was stomping down the hallway toward them with her forceful stride.

'You,' she called. 'Mister Winston. Here's Ty's drugs and a note for him. If you don't deliver them, I'll find a way to send you to a nasty California prison for the rest of your life.'

'Why you be that way?' Winston took the pill bottle and an envelope. 'I do everything smooth and sweet.'

Thoughts of Miss Bell Gardens had addled his judgment a bit. He saw her on the other side of the room glowering, but he didn't believe her furious air any more.

'I'll have Tyrone call you.'

Mrs Bird stalked away, and he turned his attention to the better human being in that house.

'Solitude heavy on my soul,' the maid said softly. Her words gave his penis a little tweak.

'Life is sugar, for true, ma'am,' Winston said to her. 'You widout friend here, in dis canyon of no-NIBs. I be back and be a friend.'

*   *   *

Jenny Ezkiaga pulled the steel crackhouse screen farther open
and then pushed on the main door and went in just ahead of
Sonny, then backed hard into him as if she'd been hit by a
cattle prod.

'Hey, there. Don't be blindsiding me. I only weigh in at
one twenty-seven.'

She moved aside a little, in no mood for jokes. Sonny held
on to her shoulders and bodily moved her bulk a little farther
so he could get past. Immediately he wanted to scream out
something, but his hard-as-nails old cop armor took over, and
he only grunted. It took some assimilating, this bloody tableau
that surrounded the unconscious woman he loved to distraction. The sunlight dazzle through the blinds helped etch it all
onto his retinas. An image that would last for the rest of his
life, he knew that.

His ears pricked up for sirens or some cry of rage from
Saldivar outside, but for the moment they were on their own,
and maybe he could gather himself together enough to sort
this out. As fast as he could, he started organizing in his head
what he saw in that room.

Gloria Ramirez lay half unclothed on the big bed, with her
left arm handcuffed to the brass headboard. Her clothes
appeared to have been torn open more than removed, and she
was covered with blood and large purpling bruises on her dark
skin. Her nose was apparently broken and had poured out
blood that was hardening on the mattress. She'd been punched
a lot, he could see, not clinically like someone had been after
information, but angrily, to punish or revenge – and probably
she'd been raped, too. His mind refused to stay in focus on
the white cotton panties that had been ripped apart. He tried
to get some distance so he could sort this out, but he could
feel tears rolling down his cheeks. He saw Gloria's chest rise,
a bloody bubble forming in the corner of her mouth, and he
thanked whatever God there was that she was alive. No small
favor given the extent of the beating she'd obviously received.

The rest of the tableau was even worse. On either side of
her, two large and pants-down cops were quite dead –
Etcheverry had a black bullet hole centered in his forehead,
and he lay on his back on the bed, his unseeing eyes wide
open. Another not-so-bright cop whom Sonny recognized but
couldn't name had several holes in him and was lying still on

the floor in pools of his own congealing blood. The wounds on the second one suggested a weapon fired again and again in a rage & not aimed too professionally. And there it was – right next to Gloria's right hand on the mattress. A shorty Smith & Wesson Chief's Special .38.

Sonny guessed that he'd find a holster for a backup piece on the ankle of one or the other of the Bako cops, if he looked, but he had no interest in looking. She'd undoubtedly grabbed it and used it immediately – more power to her. If they'd finished their . . . business with her, her life would have been just as forfeit, and her body would have disappeared forever down a dry well out near Wasco or Buttonwillow. He couldn't help it – the tears kept welling over and running down his cheeks.

Jenny finally came to some sort of consciousness and stopped her gasping and gulping behind him. 'Ohhhh. Sonny, what happened here?'

'Hush,' Sonny said. 'Oh, hush. We don't have time. That one will have the handcuff key.' He pointed to Etcheverry. 'Find it and release her. Wrap her in a blanket or anything you can find and bring her out to the car. Rip down a curtain if that's all you can get.' He wiped his face on his sleeve. 'I'll be talking to Saldivar when you come out. Just ignore us and lug her to the car. Don't stop, no matter what he says. I'll deal with him. You can do this.'

'Oh, God.'

'Do it now.' He could hear the unearthly calm in his voice, amazed he'd got it together. 'Our future in this town depends on our composure for the next two minutes.'

'Are we going to have to pay for this forever?'

'Nobody in Bako wants two local cops to be remembered for kidnap and rape of another cop. I'm sure they were killed by some Mexican meth dealers who ambushed them in this drug house.'

'Is Efren going to buy off on that?'

'I figure I've got about a minute-and-a-half to make it happen.'

FIFTEEN
Too Much Going Bad at Once

'How sure are you that this Marcus Stone is really your dad?' Jack Liffey was mainly trying to divert him, watching the poor kid get more and more nervous – trying so hard not to let on that he was seeing his ghostly pals moving about the motel room.

'He admitted he was with my mom at the right time. He looks an awful lot like me. Darker, of course. I suppose we could do a DNA test. But I tracked him down. It's not like he's holding me up to get my money.'

'A paternity test might be a good idea before you leap off the deep end of the gene pool. You already got your expensive car beat up pretty bad protecting him, and you're right in the middle of a dope deal from hell that seems to be going nuclear. You and Marcus Stone haven't seen the last of the Colombians, I'm afraid.' He watched Tyrone's attention go abruptly to something in the center of the room. 'Instead of getting deeper in this violent melodrama, you could be filming a fine Chester Himes novel right now, maybe make a classic movie. I'm not riding you, son, but give it some thought. I'm with you, either way.'

Tyrone Bird closed his eyes and finished off the last of Jack Liffey's coffee, which Jack Liffey had dearly wanted. Life was full of minor disappointments, he thought. It would be good and cold by now, anyway, and the Sputnik Motel had no fancy features like microwaves or hotplates.

'Could you keep the movie people off me, Mr Liffey? I bet the producer and all his little minions are having shit-fits. They're probably threatening air strikes on my home, my wife, the charities I support. Probably you, too.'

'Oh, I've been threatened,' Jack Liffey said impassively. 'But as of now, you're my man, Mr Bird. My usual profession is finding missing kids, a lot younger than you, but my rule number one is that I never take them home if they tell

me home is no good. I figure my real client is always the kid.
Or maybe my real client is just my own contrary frame of
mind.'

'Do you mean you stand up for the weak of the world?'
Only a fine actor could have said that line aloud without
sounding absurd.

Jack Liffey smiled. 'It must sound silly to you, too. I loved
the Lone Ranger to distraction as a kid. You know that poor
sad man who played him on TV, Clayton Moore – he believed
in it all, he really did. It was touching. He'd go to supermarket openings in costume and talk to kids about always
telling the truth and trying to make a better world. In that
wonderful rich voice. Years later, I hear he begged for a tiny
role in the movie remake, just a walk-on to pass the baton,
but the Hollywood assholes didn't want the guy around. Serves
them right – the movie turned to shit.'

'He was before my time, but I've seen the old black-and-
white TV. I think I qualify as the weak here. Do you want
me to list my vulnerabilities?'

'No, not at all. I just want you to believe I'm on your side.
And tomorrow morning, I want all of my own coffee.'

'God, I'm so sorry. I didn't think. I really needed something
strong.'

'It's OK, son. We can get more. But I mean it about being
on your side. I don't give a goddamn about Meier Reston
or Joe Lucius and all their self-important movietown boasts
about their power. Money has its power, I know it, but I
have enough to eat tomorrow. That's plenty to keep my
ethics out of the gutter. They came to me and rented my
experience to find you, but it was just a rental – nobody
buys me . . .'

Ty smiled, between furtive glances at the strange empty places
in the room. 'I wonder sometimes if those movie hotshots have
souls. One of the writers I pokered with used to call them empty
barking husks. Thank you, Jack. I know I'm sliding down a bad
glide in my head right at the moment, and you know it, too.
When Winston gets back, I'll swamp everything inside me with
the dulltime drugs. It's no fun, but it makes me appreciate people
who know about failure.'

'Oh, that's my middle name, son,' Jack Liffey said.

They heard a backbeat rap at the door that could only have
been Winston Pennycooke.

'That should be my meds, bless his Jamaican soul.'

Joe Lucius' personal cellphone rang its ta-daaa, mimicking
the racecourse trumpet, and it meant he'd better get it. 'Hold
on, girls. This better be important,' he barked into the phone.
The hookers rolled away and waited patiently.

'Joe, I got a bead on Tyrone. It took a whole FBI under-
taking to track the GPS in his cellphone.'

'No brag. Just tell me.'

'He's still close. I think he's on his mission from God to
find dad. Should I go drag him in?'

'Meier . . .' There was a very long pause, his imagination
filling with naked producers tossed into active volcanos. 'Did
you not hear me earlier? What was it about ripping out your
lungs and eating them that you didn't understand? I said we
shoot tomorrow or else. Hire some muscle – hell, hire some
brain. Fuck up anyone who gets in our way. Bring me Tyrone
Bird at nine a.m.' He hung up.

Marcus Stone stood on the highest ground he could find and
looked out over the small campus-sized Jewish cemetery that
had been shoved up against a shallow curve of the 405
Freeway. The cemetery was built on rising hills that were cut
up at angles by a dozen sturdy columbarium walls, or whatever the hell they called those long blank structures that held
urns full of ashes. There was a big mausoleum below and,
weirdly, a tiny Greek temple and a stepped waterfall dedi-
cated to some singer from ancient time named Al Jolson.

Stone knew the place because he'd had a friend buried here
years ago. Because of some misunderstanding Marcus Stone
had been stuck waiting two hours, so he'd wandered around,
looking at things. It was better than he remembered as a place
to defend, which was certainly a new way of thinking about
a cemetery. The patchwork of thick walls looked impregnable
from up the hill, you could get up high above the entrance,
and the hilliness let you and a chosen squad or two sprint
from one columbarium to another.

He turned and nodded to the dozen or so young black

men behind him. They'd all parked outside the cemetery
on the uphill side, two-thirds of the Rollin' Seventies,
carrying crumpled shopping bags and sports satchels with
multiple weapons in them. Looking totally out of place, they
gathered near him. 'My po-lice say the Colombians be
coming here at three, lookin' to catch a fade with us. They
think they be here first, and they be coming in the front,
down there off Centinela. So we keep the high ground. We
go up top of these wall-things, both sides of the road. Get
on the roof. Wait till they got to spread out. We use only
text on the cells to communicate.'

'Ain' be no Eighty-Three Hoovers, Stone-man? Promise
this be all crackers.'

'It's the same Spanish crackers that hit us at the Costco,'
Marcus said. 'You wasn't there, Ace-high. Most of them black,
but that's just the Colombian way. Don't let it confuse you.
They don't even speak English. We got them outmanned and
we got grenade launchers and shit. We the cavalry here an'
we gonna get us some Injuns.'

He let Harper take half the crew across the narrow cemetery roadway and boost themselves up on to the roof of a long
two-story columbarium that looked as thick as the Great Wall
of China. Oh, here it is, Stoney thought. I guess I been moving
toward this badass showdown all my life. They didn't show
us respect at Costco, and then they killed Li'l Joker like a
dog. So there's no grays here, no in-between thinking, no old-
school mercy. Just the Colombian ass-clowns and us, and
we're going to waste them all.

'Let's bust a cap on these *cholos*,' he said to the squad of
foot-soldiers who'd stayed with him, most of the bangers from
the Costco. 'Anybody got an extra strap with some distance
to it? I only got this.' He showed his Desert Eagle pistol. It
had never seemed important, or even practical, for him to
have a rifle. He wasn't some peckerwood deer-hunter.

'Jeez, Stoney, you don't go to no sock dance without no
socks. Here.' G-Dog handed him a little Ingram spray gun
and a couple of extra 30-round magazines, no more accurate
at distance than his pistol, but at least it could fill the air fast
with a lot of metal.

'OK. Let's get up on top of this thing and we the boss.'

*   *   *

Jenny Ezkiaga stood in the doorway of her spare bedroom in Bakersfield.

Gloria lay on the spare bed, utterly naked now and showing the bruises merging into one huge discolored mass. The blood had been gently sponged off, but she moaned and shifted a little from time to time like some form of sealife driven by invisible ocean currents. Jenny's partner Teelee Greene knelt in the corner of the bedroom clutching her daughter, mesmerized by the sight of Gloria and watching over her like a helpless guardian angel. Teelee was reminded of her own miserable marriage with its irregular beatings with no warning, not so many years ago.

A female gynecologist had come to the house in the afternoon, sworn to eternal secrecy, and had examined Gloria's wounds carefully, sewn some and salved others, and then left behind two syringes of morphine, to be used only if the double dose of ibuprofen failed to kill the pain. The doctor promised to dummy up some medical forms for a series of Jane Doe X-rays and ultrasounds in a clinic where she sometimes worked. But next morning – before it opened.

Jenny watched a few more restless twitches, caught Teelee's troubled eye for a moment, and then went back to the kitchen where she'd made Sonny wait. 'Shouldn't we call Jack?' she asked.

'I don't think so.'

She glared for a moment. 'You're going to have to handle your own complications, Sonny.'

'Don't you think I know that? We need to keep our heads down until we can get her out of here. He'd go berserk. He would, you know. If he saw her now, he'd probably go to the big cop funeral that's coming up and shoot those two again in their coffins, and then he'd die in a rain of lead from the assembled Bako P.D. Not to mention the sheriffs and all the other P.D.s around who'll be sending their envoys. Jack's not very popular here.'

She nodded. 'I know it. And I hate to think what Gloria's own pals in LAPD would do to this town if they knew the real story. They've got Navy SEALS and all that shit. We could have a guerilla war between cities. What a mess. If we get through this, please don't bring her back here for your own pleasure.'

'You know I'm really in love with her. It's not just random fun, OK?'

'She'll be wherever she is, and you and Jack can fight it out with machetes if you want. But not here. We already owe too much to Lieutenant Saldivar. I'm still surprised he let us out of there.'

Neither of them had to mention her other handicap: being the most open and public lesbian in a city that was more or less run by conservative Evangelicals.

'Sooner or later, I'll run out of bonus points for my great-granddad and granddad, the sheepherders, and for going to Bako High, and then Teelee and I will have to skedaddle.'

'Why don't you leave now and go to the coast where you'd have a real community? Inland is another state, maybe another century.'

'This has been my family's town since 1910 when Domeka Ezkiaga was plucked out of the Pyrenees and brought here by a rich landowner and turned loose on the Kettleman Hills with a crappy little tent and a thousand sheep to watch. Once a month, the first Sunday, poor Domeka got to dress up in his only suit and be driven down to Bako for a meal at Noriega's with the other herders. Think of the loneliness, man. My family earned its place in this town before any dustbowl Okies.'

He'd heard the tale before. 'Those intolerant assholes all deserve scorpions in their boots.'

'You learn to acclimate by not expecting any better.'

For some time Tyrone Bird had sat and stared at a handful of long pale green medicine capsules on the table with a glassy-eyed smile of cartoon lunacy, like Bugs Bunny with a spinning ring of stars over his head, occasionally looking up at some vacancy in the room that was probably not vacant for him.

Who knew what tricks his Skinnies were getting up to to stop him from downing the pills that would probably push them down into some dark recess of his tortured psyche, Jack Liffey thought. In the end Ty offered the vacancy in the room his middle finger and swallowed one pill, then another. He didn't even need water to get them down.

'Your wife send a note,' Winston announced. He'd waited discreetly.

Tyrone poked his index fingers together for some reason,

gingerly, as if they might spark. He ignored the envelope.
'Not yet.'

Jack Liffey thought that this poor man would probably
never experience a moment's peace in his life without medications – and using the powerful psychoactives, who knew what
side effects he had to put up with? He'd heard complaints
from other clients. A dulling, a clouding, a kind of dementia
that left you grasping anxiously for words or memories, strange
internal wrestling matches that the anti-psychotics could set
off. Most of all, the feeling of having your psyche inhabited
by some consciousness that was not really your own.

'You OK, Ty?' Jack Liffey asked.

'Not really. The Skinnies are fleeing for safety. Some other
creatures may come forward soon. But they'll be calm and
well-behaved, no worries.'

'You've been well-behaved yourself.'

'You don't know the chaos and fear inside.'

'No, I don't. Take your time, man.'

Jack Liffey took Winston into the bathroom where they could
talk about Stoney without Ty hearing. Winston had no idea
where Stoney had gone. He'd been given a disposable cellphone by Stoney's lieutenant, Harper, but no number to call.
We call you, Ratchet. You put your thumb up your ass and wait.

Jack Liffey took it from him and keyed back through the
menus to find recent calls. He knew a bit of the technology
from some help Maeve had given him once. But the numbers
he found were just strings of asterisks, and there was no way
to select one of them. He assumed that meant the phone was
blocked in some way.

'Stoney's in trouble,' Jack Liffey said. 'We know that.'

'Him done da ting himself, Jack. Dat man built of trouble,
you noseeit? You think Ty his real-an-true son?'

Jack Liffey opened the bathroom door a little and peeked.
Tyrone Bird was constructing small diagrams on the motel's
kitchen table with the remainder of the capsules.

'I don't know. Frankly, I don't think it's very likely. Everybody
fucked everybody at this creepshow. And every single sperm is
out for itself. What are the odds? I think his mom may have
liked Stoney special and dropped precautions, but who knows?'

They heard powerful cars revving in front of the motel and
looked at one another. 'Think anyone followed you?'

'Can't swear naa, ma'an.'

Then there was a heavy and persistent knocking at the door, and even Ty looked up, but rather blankly, as they came out of the bathroom. Quickly and surreptitiously, Ty herded his pills back into their vial as if Big Nurse might come to take them away.

'Open the fuck up! Or we'll kick it in and charge it to you.'

Jack Liffey recognized the self-important voice of Meier Reston. It took only an instant to realize that Ty was going back now, no matter what anyone wanted. There would be heavies out there, for sure. He guessed the film folk would have a hell of a time getting much of a performance out of him on the medication.

The door banging went on and on, like a crazed man who was in it for the long haul.

'You want to go back to the set, Ty?' Jack Liffey asked softly. 'It's up to you.'

The man shrugged lethargically. 'Sure.'

'We'll do what we can for Stoney.'

Somewhere, not far behind Tyrone's eyes, an opaque shutter had fallen.

'I don't suppose with that famous face you could have hid out much longer. It doesn't even matter who snitched. Get the door,' Jack Liffey said to Winston.

He wanted to see what would become of Reston's aggressive demeanor – all of a sudden facing the giant Jamaican. It was just mischief. There was nothing to be gained by balking the man or hustling Ty out the bathroom window, and if the actor went back to the set, at least he'd be out of the Marcus Stone orbit of trouble.

'What I do?' Winston asked.

'Just look tough but don't do anything. Go on.'

Winston opened the door a few inches, and two very big white guys pushed the door all the way open, twin wrestlers. They glanced at the Jamaican dismissively and turned to Jack Liffey. Conspicuous bulges under thin jackets showed that they were armed, too, should it be necessary. The whole package was just a boast of power, the expensive jewelry of coercion by the rich. Jack Liffey ignored them and looked at Reston, who waited calmly behind.

'You didn't need the Air Cav, Meier. Ty's not in running shape.'

'Fuck yourself, Liffey. You never phoned us. You can kiss your fee good-bye.'

'I did that a long time ago. Ty'll come peacefully. I want you to take good care of him. He's got the meds he needs now. If you take them away, you may do him real harm.'

'We got plenty of doctors with the right feelgood to help him work.'

'If you hurt him, so help me, I'll make you sorry.'

All of a sudden someone outside was shouting, '*¡Puta! ¡Puta!*' but no one took notice.

The wrestlers grasped Ty's arms, about as gently as gorillas, and lifted him to his feet.

'You're over in this town, detective,' Reston said.

'I was born over. I'm an old man now, Meier, but I don't walk away. I like Ty a lot. Treat him like your son. Please, man. For the good of your own soul.'

'Bring him along, gents. You two back off and stay inside. Have his luggage sent along.'

Jack Liffey watched uneasily. The sight of Ty Bird being frog-walked slowly toward the door cauterized something deep inside him. Defend the weak, hadn't he just said it to Ty? At least when you could. But maybe even more when you couldn't.

Outside, a big Hummer was parked beneath the moronic Sputnik on its pole.

'What do I do?' Winston asked Jack Liffey as the giant wrestlers pushed Ty past him. He put on a fierce expression as if he might have a secret karate way to overwhelm them.

'It's OK, Win.'

Reston stared back into the room from the forecourt. 'You just did something smart for a change, asshole,' Reston said.

'Remember, the guy's hurting.'

Reston frowned. 'It's so nice to see a real loser really lose. Don't get in our face again.'

'I'll be around,' Jack Liffey said.

Reston made a dismissive shrug, and the twin wrestlers half-carried Ty across the parking lot toward the Hummer as Reston slammed the motel door.

'I din't like that,' Winston complained.

'Me, too. We're not through, *caballero*. Can I have your phone?'

He may as well use Stoney's dime, he thought. Jack Liffey called his home first, for messages that didn't exist, and then he called Sonny in Bakersfield to try to find out about Gloria, but no one picked up. At the message tone he said, 'Sonny, for Chrissake! Put me in the picture or I swear to God I'll drive up there and barbecue you.'

Too much was going bad at once, but that was always the way it was.

WHER THY AT? The text message came in after an unobtrusive clunk on Stoney's cell. From what he'd taken to calling Squad B across the road, probably from Harper. Poking his forehead over the parapet of the facing columbarium, he could actually see a couple of Squad B lying on the roof opposite. Just like Squad A, they'd probably ascended the makeshift stepstones of the bronze flower holders pegged into the marble.

Ain no psychic, he texted back. There had been very little activity down at the Centinela gate beside the chapel and parking lot, only a few maintenance three-wheelers pottering around and one stray Oldsmobile that'd entered. But it was only an old man in a fedora who got out and strolled forlornly across the grass to leave flowers. Stoney had one Dexedrine tab in his pocket and he wondered if he should take it now to pep up his attention. Harper called it Special Forces popcorn.

H8 WAITIN-
No shit L8r

They went back to watching and fretting. Stoney wondered if his on-board Torrance cop was selling him out. Why now? And if it was some kind of sellout, he sure hoped for a no-show from the Colombians, not an ambush. From time to time he turned to look at the Green Valley Circle entrance to the cemetery. It was above them, where they'd walked in after parking outside, making their way part way down the hill between the Garden of Sarah and the Garden of Leah. The entry gate had maybe thirty feet of elevation advantage on them, not much, but enough to make things a mess if the *Colombianos* came in that way.

In the end, though, the *Colombianos* came in down below off Centinela exactly where he'd figured, though not in the Lincolns and Caddies he'd expected, or the exotic Maybach they'd flaunted at Costco. They looked like stolen cars, random street rubbish. That was his first sign that something was going wrong. It meant they had allies here to get them what they wanted – probably Eighteenth Street, the biggest Latino gang in the world. Eighteenth Street wasn't like the usual small-time local gang. They had scores of affiliate gangs, at least twenty thousand members in the L.A. *clikas* alone, but more important, they had colonized their home countries in Central America and then allied with the Colombian cartels. They had the resources of a medium-size army.

Wakey soljers!

The message probably wasn't necessary. The five old cars below had arrayed themselves in the wide spot of the entry road like military vehicles about to swarm a hostile village. When the car doors came open, Stoney could see it wasn't just the black Colombianos coming out. They had allies now, bronze-skinned Latinos, and every one heavily armed. He saw AKs and Uzis and a street-sweeper shotgun, and then a long fat olive-colored tube that he didn't like at all. He heard the sound of an explosion at least a mile away. He had no idea what it was, but he guessed with a chill that it was a diversion, meant to keep the cops busy elsewhere. Then a second explosion far to the east. They were up against real pros now, and there were a lot of them, with heavy weapons.

Retreat he keyed in, but when he looked uphill, a supermarket eighteen-wheeler truck was parked hard across the Green Valley gates to block the exit. *Shit*, he thought, why didn't I hear it? Just as another explosion went off in the distance. There'd be no help from cops.

Go! Get out alive he texted.

WHASSUP?

2 much 4 us!

An old beat-up panel van started up the hill fast. A tall Latino standing at the edge of the parking circle down below was looking straight at Stoney's roof with big binoculars. Did they have satellites? Drones? The van stopped just below them and Latino foot soldiers fanned out of it, reminding him of red ants swarming a mound of weaker black ants. A couple of his Squad B soldiers across the road broke discipline and began firing bursts at them, and whoever had the grenade launcher over there tried to take out a second oncoming car but hit only road with a useless orange burst. We're amateurs, he thought.

The Colombian team seemed to have plenty of RPGs, and three of the missiles smoked their way across the afternoon straight for Squad B's columbarium. The explosions sent thin marble and metal urns flying everywhere. The third blast, slightly delayed, brought much of the roof caving in, and the freestanding walls soon came after. These damn things weren't nearly as substantial as they looked.

'Go for home!' Stoney shouted to his own squad, and he was one of the first to dive off the back side of the roof. Luckily he knew how to fall and roll, and he did no damage to his ankles. He headed due east, uphill, to the nearest perimeter wall and the supermarket truck, until he saw muzzle flashes ahead of him, left and right – Jesus, they were there, too! The whole of L.A.'s Latinos had come down on them! He did a quick U-turn downhill. A big concussion punched him in the chest before he even heard it. Something more powerful than the RPGs had hit the columbarium he had just leapt off, and the building was now collapsing like a wall of mud bricks.

How could this be happening in the middle of a big American city? Surely, we have law and order here. He almost laughed aloud at himself – remembering that not long ago he'd thought he had the Colombians outgunned. He loped downhill across grass and grave markers toward the little temple and waterfall, while all the gunfire seemed to be still above him and east. He heard two more explosions behind him, probably grenades, and then another of the really big bursts, which seemed to stop most of the answering fire as definitively as pulling a plug. Shit, guys, run! Rule one of the ghetto is never kick a bear if you can't kill it. But he knew some of these guys lived in a tightly wired world of their own self-respect, where you had to guard your props every minute. Some of the Rollin' Seventies would rather die than look gutless.

He stumbled over a brass vase planted in the earth and heard individual gunshots not far away, then the crackles of high velocity bullets passing near his ears. All his attention was on attaining the little temple below, though really, it was no more than a low wall and skinny columns, probably no more substantial as refuge than the columbariums, but it offered some kind of irrational escape from the madness.

'Stoney!' a magnified voice called from down the hill. 'Come to *papi*, now! Medicine time, *amigo!*'

He thought of the big Desert Eagle pistol, in his coat pocket now and banging his hip, but knew it would do him little good. It was just a dead weight. He'd lost the submachine gun in his jump from the roof a long time ago. Just as useless. He felt the sun on him, the light breeze as he ran, the smell of mown grass, and wondered if he'd ever experience these wonderful things again. He knew he couldn't be taken alive.

There were a few more isolated shots from uphill, not at him but far behind, terribly like a ruthless platoon finishing off the wounded. He leapt the low wall into the temple, and before he could brake himself, he almost ran straight into a two-thirds size metal sculpture of Al Jolson on one knee with an insipid smile, his arms outspread as if welcoming the sudden embrace of something terrible. Who the hell was Al Jolson, he thought. A singer, back in the mists. The word 'Mammy!' swam in his near-consciousness, from long ago, and a sense of early talkies. A gunshot pinged crazily off the bronze sculpture.

'*¡Alto! ¡Pare disparar!*' He knew enough Spanish to figure that one out – Stop shooting. The asshole wanted him alive. Gunfire began to taper off and then sputter out.

It had been Oreteguaza's voice, all right, but the cheap megaphone sent so much reverb off the surrounding hills and structures that Marcus Stone couldn't make out where the man was standing. The parking area below was filling up incongruously with a tangle of shiny new cars with stickers on their windows, the black sedans and limos of a genuine funeral.

'You my fre-en', Señor Estooone! Come to my arms for mercy! We can make us a new treaty.' The voice, overamplified, was almost impossible to decipher, but he could just make it out. Fat chance he'd surrender with the image of Li'l Joker fresh in mind.

There were sirens all over the map, and some of the cop cars had to be coming their way – the first time in his life police sirens had been welcome. 'Law and order is near!' he shouted.

'In Los Yunaites? You make a joke!' A crude and humorless laugh hawked and hawked, like a donkey braying into a bucket.

Below him, Stoney saw a large Jewish burial party in homburgs and sidecurls accumulating around the mortuary and chapel near the biggest pool – the bottom of Al Jolson's stepped waterfall. The more recently arrived cars were parked anyhow, jammed at angles into the driveway and lot, and dozens of dark-suited men were getting out and standing beside their cars trying to decipher what had gone on up the hill. The men all had baleful looks, and a few women who had stepped out had full-cover black dresses. Those near the street jumped back into their cars and backed away, but most stood transfixed, as if witnessing some odd but possibly explainable ceremony. Maybe it was a movie being shot.

'Come out, Señor Estone! We know right where you hiding.'

Stoney was starting to feel faintly sleepy, and he knew that was a really bad sign. He should have taken the dex. He tried to get a glimpse of his arch-enemy, looking down over the wall and then toward the jalopies of the enemy brigade, and what he saw gave him a chill. Two men knelt just off the roadway with RPG rocket launchers; their bulbous olive noses aimed straight for his little sculptural hideout.

'Shit!'

Just as smoke trails closed on the tiny round temple, he leapt over the far side out on to grass. He flattened to the ground as the explosions went off and hunks of stucco flew everywhere, but still his lucky shield held. A big section of column flew past him, and the domed temple roof crashed straight down, the sound like a huge jaw biting through a thousand stale crackers. Stoney raised his head an inch and saw – only a few inches away – the head and shoulder and one outstretched arm of the bronze statue of Al Jolson, wide-eyed with surprise. Bye-bye, dude, whoever you were back in the day.

There was only one way out of here now that might protect him. Water still splashed down from one pool to the next, disturbed a little now by clots of debris. Fortunately, there was a lot of foggy concrete dust in the air. Stoney jumped into the first pool without even thinking, took two steps on the slippery concrete and leapt over the weir. His front foot skidded and he came down on his ass in two feet of water.

Some of them had seen him, and bullets made that nasty bullwhip crack near his head. He jumped to the next pool, landed better, and then the next. Two more pools to get to the bottom, to the parking lot.

There was another blast, far up at the columbarium where he'd started out, and he assumed someone else was still alive up there, or had been. Stoney felt bad for Harper and his crew, but only momentarily.

As he jumped the next weir, he heard a quiet sizzling go by his ear, and he guessed someone had a silenced rifle, not too far away. Subsonic rounds from a silencer didn't give off that signature shock wave, the snap-pop. He'd been around long enough to know that.

He jumped into the the big round pond at the bottom, caught himself on spread feet that slipped a little on the algae-slicked cement and immediately took two steps and jumped out and ran across a few feet of grass toward the crowds of men in black suits and homburgs in the parking lot. They cleared a path as if he had the plague. The cars were so jammed in now that he gave up the idea of stealing one of them. Cars were backed out double on to the street, and he'd never get a car out the gate. The firing seemed to have stopped for the moment, as if someone had decided that accidentally killing these weird-looking Jewish civvies was a bad idea.

'I mean you no harm!' Orteguaza's braying voice called.

'What's going on?' a man nearby asked him, plucking at Stoney's coat.

'They love to kill!' he shouted. 'Drug lords!'

The words were black magic, and people started diving back into their cars or into the mortuary for safety. He ran through those who were too stunned to move, and they still parted for him like the Red Sea.

One man stood his ground and held out both hands toward him, with his fingers spread. '*Barukh ata Adonai Eloheinu melekh ha-olam . . .*'

'Thank you, man,' Stoney mumbled as he dodged hard past him, hoping it had been a blessing, and headed toward the front gate. A few gunshots crackled past. He could tell that the tangle of cars in the entrance would keep anyone from coming after him, at least for a minute or two. Bless you all, Jews!

Outside the gates, he ran to the left so the stone walls around the cemetery would give him cover, then he jumped into the street, across a lane, to where a woman with her hair in curlers slowed her station wagon full of children for him, startled. He banged his huge pistol against her window. 'Move over, ma'am! I won't hurt any of you. I need your car *now*!'

Everyone inside the car screamed at once.

SIXTEEN
A Beet on Fire

Jenny fed Gloria tiny dribs of rich beef broth, letting her sip it off the tip of the spoon. They'd given her one of the doc's syringes of morphine eight hours back, before she was fully alert and able to refuse, but she was adamantly refusing the second shot even though her face contorted now and again with pain.

'Should have taken your morphine, officer.'

'We're very tolerant of pain,' Gloria said, her tight expression saying otherwise.

'You mean we as in women or we as in Native Americans?' Jenny asked.

Teelee Greene was still in the corner of the room with her napping child, rocking a little on her heels where she squatted barefoot, watching only nominally, her eyes in fact fixed on some place on the far wall, like a cat's, like a shaman seeing some other thing entirely.

'We made of cast iron,' she said, without specifying further.

'Are the cops in Bako looking for me?'

'Sonny is out trying to find out our situation. If the doc hadn't told us not to move you yet, we'd have you back in L.A. and out of their reach.'

'Those two cops . . . ?'

'They're dead, hon. Don't talk about it unless you need to.'

'Umm.'

Which could have meant anything.

'Never been . . . ' Gloria said, and then took a very long time puzzling over the next words. 'So powerless. Such hopeless rage.'

'Hush. Life can hand you too much sometimes, honey.' Jenny rested her hand on the woman's cut and swollen hand on the blanket.

'Mortification,' Teelee enunciated all of a sudden. As a child, she'd been a Catholic, and maybe that was a word out of some deep recess of bygone beliefs.

They both looked at the small fragile woman hugging her sleeping child, but her eyes were still off somewhere else.

'What does Jack know?' Gloria asked. In speaking, she was moving her jaw as little as possible.

'Not much. But he calls and calls.'

'Keep him away. Don't tell him a thing. Or make something up. They'd really hurt him.'

'We know that, hon.'

'Spoon me some beer. I command it. I need to relax to think.'

Jenny chuckled. 'Then I obey. Teelee, honey, could you get a Heineken from the fridge and pour it into a soup bowl?'

Teelee came to life and rose gracefully to her feet, clinging hard to her groggy child as if something unspeakably evil might pop out of nowhere at any time to claim the little girl. 'And one for you, love?' she asked.

'No. You're bananas, Gloria.'

For all the pain she must have been in, Gloria offered a weak smile. 'Don't worry. My only mission now is trying to keep L.A. macho men with too many weapons from coming after Bakersfield macho men with too many weapons. Jack could be pretty hard to deal with, but think of LAPD SWAT declaring war on Bakersfield. Sixty-seven Rambos in 3D!'

'We've envisioned all this, hon. It's never tidy with men.' Jenny Ezkiaga moved her hand to the woman's forehead, felt the fever. 'Women together can tame this.'

'I wish it were always true.'

'We make it true.'

Teelee brought in the opened beer bottle and a bowl and fresh teaspoon.

'This home right here, your home, is a holy place,' Gloria declared.

Jack Liffey and Winston Pennycooke sat on the uncomfortable Adirondack chairs that had been provided outside the motel rooms for those who wished to watch the Pacific Ocean sunset and weren't very particular about the unsightly scene intervening – the parking lot and busy highway, plus a row of beachwear shops on the far side. The mock Sputnik on its steel pole, leaking glimmers from dozens of pinholes, pretty much ruined the sky, too. It was actually the kind of

memorably trashy L.A. vista that Jack Liffey usually saved
up to share with Maeve. Beyond all imagining. They hadn't
had the TV on and knew nothing of the shooting war going
on at the cemetery.

'I hate feeling like a fifth wheel,' Jack Liffey said.

'I-an-I don' know what dat mean,' Winston said.

Jack Liffey noticed that he'd reverted all the way back to
his comfortable vernacular, but always with a bit of a cocky
grin.

'A third tit when you have twins.'

'Ah – wurtless. Can we help Ty someway? Him OK in my
esteem.'

'Mine, too. When Stoney's man hired you to chase Ty off,
did he take you to meet Stoney?'

'No, but I seeit. Over de hills in dat big valley dere, in a
bunch of rich-man houses. Wood . . . lawn?'

'Woodland Hills?'

'Dat it!'

'Some of that's big money.'

'Not dis guy. He live in de servant house, out by de swim
pool. Nice servant house, but him not stoosh with no easy
money.'

'OK, let's go talk to Stoney, or look at the house, if you
can find it.'

Winston puzzled a moment, blocking out with a palm the
last of the blood red sunset light. The sun was just touching
its burning disc on to the black ocean, visible between two
shops. 'I know there a reason we gwine talk to de mon, but
I don' overstan' what it is,' Winston Pennycooke said. There
was no expression at all on his face.

Jack Liffey looked up at the bogus satellite, as the entire
sky reddened over their heads. He smiled. He might have been
smiling at anything. 'I don't know either, my friend. It's a
rare damn day when I know exactly what I'm doing.'

'Tennessee Williams is so hard to get your head around,' Bunny
complained. 'I'm sorry, it's not PC to say it, but he's so damn
gay. Even some of his women have the sensibility of gay males.'

'Which one are you doing?'

They were outside on the narrow rock patio, facing the coming
sunset and drinking Bunny's favorite cocktail, a Cosmopolitan,

mainly vodka plus cranberry, lime and bitters, which Maeve figured Bunny had picked up from some trendy bar.

'We only do scenes. It's just a workshop.'

'You've never had a gay experience?' Maeve asked vaguely. She thought of her own brief but all-consuming passion for Ruthie Loew in her last year of high school. Ruthie had been a notch or two up the social register, had lived in the richie-rich Palos Verdes Hills, and had taught her how to drink absinthe – dripped through a sugar cube that rested on a special perforated spoon – while most of her classmates were still learning to drink beer without making a face.

'Is that an offer?' Bunny asked.

Maeve made the most ambiguous expression she knew how to make. Bunny was big and a bit masculine but very attractive, and she appealed a bit to both sides of Maeve. 'Not at this exact moment.'

Bunny chose to laugh.

'I think about it, of course,' Bunny said. 'Maybe I'll have to work my way to the end of men first. The Stanley Kowalskis and their ilk.'

'I think I've been near there,' Maeve admitted. 'It's very consuming.'

They sipped their Cosmopolitans, which Maeve wasn't all that crazy about, but she was nothing if not obliging.

'Whoa. You can't start up and just stop.' Bunny's eyes bored into her.

What had she gotten herself into? But she liked Bunny – the woman was so big-hearted. 'I can't back into this gently, Bunny. For a time I was the girlfriend, the property really, of a gangbanger who was the leader of a Latino gang in East L.A. The Greenwoods.'

'Girl, never!'

'It's true. My weak heart went so crazy I let him jump me into his gang – but I'm sure I was nothing more than a mascot – but then he got me pregnant. It's beginning to feel like it all happened to somebody else long ago.'

'I don't believe you.'

'I wouldn't believe me either, but look.' Maeve unbuttoned the top of her blouse and pulled her bra cup down enough to show off most of the ornate Olde English letter G crudely tattooed on her left breast. She covered up quickly.

'Merciful heavens!'

'Please keep my secret. I don't know how others would take it all. But I've got a past, Bunny.' And you don't know the half of it, she thought. Well, maybe she did know just about half of it. If Maeve had another Cosmopolitan she'd be talking about Ruthie, too.

'How amazing! If you were in theater arts, you could really work with that. They always tell you to use your own experience.' Bunny rested a big rough hand affectionately on her wrist, and it meant a lot. 'Are you OK, now? You seem so sensible. I just can't believe you ran with the Mexican bangers.'

She thought of telling Bunny that she'd dyed her hair black and run away from her dad and even scraped together a kind of apartment home for Beto for a while, stuck amidst all his stolen merchandise, teaching herself forlornly to cook Mexican to please him. And waiting a terrifying forever every evening for Beto to come back. It really had been another time and place, and maybe she'd been someone else. 'I think I'm a bit impulsive,' Maeve said. 'Probably something I can unlearn in college.'

The front door slammed, probably Axel. Maeve made a shush gesture and Bunny nodded.

'Who's on deck?'

'The rest of the Hillbrow crew.'

'Want a Cosmo? I'm good at it,' Bunny offered.

'I'm too beered up. I'll grab a sparkling water.'

There was a lot of banging in the house and Bunny and Maeve smiled at one another. Axel never did anything quietly, setting a frying pan down on the stove or even taking off a sweater.

Axel slammed open the French door to the darkening patio and announced, 'That pretty well puts paid to Jean-François! People don't always do what they promise. Make a note of that.'

'No!'

'What happened?' Maeve asked, realizing with relief that her own past was a closed issue for now.

It seemed Axel's boyfriend had refused to introduce her to his French parents. They did their best to placate Axel for a while, plying her with snacks, and then as the big red sun sank behind the hills, Maeve slipped away to study. It was hard to concentrate, and she lay down for a bit, trying to let her mind clear. But the big blowzy kindly face of Bunny stayed with her.

Stoney should have pushed them all out of the car immediately, but he hadn't. He'd driven the whole load of hysterics over the hill, his nerves going jangly with it, and he'd locked the parking brake and jumped out a half mile from his home. Then he'd leapt fences and jogged through yards and gardens in the dusk, avoiding any police cruisers – or anyone else – who might be after him. A gunbattle could gel-up the sense of self-preservation wonderfully, that was for sure. He still carried the Israeli Desert Eagle pistol in his coat pocket, unfired as far as he remembered. He wondered who was still alive from the Rollin' Seventies. Harper? He was so addled he couldn't remember seeing any of them running away, as he'd ordered.

Hurriedly, in his little cabana, he packed a sports bag with underwear, a prepaid cellphone in the name of E. Manny Kant, and his emergency stash of twenty dollar bills that he kept in a hollowed-out old philosophy textbook, cut out initially as a dope ditch for his office at Valley JC. He'd lived outside the law so much of his life – but not quite like this, not on the run from stone crazy killers who seemed to skin their enemies alive. Why would they do that? To make a point? You *Colombianos* don't much like me and my friends. Man, I get it, truly, he thought. Can't we all just get along? He could feel his mind starting to go off on a free float, but he dragged it back to the business at hand. He was utterly unused to this recurrence of the state of panic.

He grabbed his car keys and headed out the door, but where to . . . ? He didn't want to go too far, because he knew the tacos would have to bounce out of the country pretty soon, given all the carnage they were leaving in their wake. And he wanted to try to pick up the pieces of what was left of his poor crew. It wasn't just every day you could build up a functioning distribution network for the weight that he'd been dispersing. Too bad the profit had mostly been reinvested in more goof, but that had always been his way. Pay the guys well, no show-off flossin', no spinning rims on his car, no leopard-fur jackets. A modest little place to stay and a modest lifestyle, befitting the good reliable community college man (and befitting his modest IRS payments). Preening goeth before a fall. Being with the Panthers in L.A., in their most abstemious phase, had primed him for it. He still had true respect for a lot of them. Bunchy from the Slauson gang, Masai, Geronimo Pratt, Ericka, Angela, Franco and John Kelley. People you could have built a whole world with.

But where to hide out now? You could never tell – a lot of motels wanted a name these days, a real DMV name. And he didn't want to risk staying at the home of anyone he knew – the risk for them. They'd probably all be listed on his police jacket, and he was pretty sure the *Colombianos* or their Eighteenth Street allies had their own dirty cops to access that. For just an instant he thought of his new-found son, if he was his son, Tyrone Bird, but he had no idea where Ty lived, and looking for a movie star in L.A. was like wearing a neon hat saying, Look at me! I'm an asshole from Kansas!

Thinking of Ty brought to mind the whole spiral of feelings about Mel and the Sandstone Retreat in the hills. He knew the place had closed down long ago, and the whole isolated campus had been left abandoned, probably overrun with its own special ghosts and vampires – the tormented spirits of all that freaked-out sex. Hell, he thought all at once, that could be just the hideaway crib he needed. If he could remember the way to get there and then break in.

On the way to Woodland Hills, Jack Liffey and Winston listened to the local twenty-four hour radio news – not much choice since his frazzled old car radio had been stuck on that AM slot for years – and they finally heard about the astounding gunfight at Hillside Cemetery in Culver City, and the police hunt going on for two warring drug gangs – one from South Central and another from Latin America.

'That's our lads,' he said.

'For true, ma'an.' Winston punched Jack Liffey's shoulder softly. 'Cha, stop! Dat de place. Right dere. Wit' de big black Bent-Leg in de drive.'

Jack Liffey stopped the car across the pseudo-country lane, Topochico Road, no sidewalks but pretty fancy homes. A small building jutted above the low wall in the dusk, clearly not the main house on this property, especially with the Bentley coupe in the drive. 'Are you sure, Winston?'

'Mos' def.'

He was getting tired of the patois again. 'How about going back to Standard English, just for me?'

'Definitely, sir,' Winston said, grinning from ear to ear.

'Let me go first here. People who look like you and jump over a wall sometimes draw a stray shot or two in this country.'

'You do what your heart say, Mr Jack.'

'My heart says, Send in the First Armored ahead of us.'

He walked cautiously up the gravel driveway to what it soon became obvious was a pool house in front of a much bigger pseudo-Tudor mansion that lay back across fifty yards of lawn and an even more substantial gate. The Bentley was in a wide spot of the drive before the second gate. A light was on in the pool house, leaking across the flagstones beside the shimmery water that was lit weakly from below. Jack Liffey had brought his old .45, but he left it in the creaky leather shoulder holster under his armpit. He'd bought the holster and pistol at a firearm swap-meet many many years back when those things were still allowed by the gun-sale laws. By and large, he'd found that waving a big gun around was more trouble than it was worth, but it had occasionally been useful in his job.

Winston was dutifully a few feet behind him as he arm-vaulted the low wall. The front door of the pool house wasn't quite closed, which gave him a chill. A vertical crack of light fanned its glow through the faint mists off the heated pool, like an entry to another dimension. He reached back and held his hand briefly on Winston Pennycooke's chest to stay him. No sense in both of them getting killed here.

Jack Liffey pushed the door open slowly. 'Mr Stone, I'm a friend.'

But it was obvious right away that the place was empty. Drawers were standing open, suggesting a rush to depart, but not enough drawers to suggest a burglary.

'He's running,' Jack Liffey said. 'I bet he was at that shoot-out and decided not to stay here.'

'You say that with satisfaction?'

This Jamaican had a sensitive radar for tone of voice. 'Lord, did I? I guess I just get pleased with myself when I figure anything out. I'm not much of a detective, Winston, but I keep coming. That's my virtue.'

'Like Mr Steam Train.'

'Just like Mr Steam Train. Now let's see what we can find out about Mr Marcus Stone.'

'*Jefe* . . .'

Orteguaza was deep in thought and did not want to look up. He and his *compadres* – a restless army who'd been yanked out of the battle before they could deliver the final blow – were sleeping or waiting restlessly in the big room that was jammed with old sofas and threadbare easy chairs. Eighteenth Street had dropped them in this Pico-Union basement near downtown, to hide them away from the prodigious police search that was going on all over the city, and then all the Eighteens had gone away, vanished off the earth. Sirens were keening near and far like the *Keystonéttos*, on their big slapstick hunt.

Estuardo, their contact from Eighteenth Street, had come back to bring them a large cardboard tray of Mexican food, burritos, tacos, tamales and little plastic tubs of an inedible fiery red sauce. They'd found the food rather exotic and just palatable. To a man, they'd have preferred McDonald's burgers.

'*Jefe*, we going to be able to get back on the airline?'

'Of course not, Andrés. *El Diablo* will send us a plane out in the desert where we don't have to show our passports. We'll fly out low and fast in the dark. *El corporación* takes care of its own.'

'That's good, man! We really shot the shit out of *El Los*, right?' He was grinning.

'They're used to it. You've seen the movies. *Heat* is the best. Pacino and De Niro both.'

'No, "Say hello to my leetle fren"',' somebody shouted in thick English – the Al Pacino line from *Scarface* about his assault rifle with a grenade launcher, a line that every gang-banger, roughhouser and petty criminal in the world repeated endlessly.

Ferdinand looked up slowly from his comic book. '*¿Pasaportes?*' Then in English: 'We don' got to show you no stinkin' passports!'

Jhon Orteguaza had seen *The Treasure of the Sierra Madre*, too, but he refused to smile. 'Shut up, everybody. This isn't movie night. We'll get home safe as doves, I promise. But our honor is still in the smoke. We've got to make sure we leave the big Mr Marcus Stone kicking his little feet in the air. So everybody knows we did it.'

The house was down in a canyon, but the bands of haze boiled up behind the eastward hills and they were lit up a dull purple neon a half hour before the local sunrise. Stoney had slept restlessly on the fetid mattress facing the curtainless wall of windows downstairs at Sandstone, one of the original fuck-mattresses from the 'ball-room,' judging from the odor. The seemingly abandoned place had had a caretaker after all, some aging and rather dense cowboy in a strap undershirt who'd offered him a tour of Sandstone the night before for cash money, and money meant nothing to Stoney just then. He had plenty from his just-in-case running stash. A little ready money and a sharp word or two had transformed the sightseeing tour – the last thing he wanted – into an untroubled sojourn.

Stoney tossed off a prickly blanket and sat up on the mattress to watch as a pinprick of bloody light caught fire above the hills, and then, slowly, an arc of the red disc formed. He couldn't remember the last time he'd seen a sunrise, and this terrible fiery spectacle couldn't be a normal one or everyone on earth would go straight back to bed.

A few pills and a bottle of Scotch offered by the old geezer had calmed him down the night before, but they'd worn off now. He was as edgy as he'd ever been. He'd have to find out if the place had a TV and try to catch the news.

A dark figure at the top of the internal staircase gave him a fright. He really was jumpy, he thought, his mind leaping about like a scalded grasshopper. But why not, after getting shot up and rocketed by these *Colombiano* madmen?

'Coffee, mister?'

Was hell run by the father of your lies or the father of your wishes? Stoney wondered. An old Philosophy One question. What an unruly mind he had going now – the fault of too much reading when he was too young.

The pounding noise finally awoke Joe Lucius, and he staggered to the flimsy door of his trailer, where he'd never before spent the whole night without going home, but last night's whores had exhausted him.

He opened the door on one of the last faces he wanted to see:

Meier Reston, looking for some reason like he'd just swallowed the canary. Behind Reston, a gigantic dull red moon
– no, by god, it was the sun – was rising over the pathetic
little skyscrapers of Long Beach, burning its way through
ribbons of crimson cloud stretched across the sky. Maybe I
should reshoot *The Red Balloon* – is that what the world is
telling me? That old French chestnut was so full of pathos
it would make a tree vomit. Jesus, Joe. But just as his mind
was trying to grapple with the little boy and his willful sentient
balloon, one of the whores shoved past him and then past
Meier and ran clutching her half-buttoned clothing toward a
yellow Corvette.

'I hope you got Tyrone Bird in hand, not bush, fuckhead.'

'I got him long ago, Joe, and he's sleeping in his own trailer
right over there with two gorillas outside watching the door.
But I wanted to warn you he's back on his psych meds, and
we'll have to talk about that. But you look like you ought to
get a little more rest first.'

Lucius realized he was utterly nude except for his Breitling
wristwatch, and he had a full woodie morning erection, Cialis
leftover, which Meier was trying hard not to stare at. 'Ah,
Reston – aren't you afraid of growing old?'

The whore's Corvette growled to life.

'Yes, I am, sir.'

'I'm more afraid of *not* growing old.' He slammed the
flimsy door, which bounced all the way open, to summon the
attention of two girl stagehands who were walking across the
parking lot, both of whom started giggling at his erection.
Lucius closed the door again with two steady hands.

Despite the dulling effect of the drugs and some muddled
dream-memories of a lot of excitement the day before, I wake
up early and realize that I'm in my own star-trailer on the set
on Terminal Island, surrounded by my old clothes and various
other effects of mine. All those workshirts, a pair of Farmer
Johns, that damn *Vanity Fair* with my interview that I've never
been able to read all the way through, the makeup kit like a
fishing tackle box, even the black wood Makonde sculpture
of a distorted Picasso-like face that I usually bring along. Why
do I bring that? Ugh. The motels with their junk art had been
a relief. I've come to hate my own things, and I get so I never

really want to see any of them again. They remind me of a
bubble of intolerable loneliness and pain, surrounded by chatter
so rapid and shrill I can't even make it out. The usual movie
set, I guess. I'd almost rather see one of the Skinnies cart-
wheel past now. But I feel a woozy heaviness all over and
know I'm deep into the med.

I can just barely think straight. I feel it's time for a real
break in my life – dropping a great knife across the track of
my actions to mark a new era – maybe something to do with
a normal person who has a father. But I know I'm expected
to jump back into playacting this morning, as if I never left.

The Himes script is tented on the little built-in kitchen table,
bristling with Post-its, but I can't bear the idea of studying lines,
and I go to the trailer door and open it and sit on the stoop,
watched abruptly by the two thugs from last night, sitting on
folding chairs and eating off paper plates, very alert now. I ignore
them. Already, set dressers and best boys and face-dabbers are
scurrying to and fro, and in the distance I see a whole crowd
of 'atmosphere' talent in dated-looking work clothes waiting
patiently behind sawhorses. Caterers are setting up under a long
awning – it'll be coffee, danish and doughnuts, bagels and the
trimmings, maybe even a steam tray of hard-boiled eggs.

Above the food awning, a surreal red tennis ball is entrapped
in bands of horizontal crimson netting, rising slowly and burning
my eyes. I've never been able to look away from things.

'Morning, Mr Bird,' a man in an electric fetch-cart calls
cheerily as he burrs past.

I nod. I'm not sure if I can speak at all.

> How can I still be so confused? Is it boys or girls? Anthro
> or something else? School or run off to Europe? I don't
> even know if Bunny would want me, and I'm not sure
> I can get out of anthro. I'm torn between memory and
> desire. Who was it said that? Today will tell on anthro,
> I guess. All the art history classes are closed, but I have
> a lead on a sketching class if the old Czech who teaches
> it will let me in. I wonder what would be best to convince
> him? A beret? A short skirt? Cleavage? Be serious,
> Maeve. Confusion and I speak a common language. Gotta
> get out of bed and get going.

Maeve hid the new diary away under the mattress, and, in her bathrobe, she went to the kitchen and brewed the first pot of the day. The kitchen was untouched since her midnight snack of Cheerios – this was just supposition from the abandoned bowl that was still on the table, not a sly hair taped to the fridge door as a test. She wondered if she got that sense of detective melodrama from her dad. Where else?

The coffeemaker was too slow. She poured a tiny glass of pomegranate juice and wandered out on to the patio. With the steep hills opposite, the sun wasn't up yet, only bands of dark cloud with maroon linings underneath. In Topanga there would always be long teasing twilights at both ends of the day, she thought. It was the price of living in a canyon.

Then as she sat down, the first crimson ray shot upward from the slope near the top of the tallest hill, loosed from a tiny burning hole in the sky. Wow! She watched the dot swell into a thin slice of a molten red disc. She'd never seen the sun quite this deep red and wondered if it had to do with firesmoke somewhere nearby. Everyone she'd met in the canyon lived in utter terror of fire.

The night before, Loco had been ecstatic to see him, uncharacteristically doggy in his affection, licking his hand and mewling and banging his rump against Jack Liffey's leg for a petting. Señora Campos across the street had made her way over to tell him – in their muddle of broken English and broken Spanish – that she'd noticed the lack of cars in the driveway and decided to come across and feed the ailing dog. She kept the key for emergencies, and he'd felt guilty for letting himself get distracted and not calling her to ask her to look in on Loco.

Jack Liffey made himself the strongest coffee he could manage. Winston was crashed face down on Maeve's bed, still fully fluorescent in his Jamaican outfit, sleeping off too much rum and Coke. She wasn't likely to scurry back from UCLA midweek, and if she did, he knew she'd be a good sport and take the sofa.

He carried the cup of brown mud out on to the front porch to try to think, a nearly hopeless enterprise on four hours sleep. As usual (in the rare instances he was up this early) he was astonished by the spirited activity at dawn in Boyle Heights,

Latino east Los Angeles. Under an unusually eerie red sky, men bicycled off to work, women dragged along big plastic ice-chests of tamales on lopwheeled wagons, young men under hoods banged on car engines. His whole being was in an uproar over Gloria, who owned the house along with his heart, and should have been there about twice over by now. He figured he'd been getting nothing but lies and evasions from Bakersfield, but this was the last day he was going to put up with that.

Then, like an aggressive challenge, a ruby laser beam flared straight at him from over the Campos house. The air around him filled with a kind of unidentifiable reddened foreboding. A spark at the base of the laser beam spread slowly into a burning wafer, then a furnace door left open. He sat on the steps and nodded as a young Latino he probably should have recognized, but could barely see against the glare, walked past and waved to him.

The blood-and-fire sun formed itself unbearably at the bottom of a striped purplish sky as he began to wonder which crisis demanded his attention first. And was the arrival of too many crises all at once just the human condition?

They had got her up out of bed, and dragged her feet as far as the front porch of Jenny's house in Bakersfield and then had to take a rest so they sat her on the old barrel chair there. Gloria was partially awake but obviously in trouble and couldn't help them much with the shifting of her weight. Sonny Theroux and Jenny Ezkiaga had been informed the night before that if they got Gloria to the Harrison Memorial Women's Center by seven o'clock, well before it officially opened at nine, their friendly doctor would meet them and take some discreet X-rays and other scans of her injuries.

As they waited, panting, on the verandah, the sun began to peek over the Sierra foothills to the east, discolored only a little by the ugly veil of Central Valley smog that had matured over the last two decades of runaway growth.

'We may need more help with the weight,' Sonny said, panting with effort and soured by lack of sleep.

'Bite your tongue,' Jenny snapped. 'Let's find out if she's going to live.'

'I'm alive,' came a weak voice, her eyes still shut. 'I plan to stay that way.'

'Another country heard from. I meant nothing, my sweet. I love every ounce of your abundant body.'

'Shut up, Sonny! Back your van up on to the grass.'

On the TV news the night before they'd seen frenzied reports of some big drug war going on in L.A. ninety miles to the south, apparently a kind of shoot-out usually only seen in films, but they had no idea at all that the insane drug war involved Jack Liffey, if only indirectly.

Orteguaza was sick of being cooped up in the basement, and he took himself up the stairs to the street door of the tenement. His men were all snoring away on the sofas and chairs below, but he never slept more than an hour or two at a time, and then only lightly. He figured he was part vampire or maybe the famous animal-sucking *chupacabra* of Mexico, and he would eventually have to go wandering the nights in search of blood. He was only half joking when he worked himself into this mood. Jhon Orteguaza read his horoscope every day in the Barranquilla *El Heraldo*. He believed almost everything he read, especially when it had to do with disasters or betrayals. Betrayal was his great truth of life, and only fools refused to anticipate it from every direction.

He opened the street door and stepped out boldly, as befits a man of special gifts. Shorter people of approximately his own skin color, mostly contemptible Central American *mestizos*, were rushing left and right, carrying baskets and boxes of common things to sell or hurrying to the bus to some menial job far away. One man was inexplicably dragging an engine block along the street with a rope, making a terrible scraping sound. He wondered when Eighteenth Street would get back to him with news from their own dirty cop. There was a tension in him: he had no choice, but these gangbangers, like so many others here, were not fully honoring his status, or even his manhood.

Then he was hit in the face by the god of fire. In the narrow gap between two tall buildings, across that ugly street, a red eye opened suddenly to him alone, pinning him in place with its scorching regard. The eye began pumping into him a boundless wrath that came from very ancient times – the times when games had been played with human heads for balls, and the losers became the next game.

Yes, he thought. Do not trouble yourself, great *Fuego*. He recognized Fire himself. I am of your belief. I will do my duty to our joint wrath before I leave this city, or you may incinerate everything.

SEVENTEEN
I Can't Go On I'll Go On

The old man staggered bowlegged down the stairs with a cup of coffee that, after the first taste, Stoney knew could only have been boiled grounds, cowboy-style, tasting like battery acid.

'You may not credit it no credit, but I recollect you, Mr Stone, from so long ago. You was always polite as the barkeep to a sheriff.'

'Was I?' Stoney wondered how many blacks had come though this stinker, after all. 'I may not be so damn polite any more.'

'I got a good think-box still 'cause I got out of stunts in time,' he said, apropos of nothing. 'I worked on the TV oaters in the early sixties but I quit the horse tricks before I got throwed too much. Lucky to get this gig, sir. I remember it all – the movie stars, the senators, the famous folk. And the bad nights with some poor girlie going crazier'n a biting boar. A little too much sex for some. Some nights it was a young husband, thought he wanted to see things he really didn't.'

Stoney sipped his boiled mud as the sun outside rose out of the murk and became a big yellow traffic light. Caution.

'A little too much privilege gone berserk for me,' Stoney said. He might have said 'white privilege,' but he rather liked the old fart and saw no point in needling him with stuff he'd only take the wrong way.

'For sure, some's got more money than they can keep dry. They wasn't all so pretty in their behavior, I tell you.'

'But you put up with a lot of it, didn't you?'

The old cowboy shrugged. 'I saw more tits and pussy than a gyner-cologist. Got my share of nookie down here, too. But here's the thing I used to exercise my think-pan about. Say you build you a really big room, like this room, and you put up four of these new flattie TVs on the four walls. One of them's got a fancy sermon on saving your soul, all in rousing talk. Next one's got Mr Shakespeare or suchlike, a really good one with good actors. The next one is showing a talk about science and ee-volution, interesting as hell with platypuses and aardvarks. And the last one's got a loop of one of them classy pornos of the seventies – *Behind the Green Door* or *The Devil in Miss Jones*. Where do you think most people gonna end up when you let 'em loose in that room for a while?'

Stoney laughed. 'That supposed to be your contribution to philosophy, old man?' He tried to drink another sip of the dark sludge. The old fart wasn't quite the bumpkin he feigned. Stoney wouldn't have minded settling back with the old poop and some genuine coffee, maybe a hair of Jack Daniels, and have a nice bar yak, but it was important not to relax this morning. Too much to worry about. 'Anybody from those times ever come back here for a look-see?'

'Not so much recent-like. Things around here got quieter'n a hole in the ground after the last boss lost heart for the sex game and left. All the true believers went like cats runnin' from a broken vase. Later the property owner got some renters in over in the east wing for a while, but they gone. Ain't no buyers. I like the peace. I can't never seem to move my draggy carcass on.'

'Visitors. Think.'

'That movie star showed up a week ago, but I told you that. Tyrone Bird.'

'I'll pay you generous room rental, old man, for a few days' stay, but you've got to keep your trap shut about me. Got a TV?'

'Nothing fancy but she works. Up in the old kitchen. I practically live total in the kitchen.'

'Any weapons here?'

His eyes slitted a little. 'You be the huntee, Mr Stone?'

'Call me Stoney. What does it look like with me nervous as hell? If they find me, these crazy assholes will skin us both alive and crucify us to the wall. And that's not a fucking metaphor, Mr Cowboy.'

'It's them Colombians from the TV news. Betcha.'

'I asked – weapons?'

'One old double-barrel that been sawed off, and one box of 12-gauge shells. Never used. Ain't much.'

'Keep it close to you, friend. That's yours. I've got my own. This is just like the worst of the Indian days. The last round goes in your mouth.'

Reston has set up shop under a freestanding awning that he's co-opted from a makeup crew. We're well off shot. He's the troubleshooting producer, but he seems to be wearing an assistant director's hat as well to coach me on my lines for the first shot, while makeup dabs annoyingly at my face. Right in front of us the best boy and the gaffer are unrolling cable for an arclight, and two other crew are playing with a collapsible reflector, trying to see where their mischief can send the big glary circle of sunlight among the waiting extras who turn their backs or give them the finger.

'"Are you the kind of guy to jeopardize his whole future because some ignorant white guy calls him a nigger?"' Reston reads in a tinny unconvincing voice. It's supposed to be my white lover, Alice. Conny Hughes is playing her damn well, and she's been a good sport about my absence.

'"Hear my story first,"' I say without much acting.

His eyes contract with worry, but he goes on: '"If the white people hated you as much as you hated them—"'

'"They'd kill me now and have done with it,"' I say. I can tell it's got no real conviction. I always save that up. '"And that'd be fine."'

'Hold on,' Reston says. 'Ty, your feelings are a thousand miles away.'

'I got the lines, man. The rest will come when we're rolling, trust me. I *am* Bob Jones. I know him like my brother.'

'You've got no brother. Bob Jones is broke and angry, and he needs this welding job desperately, and his white lover is just starting to realize that he's wrapped so tight he's inevitably going to blow up and turn himself into a loser.'

'Yeah, yeah. You don't think I grew up with three or four angry and self-destructive niggers in every school class?'

'Don't make this a black thing, man.'

'*What*? The whole movie is a black thing!'

'Sorry, sorry, sorry. Ty! I didn't mean it that way, man. I meant a thing against me. This is a big moment in the movie. Joe is going to make fifty retakes until he sees something he really likes. He's already pissed off at you. I'm on your side, believe me. This is the scene where Bob just begins to kick back at the whites, when he doesn't even have to yet.'

'I get it, man. You know, it's wrong that they moved this scene to her car. It should be at the party at her house, with all the white Commies doing their best to get down with the blacks.'

'You know that's gone, Ty. Commies is totally gone. It is what it is. I promise you, the new script works. You been around long enough to know you can't ever film a novel word for word.'

'Maybe that's the problem,' I say.

'Maybe you shouldn't be taking all those mind-killer drugs when you're trying to do real work.'

'Pecker – you got a real knack for saying the wrong fucking thing.' I turn away from this geek and walk back toward my trailer, wondering if I can get into my dented Porsche behind the trailer before a dozen grips tackle me. At least the two gorillas are gone, which makes better odds.

'Most Señor Orteguaza,' the unexpected voice from the street called him away from watching a young long-haired beauty who was walking toward him with some of the most immense bouncing *chupas* he'd ever seen.

'What is it?' He saw it was Estuardo, leaning out of an old Chevy, with someone else driving. He was obviously unwilling to get out of the car and stand near him, as if Orteguaza carried some disease. He wondered if Eighteenth Street were about to cut them loose, or worse. Betrayal was always the most probable act. The horoscopes had warned him about this trip.

'Man, I got what you want,' Estuardo said.

'What's that?'

Estuardo glanced around first. He saw the same woman still approaching, and waited while she walked disdainfully between them, his head almost bobbing with all that soft flesh. '*Alma mía, te adoro intolerablemente*,' Estuardo called out. She made a shooing gesture and went on without pause.

'Friend,' Orteguaza said gently. He touched the pistol in his coat and was very close to blowing the kid away unexpectedly, almost always the best policy.

'*¡Tremenda!* I bet that *puta* has nipples the size of *béisbols.*'

'What is it that you have for us, *amigo*? Are you sending us to hell?' Orteguaza's hand fished slowly into his jacket pocket and curled around the .357 Magnum.

'*¡Ay, coño, no!* Man, our cop says all the known cribs of this American nee-gro are clean as Tide Soap, and that he is in the wind. Every *policía* in ten cities is looking for his gang, those you didn't kill, plus the *federales*, and they look for you, too, of course – you got to know that, you all over the TV. But my good friends offer you three places from the man's distant past, where he might run, out of love for you. Don't ever call me or Eighteen again.' Estuardo dropped a piece of folded paper on the sidewalk contemptuously, and the car accelerated away.

Orteguaza stood with his legs braced and very nearly pulled out the pistol to let off a shot at the heads as the car receded, but the growling old muscle car got away fast, and he didn't do it. He knew the alliance with Eighteenth Street, that *El Diablo* had worked so hard on, was over now. Best to finish business here and get home, and they could start over from a new genesis, with advice from new witch-men and new horoscope. *El Diablo* in Medellin could betray, too.

He sighed and picked up the note off the sidewalk.

Pierce College, Philosophy Department, the first line said. And then it gave two addresses, one identified as **old residence**, and the other as **famous free-sex cult: Señor Stone was known visitor**.

Time to wake up the boys, he thought.

'Time to rise and shine. What do you want for breakfast?' Jack Liffey shook the Jamaican's shoulder, and he could feel how muscled and young Winston was, without too much envy, though the lad was still dead to the world. He shook some more and waited. Winston eventually turned over and sat himself up on Maeve's bed like a mechanical vampire. Jack Liffey gently handed him a cup of coffee.

'Take it slow. Do you have a breakfast order?'

'Okra and boiled banana.' He sniffed the cup. 'You got tea, mon?'

'Okra's all run out, but tea I can do. Maeve has some English breakfast tea somewhere. You want it strong with milk?'

Winston nodded and tried to focus. 'I dream of that poor man on TV. The one they peel off his skin. Why they do that?'

Jack Liffey paused at the door. 'Come to the kitchen and talk to me while I'm brewing. You can tell me if you've got a convincing theory of evil. I sure don't.'

Jack Liffey hunted in the cabinets until he found the English tea. Right beside Maeve's guilty stash of apple strudel Pop-Tarts. It was in round teabags without the danglies, and he rinsed out the china pot with hot water, as once instructed, and put several of the bags in the ugly Wedgwood pot while he boiled water in a saucepan. Fancy teakettles were in short supply in Boyle Heights, right along with okra. Lord, does anybody really eat okra and boiled bananas in the morning, he wondered, or was Winston pulling his leg?

He could hear Winston peeing hard for what seemed five minutes with the bathroom door open. Jack Liffey resisted the urge to step into the hall and see if his dick really was a whole lot bigger. Eventually the Jamaican wandered into the kitchen, tugging up the waistband of his striped wrestler pants, and sat wearily.

'I believe Mr Marcus Stone is in dread and trouble,' he said.

'No shit.'

'Rituals of blood in the burning,' Winston chanted.

'Jesus Christ – what's that?'

'Just a song that come to me, Mr Jack.'

'Just Jack, please. You know anything about these Colombians? They sound more than unusually crazy to you?'

'Back on J, we say Colombians got the money sickness. It's about all those drugs emanating from their country and all that money emanating back the other way.'

'Neither of those things emanate, Winston,' Jack Liffey said. 'People carry them. Some poor souls in Colombia, trying to get to America, are made to swallow rubber balloons of pure coke and then fly up here to shit them out and make a few bucks. Or die, if the balloons spring a leak.'

'I know all dat stuff. But, Jack, why some ma'an go cut de skin off another ma'an? That a sickness, for true.'

'I used to think evil like that could only be a sickness,' Jack Liffey said. 'But then you meet some very sick people, like Tyrone, that don't have an atom of cruelty in them. You've

got to think, Why is this sick one evil, why not that sick one?
Are we stuck with the way the dice roll? You believe in a
God?'

'Not so much,' Winston said.

The water started boiling noisily in the saucepan and Jack
Liffey poured it into the teapot. 'Me, neither. I used to think
I had a grasp on things like cruelty and mean spirit, but the
whole idea I had then is just gone, poof. I don't seem to have
a clue any more.' He gaped into the teapot and watched the
turbulence start to settle out.

'My life slowed way down last year for a while. I was
without my voice or working legs after a bad accident, and I
had to really listen to everything, to wood floors creaking,
refrigerators starting to hum, windows just making their little
pops in the sun, to the grumbles deep in my own body. Even
my woman confuses me now. I know it's deeply dangerous
to start attributing reasons to things that just happen, but I
think I've started to want reasons.' He knew he'd better just
let the tea brew and stop brooding, so he sat down in silence
for a while, with the redness turning to yellow in the sunlight
flooding into the kitchen.

'Maybe there's got to be great suffering to weigh up in the
scale so that good can exist,' Winston Pennycooke said.

'You got a plausible reason for that?'

Winston considered, then frowned. 'Not really.'

'I wish I believed in a world with giant gods who look like
elephants and play jokes on people – like the Hindus,' Jack
Liffey said. 'But only playful jokes.'

Winston smiled. 'I know Ganesha. My good mate in school
was an East Indian.'

'What do you believe?' Jack Liffey asked. 'You don't think
Haile Selassie is a god, the way your brother did?'

'Oh, no. That's so dimwit. At school we all say it's the
homemade philosophy of the poor.'

'Nice.' Jack Liffey stood up. 'I'll make us some toast. Sorry
that's all. No okra here, mon.'

I guess I believe in Samuel Beckett, Jack Liffey told himself,
as he worked deliberately at slicing the whole-grain bread.
Neither of them said a word for a long time. I can't go on
I'll go on.

*   *   *

'Watch the bump at the door.'

They pushed Gloria's wheelchair over the slight hump out of the X-ray room and on into a small side office in the dark building. She looked pretty used up, almost a zombie, after a thorough series of standing, sitting, lying and tilted exposures, and a lot of prodding of sore spots with the business end of an ultrasound.

One of the techs had been called in early, and she'd proven a good sport and helped out a lot after she'd heard Dr Morretti's spin on events. The doctor was developing the X-rays herself in the darkroom.

'How do you feel, Gloria?' Jenny asked.

'Like a million dollars,' she said, but her tightly closed eyes belied it.

'If they let us go, you can sleep all the way home.'

A million Confederate dollars, Sonny thought. He rested his hand on her shoulder, knowing that he'd soon be losing her, at least for the foreseeable future. It meant a lot to him when she reached up blindly and pressed down on his hand briefly. She'd been lusty enough in bed but had rarely shown him simple affection. An angry stubborn beast at bay.

'After we get you out of here, is there anything else we need to know about what happened?' Sonny asked her. Any other dead bodies, he meant.

Jenny tried to shush him.

'No, we need to know,' he insisted.

Gloria seemed to be trying to focus her attention and not having a lot of success. 'Those horrible men who assaulted my mother in Lone Pine. Then left her in a gutter in freezing weather,' she said softly. 'That was forty years ago. I wonder if those two damn cops knew I'm Indian. So they could fuck the old squaw any time they wanted.'

'We're never going to know what they thought,' Sonny said. He wasn't sure if the news of their death had percolated down through her pains and dreams. 'You took care of that, Glor. Those pricks are dead as corned beef. You were lucky you got to snatch an ankle piece. They'd have killed you sure.'

'I don't remember much, I think they drugged me.'

'Keep it that way,' Jenny said, pressing a hand to Gloria's warm forehead.

'We'll deal with the leftovers,' Sonny said. 'Where's that doctor?'

She must have heard him from the open door to the hall. 'Just let me write it up for her own doctor.'

'We can fax later,' Sonny said. 'Right now we'll take the X-rays wet and whatever it is you get out of a sonogram. We've gotta go before there's trouble.'

The doctor came in. 'Then I have to wrap her chest. You've got three broken ribs, Gloria. Can you hear me?'

Gloria nodded.

'The rebuilt breast. It was cancer, I guess. The sac is smashed and the silicone is on the loose. You'll want that drained and fixed, but it's not critical. You might need your spleen out. I'd have an MRI when you get home. You were really worked over by at least one strong and angry male. The bruises and edema you can live with, but the ribs are going to hurt. Here's some genuine painkillers. Be careful of them, they're addicting.'

'Don't want 'em.'

'Take them and be brave later.' She tucked the bottle into Gloria's shirt pocket, an old shirt of Jenny's, far too big.

'Who's driving her?' Dr Morretti asked.

'I am,' Sonny said.

'No, I am.' Jenny looked daggers at Sonny. 'What do you want – a comic book fistfight with Jack when you get her home? Go away now, Sonny. You've got duty and love all mixed up, and it can sort itself out later.'

He made an angry face, but realized that she was right. He couldn't bear to deal with Jack, not right now. And, in truth, it was a torment to hear Gloria moan now and then with some indescribable pain as her wheelchair moved. Besides, Jenny had a cushy station wagon, an old Buick, and Gloria could lie down in back. He made a mental note to grab a mattress, maybe swipe one from the clinic.

'Whatever I can do, Jenny.'

Gloria's eyes slitted open for a moment.

OK, Sonny thought to himself, quit spittin' on the handle and get to work. 'I love you more than myself,' Sonny leaned in and whispered. 'I'll see you again.' And to the doctor, quietly: 'We've got to snag a mattress or a foam pad. Right away.'

*   *   *

I have no idea where to take myself once I sprint off the
rancorous film set to my car and then accelerate noisily past
the guard at the gate. By default I head east off Terminal
Island over to the Long Beach Freeway, and then I use my
cell and ask for Jack Liffey's number. The operators usually
don't help much, but I give her an extra boost of charm in
that instant before she can switch on the talking robot, and
she gives me his address off her screen. I've got GPS in the
Porsche so I know I can find him easy on Greenwood. My
life has changed, and there's no going back to Joe Lucius'
venomous movie world for now. I need my father. My next
anti-psychotic pill is due soon, and that'll be another big decision. To submerge into the woozy half-light or dance in the
sun with the Skinnies.

From a storeroom, they'd grabbed an inch-thick foam pad, in
a durable blue plastic cover, one of maybe fifty that the clinic
had held there for half a century for civil defense emergencies. They emptied various odds and ends out the back of the
station wagon into a dumpster. Then the four of them helped
Gloria off the chair and on to the pad and covered her with
a pink thermal blanket.

'Make your own way home,' Jenny said to Sonny.

'I'll take him,' Dr Morretti said.

For some reason, Sonny seemed to be in a hurry to get
away from there and he hurried the doctor up.

Jenny had to stop for gas and then the green-and-white
sheriff car started tailing her as she passed Panama Road at
the very south edge of Bako, one car and a motorcycle.

Luckily, Jenny thought, it was town cops Gloria had killed,
but that fact didn't provide much comfort when the flashing
red light came on in her side mirror, and even her toughened
heart missed a few beats.

Highway 99 was a freeway here, but you could just pull
off against the oleanders and be clear of traffic. The motorcycle cop went on past and stopped diagonally right ahead of
the station wagon to block her – in case she decided to run.
Her apprehension was going a mile a minute. Traffic laws on
state highways were the jurisdiction of the California Highway
Patrol, who mostly worked out of overpowered Mustangs, so
this wasn't about breaking the speed limit.

He looked in his late twenties, standing in the window, as she ran the glass down to let in the gathering Valley heat. He had the usual trim mustache, and that uninflected We-both-know-I'm-the-boss voice. 'License and registration, please.'

'I'm a Bakersfield attorney, sir. Which makes me an officer of the court. I need to know why you've stopped me.'

'No, you don't, ma'am. But as a courtesy to an "officer of the court", I can tell you that we received a radio call about your plate from the Bakersfield PD.'

'That's all I need to know,' she said. She sighed as she reached for the glove box.

'Freeze! Step out of the car now!'

'That's where my registration is, sir. Like about a hundred per cent of the car-owning population.'

'Step out of the car now, or I'll have to arrest you for refusing a request from a peace officer.'

'California Penal Code eight-three-two, seventeen,' she suggested. 'Broadly.' It would never have stuck, not in a million years, but it was the Catch-22 they always had. She didn't want to sit in a sheriff's substation for hours with poor Gloria wrapped in a blanket, in pain and in danger of far worse. 'OK, sir. You'll have no trouble from me.'

She showed him both palms and then opened the Buick door. His hand was resting hard on his sidearm, but he hadn't drawn it, though the keeper strap was unsnapped.

'Come out slowly, ma'am.'

'Yes, sir.' She would have said a lot more, but she knew she had to kiss ass for two, now. The last thing she wanted was Gloria dragged out of the back because she'd sassed a cop.

'Please turn around and put your hands on the hood. What's in back?'

'A very sick woman I'm taking home to L.A. on the authority of Dr Carly Morretti in Bakersfield.'

'Is the rear unlocked?'

'Yes, sir.'

'Stay right there.' He walked to the back of the car, glancing to the side quickly when dust whuffed up off the shoulder as an eighteen-wheeler blasted past on the near lane. He opened the tailgate and studied what he saw for a while, then grabbed the mattress pad and yanked it toward him several times until half the pad and Gloria's legs dangled off the tailgate.

'Sir, that woman has broken bones. She's in very bad shape.'

'So you say. We say you're using her to conceal drugs.'

'Oh, don't do this, deputy. We both know it's not true.'

Looking back at him, she noticed a familiar white panel van pull off the road behind the sheriff's car, stirring a new cloud of dust. Everybody took note immediately, and then she realized it was Sonny, and the thump-thump of danger in her chest redoubled. He hadn't gone home after all, but only a few blocks to her house to collect his van.

Sonny could get them all killed with one of his intemperate outbursts. There would be apologies later, of course, many expressions of regret, but nothing of consequence would ever be done to the deputies who'd 'accidentally' killed him and her and Gloria Ramirez.

A husky man climbed out of the passenger side of Sonny's van, carting a TV camera with a big rectangular hood on its lens. He looked like a local football hero, and Jenny thought she recognized him from a local TV crew she'd seen several times. Sonny climbed out of the driver's seat with a microphone mounting a shield that carried the number seventeen. He must have called in all his favors, she thought, and awfully fast.

'Roll tape! KGET,' Sonny called out. 'This is Bakersfield channel seventeen. Rich Arnold, reporting from the scene south of town just past Panama Road on 99, where several sheriff's deputies have stopped a mission of mercy on its way to UCLA medical center for the operation that just might save a woman's life.'

She didn't think they could actually transmit from this far out of town without a microwave truck, but she didn't know if the young deputy would realize this.

'Get out of here!' the deputy called to Sonny.

'Can't do it. We're told to follow this woman to emergency surgery at UCLA, where they're setting up now.'

A Humvee burst past in the near lane, offering them all a moment or two of pounding rap music.

'We can change your career forever, deputy,' Sonny Theroux said softly. 'Or we can shut the camera off and go on our way. It's your choice. I like the story for the noon, five and

six o'clock news, eleven if she dies. Would you identify yourself, please?'

Jenny lifted her hands from the hood and glanced at the
deputy who appeared undecided about what to do next. He
seemed half ready to draw down on Sonny, or maybe throw
his head back and bray at the sky. When his attention came
around to Gloria, he had that slightly wild expression in his
eyes of someone who was about to delaminate.

'Please, deputy,' she said softly. 'My friend is hurt bad. Be
generous. You have no idea what this is all really about.'

He looked at her blankly and gave a single shudder.

'Please push the woman back inside so we can get her to
the hospital.'

The deputy took on a businesslike manner and made a point
of feeling under her body and patting her down under the thin
blanket before pushing her back inside.

Jack Liffey wandered into the living room and turned on the old
TV. The world had gone digital, but their house hadn't. Except
for the cheap converter box that rested on top of the forty-year-
old white wood console TV the size of a tipped-over fridge. The
other half was a record changer; coming back into fashion he'd
heard. There was nothing on TV he ever wanted to see, but
Maeve watched PBS once in a while, and Gloria watched, too
– a couple of cop shows, strangely enough – and he realized this
was the way most people in America got their news.

He tuned to the locals, five, then eleven, then nine, then
eleven again, as something was dominating all the local channels. Cameras in helicopters were circling what looked like a
small flat campus somewhere, and he punched the sound up
until he could follow what was happening.

'Winston, you'd better come in here,' he called. 'Something
big is up, and I have a funny feeling.'

'I don't think I'm liking your country as much as I thought
I would,' Winston said as he came in with his steaming cup
of tea. 'I was just reading your newspaper. Even a grown man
has to cry for all the pain here.'

'There's no pain in Jamaica?'

'Almost all of us is poor together. And we don't hate so
much. Even the bad boys don't shoot into schools. Life is all
war and hate here.'

'Yeah, what is it about the well-off middle class that makes them hate so? I've never understood what's grieving them. They've got possessions and houses and tons of entertainment. Everything except grace.'

Orteguaza and his crew drove away from Pierce College in the nondescript old cars, just ahead of an arriving armada of police cars and SWAT wagons. They'd been through the philosophy department, right on through it like locusts, and they'd had to kill three professors, the hard way, before they found a woman who admitted knowing Professor Marcus Stone. This one was very old and gray, and she said the man had been gone for more than three decades. And the smart-mouth had never been as good a teacher as he thought he was, anyway. She'd clearly told the truth and earned a quick and easy death.

'Which way, *jefe?*'

'Pull over a moment.' Their short cortege stopped on a business street full of shops with Spanish words either in the store name or invitingly on the windows, and it made them feel less uncomfortable. Orteguaza studied the note. The school was eliminated. The home address was certainly out, too, if he hadn't taught at the school for thirty years. But a famous free-sex clubhouse. At least it might be entertaining. '*Buenos, muchachos.* Turn left at the next street, and we'll get on that *autopista.*'

'That's the community college where Stoney taught ages ago,' Jack Liffey said, pointing at the ever revolving aerial view. 'But that was ancient history. My God. He's been all over the world since then. Maybe he still has a friend there. He's maybe a year or two older than me, and almost nobody that age is still teaching.'

'Oh-ho,' Winston said. 'I slap your back – you turn to dust like a mummy.'

'Fuck you, Winston.' Jack Liffey chuckled and slapped his own cheek to demonstrate his solidity. 'Nothing fell off, right? Not even a moldering ear? Yeah, I'm getting old, and it's scary, too. What scares you, *mon?*'

'Nothing, ma'an.'

'Not even death?'

'I don't believe in it.'

'You will one day, I promise. I wish you had a weapon.'

'I don't like guns. Guns let fools kill heroes.'

'I've got to get you one. Sometimes the heroes have to shoot back. Let's go.'

EIGHTEEN
Luck Pays Its Dues

Before they left the house, Jack Liffey flicked through the TV news to check for any more updates on what those helicopters had spotted. It turned out to be the Colombians, for sure. About an hour ago, they'd killed an off-duty L.A. cop, some poor old desk guy who was moonlighting as security at the community college, then several teachers. It all sounded crazy as could be.

Damn – he hadn't checked up on Gloria in an hour.

He called every number he knew in Bako, while Winston waited impatiently, drinking Jamaican ginger beer, but they all just rang forever or went over to voicemail. There wasn't much point in threatening Sonny again on the tape. He'd already yanked out his left lung through his ear.

Then – what a surprise! – an immediate ringback.

'Listen to me, Sonny!' Jack Liffey snapped. But the annoyed screech meant it wasn't Sonny, after all.

'Shutup, shamus! Tyrone's gone again, running like a jackrabbit. This is going to be your last chance to earn some bread and get out of Dutch in this town. Bring in Ty Bird today and all is forgiven.'

'Meier Reston. As I live and breathe. You already consigned me to the lower circles of hell. What are you going to do now? Send me to Vietnam?' It seemed to be a day for phone threats.

'I can find something you won't like much, I bet.'

'Meier, you know the main trouble with the film business?'

'What?'

'It's full of film people.'

Sonny and his TV cameraman followed Jenny Ezkiaga's station wagon to the very foot of the Grapevine, the historic designation for the four thousand foot ascent that led out of the Central Valley toward L.A. He was pretty certain no

Bakersfield officers were following her – and the Kern County jurisdiction gave way to Los Angeles County at the top of the grade – so he felt it was about as safe as it was ever going to be to take his very annoyed captive home.

It was amazing how intimidating the presence of the TV camera had been. After a little more prodding, the deputy had grudgingly pushed Gloria into the station wagon, then glared at Sonny and the cameraman a while, as if they'd just taken his lunch, which they basically had. Then he'd refused to talk at all and driven off fast – with that spurt of raw acceleration cops always kept in reserve when they needed to say, I can always do this and you can't.

Tony Zabatta, one of KGET's prime cameramen, was looking away from Sonny in the passenger seat, still pretty pissed off at being drafted into a war he wanted no part of. The promise was a really big story.

'Sorry, man.' Sonny couldn't even remember quite what lies he'd told to get Zabatta there. He turned the van around at the little coffee-clatch of gas stations and fast-food shops at the foot of the Grapevine.

'What's this all designed to do for me?' Zabatta said.

'All my hot tips are yours exclusively from now on. And I'll watch for openings in L.A. TV, if you want the big time. And we may have saved a life.'

'You say.'

'Come on, you remember who she was. That whole business a few months ago of the mass arrest of the goth kids. Gloria made the cops look like idiots by finding the actual child-killer in two days of real police work.'

'Yeah, she came up here and stepped on every sensitive toe in town.'

'She did it in the interest of justice, man. Real justice – for all those messed-up kids – and for one baby-killer, too. Isn't justice what journalism is about?'

'I thought it was about keeping me in a well-paid career.'

Sonny gave him a big fish-eye. 'Maybe I misjudged you, Tony. I thought you were one of the good guys in TV news – they're scarce as bird-dung in a cuckoo clock.'

That did it. Zabatta laughed out loud and shook his head ruefully. 'Oh, my Sonny. Where do you get this corny-pony stuff?' He smacked Sonny's shoulder, but not too hard, just enough to dislocate it a little. 'Somebody says "justice", I think of my old man. It never worked out for him when he tried to get his life savings back from a shyster contractor and shyster mortgage outfit. Dad just needed a new roof on one side of his cottage down in Magunden, and the fine print saddled him with a balloon refi that he could never pay.'

'Hell, the mortgage crooks took the whole world economy down. Your dad's in good company.'

'There's a CHP car, Sonny. Maybe you could sideswipe it and get the state cops after our ass, too,' Zabatta suggested. 'FBI, CIA, what the hell.'

'I think you're the only Jewish cowboy I ever met,' Stoney said.

'It's just a name,' Karl Rubin said. 'I guess it's Jewish. I never went to no special sing-along.'

'Not your parents?'

He shrugged. 'Dad used to talk about his folks coming from a *shtetl*, but I don't even know what the word means. I didn't see much of him after he left us and I was sent to all the asshole fosters, which finally made me run off. I was fourteen and tried to join the Marines, but they weren't buying the fakest ID you ever seen. I ranched for a few years. It's every kid's dream, but I found out most all the cowboys are Mex now, and I just didn't fit in. Then I came out and tried to be a Hollywood cowboy. It wasn't the smartest thing I ever done. At first I got propositioned a lot by old guys in Lincolns, when I still looked young and pretty, and then I got my body mashed up doing stunt falls in the glory days of the TV Oaters. I did dozens of *Bat Masterson*s and *Wyatt Earp*s, even a couple movies. I still get residuals.'

They sat in the big industrial kitchen, with stainless steel counters and open shelves everywhere. Two industrial ranges, two wide steel fridges, a wine cabinet and a horizontal freezer chest.

'Does all this shit work?' Stoney asked, waving vaguely at all the kitchen machines.

The man shrugged. 'Owner wants to keep it all here in case there's a sudden rush of buyers. I dust it a bit.'

'How come nobody's bought the place?'

'It's only any good for a resort, or maybe a nursing home.

The house sure isn't a looker, and it's way too expensive with all the land attached.' He smirked a little. 'And nobody likes that smell downstairs. Fifty thousand loads of semen seeped into the wood floors.'

Which reminded Stoney of Tyrone Bird, who he was beginning to believe was truly his son, for all his first doubts.

'More coffee, friend?' the old man asked.

Stoney pushed his cup across the table. He was in a funny, fatalistic mood, and he took out his untraceable prepaid cell and called the number Ty had given him. He got an annoying snatch of music and then a robot voice asking him to leave a message. No name at all. 'Kid, this is you-know-who,' he answered. 'I'd like to see you. I'm at that place where you were a glint in your mom's eye. Be extra careful and don't let anybody follow you. I mean it. There's some real wigged-out Latins out there.'

When Rubin came back, instead of coffee, he set down a presentation bottle of Kentucky Spirit Wild Turkey, weirdly crenulated across its shoulders, some special brew-up of bourbon that he'd never seen before.

'There's nothing better on earth than once in a while getting a little schnocked before noon,' Rubin said. 'Guys from the old Hollywood used to tell me how Faulkner was the whizz master of Jack Daniel's over in the Garden of Allah, but I don't think he coulda touched the stunt guys I knew for quantity. Go on, paint your tonsils.'

The last thing Stoney wanted to do right now was buzz himself down, but he figured a sip might even put a little edge on, keep him alert. He was curious, too. He'd never been a bourbon man, but this was obviously special stuff. Rubin slid a jam jar with an inch of the stuff toward him.

'To good character,' Rubin toasted, holding his glass up.

'To good luck,' Stoney countered. 'Luck is the only thing I ever found that pays its dues.'

After he'd dropped the cameraman off at KGET on L Street, Sonny headed up Chester toward home across the riverbed. He was bone tired and, with Gloria gone, he felt more alone than he had in years. He was getting a little old to think he still had an endless supply of options ahead of him, just up the road. His job hadn't opened a lot of romantic doors for him, this legwork for the most notorious lesbian lawyer in town. The women he'd met were an unending parade of lonely drunks and demanding hysterics and self-centered spiritualists.

Across the marshy whipwillows poking out of the sand, he turned on to his own street, McCord. With a small frisson of alarm, he spotted Gloria's RAV-4 in his driveway. Last he knew, the cops had towed it away from the zoo to impound. How he wished he'd never showed her that bald eagle.

Sonny approached slowly and eventually parked and got out as a local Harley ratcheted past with its almost unbearable potato-potato din. He noticed a small note on her front seat, tucked under the spray of her keys. The door was unlocked.

NEVER A FUCKING WORD, CAJUN. Or its el Slammer forever.

The art teacher was an aging long-bearded hippie.

'We had a dropout. The class is open again,' he said. 'Leave your reg card on my desk. If you haven't got any supplies, that easel is open, and Dodd left all his stuff. One day you can thank him. He told me his Kentucky Christian upbringing wouldn't let him stare at a nekkid lady. The catalog plainly says figure studies.'

'Thank you, sir. Thank you, so much.' She was so relieved to find a slot to replace anthro that she was overwhelmed with gratitude. She'd never felt she had any particular aptitude for painting, but she figured she could work her way into art history this way.

'Are you any good, Maeve?'

'I don't know, sir.'

'Do some outlining in pencil first.' Indicating the over-abundant nude on the platform up front. 'Or not. I'll be back in half an hour. We'll work on technique as we go.'

'Jesus, this is very good stuff, my man,' Stoney offered. 'I almost never tried bourbon. I was a Scotch snob.'

'This is better than your average corn likker,' Karl Rubin said, slurring a little.

Was it three or four slugs they'd had already? Maybe even five. 'Thanks for sharing, man. You're right – once in a while, a man's got to go down the wet road before noon.' He closed his eyes and found his phone, and, when, after pondering, he figured it out, he hit redial for Ty's number. The imaginary resonance of long, long phone wires humming in the warm dry Santa Ana winds held his attention as he waited. When the phone seemed to come alive, he closed his eyes. 'Ty, this is Stoney,' he said.

'Hi. I'm driving up PCH right now, sir. I shouldn't use my cell in the car. I don't want to risk the cops.'

'Let's make it all up,' Stoney said, feeling how tipsy he was. 'I mean it, son. My only excuse is I didn't know. I didn't know – honest to God. Your mom never said she was carrying you. We could be terrific, you and me.'

Just then an explosion went off against the north side of the Sandstone Resort, and Stoney slapped the cellphone closed. 'What the fuck's that?' he demanded of Rubin.

'Mice?' Rubin said, with a plastered smile.

A second rocket-propelled grenade took out a lot of the windows in front of the ballroom down below them, with a great shattering of glass, and now Stoney guessed what was going on.

'Get yourself together, man,' Stoney said. 'That's gotta be the Colombian flippos. Last guy they took alive, they skinned.'

Rubin's eyes went wide, but Stoney couldn't tell how seri-ously he was taking it.

'Is there some way out of here?' Stoney demanded. He felt himself slurring a little and patted for the big Desert Eagle that was still in the pocket of his coat slung over the chair. 'I mean secret and right now!'

'Follow me.' Rubin hurried straight into the front room and then waddled down the steps to the ball-room. Stoney was suddenly enraged at himself for drinking. He was having trouble keeping up with the old man and not stumbling. When he got downstairs, he saw broken glass littering the whole room and sniffed the explosive. He'd seen the same damn things take out several buildings at the cemetery.

Automatic weapon fire was slamming into the rock walls now, wap-wap-wap, quite a lot of it, as he saw Rubin dead-focused on rolling up a section of carpet and then lifting a trap door. Rubin had picked up a sawed-off shotgun from somewhere along the way.

'You're a genius, man,' Stoney said. 'What is this?'

'At some point, the last bossman read a book about the Chinese in California. Every Chinatown had underground escapes because angry mobs came in and tried to wipe them out.'

Another explosion went off against the stone side wall of the house, and he felt the shudder in his feet. Thank heavens the place was well built. 'Too much information. Go now.'

Rubin was already half way down a staircase, calling back, 'Roll the rug and throw the bolt behind you, Mr Stoney.'

Jack Liffey had had a quick call from Ty about where he was headed. Winston sat in the pickup in the driveway, antsy to get a move on, but Jack Liffey had to make one more try first. He was worried sick about Gloria. He used the house cordless from the living room and punched in the number again for Sonny Theroux in Bakersfield.

'That's Jack, isn't it?' Sonny's voice came on surprisingly down the staticky connection, and he realized Sonny's phone must have caller ID.

'Where's Gloria? I don't have time to shilly-shally.'

'I'm trying to stay square. Jenny is driving her to you right now, and I just tracked them to the Grapevine to make sure they're safe. She pissed off the Bako cops really bad, Jack.'

'Don't be familiar, wifefucker. We aren't friends any more. Why isn't Gloria driving herself home?'

'Ask her to tell you. She'll be OK. But it's her business, Mr Liffey.'

'You bet,' Jack Liffey said. The man's voice had been steady, but you couldn't know what that meant, not with a pro. 'Maybe you care, too, guy. OK. I'll go nuts right now if I don't know what's happened. You can appreciate that.'

'You have to trust me now. Gloria's going to be OK, she's with Jenny, and she's on her way to you, but what happened is something she's going to want to tell you herself. Maybe after a long sleep. She got beat up.'

'You fucker – don't play with me.' Then there was a roaring in Jack Liffey's ear, as if something like death were flying down the telephone line. He realized it was only the howl of all those space satellites and wires and relays that made up the broken connection.

Winston was starting to nod off when Jack Liffey got in and whacked his chest with the back of his hand. 'Wake up, mon. I need you now. I don't know why I'm heading for Topanga when I should be waiting right here for Gloria, but I trust the women to take care of themselves. Have you ingested any drugs this morning?'

'Oh, no, sir.'

'I want us both on top. I mean it.'

'Did you have a bad childhood?' Winston asked, apropos of nothing.

Jack Liffey started his pickup. 'Not so bad, did you?'

'Yes, sir, pretty bad. One day I tell you the story of my life.'

'And how does it turn out?'

Winston grinned and laughed. 'I think I find some help. I think a guy with a heart.'

Jack Liffey smiled. 'Heart's not always so great. It can be a real pain in the ass sometimes.'

I drive up to the gates of the Sandstone Ranch that I still think of as my birthplace. Ominously, the gates have been ripped open. The iron grid is torn off its track and lies in the dry weeds. In the distance I can hear a lot of gunfire – reminding me of an action film I shot near here once out in Malibu, on the old *M.A.S.H.* set. I can see smoke rising from where the house is, over a crest of the graveled road. My father is in trouble, certainly. What would a movie hero do? Fly to the rescue, of course.

A small brushfire was brewing up near the north wall of the house, cemented stone, but it was nowhere near enough fire for Jhon Orteguaza. The gods he served wanted much more. If you were going to have an inferno chasing down your enemies, you wanted a real roar-voiced firestorm, flicking its long red tongues far into the air and sending out the kind of heat you could feel for a kilometer. A dozen of his *compadres* had found the best cover they could, rock outcrops and small trees, and were firing AKs and fancier weapons at the much damaged house, which had stone side walls that seemed not to care very much. Another grenade went off where the lower floor windows had already been blown out, with little discernable effect.

He rapped Andrés on the shoulder and said, 'You got a Willie Pete, *hombre*. Use it.'

'*¡Ay, que, es feo!*'

Willie Pete was universal military slang for white phosphorus. It was precious here, they'd only been grudged one rocket round by Eighteenth Street. But it did fit their big launcher. Willie Pete would loose a glorious white starburst of phosphorus flakes burning at five thousand degrees Fahrenheit, a blazing flower the size of a pretty big hill.

'Boss, it'll bring the cops.'

'You think they don't see this?' He indicated the pillars of dark smoke from the brushfire and smoldering house. Already a speck of a noisy helicopter was heading in their direction.

'Then how do we get away?'

Orteguaza placed the barrel of his pistol against Andrés' forehead. 'This is important business, *amigo*, but business has got to be done right. You want to die now or worry about later?'

'I'll get the W.P. Yes, sir. I don't like this *el norte*. I am too far away from anybody who cares about me.'

'I care, dear Andrés. *Hombre mio*, I want Willie Pete now.'

'*¡Caballero!* Your wish is my deed.'

Stoney followed the old man along the low underground passageway, bent over, as they heard muffled explosions behind. How could the police let this go on?

Every once in a while, Rubin paused in his flight to wave the flashlight ahead of him and do a little intricate foot-dance, and Stoney could tell he was drunk as a skunk.

'Cool it, man. Get me out of here or I'll shoot you in the ass. I hate tight places.' He'd had a small case of claustrophobia since he was a child and could never bear an MRI.

'Almost there, pard,' Rubin said briskly.

He didn't ask what 'there' was. Maybe an underground casino built by the Chinese.

Rubin reached a crude staircase of metal rungs up against a mud wall where the tunnel ended. He climbed slowly without handrails, splashing his flashlight against the ceiling above him. Rubin shouldered hard against what appeared a small wooden tray set into the roof. It slid aside and soil dribbled down from above as daylight flooded the tunnel. The sound of gunfire entered with the light. The tray wasn't hinged, but was obviously heavy as Rubin shouldered it another foot to the side. Then he pushed hard with both hands to expose a full rectangle of blue sky. Stoney noticed that the sawed-off was gone, dropped who knows where?

Karl Rubin raised his head slowly into the world to look around. He yanked his head back down. 'Into the mouth of safety,' he slurred, and beckoned to Stoney. 'They're far away.'

Jack Liffey parked as close as he could get, forcing the pickup off the narrow pavement and against the dirt roadcut to let pass anything that needed to pass. He saw the smoke rising in the distance, straight upward in the unnatural stillness of near noon. A bit farther along Saddle Peak Road, there were several cop cars with their light bars flashing away like flying saucers, and a helicopter was circling. When he opened the window of the pickup, he heard the distant popping of automatic gunfire, a far explosion, more gunfire.

With a chill, he glanced at Winston. He looked so much like Trevor who had been killed running from a raging brush-fire, a firestorm really, not too far from here. The parallel was too eerie to think about.

'I'm not sure why I brought you with me, my friend,' Jack Liffey said. 'But we know this is where Ty's going. I owe it to you to tell you that we're only about three miles from where your brother was killed. I think I'd rather you stayed in the car.'

'Mr Jack, there was no one better than Trevor, and he said he trusted you. You don't know the end of this at all. I got to watch your back.'

'Thank you, Winston. I didn't do so well watching Trevor's.' He studied the lay of the land now. 'We can't drive past the cops. I think we can get to the ranch on foot that way.'

'Is Ty really crazy?' Winston asked. 'I mean, in his head?'

'Don't think that. It's a way of dismissing someone who's troubled and maybe ill. I'll stand up for him.'

'I will, too, ma'an,' and, with his door opening only an inch against the cliff, Winston had to slide across the seat to follow Jack Liffey out of the pickup. Surprisingly, he stuck a big revolver from a paper bag into his waist. Stoney's associates must have given it to him at some point.

*   *   *

I drive extremely fast in the Porsche along Mulholland and for some reason the gate is open west of the 405 so I can enter dirt Mulholland at the old Nike Station – mainly just a fire road for the next six miles. I enjoy drifting hard through turns like a Southern moonshine runner, terrifying the poor teenagers who are just out for a day of truancy – mountain bikes, beer and sex.

I cut over Santa Maria Road, another fire road, and then Topanga Canyon to Fernwood. Almost home, Dad. I pull up when I see a big Highway Patrol Ford crosswise ahead, and the brushfire smoke rising beyond.

Time to hike, I think. I'm overdue for an anti-Skinny pill, but I decide to let it go. Maybe my Skinnies will enjoy a little spectacle.

For anyone watching the smoldering Sandstone Resort just then, it was a moment that was never to be forgotten. It began with a smoke trail coming inward from the north, a rocket grenade of some sort, then pure white eye-smarting flame bloomed inside the house and burst through the roof. An immense fountain of flaming debris belched upward and outward, slow as a dream, spreading across half the sky and arching over out at the tips of the trails of so many individual white-hot cinders as the fire-god unfolded himself into a perfect chrysanthemum of annihilation, dimming the sun. Embers sizzled their way downward all around into the summer-dry brush, igniting scores of brushfires.

Jack Liffey and Winston Pennycooke had stopped in their tracks at the sight. Jack Liffey's mind had been drifting as they hurried across the uneven ground, fretting over so many worries, but it was focused now.

'Dat so dread, ma'an!'

'White phosphorus,' Jack Liffey said. 'Really bad shit.'

As he and Winston watched the fireball subside, the roof and second story of Sandstone Resort began to sag and then it all started to fall in big chunks into the story below. All that ecstatic sex, all those forbidden secrets in the ball-room, being extinguished by an inferno that didn't give a damn.

NINETEEN
Hellfire

J hon Orteguaza was mesmerized by the gigantic blossom of
burning phosphorus. Shangó, the Orisha of fire, one of his
mother's favorites. He felt like falling on his knees to
worship, but his discipline prevailed and he lifted the binoculars. He was keeping a careful watch through the heat-wavery
air, and he saw the small punctuation marks of two men running
downhill ahead of small brushfires. The one in back actually
appeared to be aflame himself.

'The hunt is on,' he said in Spanish. '*Ándale. Compañeros*,
there go the rabbits.'

Lieutenant Jimmy Harrison waited, almost trembling with frus-
tration. His hand rested on the torn-open wrought-iron gate of
Sandstone Resort, awaiting orders to deploy his squad and
stabilize the situation. The command to stand down, to wait,
was truly unusual. He ground one toe in annoyance. Latin
American terrorists were running amok in his city, they'd
already killed a cop, off duty or not, and killed quite a few
other people, and they'd badly desecrated a cemetery. His
SWAT team wanted to move immediately, each man wanted
to move – they were all as restless with it as he was. There
was no Zen at all in waiting.

Jimmy Harrison had trained with Navy SEAL Team Six
many years ago; he had almost fifty hostage rescues and barri-
caded suspects to his credit, none of his guys had ever been
hurt, and rescue was his sworn duty, his purpose. He had
never before been told to stand down when a civilian was in
danger. They were strung out along the Sandstone wall, each
man a safe distance apart, two eleven-man metro SWAT teams
wearing full body armor and the dark blue Kevlar 'Fritz'
helmets that unfortunately made them look a bit like SS
troopers. Each man carried a Kimber updated version of the
old reliable 1911 .45 auto, a pistol that would immediately

stop any argument. Most of them also had Car-15 assault rifles or Heckler & Koch MP-5Ns, and a few carried sophisticated sniper rifles or shotguns or flash-bangs, but nobody had grenade launchers or missiles or tank-killers. Maybe in the next dispensation, their armament would finally catch up with the bad guys.

A big tanker truck would have been necessary to replenish the testosterone they were burning off, just exercising their violent thoughts. Each team did have an armored BearCat truck. But several of the terrorists seemed to be carrying those Iraq-war rocket-propelled grenades, probably with HEAT warheads that could punch right through their trucks. He guessed all the hesitation back at 'Upstairs' had to do with finding some kind of backup to protect them, but he knew they could deal with it on foot. They were pros and they could always deal with amateurs.

Clearly, 'Upstairs' didn't want a repeat of the chilling North Hollywood firefight of 1997 – that horrible street battle in which two goofball bank robbers wearing full body armor and carrying automatic weapons with Teflon cop-killer ammunition, had sprayed more than 1,600 rounds all around them as they walked coolly away from the bank, miraculously not killing anyone, but badly wounding nineteen cops and civilians.

Both SWAT teams stilled in reluctant awe to watch what they could see of the white phosphorous starburst. How many more of those rounds did the suspects have? They had no protection for that. Where were they getting this stuff? The arching lines of the incandescent metal scalded their way unnaturally through the morning and eventually touched down to start new brushfires, or maybe to burn all the way to China.

'We gotta go *now*!' Harrison yelled into the cell. 'I'm taking responsi—'

'Wait at that gate! That's an order,' his phone crackled. 'It's still a hold, Jimmy, still a hold. Command's doing a square dance upstairs. Do-si-do and cover your ass. To be honest, I think something big is on its way.'

'For chrissake, captain. I seen civilians in the line of fire. Upstairs got two minutes. Two minutes and I'm gonna lose radio contact, and I go.' He made the hissing sound of a dead line, but it was only a threat. Orders was orders.

*   *   *

I climb the low stone wall easily and cut cross country toward the house. My meds are wearing off, and a single Skinny squats in the brush watching me, wiggling his hands with fingers no thicker than pencils, then jumps up to trot along parallel to my course.

'Eat me,' I say aloud. 'Go away. This is bigger than you and all your buddies. This is my father.'

Just as I come over a hill, I see a horrendous fireball go off all at once at the house, like one of those TV clips from Vietnam – that terrible photograph of the little Asian girl with all the burn scars on her naked body, running screaming up a dirt road. The house won't survive this. I watch closely, and as the burning remnants of the explosion arc over in the sky and descend, leaving their tails of smoke and fire, I think I see two faraway people who haven't quite made it out of their range. Damn. Sure enough, one of them seems to be hit by an ember and spins around madly, winding trails of smoke off his body.

In a near panic I run through a grove of sumac toward the fire, fearing it's my father who's burning. Why? Why not? I've lost sight of him but I know the world is always trouble for the guys who don't control the storyboard, and something about the way he spun and then ran again suggested the Marcus Stone I was only getting to know.

Joe Lucius and Meier Reston can go to hell, I decide, along with the whole *If He Hollers* project. I'm so sorry, Chester Himes. I love you to death, a credit to our people, a great writer, etc., etc., but I don't have time for you now. I don't have time for movies at all. I finally admit to myself that 'Let's Play Pretend' is making me ill deep inside. I need something real.

Saying that to myself makes me feel a bit panicky for a moment, as if someone might hear and cut off my air. I know I'm deeply impaired, and I'm probably casting away some last chance in the movie world. So be it. I am impaired – I'm a half-controlled schizophrenic, I'm a lost working stiff, I'm a black orphan – but I won't let any of that damage me as a moral human being, even if they call me crazy as a loon. I watched this Jack Liffey make his decisions, and I liked the way he stuck with what mattered to him, what mattered period.

I run fast now over a little ridgeline and see two men, across

a shallow ravine, running hard in a meadow of yellowing
fieldgrass. The rear one is still smoldering off his back. Gunfire
echoes horribly from the hills again, acoustics from far to the
right and behind them, ugly and rapid. I really hate that sound,
though for years I've heard it over and over as make-believe.

Jenny parked her station wagon in the driveway of the Boyle
Heights house. Jack's pickup wasn't there. Gloria seemed
to have passed out pretty thoroughly during the fifty mile
passage through the mountains and down into the San
Fernando Valley, but luckily Jenny had the address and a
Thomas Bros. mapbook. She liked the look of the area off
I-5 that the book called Boyle Heights, with its old frame
houses and Latino street life, and she wondered how it was
that she could identify it almost immediately as a Latino
neighborhood. Lots of flowers in the yards, front fences made
of ornamental wrought-iron spears, a bit too much rubbish
in the street, an ice cream pushcart on the sidewalk with a
little bell on the push bar. She envied Jack the daily fasci-
nation of a non-Anglo suburb.

She turned in the seat and called behind her. 'Glor? Anybody
home?'

No answer. She'd need to go through any address book she
could find inside for Gloria's doctor. But first she had to get
her into the house and into her bed. She didn't think she was
strong enough to do it by herself, but she bet neighborliness
prevailed here. As long as she didn't pick out a home with a
running feud against the local cop.

Jenny picked a two-story house across the street, and she
walked over, hearing a vacuum cleaner roaring inside, and
knocked hard on the open doorframe. '¿Cómo estamos,
señora?' Jenny tried, as colloquial as she could get.

An old woman, holding a strange-looking hose vacuum in
rusted chrome from the 1940s, smiled back and, just as she
deserved, launched a burst of idiomatic Spanish back at her
that contained norteamericano words and strange construc-
tions that Jenny had never heard in her college classes.

'Speak slowly, please,' she begged. 'I'm still learning.'
Actually she knew Castilian and Basque-Aragonese Spanish
very well (though not much Basque itself), but she had trouble
with L.A. Norteño – which was called caló on the street.

'Sorry, señora. What do you require?' the woman said in labored English.

'I have brought Mrs Ramirez home from far away, and she is hurt and unconscious,' Jenny said in slow Castilian Spanish. 'She was beaten by some bad men. I need help getting her into bed in her house and finding her doctor. Are you a friend?'

'*¡Por supuesto!* Of course!' The woman dropped the vacuum instantly and shouted, 'Agusto! Come here right now!' She pounded on the wall. An eighteen-year-old with earbuds buzzing like insects appeared from within the house. He yanked them out, and they followed Jenny across the street, with the woman talking fast again, just beyond Jenny's capabilities.

The three of them managed to slide Gloria out and stagger-carry her to her bedroom. In searching later for an address book, Jenny found Jack Liffey's note on the fridge: 'Rescue in Progress. Back soon. Jack.'

It was incredibly annoying, but what could she do but wait and keep hunting for a doctor's phone number somewhere in a drawer or notepad? She would slap Jack Liffey silly the very next time she saw him.

Luckily I'm still young so I can outrun even a man who's running for his life, especially this man ahead of me who's staggering now with pain and is clearly Marcus Stone. He's showing ugly ropy burned flesh through the charred-away holes in his jacket and shirt. He must have been hit by a fleck of the horrible fire. The other man is gone, I don't know where. Probably saving himself.

Short rips of gunfire are going off behind us, and I hear a helicopter overhead. Will it be our savior or just TV looky-loos?

'Dad! Hold on!' I call. 'It's Ty.'

Shouting at him from nearby is like swatting him with a two-by-four. My outcry has destroyed some fragile equilibrium holding him upright. His limbs flail out of control and he falls awkwardly into the tall dry grass.

He moans and bangs his forehead repeatedly on the dirt. Yes, this is truly pain. I wish I had morphine.

'Dad, we can't stay. I'm sorry about the pain. They're getting closer.'

I don't know if he even recognizes me. His eyes are wide

with shock. I help him up, and I feel he's almost insensate with the agony and panic. We stumble only a few steps before we both go down, and bullets are crackling past us, a few burying themselves into the earth around us.

Marcus Stone levers himself up to a sitting position, having found somewhere in his jacket the biggest shiniest pistol I have ever seen, and he uses two hands to fire it back into the grass in a monumental aimless rage, again and again, until it's empty. I doubt if he's seen anything to aim at. It may even be an attempt to kill the monster of pain that's clawing at his exposed back. I can see one wound too clearly, burned right down to a flash of white, which can only be the bone of his shoulder blade.

Jack Liffey and Winston Pennycooke could see the drama clearly. Insects going to war across the canyon. The semicircle of hunters were firing away and drawing closer to the two men who were up now and trying to run together, like hopeless drunks. He had no binoculars, but presumptions of identity were enough. They had clearly seen Tyrone Bird come out of nowhere to join the wounded man who had to be Stoney.

A police helicopter seemed to be harrying the relentless hunters, a loud voice shouting something unintelligible on a P.A. and flashing their big sungun lamp at the men below, but an LAPD helicopter carried no weapons, by law. And the peculiar old Posse Comitatus Act from the end of Reconstruction in 1878 had banned the use of any military weapons against civilians – unless Congress declared an outright insurrection.

A startling smoke trail soared out of the grass where one of the Colombians had fired an RPG at the helicopter. Jack Liffey was amazed at their arrogance, to take on the police in a faraway land. The rocket grenade contained no guidance system and had no chance of hitting the helicopter. It burst harmlessly in the air, far past the aircraft. But it was enough for the pilot. The helicopter scooted away.

'OK, Win. What are friends for?'

'For help when help is no other way.'

They took off down a shallow ravine along the hillside, high-stepping to use the momentum of their descent and dig a stabilizing heel into the soil at each leap. At the bottom, Jack Liffey thought he'd seen a rattlesnake momentarily but kept right on going and labored up the other side. Then it was really hard work, his years making him huff and puff, climbing into the whipping cheek-high grass and mustard. A few of the weapons had clearly turned in their direction now, and he heard the pa-zing of rifle rounds passing at head level. Part of his mind reminded him it was tiny little supersonic shock waves that he was hearing, from little tubes of hot metal doing their best to slam into him and make a mess of his body, and another part tried to tell him about the very long odds of being hit at this distance.

Where were the cops? He'd seen innumerable black-and-whites parked outside. And down the road, two whole SWAT trucks, for chrissake.

'Mr Jack. Can I shoot back?'

'Hell, yes.'

As they labored uphill, Winston took little trouble aiming at what couldn't be seen anyway through the tall grass, but he fired two, three times in the general direction of the hunters with the big revolver that someone had given him. Maybe it would keep a head or two down. Jack Liffey didn't waste any shots from his own .45. He might need them later when he could see something.

He'd directed their run well – he could see Tyrone's head facing backwards fifty yards dead ahead, going much slower now. The young man was dragging something behind him, making futile progress.

'Mr Jack?'

'Yes?'

'Something bad is going on here.'

Jack Liffey wanted to laugh, but didn't. Yes, indeed. Something bad. He knew Winston had no way of seeing the past. A brushfire, a gunfight, a run to escape, and Winston's brother Trevor had died all at once of one unexpected gunshot. How could he let that happen again? Mrs Pennycooke would never forgive him.

'Where the coppers?'

'It's like they all decided to go on vacation.'

As he gasped uphill, Jack Liffey fell behind and became aware of the sun beating down, merciless. The whole insane firefight was complicated by so many things he didn't understand, and by a duty he didn't really want. Why wasn't he with Maeve and Gloria, helping with their problems? But his whole life, his sense of duty had trapped him here.

'Ty!' he yelled. 'We're with you. Stay low.'

'Mi arse!' Winston screamed in pain.

'What is it, Win?'

'Worry not, ma'an. I got a damage of no importance. In mi bati, where I sit. Is likkle nothing.'

The two of them tumbled unexpectedly into the grass hollow where Tyrone Bird lay gasping next to the unconscious Marcus Stone. Stoney's skin looked a greenish gray, and that was worrisome. Shock, Jack Liffey knew.

'OK,' he said. 'We're under control now, Ty. You and I take his arms and shoulders. Win, you're stronger, you take his feet. Your new wound going to prevent that?'

'Never. Don' pay no heed.'

'I won't forget this,' Tyrone said. 'I guess you can't ever try to fly solo.'

'You say it, brah,' Win replied.

They stooped and managed to pick up the limp Stoney, but it was going to be quite a carry. He weighed at least two forty. Jack Liffey wished they had time to make a stretcher or even an Indian travois, but he heard the repeated coughing of the assault rifles behind them, closer now, and a few crackles of rounds passing nearby in the tall grass.

'L.T., they're on the satellite phone.' Jimmy Harrison took the phone that they kept in a recess of the BearCat. It was about the size and weight of a big brick with an antenna like a long fountain pen. Unlike cells, it communicated directly through an overhead satellite – a system once known as Iridium.

'Harrison here.'

'Jimmy,' his commander's voice said, 'We know they can't monitor this phone. Stay backed off, that's an absolute order. These are Colombian drug-pushers, you and I both know it, the chief knows it. But Homeland Security has declared them a foreign terrorist invasion—'

'Andy, that's bullshit. My men could put an end to this in fifteen minutes.'

He heard another laugh. 'Jimmy, there's going to be no end of blame and trips to Washington to testify, and they'll construe it all wrong. Consider yourself lucky to be out of it.'

'Lucky isn't standing down and watching these skells kill citizens.'

There was no more laughter. 'Well, you've got your orders, J.H. There's fancy aerial support coming in fast, and there's always a lot more citizens where those came from.'

Maeve was sitting in her room in Topanga, a little dazzled still by the hairy artist looking at her first painting and telling her she had 'real talent.' She'd never had the faintest idea.

Bunny summoned Maeve to the crummy little TV they kept in the living room. 'This is all going on right here in Topanga. We better lock the doors.'

It was a local news channel, most of which had abandoned showing anything but celebrities punching paparazzi, goofballs trying to fly in beach chairs with hydrogen balloons, and baby animals at the zoo. A news-copter was distantly circling some kind of gunfight up toward Tuna Canyon, misidentified on screen as 'Tuno Canyon'.

Maeve saw a replay – 'Earlier Today', the on-screen type said. A big explosion that created a burning firework star right on top of a rambling flat house. 'Live', the screen said now, and a jiggly shot showed a group of men with rifles chasing a few other men carrying someone through dry grass.

Maeve looked away. Too many times in her life she'd picked out signs of her father in TV scenes just like this – it took so little: a distinctive way of moving he had, a bald spot at the back of his head. This time she made sure she wouldn't work herself up unnecessarily. She stared at Bunny instead, that big huggable woman.

The TV voice was babbling away, but she managed to tune it out.

'Bunny, you're really nice.'

She looked over, startled. 'Are you making fun of me, Maeve?'

'*God*, no. I'm trying not to look or think, just in case my dad is down there. That's the whole truth, so help me dog.'

Bunny stared hard at her. 'You told me the cord was cut.'

'I'm trying. What are the odds it's him, anyway?'

Bunny flicked off the set. 'OK. I'll help. Let's go have a Cosmo.'

*   *   *

'Down the ravine,' Jack Liffey said. 'We'll go faster down-hill, and we might find somewhere to hole up.'

They bent their course downhill, as the gunmen fired and fired. Remarkable how much missing there was, and he remembered reading Che Guevara's memoir and the firefights during the Cuban Revolution that had gone on for what had seemed hours with no one hit at all. Adrenaline and amateurism.

Jack Liffey headed them toward a small outcrop of rocks he saw below in the gully that would afford some protection. They couldn't carry Stoney much farther. They scrambled over the sandstone outcrop and set Stoney down in the lowest swale of the bone-dry streambed. His skin was even more gray-green than before.

'He's cold,' Ty said, feeling his forehead. 'My god, his lips are blue as a crayon.'

'Cover him with anything we've got,' Jack Liffey said. 'Turn him around so his legs are uphill. And keep checking his breathing. He's lost blood, maybe internally. Maybe it's just the pain. But he's in shock, and shock is no joke.'

Jack Liffey and Winston took flat cover behind the sandstone and aimed their pistols back uphill. The grass was too high to see very much, but the shrubs were much thinner toward the bottom of the arroyo, particularly the last thirty yards or so.

'We'll get off a few shots if they come close,' Jack Liffey said. 'Make them count.' He didn't think Winston had any shots left.

Winston reached over and touched Jack Liffey's shoulder. 'Remember that movie, ma'an? Some Red Indian he say, It's a good day to die.'

'Winston, it's never a good day to die.'

Lieutenant Harrison's satellite phone squawked. 'Here it comes. Have your men take good cover, Jimmy. You got incoming.'

'What the hell?' He swallowed his anger. 'Cover up, men! Use the wall! Incoming!' But incoming what?

Captain Lon Schuster made a V-gesture over his shoulder briefly to his copilot/gunner who sat directly behind him and about eighteen inches elevated in the Longbow Apache. They were conscious of flying some of the first state-of-the-art attack helicopters entrusted to the Air National Guard, and all they'd been told was that insurrectionists were down there, and they'd be guided in.

'Handyman Two, this is Handyman One,' Schuster said into his throat mike. 'Target's in sight. Nine-ten men with auto weapons and a couple big RP sticks. Clean 'em up and green 'em up.'

The two attack helicopters worked quickly to arm their weapons systems and their defenses, green indicator lights coming on one after another. The copilot worked his laser joystick to paint the tallest man down below with a bright red laser spot.

Jack Liffey heard a tremendous roaring, thumping sound coming up the hill behind him and chanced a look. A chill took his spine hard. This is like Nam, only doubled. He'd never seen a chopper so crammed with outriggers full of missiles and cannons and other weapons. It had to be the meanest-looking machine ever made.

The Colombians saw the black helicopters coming, and suddenly Jhon Orteguaza noticed an incandescent red circle the size of a 200-peso coin joggling on his chest. The helicopters slowed and their tails bobbed like big stick insects as they came to a hover, maybe fifty meters away.

'Shoot them down!' Orteguaza commanded. 'We have Shangó with us!'

All of the Colombians trained their rifles on the helicopters and went on automatic fire, feeding in new magazines as necessary. The two last RPGs they had fumed away fast, directly at the haughty, stilled flying machines.

Captain Lon Schuster smiled when the Apaches' automatic defenses kicked in and smacked the rocket grenades into useless puffs of smoke with intensely concentrated bursts of chain-gun fire. The other rounds from the ground fire just deflected harmlessly off their underside armor. Now and again one snicked off the thick cockpit plexiglass and bounced away. So much for the defensive phase. 'What do you want, cap? The chain gun?'

The chain gun was capable of firing so many rounds so fast – more than ten a second – that its distinctive groaning sound would have filled the air near the insurrectionists with a near solid wall of moving metal slugs.

Back at the gate, the infrared binoculars that Schuster carried gave him a clear view of the tall Latino facing the Apaches. Defiantly the man took out of his pocket and tugged on a goofy-looking pointy knit cap. Then he spread his arms like Christ on the cross. Do your worst, he seemed to be saying.

'Look at him. The guy wants to play. OK, let's play. Give him a Hellfire.'

'Jesus, cap. That's so overkill. It'd blow open a bank vault.'

'What isn't overkill, Tommy? You can push one button back there, and this damn beast goes auto and engages hundreds of different targets in less than a second. Should we set her down and fight them with swords in order to fight fair? Look at the guy. He wants your Hellfire so bad. He's begging for it.'

The Hellfire was a missile designed to penetrate a heavily armored tank, a cement bunker, a refuge cave. The god Shangó must have loved it when a Hellfire flamed downward directly toward one man wearing a cotton shirt.

EPILOGUE
You Can't Fix Everything

The Fire Department helicopter out of Van Nuys couldn't touch down because of the angle of the ravine, but it hovered busily in the wind gusts, a foot or less off the slope, and three SWAT cops lifted Stoney into the metal basket locked to the skids. They strapped him in.

'Take me. If he needs blood, I'm his son,' Tyrone told them.

One of the cops looked skeptical, but reached out and boosted the young man aboard the half-open door.

For about the fifth time in the last ten years, Jack Liffey had his Ballester-Molina .45 pistol taken away from him by the authorities. Winston had quite sensibly lost his empty revolver some time ago in the weeds.

They sat on a bench in the Lost Hills Sheriff's Station in Agoura, waiting for the obligatory debriefing. Or browbeating.

'Do you want to meet your brother's girlfriend?' Jack Liffey asked Winston. 'I can take you.'

Winston seemed to think about it for a while. 'I got my own girl on Jamdown, and I already got ideas about here. Let's let this woman have her new life. I think any avenging and reckoning and all that stuff is finished. America is chaka-chaka.'

'What's that?'

'A big mess.'

'You can say that again.'

'Liffey!' a voice shouted, unnecessarily.

He looked up to see a heavyset deputy with an air of angry fatigue and figured the man was going to be pretty much unreachable as a human being. Just the facts, man.

The two Mexican laborers who'd been hired that morning at a *mosca* with a dozen others in Long Beach were on Terminal Island now, pulling out double-head nails that held a giant flimsy replica of a freighter upright against substantial four-by-four buttresses. They had no idea that what they were doing was known as 'striking a set'.

'Gringos are crazy,' one said. 'What is all this phony crap?'

'Who cares, *compa*? It's good day-money.'

Maeve parked at the curb on Greenwood. She had no idea what the old Buick station wagon was doing in Gloria's driveway. She'd crammed her backpack, preparing for a weekend at home, and now she lugged it up the sloping yard to the door.

'God, I know you,' she said, when Jenny opened the door. 'You're from Bakersfield.'

'It's not like Transylvania.'

Maeve smiled, remembering all that had happened in that town. 'Is Gloria home?'

'You've got to prepare yourself. She's been beat up pretty bad. She's sleeping now.'

'Oh, no!'

'Do you know her regular doctor's name? I'm having trouble finding out.'

'Sure. I'll show you. She's got reason to keep it private. She says the police management hold everything medical against you. Even your period.'

'I understand.'

'But the deal is: you've got to tell me what happened.'

Jack Liffey brought Winston home late that night after they'd been released by the sheriff's station. He found the house surprisingly filled with all sorts of people: Jenny Ezkiaga, for God's sake; Maeve, Señora Campos from across the street; and, worst, a very unconscious, almost comatose, Gloria, covered with bruises and bandage wraps after her adventure, whatever it had been. So much sex in the world, he thought, and so much violence. How could you keep them apart?

'Who's going to explain this?' he demanded, when he couldn't wake Gloria.

'Jack, calm down,' Jenny said. 'Things go wrong. You can't fix everything all by yourself.'